BROTHERS OF THE CROSS TIMBER

BROTHERS OF THE CROSS TIMBER

A Novel

Bob Perry

Brothers of the Cross Timber

www.bobp.biz

A friend loves at all times.
A brother is born for adversity.
There are friends, who pretend to be friends.
But there is a friend who sticks closer than a brother.

SOLOMON

PART I

CHAPTER 1

"Ya' think he's asleep?" I asked peering across the moonlit field.

"Must be," Arty Martin replied crouching next to me in the tall grass, while katydids and tree frogs sang from the thick woods behind us.

"What do you think, Lance?" I whispered to my other friend Lance Carrington.

A warm breeze whistled through the muggy air as Lance smiled reassuringly and said, "Patience, Gill."

"I don't know what you got against old Haskell?" Arty muttered as we waited restlessly in the shadows.

Lance did not respond, but we knew the reason. This farm once belonged to Lance's mother and he resented Haskell Holiday owning it.

Moonlight glimmered off ripened watermelons, as we watched the amber flicker of an oil lamp from the farmhouse across the darkened field. Another fifteen minutes in the quiet darkness seemed like an hour, when suddenly the distant light vanished.

"Let's go," Arty whispered eagerly.

"Wait a little longer," Lance calmly replied.

Five minutes passed before Lance commanded in a stern whisper, "Now!"

The three of us crawled quickly to the edge of the melon patch. My heart pounded as I calculated the effort it would take to carry a twenty-pound watermelon to the trees. Arty Martin already had a smaller melon under his arm as Lance ventured close to the house. I let out a muffled grunt while lifting my watermelon and took a step toward the safety of the woods. A string of obscenities from Haskell Holiday, however, caused me to drop my melon as it smashed on the hard ground. Haskell Holiday, a man of nearly forty with a graying mustache, potbelly, and mean disposition, barged out of the house. The explosion of a shotgun ripped through the quiet night.

"Run!" Arty screamed as we darted toward the wall of trees fifty yards away.

Arty and I scampered away empty handed while Lance cradled a nice size melon under his arm as he passed us before diving into the thick woods. Lance moved as smoothly as a man might navigate a trail in the daylight. Arty and I followed his lead, while low-hanging branches scratched and scraped us. Another blast from the shotgun echoed in the leaves above, encouraging us to move quickly through the brush as we tried to keep close to Lance.

The thick Cross Timber forest continued a quarter mile before we entered an open meadow a short distance from Salt Creek, a small docile stream surrounded by thirty yards of rusty-red sand.

"Where's your melons, boys?" Lance Carrington smirked as we gasped for air.

Lance Carrington stood on a large flat sandstone positioned above the riverbank while the evening wind caused his dark hair to dance in the moonlight under his always-present floppy hat. The shapeless, felt hat was crusty with dirt but Lance was rarely seen without it. His darkly tanned skin caused the whites of his eyes to glow mischievously in the night.

"You nearly got us shot!" a puffing Arty Martin charged.

Lance grinned, "Old Haskell couldn't hit a barn if it was painted red."

"Sounded pretty close," I observed.

Lance produced a worn pocketknife and in one smooth movement sliced the large melon he had carried from the field.

"It'll make the melon taste that much sweeter," Lance proclaimed.

Arty smiled at his friend's confident appraisal and took a piece of melon from the knife blade.

"It does make it taste sweeter," Arty agreed with a smile, as he slurped down a slice of the watermelon.

"You think Haskell's still after us?" I anxiously asked.

"Naw," Lance assured. "I doubt he could get through the Cross Timber in the daylight, much less the dark. Don't worry about Haskell; it's his cousin Leland I worry about. He's mean as a rattlesnake and sneakier than one too."

"Haskell ain't coming," Arty confirmed as he looked at me. "Have a taste."

The warm melon was sweet and wet as it melted in my mouth like candy.

"You need to be careful with Leland Holiday," I stated seriously. "I've heard stories."

"They're all true," Lance replied factually. "He's got his hands in a lot of things in this county. Worst of all, Leland's as smart as he is mean."

"We don't have to worry about Leland tonight," Arty interrupted.

As the adrenaline rush of dashing through the dark woods began to wane, we enjoyed a majestic summer sky relaxing at our boyhood sanctuary. It was always the three of us in those days. We were brothers of the Cross Timber, at least during the summer of 1915. Leland Holiday seemed only a character in our youthful adventures—a villain only in our minds. We did not realize at the time he would steer events so dramatically in each of our lives.

"The sky's alive tonight, ain't it?" Arty Martin proclaimed looking up at the stars above.

"Nothin' like it," Lance affirmed.

"What's you doin' tomorrow, Gill?" Arty asked me.

"Weedin' the cotton fields," I replied.

"Pa will probably have me tendin' to the mules," Arty sighed, as if this chore would be an inconvenience to his day.

"Must be nice havin' a team of mules do most your work," I mused.

Arthur Martin's father farmed a quarter section of the Salt Creek bottomland south of the small town of Romulus in Pottawatomie County. Arty, as we always called him, was a handsome boy with sandy hair, blue eyes, and an easy smile.

"The mules help, but they take a lot of care and a lot of my time." Arty explained. "Pa's been looking at a tractor."

"A tractor!" Lance exclaimed. "What for? You already got the best team of mules money can buy and four brothers to boot."

"Pa's always plannin' for the future," Arty shrugged.

Lance shook his head, thinking the cost of a tractor would feed him for a year.

"Where are you headed tonight?" Arty asked Lance.

Lance took a moment to spit out a watermelon seed and said, "Don't know…probably just head to the rail bridge over the Salt Creek and sleep there tonight. It's too late to head home, and it's warm enough to sleep under the stars."

Lance's father had tried farming, but spent most of his life running liquor. His father lived in a place called Violet Springs, on the border of Seminole County. Towns like Keokuk Falls, Corner, Young's Crossing, and Violet Springs lined the border between the former Indian and Oklahoma Territories. The distilling of liquor was legal in Oklahoma Territory before statehood and the marketplace across the border provided an adventuresome, lucrative, and often violent occupation for many men like Lance's father, Eli Carrington. Cowboys visiting these wild saloons along the border would put flat bottles of whiskey in their boots and travel back through Indian Territory for extra cash. "Bootlegging" continued as a profession when the new state of Oklahoma prohibited all liquor.

There was not much left in Violet Springs by 1915, but Eli Carrington lived in one of the abandoned buildings. Lance, nearly sixteen-years-old, rarely saw his father and lived mostly on his own, away from the old, notorious border towns his father frequented.

"You can sleep at our place," I offered.

Lance smiled under his floppy hat and said, "Thanks Gill, but your brother Lloyd snores something awful. I'll come stay when the weather turns cold."

I chuckled at Lance's candor because Lloyd did snore like a bear.

We finished our melon, and reclined on the banks of the trickling river. I was thinking about the next morning and heading home. The late August night was pleasant, but I would be up early working in the fields.

"Guys!" Arty said, breaking the silence with a tone of urgency. "We need to make a pact."

Arty, the most outgoing of our group, instigated most of our boyhood adventures. We were on the brink of being men, but still held to the boyish life we were accustomed to that summer.

"A what?" Lance asked.

"A pact…an agreement that we'll be friends forever," Arty clarified. "We need to agree that every ten years we'll meet back on this rock…meet back at Salt Creek no matter what."

"Sounds good to me," I replied.

Lance, taking a little more time and in a more serious tone, said, "Ya'll are about all I count as family. I'll be here."

Arty Martin leaped excitedly to his feet. He was always the most energetic and imaginative of our group.

"It's settled then!" Arty stated while slapping his knee. "We'll meet here no matter what on August 19, 1925!"

"August 19, 1925," Lance echoed. "Consider it done."

We talked a little longer that night about things boys talk about—our hopes, dreams, plans for the future, and about the local girls. None of us had the courage to talk about the one girl we all knew was the prettiest in the county, Gwendolyn Peaudane. A shapely and poised young woman, Gwen Peaudane's shoulder-length, brown hair seemed to reflect the brilliance of the sun. Captivating blue eyes balanced her perfectly proportioned face. She had a hint of vulnerability to her soulful gaze, while her perpetual smile created matching dimples on her creamy smooth cheeks.

That night we three were as one, bound together with a camaraderie that seemed unbreakable. Arty and I left together since our houses were close to each other, while our good friend Lance stayed on the rock by the river to contemplate the reality of his situation before heading to the rail bridge over Salt Creek to sleep for the night.

CHAPTER 2

Pottawatomie County, named after the Citizen Band of the Potawatomi Indian Nation, was located at the southeastern corner of the old Oklahoma Territory. The county bordered the Seminole Nation on the east and the Chickasaw Nation to the south. The state of Oklahoma, being only eight years old in 1915, had originally been two distinct regions separated by an ancient forest called the Cross Timber.

The Cross Timber varied in width from five to thirty miles and ran the length of Oklahoma from south to north. It separated the vast, open plains of the west from the wooded hills of the east. Washington Irving in his travels through the region called the thick Cross Timber "The Cast Iron Forest." Irving marveled that the short forest—comprised of pin oak, hickory, and blackjack trees—started so abruptly and was so difficult to traverse.

The edge of the thick forest followed a geological boundary between the sandy soil of the grasslands to the west and red-clay soil of the Cross Timber to the east. The trees native to the Cross Timber were short and tough, able to resist the wild grass fires of the prairie and severe droughts. Occasional ice storms in the region added to the tangled mess and made the area almost impassable except by foot. The Indians of the plains called the forest "The Emerald Wall," and it represented the eastern boundary of their hunting grounds.

By 1915, much of the Cross Timber had been cleared for cotton farming and some ranching. Remnants of the forest remained where the terrain was too rough to farm. The dried up creeks and gullies made good hunting grounds for squirrel, raccoon, and deer. The Cross Timber also provided sanctuary for those hiding from the law or distilling whiskey in a state that prohibited the manufacture, distribution, or consumption of liquor.

The inhospitable Cross Timber covered most of south Pottawatomie County to the North Canadian River. The land comprising the county was the final exile for the Sac and Fox, Shawnee, Potawatomi, and Kickapoo Indian tribes. The new city of Shawnee, located on a peninsula surrounded on three sides by the North Canadian River, was north of the river and beyond the Cross Timber we knew.

Shawnee, the largest city in the county, tried becoming the state capital, going so far as to build a mansion for the governor. Missing out on that opportunity, the enterprising city tried to wrestle the county seat away from the smaller town of Tecumseh. Shawnee won an election to move the county seat, but when the citizens of Tecumseh complained about the tactics used by the businessmen of Shawnee, the state's Supreme Court ruled the election invalid and the county government stayed south of the North Canadian River in Tecumseh.

Although less than twenty miles away, Shawnee seemed like a different world from the Cross Timber forest which we knew. The city boasted large churches, tall buildings, and three railroads giving it access to the world. Arty, Lance, and I had planned for months to take a trip to the city, but we would have to wait until after the grueling task of the cotton harvest was done.

CHAPTER 3

Arty Martin and I left Lance Carrington on the banks of the Salt Creek after our watermelon raid on Haskell Holiday. Lance would sleep under the stars most nights or under the rail bridge if it happened to rain. Only the coldest weather would find him back with his father.

"Ya' ever worry 'bout Lance?" Arty asked seriously, as we walked on a trail from the river to a road leading to Arty's house.

"What do you mean?" I quizzed, thinking Lance was better equipped than anyone I knew to take care of himself.

"You and me…we got family…we got some roots," Arty explained. "Lance…well, Lance has got no one, but us."

"I guess," I replied. "But Lance seems to make out okay."

"Lance is best at everything…but school," Arty agreed. "I shouldn't worry 'bout him I guess."

Lance Carrington never applied himself in school and spent more time in trouble than in class on the rare occasions he bothered to attend. We all went to the schoolhouse near Romulus until the eighth grade, but the antics of Lance Carrington were notorious and caused one schoolteacher to call the rowdy place a "Fuss Box."

If not for Gwendolyn Peaudane, or Gwen as we called her, Lance would have quit school years earlier. Although I always liked school, Gwen's presence added to my enthusiasm for education. When Gwen left school after the sixth grade to help her mother at home, Lance Carrington lost all interest.

"Gwen Peaudane's gonna be at the house tomorrow," Arty stated, interrupting my thoughts about Lance Carrington.

"What?" I replied, not wanting to sound overly alarmed.

"The Peaudanes are comin' to supper tomorrow, and she's sure to come."

"Maybe," I muttered, hoping Gwen would not come to the Martin house where Arty would have her all to himself.

Arty Martin, Lance Carrington, and I had known Gwen Peaudane for years. We talked vaguely to each other about Gwen's charming qualities while acting as if we had a lukewarm interest in her. Away from my friends, however, I took every opportunity to impress Gwen and was particularly concerned about Arty. Tall, good-looking, and by far the most personable boy around, Arty received his share of attention from the girls. With his family's status, Arty would be a formidable rival for any girl's affections.

"Maybe I'll stop by and say hello," I offered. "I have a book I borrowed from Gwen that I could return."

"Thought you had to weed cotton tomorrow," Arty reminded. "They'll be gone by dark."

"Yeah," I sighed more disturbed that Arty seemed to be maneuvering to get Gwen alone than I was about not getting to see her.

Arty knew my father would not let me out of the fields before sundown.

"I could come by your place and get the book," Arty offered in a smug tone.

"Naw…I'm…I'm still reading it," I stammered.

"Oh," he wryly smiled, sensing my desperation to see Gwen.

The Martin home stood on top of a small hill overlooking the fields stretching toward the rich bottomland. The two-story house featured a porch wrapping around two sides. The fresh, white paint made the house almost glow in the moonlight. A large rusty-red barn with a new tin roof was situated about fifty yards from the home. The

Martin place always looked in perfect order reflecting Mr. Martin's demanding attention to detail.

"Hey, Gilbert," a soft voice greeted from the shadows of the dark porch.

I immediately recognized Arty's sister, Marilee Martin. Marilee was almost two years younger than Arty, but without his personal charisma. Her eyes had a continual squint, as she looked through gawky, eyeglasses. Marilee's slender frame and hair, which frizzed in the hot wind, caused her to look gangly and clumsy. She was always friendly and hospitable, but more shy and reserved than Arty.

"Hey, Marilee," I replied apathetically.

"Guy Peaudane was askin' about you," Marilee revealed.

Guy Peaudane was a successful young businessman in Romulus. More importantly to me, he was Gwen Peaudane's older brother. Nearly ten years older than Gwen, Guy was actually a stepbrother. His mother had died years before Dr. Peaudane married Gwen's mother. Guy was married and managed the family store. Dr. Peaudane was the patriarch of the family and owned a small farm on the outskirts of Romulus. Although Dr. Peaudane did not practice medicine, some said he had been a doctor as a young man during the Civil War. Dr. Peaudane did not talk about his past, which added intrigue to the story.

"Why don't you stop botherin' us?" Arty curtly asked his younger sister.

"I don't have to," she replied.

"Ain't no one want to hear your stories," he reasoned.

"I wasn't talkin' to you. I was talkin' to Gilbert," she defiantly defended. "Besides, Momma's told you not to say 'ain't' hasn't she?"

"You old cow," Arty muttered.

"Marilee!" the stern voice of Mr. Martin rang out from the front door. "You know it's not proper for you to be talking to boys after dark."

Mr. Martin was a tall man with a foreboding appearance. He wore trousers with suspenders instead of the overalls preferred by most farmers in the area. Mr. Martin had come from Texas and prospered more than most people in the area. He was strict with all of his children, but particularly Marilee. I spent as much time with Arty Martin as anyone, but was always uneasy around his father. Never feeling completely welcomed at the Martin house, I avoided Mr. Martin whenever possible.

"Arthur, you're out late again," Mr. Martin scolded.

"Yes sir," Arty answered in a less swaggering tone than was his custom.

"You better get home, Gilbert Brooks," Mr. Martin instructed me in much the same tone I had heard him use with his prized mules.

"See ya," Arty whispered.

"Yeah," I replied.

Arty stepped onto the porch to receive additional instructions from his father while I took the opportunity to walk quickly away from the Martin house and to my more humble home.

CHAPTER 4

I walked down the hill toward my house, as the flicker of an oil lamp danced in the distance. Dad and my two brothers sat on the porch. Gordon, my youngest brother barely ten years old, listened to my older brother, Lloyd, keep time on the washboard while Dad played a lively tune on his harmonica. This scene contrasted dramatically with the Martin home. Laughter and music were common with my father, while Mr. Martin would have seen such frivolous activity as wasteful.

"Look who's draggin' in," Dad greeted as the music stopped when I approached.

"Hey, Dad," I replied.

Unlike Arty, I would not be questioned about where I had been or lectured about the wasted effort in spending time with my friends. My father had a pleasant cynicism in the way he lived his life. He always considered a good story, colorful conversation, and entertainment a good diversion from the harsh realities of the farm.

"We were playin' some tunes and talking about the fields," Dad explained.

"Sorry to be out so late," I apologized.

"You're only young once," he shrugged.

"Yeah," I replied.

Lloyd rolled a cigarette, while Gordon sat quietly with his foot dangling off the small porch. My mother was inside trying to sleep, I assumed.

"Guy Peaudane came by earlier," Dad casually informed.

"What for?" I asked.

"Didn't get to see him, but Lloyd did," Dad replied. "What did he want, Lloyd?"

Lloyd took a drag on the cigarette and said, "He wanted to talk to you."

"About what?" I anxiously asked.

Lloyd blew thick, white smoke into the night and with a big smile replied, "Don't know…but don't worry none…he didn't bring that sister of his you're sweet on."

My cheeks flushed in anger as Gordon and even Dad laughed under their breath.

Before I could respond, the easy-going Lloyd smiled and continued, "He said come see him at the store sometime."

"Don't be thinking you're going to Romulus tomorrow," Dad scolded.

"I know," I acknowledged. "We got weedin' to do."

"That's right," Dad nodded in a stoic tone. "Maybe if we get caught up we can head to town Saturday."

My eyebrows rose with excitement at the prospect of going to town and the possibility of seeing Gwen Peaudane.

"For tonight," Dad continued, "we better turn in."

Dad, always playful with his boys, told a few more stories before commanding us to go to bed. My brothers and I slept in the same room, but during the warm summers, Lloyd and I usually slept outside on the porch. Lloyd was only two years older than I was, but he always seemed much older.

Lying in bed, I almost laughed out loud thinking of the look on Haskell Holiday's face as Lance Carrington toted off that big melon. A warm breeze and a few flashes of lightning in the west promised potential rain, as I drifted to sleep hoping for a downpour that might keep us out of the fields and thinking how I might impress Gwen Peaudane if I had a chance to see her tomorrow.

CHAPTER 5

Lightning and wind threatened during the night, but the downpour I hoped for amounted to only a brief shower. A little after dawn, we headed to the fields with hoes in hand.

Each row of cotton stood less than waist high in our forty-acre field. With more rain than normal during the hot summer, the weeds looked healthier than the cotton. A haze hung over the field in the soft light of dawn. The ground was damp, and the heat of the day would bring humidity. With a sigh, I took my worn hoe handle with a sharpened blade and attacked the weeds threatening to choke our cotton.

My brother Lloyd could use the hoe and almost any other farm tool as if it were an extension of his body. Working with a steady rhythm, he completed row after row at almost twice my pace. Gordon hauled water, while Dad oversaw our labor, occasionally admonishing my output. Mother brought sandwiches at noon, as we took a break under the shade of a pecan tree. I suggested we were progressing enough to finish the field before dark, as Lloyd grunted, while Dad laughed at my veiled attempt to see Gwen Peaudane at the Martin farm.

Heat shimmered across the field in the afternoon, while my shirt crusted with sweat and dust. The pre-dawn rain, which had provided a cool morning, caused a muggy, miserable day. Dad let us take a break late in the afternoon. I thought about running up to Arty's to see Gwen, but my part of the field was far from finished. Feeling dirty and worn out, I reluctantly reclined in the hot shade.

"We should be pickin' in three or four weeks," Dad stated as he looked over the fields while casually chewing on a blade of grass.

Lloyd rose from his reclined position and said, "Look's thin."

Dad spit on the ground and sighed, "Look's real thin."

My concern for the cotton harvest was less than it should have been. The garden and livestock might feed us, but paying the rent, buying seed, getting equipment, and purchasing household items depended on the cotton.

"You boys see if you can finish those last three rows. That'll put us nearly half way, and we'll finish tomorrow," Dad instructed. "Lloyd, you're in charge."

Gordon and I groaned at the prospect of working for Lloyd. Dad was benevolent compared to our older brother. Neither of us could match his pace, and now he would put us out to hoe while he barked orders.

Lloyd nodded as he rose to his feet. Dad gave one last stern look at us before heading back to the barn to mend equipment and prepare for the next day. Looking over the sweltering field, I knew finishing before dark was hopeless.

"What are you sulking for?" Lloyd mockingly asked as I grudgingly walked toward my unfinished row.

"Nothing," I assured, not wanting to provoke Lloyd's wrath.

"He's wantin' to see that girl, I bet," Gordon teased.

"You still sweet on that Peaudane girl?" Lloyd asked as he reached in his pocket for a cigarette.

"No!" I defiantly replied.

Lloyd gave me an easy smile as he continued digging through his pockets.

"I just don't like wasting my time hoein' weeds that'll be back next week," I explained.

"You're pretty stupid then," Lloyd said as he was becoming agitated over not finding his cigarettes.

"Who are you callin' stupid?" I shouted, as Lloyd drew me into the conflict. "You didn't even finish fourth grade."

I braced for the fight that was likely, when Lloyd removed a crushed cigarette from his pocket and struck a match.

After deeply inhaling his newfound prize, Lloyd smiled and said, "I didn't need more than the fourth grade to find me a girl and to know the Peaudane girl's as pretty as a peach."

Smiling at Gordon, Lloyd continued and said, "In fact, I've got a couple of girls around."

Lloyd having more than one girl was probably a lie, but he did have at least one girl. Neva St. Clair had been sweet on Lloyd since I could remember. She lived close to the Sacred Heart mission and had been chasing Lloyd for nearly a year. Lloyd's enthusiasm for her was well disguised, but she coaxed him there once or twice a month.

"Bull," I whispered under my breath just loud enough to hope Lloyd would not hear me.

"What was that?" Lloyd asked with a mocking grin.

"Nothing," I replied. "Dad said to get those fields done."

"At the rate you work, that'll be midnight," Lloyd teased as he walked closer to me.

"Leave me alone," I threatened. "I got work to do."

"Let's think about that," Lloyd said as he put his arm around my shoulder.

"Think about what?" I asked suspiciously.

"I know for a fact that Gwen Peaudane was headed to the Martin place," Lloyd calmly explained. "Her brother Guy told me yesterday. I know for a fact you're sweet somethan' awful for that girl, though I can't imagine what use she'd have for a turtle headed-looking guy like you."

"I—"

"Now don't deny it," Lloyd continued. "I know it to be true."

I was forced to listen to his teasing. He was right and had the ability to wrestle me to the ground to make me admit it.

"I could probably hoe that field with Gordon's help and finish before dark with no problem."

"I'm not doin' his work," Gordon defiantly stated.

"You'll do what I say," Lloyd sharply corrected. "Besides you ain't heard my terms."

"What terms?" I warily asked.

Lloyd smiled and said, "I'll finish the field and let you get cleaned up to see your sweetheart."

"I don't have a sweetheart," I restated.

"Of course, you don't," Lloyd teased. "But that's part of the deal."

"The deal?" I confusingly replied.

"You admit you want to go see Gwen Peaudane and buy me two packs of Camel cigarettes. I'll finish the field and even tell Dad you did a bang up job."

"Two packs?" I defended. "They're ten cents apiece!"

"Two packs of Camels is a fair price to finish that field and let you go romancing," Lloyd explained.

"I won't do it," Gordon interrupted. "I'll tell Dad."

"You're not tellin' anyone," Lloyd threatened. "Gill's goin' to get me two packs of Camels and you a chocolate bar."

I had about a dollar saved, and this extortion would cost me nearly a quarter. The prospect of getting out of weeding the rest of the field and seeing Gwen was too enticing not to think about, however.

"I'll do it," I blurted out after a few seconds of thought.

Lloyd rubbed my head and said, "I expect my Camels by Saturday."

"I want a Hershey if they have it," Gordon added.

Nodding in agreement, I headed to the house to clean up and change shirts without Dad seeing me. After only ten steps, Lloyd interrupted me.

"Aren't you forgetting something?" he smiled while Gordon smirked beside him.

"What?" I asked.

"The rest of the deal," he said.

"What?" I asked again before I realized what he wanted.

"You know what," Lloyd chided. "Say it."

With a sigh, I said, "I'm going to see Gwen."

"I didn't hear you," Lloyd teased. "Did you hear it Gordon?"

"Nope," Gordon added under Lloyd's protection.

"I'm going to see Gwen," I stated louder.

"And—" Lloyd continued.

In resignation I said, "I'm going to see Gwen…because I'm sweet on her."

While Gordon giggled like a girl at my embarrassment, Lloyd said, "Now that wasn't so hard, was it?"

I did not reply and stepped quickly toward the house. Although embarrassed, it felt good telling someone, even my brothers, about Gwen. In less than half an hour, I was sneaking out of the house with a clean shirt and the possibility of seeing Gwen. With a bounce in my step, I headed to the Martin farm.

CHAPTER 6

The sun hung low in the afternoon sky, casting long shadows across the country road as I hurried to the Martin farm. Even in the shade, the hot, stagnant air spotted my shirt with sweat.

I stepped quickly past the gate to the Martin house, but my pace slowed as I noticed a strange quietness. The Peaudane surrey was not hitched out front, and there seemed to be no one around. Moving cautiously forward, I froze when I saw a frail, old woman sitting in a wooden wheelchair.

Grandma Nance, Arty's grandmother on his mother's side, was the oldest and oddest person I had ever encountered. Small in stature, Grandma Nance had dark, wrinkled skin, and erratic eyes, while her teeth were nearly all gone except for three sharp protrusions visible when she occasionally spoke.

All the Martin boys, including Arty, were wary of the spry, old woman. Arty often talked of her sharp tongue and demanding ways, but most had rarely heard her speak as she seemed content to stare silently and listen to the happenings around her. When she did speak, she often talked in strange riddles, and some whispered she was a witch or some kind of mystic.

"Who's there?" she hissed in her shrill voice.

"Who goes there, I said?" she repeated in a more demanding tone.

"It's me..." I stammered. "Gill...Gilbert Brooks...I'm a friend of Arty's."

She quickly looked toward me, while her eyes focused in the general direction where I stood.

"I know you," she precisely spoke. "Gilbert…Brooks. What business do you have here?"

"I…I just came to see Arty," I timidly responded.

The old woman laughed in a way that made me feel uneasy as she said, "Gilbert Brooks comes to see Arty? I don't think so."

"No…I mean Yes ma'am…I came to see Arty," I defended.

"Come closer," she said in almost a whisper. "Come closer so I can see you."

I cautiously stepped on the porch, trying to keep my distance.

"Come closer," she demanded in an insistent tone.

Reluctantly, I moved within a few feet of Grandma Nance.

Still looking as if she did not see me, she said, "Yes…Just as I supposed. You did not come to see Arty at all…you've come to see the girl."

"Huh?" I grunted, struggling to understand her strange cadence of speaking.

"The girl!" she shouted in an overly loud voice. "She will see troubles more than you know."

After a moment of silence, she responded with her uneasy laugh and in a softer tone said, "You don't believe, but I know…I know what I've seen, and I've seen it happen as if it happened again and again."

Regaining some composure and realizing I was listening to the babblings of senility, I answered in a calm voice, "I've just come to see Arty."

Like a rattlesnake striking without warning, the old woman suddenly reached out and grabbed my arm, holding it tightly.

Grandma Nance tugged my arm to move me closer while showing her sharp-looking, chiseled teeth as she smiled and said, "I've seen it before…I've seen it again and again…and I will see it again. The poor girl is destined for trouble I say."

"What girl?" I asked.

"The Peaudane girl!" Grandma Nance shouted in a harsh tone. "She's who you're here to see? I've seen it in the girl's eyes…her unhappiness and trouble—"

The seemingly blind woman's erratic method of speech made me uneasy. Her ability to deduce I was there to see Gwen Peaudane stunned me.

"Grandma!" the stern voice of Marilee Martin scolded. "Why are you talking so loud?"

The old woman who had spoken so assertively suddenly greeted Marilee's question with silence as if she could not hear. Chewing something invisible, her lower lip contorted in an odd way as she ignored her granddaughter.

"Mother would not like you making a fuss, would she?" Marilee kindly reminded the old woman.

Grandma Nance continued to greet her granddaughter with silence and stared blankly as if neither of us were there.

"I'll bring you tea in a little while, but you leave poor Gilbert alone," Marilee concluded, as she motioned for me to walk with her around the corner of the house toward the back porch.

Taking the opportunity to leave Grandma Nance behind, I gladly followed Marilee.

"I'm sorry Gilbert," Marilee explained. "Grandma gets worked up sometimes."

"It's fine. We were just having a talk," I said, still looking back over my shoulder.

Marilee smiled, causing her nose to wrinkle. Her hair was tied back tight, and she had flour decorating her forehead making her round face look silly. She did not seem to know what a mess her face was, which made it difficult for me not to laugh at her.

"What'cha doin' here?" she asked.

"Oh…I…just came to see Arty," I lied.

Looking suspiciously at me, she said, "I see...He's not here."

"I kind of figured that," I said, looking around at the vacant property. "Don't look like anyone's around."

"No," Marilee confirmed. "No one but me and Grandma. The rest went on a ride...in the Peaudane's new car."

"A car?" I asked.

"Dr. Peaudane bought a new car...a big one!" Marilee excitedly explained. "They all went for a ride leaving me with Grandma...Even Mother went."

"Must be a big car," I said, calculating how many people might squeeze into the automobile.

"She didn't come," Marilee coyly stated.

"Excuse me," I replied.

Marilee sighed, "Gwen didn't drive out...only Dr. Peaudane."

I listened awkwardly to Marilee's scolding tone. Marilee was almost two years younger than Gwendolyn Peaudane was, but the two had been friends since they were small girls.

"I'm not deaf," Marilee pouted. "Me and anyone within a mile could hear Grandma talking to you about 'that Peaudane girl.' It's a sure bet, she wasn't trying to keep you away from me!"

I could not help but smile at Marilee's candor. As I smirked, the ridiculous smudge of flour on her forehead became more humorous.

Trying desperately to change the subject from Gwen Peaudane I asked, "You've been baking?"

Marilee smiled shyly at the attention and proudly said, "Yes, I've been makin' fried pies."

Her enthusiasm for cooking and the flour stuck on her forehead prevented me from looking away, and before long, Marilee noticed my awkward stare. She grinned momentarily at the attention before rubbing her forehead, causing her to remember her appearance. With a slight squeal, she retreated into the house.

The afternoon was quickly turning to evening as I stood alone behind the Martin house. Not knowing how long Arty would be riding in Dr. Peaudane's new car, I stood for a moment wondering whether to stay or go. The dejection of not seeing Gwen was tempered somewhat by knowing she was not with Arty Martin.

I slowly turned to make the walk back home when Marilee shouted in a stiff and formal tone, "Don't you want to try one of my pies?"

The sight of Marilee standing on the porch with her face wiped off and her hair quickly brushed was almost as comical as her flour-covered face. Marilee was in an awkward stage of life—past being a cute little girl and nowhere near being a woman. Marilee, who did not seem likely to outgrow this phase soon, endured plenty of abuse from her rambunctious brothers, and I imagined she was relieved they did not see her covered in cooking ingredients.

"Sure," I answered.

"Good," she uneasily replied. "They're apricot."

I followed Marilee to the far side of the house away from her grandmother and sat on the edge of the porch as she handed me a hot, fried pie. Marilee plopped ungracefully beside me and watched my every reaction as I bit into the hot pie. The pastry smelled sweet and tasted sweeter as the light, fluffy crust nearly burnt my mouth.

Before I had a chance to swallow, Marilee asked, "How is it?"

"It's…musty," I teased.

"What!" Marilee squealed in horror.

Smiling at her angst, I explained, "It's musty…like I must have some more…It's delicious."

Marilee's cheeks turned rosy, and she said, "You don't have to lie."

"I'm not lying," I assured. "It's better than any candy you could buy at the store."

Marilee seemed to appreciate the complement, while blushing at the same time.

"Thanks," she finally said. "Musty…I fell for that one."

Marilee quickly added, as if frightened by the brief silence, "I'd have invited ya' inside, but Mother would not approve of me having a man in the house unattended."

I took another bite of the tasty pie without really listening.

"Why'd they leave you behind?" I finally asked. "Didn't you want to go for a ride?"

Marilee frowned and said, "I kind of burnt the first batch of pies. Besides they needed someone to watch Grandma."

"Hmm," I shrugged.

"I think the boys are a little afraid of Grandma…At least they look for any excuse not to get stuck alone with her."

As the pie cooled I enthusiastically took bigger bites. Marilee Martin might have been plain as a pancake to look at, but her pies were light as a cloud and sweet as honey.

"I don't mind her," Marilee continued as I enjoyed my pie. "She's really interesting if you take the time to listen."

"Your grandma?" I asked in disbelief.

"I know she's kind of odd to some folks, but she…knows things…I always like listening to her…and I like that the boys don't…I guess."

"Arty's afraid of her," I confirmed as I finished my pie.

Marilee smiled with some satisfaction.

"I guess I better head back," I stated.

Marilee stood up before I could and said, "So soon? Don't you want another pie…or maybe a piece of chicken?"

I had no reason to stay, but a piece of chicken and another pie sounded irresistible. Marilee did not wait for me to accept the invitation. She took my hesitation as acceptance and quickly disappeared into the house. I took the opportunity to step around the back and further away from Grandma Nance. The Martin farm was the antithesis of the Brooks' place. Everything looked up-to-date and well maintained, while our equipment was held together with baling wire and a prayer.

The corral held Mr. Martin's prized mules, Buster and Duster, which plowed the large fields. We owned two broken down nags that Dad called names I was not allowed to repeat. Our horse, Old Betsy, was barely serviceable as a saddle horse. All the Martin boys owned handsome horses, and Mr. Martin's pride and joy was a large, muscular, black stallion he named Big Blackie. The horse was reputed to be the fastest in the county, but Mr. Martin disapproved of foolishness like racing. Arty bragged about the horse to all our friends and threatened more than once to sneak Big Blackie out to race. In contrast to the impressive stallion was a smaller mare, called Little Blackie, which belonged to Marilee. The horse had short legs and a thick torso, but Marilee could ride almost as good as her brothers.

While I looked over the Martin fields, the sun began to set in the west as the turquoise sky contrasted with the salmon clouds with a rich indigo above. The hot breeze became milder as Marilee reappeared with a plate of chicken, a potato, and sliced tomato. Marilee perched on the edge of the porch, watching me devour my meal.

Noticing her scrutiny, I asked, "Did you help with this?"

Straightening up, she replied, "Help nothing…This is my supper."

"You cooked this?" I clarified.

"Momma has me do most of the cookin' for the boys," she explained.

"It's good, I'll tell you that," I complemented, while continuing to eat.

I finished supper and heard the distant rumblings of a car coming down the bumpy road as I started on my second fried pie. Without saying a word, Marilee took my dishes and disappeared into the house. Walking around the corner of the house to look for the approaching car, I had forgotten about Grandma Nance sitting there.

"Sometimes you come for one thing only to find another," she said as she continued to stare into the dusk and flashed her pointy teeth.

"What?" I asked in confusion.

Snapping her head to look my direction, she smiled oddly and said, "They're here."

A blast of the horn announced the arrival of Dr. Peaudane's new car. Dr. Peaudane, Mrs. Martin, and Mr. Martin sat in the front, while the Martin boys piled in the back. All seemed enthused by the ride, except for Mrs. Martin, who appeared glad to have her feet back on the ground. She walked directly to the porch and wheeled her mother inside as the men stood around admiring the new automobile.

"Is that Gilbert Brooks?" a pleasant Dr. Peaudane greeted.

"Yes, sir," I replied.

Taking a step toward me he said, "My son, Guy, would like to speak to you next time you're in town."

"My dad told me," I confirmed.

With a pleasant smile, he turned back to the group of boys admiring his car. Arty had one older brother, Ethan, who carefully studied every detail of the vehicle. Arty was the next oldest, followed by Marilee. Roy, Floyd, and Elmo Martin were the three younger brothers, and all displayed a confidence and pride that was a trademark of the Martin men.

"It's a beauty ain't it, Gill?" Arty whispered in a voice his father could not hear.

"It sure is," I agreed. "How fast did you go?"

Arty smiled and said, "Down in that flat stretch along Salt Creek, I think he got her up nearly to fifty miles per hour."

"Fifty!" I gasped.

"I think he would've gone faster if Momma hadn't thrown a fit to slow down."

"Fifty," I repeated.

"What's ya' doin' here?" Arty asked with a mischievous grin. "Callin' on my sister?"

"No," I quickly clarified. "Came to see if you're still goin' to Romulus Saturday."

"Oh, I'm going," Arty confidently said. "But I told you that last night."

"I know," I conceded.

With a coy smile, he said, "Gwen's not here."

Pretending to look around as if the idea had just occurred to me, I casually replied, "No, I guess she's not."

"She didn't come tonight," Arty sighed, unable to disguise his disappointment.

Feeling satisfied that Gwen had disappointed Arty, I felt a chill in my spine when he worriedly said, "I think she may have a fella."

"What?" I answered trying not to be alarmed.

"I tried to question her dad…you know he likes me, but I couldn't get an answer," Arty surmised. "I bet it's one of those fellas from Shawnee."

"No way," I defended, knowing Gwen could not have anything to do with someone from the city.

"I don't know," Arty sighed. "Somethan' distracts her."

"Arthur!" the stern voice of Mr. Martin interrupted. "Don't be getting any ideas of running off tonight. You were out late last night and not good for anything today."

"Yes, sir," Arty replied.

"I better go," Arty whispered, as his father continued to stare at us.

"Yeah," I agreed. "I'll see ya' Saturday."

"See ya' Saturday," Arty whispered while walking toward his house.

Heading down the dark hill, a kaleidoscope of emotions flooded my thoughts on the walk home. The assertion that Gwen might have an interest in someone else tempered any relief I felt at discovering she was not with Arty. The apprehension would build until Saturday when I finally had a chance to see her and possibly say something clever and memorable.

Not more than a hundred yards down the road, thoughts of Gwen were interrupted by the voice of Marilee Martin calling, "Gilbert! Gilbert!"

Turning around, I saw Marilee walking quickly down the road.

"I thought you might want to take some of these pies to your brothers," she offered.

"Oh," I stammered, still surprised to see the young girl on the dark trail.

"You said you liked 'em," she anxiously explained.

"Sure," I said trying to be polite. "They were great…they'll be wasted on my brothers though…they'll eat anything…even my mother's cooking."

"Oh," Marilee laughed timidly.

Taking the sack of pies from her, I said, "Thanks…we'll enjoy them."

Smiling nervously, she said, "Good."

Without another word, she headed back into the dark toward her house. I was sure Mr. Martin did not know Marilee was out, but I had other worries. Still thinking about Gwen Peaudane, I plotted a strategy in my mind about Saturday's trip to Romulus.

CHAPTER 7

Two hot days in the field preceded our Saturday trip to Romulus. Gordon pestered me mercilessly about the chocolate bar I promised. Lloyd was more subtle but forceful in his reminders. At random times, he would punch me in the arm to get my attention, then smile broadly and point to his lips as if to smoke.

It was past noon on Saturday before we finished the chores, cleaned up, and headed to town. Dad hitched Old Betsy to our rickety wagon and bounced down the rutted road toward Romulus.

Romulus barely qualified as a town, but was less than three miles from home and had amenities like a post office, a gristmill, a couple of stores, and several churches. The town was situated on a ridge above the Salt Creek where the Rock Island Railroad ran a spur from Tecumseh to Asher on the South Canadian River. The weathered, two-story train station with an awning around the passenger area provided a gateway out of the Cross Timber and to the rest of the world.

The most important enterprise to me, however, was the Peaudane General Store situated a block from the train station. The store had a sampling of everything and provided the best opportunity for me to run into Dr. Peaudane's daughter, Gwen. Guy Peaudane, the oldest son had asked to see me, and I had been curious, as well as anxious, about the meeting.

Coming from the east, the small town buzzed with activity as farm families came to buy supplies and visit neighbors on this Saturday afternoon. The town was mainly shades of brown and gray. About a dozen wood buildings lined a grass road with wagon ruts in the center. Faded advertising for Chesterfields and Prince Albert tobacco adorned some of the buildings, but much of the paint from the town's early years had faded. The exception to the drab scene was the freshly painted green sign over the Peaudane General Store. Several wagons lined the wide space between the buildings, as Dad searched for a place to put our wagon. Impatiently, I jumped off the back of the wagon and moved through the crowd toward the store.

"Gill!" Arty Martin shouted from across the street.

"Hey, Arty," I greeted.

"Been here long?" he asked.

"Nope…just got into town."

"Seen Lance?" Arty inquired.

"Didn't see any sign of him," I replied.

"Guess he's around somewhere," Arty mused, as he searched the street. "Ya' wanna go find him?"

Finding Lance and hearing his stories would normally be on the top of my list of things to do. I had an appointment with Guy Peaudane, however, with the hope of running into his sister Gwen.

"I need to see about something first," I explained.

Arty grinned and said, "That's right. Guy Peaudane's been wanting to see you. Dr. Peaudane said somthan' 'bout it the other night."

Studying my anxiety for a moment, Arty added, "Maybe he wants to see if you'll take his sister to the county fair next month."

My eyes widened and a smile began to creep on my face, as I was about to ask, "Do you think so?"

Before I could say it, however, Arty laughed good-naturedly and said, "You don't have ta' worry about that, I've already asked Gwen to ride with me to the fair."

Panic almost overwhelmed reason, and I started to say something rash, when a voice behind me said, "There you are."

Turning around, Guy Peaudane stepped quickly toward me from the front of his store.

I wanted to question Arty in more detail about his idea of taking Gwen to the county fair, but he said, "I'll catch up with you later…I'm goin' to find Lance. Ya' wanna do somethin' tonight?"

"Sure," I said trying to hide my dejection as Arty headed down the street.

Guy Peaudane was in his late twenties. He was a dapperly dressed man who was smart and articulate. He worked for his father in the store, but most people understood he ran the business.

"Hello, Mr. Peaudane," I greeted standing in front of the store. "I heard you wanted to see me."

"I sure do," he cheerfully answered.

"Excuse me," a large woman interrupted as she headed into the store. "Can you tell me if you have any rocking chairs?"

"Yes ma'am," Guy answered. "I have two left in the back of the store."

Turning back around to me, he said, "We're pretty busy right now. If you can hang around for a bit, I'd like to talk with you."

"Sure," I responded.

"Great," he said with a smile as he headed toward his customer. "I shouldn't be long."

The store brimmed with excitement as people carefully inspected the merchandise. Compared to the dreary, hot fields, the place was an oasis. Content to loiter around the store, I looked at the products for sale, while keeping a keen eye out for Gwen.

The Peaudane General Store was a small place, barely more than twenty-five feet wide, but was as big as any store in town. The dusty wood floor was barely visible as the place was packed with all kinds of tools, hardware, harnesses, dry goods, furniture, candy—and tobacco products. Remembering my debt to Lloyd, I headed to the counter to purchase his cigarettes.

The store had all kinds of tobacco products, but I quickly spotted the Camel cigarettes Lloyd requested.

Picking up the two packs, I felt a gentle tap on my shoulder and heard a soft voice say, "Those will stunt your growth."

Spinning around, I blushed to see Gwendolyn Peaudane standing by me.

"Oh…They're…These aren't for me," I stammered.

Gwen smiled sweetly and with a little wink said, "I bet."

"No…really," I protested. "They're for Lloyd."

"Don't worry what I think," Gwen nonchalantly admonished.

"No really, they're not for me!" I desperately pleaded.

"Okay, Gill…I believe you," Gwen said in a less teasing tone.

Sensing my embarrassment, Gwen quickly asked, "Where is Lloyd? I haven't seen him in ages…I used to have such a crush on him."

My temporary discomfort turned to panic at the thought of having yet another competitor for Gwen's attention.

"He usually hangs out around Asher," I quickly explained. "Neva St. Clair lives down there."

"Oh," Gwen shrugged, appearing to be disinterested as her long eyelashes batted over poignant, azure-blue eyes.

"There you are," Guy Peaudane interrupted. "Gwen, can you excuse us? I want to talk to Gilbert."

"Sure," Gwen conceded. "I'll see you Gill."

With a flash of a smile, Gwen Peaudane gracefully spun around while her thick, brown hair seemed to float in the air. In a moment, she was out the door and down the street. Guy Peaudane discretely cleared his voice to get my attention, interrupting my gaze out the store window trying to get one last glimpse of Gwen.

"Come to the back with me," Guy suggested.

We walked through the crowded aisles of merchandise to a space in the back that served as a storeroom.

"I've been talking to Mrs. Long at Unity School," Guy began.

Mrs. Long had been the teacher the last two years I attended Unity School, or as we called it, Fuss Box. She had been a dark-haired woman with strict ways who had tried to bring some kind of order to the rowdy one-room schoolhouse.

"She tells me you're a responsible young man and have finished the eighth grade," he continued.

I had finished eighth grade a year earlier but continued going to school to help Mrs. Long teach arithmetic and reading to some of the younger students. Arty Martin and Lance Carrington thought I was crazy to continue—especially when Gwen Peaudane was no longer at the school, but I much preferred helping in the classroom to doing farm chores.

"She said you're good with numbers," Guy said, while studying my demeanor.

"I always tried to do my best," I nervously replied.

"Let me get to the point," Guy continued. "I'm looking for a boy to work part-time at the store…to take inventory, stock the shelves, sweep floors, and make a few deliveries."

A combination of excitement and pride filled my thoughts at the offer. A chance to work in a store in town seemed too good to be true.

"I'd love to," I began. "But…I'd need to check with my pa…you know…see what he thinks."

As my mind formulated the words I would use to convince my father to let me work in the store, Guy Peaudane said, "I've already talked to your father and he seemed agreeable to the idea."

"Great!" I almost shouted. "When do you need me to start?"

Guy Peaudane chuckled and replied, "Don't you want to know the terms?"

"Sure," I hastily responded, embarrassed at my uncontrolled enthusiasm.

"I'll pay you a dollar a day…to start out," he offered.

"Sounds good to me," I beamed, thinking of how much the extra money could buy.

"There's one more thing," Guy timidly continued.

I looked him in the eye to give my full attention.

"Your father owes money here at the store," Guy tactfully informed.

The excitement I felt at having a new job quickly faded at the reminder of my family's humble economic standing.

Sensing my discomfort, Guy Peaudane quickly added, "Your father's a good man and I know he'll pay when the crop comes in, but he and I were talking about him maybe saving some money after this crop to pay down on some land of his own. I told him I could pay you half the wages in cash and the other half would go to pay on your family's account here at the store."

Relieved at Guy's reassuring tone, I began to agree, when he added, "I just wanted to be up front with you."

"Yes, sir," I acknowledged. "That sounds real fine to me. When do you need me to start?"

Guy Peaudane smiled as he put an arm around my shoulder and said, "We'll start after the cotton harvest. Maybe you could come in Saturdays to start, if it works out with your dad?"

"Sounds great," I assured.

He began showing me around the back room of the store and telling me about some of his expectations, when a small commotion caused Guy Peaudane to step to the front window to look down the street.

A moment later, Gwen Peaudane burst through the door shouting, "You need to come, Guy…there's a fight!"

CHAPTER 8

A small crowd gathered around the brewing commotion at the far end of the dirt street.

"It's Arty and Lance!" Gwen shouted urgently as she tried to keep up with her brother.

Arty and Lance had squabbles in the past, but I had seen Arty only a few moments before and could not imagine why the two friends would be fighting. Peering through the onlookers, I saw Lance Carrington sprawled in the dirt with his floppy hat resting on the ground a few feet away. Standing over him was Haskell Holiday, the farmer whose watermelon patch we had raided a few nights earlier.

With a stick in hand, the large man moved toward his victim. Lance had already been knocked to the ground, and he sprang to his feet just in time to receive another blow from Haskell.

Guy Peaudane was running now with Gwen and I close behind. Haskell Holiday muttered some choice profanities as he moved to kick Lance while he was down. Two steps from his victim, Arty Martin slashed from the side and hit the heavy man with the full force of his body. Haskell Holiday nearly went down but staggered to keep his balance and then took a swipe at Arty. Arty was too quick for the first punch as Haskell Holiday swung wildly. Arty landed a blow squarely on the large man's chin.

Haskell Holiday glared at him a moment and then laughed evilly. Walking up to a stunned Arty, Haskell lifted him off the ground and threw the young man aside. Before Haskell could follow up on his attack of Arty, Lance was up and landed two quick blows to the large man's mid-section seeming to take the fight out of him. Before Lance could put him down, however, a pistol shot rang out silencing the restless crowd.

"That'll be enough!" the commanding voice of the town's marshal shouted.

The arrival of the marshal did nothing to calm anxieties. Leland Holiday had been the town marshal for two years, but many in town considered him more outlaw than lawman. Leland was Haskell's cousin and had been bootlegging partners with Lance's father years earlier in Violet Springs. He was a muscular, barrel-chested man in his mid-thirties with a thick, handlebar mustache hiding a perpetual smirk and a gold front tooth. An overall intimidating demeanor was accented by dark, penetrating eyes.

"Break it up!" Leland Holiday shouted again as the group of curious onlookers began to disperse.

Before Guy Peaudane could get to the marshal, Leland stepped between the bloodied Lance Carrington and wobbly Haskell Holiday.

Grabbing Lance by the collar, Leland said, "You're going to have to be smarter than your old man, kid."

Nodding at Haskell, Leland Holiday quickly pinned Lance's arms behind his back as his cousin delivered punches to the body causing Lance to groan and slide to the ground. Leaping to his feet, Arty Martin charged the marshal as he had done Haskell earlier. Leland, almost fifty pounds lighter than Haskell, stumbled slightly, but then tossed Arty to the ground. Before Arty could get up, Leland Holiday coolly leveled his revolver at the feisty boy, while Lance still lay on the ground trying to catch his breath.

Quickly regaining his composure and lowering the pistol, the marshal said, "This is no concern of yours, Martin."

"Marshal! Would you mind explaining yourself?" an agitated Guy Peaudane demanded.

Leland Holiday studied Guy Peaudane and calmly responded, "There's nothing for you to be concerned with, Mr. Peaudane."

Leland Holiday was astute enough to know he did not want trouble with the Peaudane family and restrained himself from saying more.

"It certainly is!" Guy continued. "Two boys are being roughed up in broad daylight accompanied by gunfire on the street. As a merchant, I don't appreciate the interruption to my customers."

Leland Holiday surveyed the situation and repeated, "Like I said, Mr. Peaudane, this really isn't your concern. This boy stole some watermelons the other night and has perpetrated numerous vandalisms on Haskell's property."

Most people around Romulus were aware of the circumstances involving Haskell Holiday acquiring the Carrington farm, originally deeded to Lance's mother when the Potawatomi nation moved to the area. When she died, Lance's father made some bad decisions in business dealings with the Holiday family and lost the farm. Many felt Lance's father had used poor judgment in his dealing with Haskell, but others in town did not trust the Holidays, who always seemed to operate on the fringes of the law. With Leland Holiday now serving as the city's chief law enforcement presence, men like Haskell operated with impunity.

"I think I have a vested interest!" the stern voice of Mr. Martin roared from across the street.

No one owned as much land or carried as much influence as Mr. Martin and the confident marshal stammered for a response.

"I see my boy's on the ground," Mr. Martin assertively charged. "I think this makes it a matter for me to investigate."

"I don't have no problems with your boy, Mr. Martin," the marshal timidly replied. "Except for the company he keeps."

"Exception noted!" Mr. Martin barked back. "Arthur, pick yourself up and get to the wagon. I'm taking you home."

Arty dusted himself off and complied with his father's instructions.

"Thanks, Arty," Lance Carrington whispered as his friend walked past him.

"I'll deal with Arthur at home," Mr. Martin assured as he walked away.

"What about this one?" an apprehensive Leland Holiday asked.

Leland Holiday was not the kind of man who was used to asking permission, but he was clever enough to understand there was no advantage in crossing a man like Mr. Martin.

Looking at the bruised and battered Lance Carrington, Mr. Martin replied, "Like you said, I don't have any business with that one."

Taking Arty by the collar and sternly talking to him on the way to the wagon, the Martin family quickly retreated from town.

"Haskell, you go home," Leland Holiday instructed.

A still agitated Haskell Holiday reluctantly agreed.

"Stay off *my* property!" he shouted at Lance as he walked away.

"The rest of you get out of here," the marshal demanded.

Everyone complied except for Guy, Gwen, and me. Leland Holiday cuffed Lance Carrington in front of us and started stepping to the city jail down the street.

"Marshal—" Guy Peaudane began to plead.

"Save your breath," Leland Holiday interrupted. "I'm taking the boy into custody for his own good."

Without giving Guy Peaudane an opportunity to protest, Leland Holiday marched a humiliated Lance across the street and into the city building as people watched from the walkway.

"It'll be all right," Guy Peaudane assured me. "You better find your folks, Gilbert. I'll go check on Lance tonight after the marshal has a chance to calm down."

I nodded in agreement and left Guy and Gwen to find my parents. Looking back to get one more glimpse of Gwen, I witnessed her picking up Lance Carrington's beat-up old hat while gently dusting some of the grime off it.

Relieved I had not been part of the fracas, I admired Arty Martin's willingness to fight for his friend. It made me proud to have a companion like him. The fight between Lance Carrington and Haskell Holiday was all we talked about on the drive home, and I listened nervously hoping I would not be connected to the watermelon-stealing incident.

Several weeks would pass before Lance, Arty, and I would be able to discuss the fight with Leland Holiday, and our reunion would happen in the most unlikely of places.

CHAPTER 9

Cotton dominated my attention the next few weeks. Working half a day at the Peaudane General Store, however, was like a vacation from the hot fields. Arty was forbidden from leaving the Martin farm for a few weeks as punishment for his role in the disturbance. Guy Peaudane talked Leland Holiday into letting Lance off with a scolding, and Lance disappeared back into the Cross Timber.

A revival meeting was held in a tent on the edge of town in late August, and my family attended several nights. Gwen Peaudane had been there with her brother Guy on a few evenings, which added to my spiritual encouragement. Although Arty was less than interested in preaching, he agreed to come with me on the last night. Even though Mr. Martin was only an occasional churchgoer, he believed some preaching might do Arty good and allowed him out of the house. It was Arty's first opportunity to escape the watchful eye of his father since the fight with Leland Holiday. Mr. Martin, however, had no idea Lance Carrington would be at the revival meeting when he let Arty come. It was a surprise to many.

Lance's arrival at the gathering shocked several of the more pious women of the congregation, while some of the men trembled at seeing the son of their bootlegger so close to their wives and preacher. Lance had only a remnant of the shiner above his eye that Leland and Haskell Holiday had given him. His dark hair was more neatly combed than normal, but his clothes were patched and looked as if he had been camping a week.

Arty and I were antsy for the invitation song and a chance to meet up with our friend. Two people came forward, one for prayers and the other to be baptized. For us, this meant more singing and more waiting to find out where Lance had been hiding. After the souls had been properly saved, we made a beeline to Lance.

"What're ya' doin' here?" Arty excitedly quizzed.

"Heard there was some preachin' I might need," Lance replied with a smile.

"Didn't think I'd ever see you in church," I quipped.

"Yeah," Lance grinned. "I guess it surprised a lot of folks."

"Where ya' been?" Arty asked. "I heard Leland Holiday threw you in jail."

Lance scratched behind his ear and smiled broadly, "Naw…He just tried to scare me some. Guy Peaudane came down and talked to him."

"I think he might have paid for that melon I got," Lance blushed.

"You didn't actually get put in jail," I tried to clarify.

"Oh yeah," Lance nodded. "Holiday literally threw me in there and proceeded to cuss at me the rest of the afternoon. I didn't care that much…the bed was going to be softer than most nights."

"But where have ya' been since then?" Arty asked again.

"Been 'round Violet Springs mainly," Lance said with less enthusiasm.

Violet Springs spawned tales that grew with time. Respectable businesses moved years earlier across the county line to Konawa. All that was left in Violet Springs were several ruined buildings once housing saloons and other scandalous establishments. Killings were so common in the area that the newspaper in Konawa noted there had been *only* 36 killings one year.

The most notorious place in the county was located south of the ghost-town of Violet Springs. An illegal saloon called the Potanole hid in an old gristmill deep in the woods. The establishment was in the far corner of the county on the border between Pottawatomie County and Seminole County close to the South Canadian River. Rumor was that no one went there without looking for trouble.

"Didn't think there was no town left." Arty continued.

"Not much," Lance admitted. "I've...been stayin' with Dad for a while...been doin' some work."

Arty and I quickly looked at each other wondering what kind of work Lance might be doing. Arty began to ask more questions before a voice interrupted our curiosity about Lance.

"Hi Lance," the voice of Gwen Peaudane greeted. "It was good to see you at services tonight."

Lance blushed at being recognized in a place so unfamiliar to him.

"It...It was good...I mean nice to be here," Lance stammered.

"It was a good lesson, don't you think?" she asked kindly.

Lance, I suspected, had come to see his friends, not to listen to a sermon. Arty and I gasped in surprise when he answered, "Very good. I liked the part about Joseph. Had all that opportunity to do the wrong things but did the right thing...I liked when the preacher said, 'Doin' the right thing's not always easy, but it's always the right thing to do.' Made some sense, I guess."

Arty and I were stunned to hear Lance recall any part of the sermon. I was quite sure neither one of us remembered that much. Even Gwen seemed impressed.

"Do you believe it?" Gwen asked.

"What?" Lance asked.

"Do you believe in doing the right thing?" she repeated.

Arty smirked, knowing Lance would have more difficulty with this question. Lance stared at her painfully as he tried to manufacture an appropriate answer.

"I...believe it, I guess," he finally replied. "But...I guess I've been a little short in practice."

With a slight tilt of the head that caused her long, sandy brown hair to dance, Gwen beamed a smile that overcame her normally reserved demeanor and quipped, "I guess practice makes perfect."

Noticing Lance Carrington with his younger sister, Guy Peaudane quickly investigated and politely asked Lance, "You've been staying out of trouble, I hope?"

"Yes sir," Lance replied. "At least out of jail…I didn't' get a chance to thank—"

"No need," Guy assured. "Just…try to stay out of Haskell's melon patch…and don't pick a fight with someone that out-weighs you by eighty pounds."

"Yes sir," Lance sheepishly nodded.

"Gwen, are you ready to go?" Guy asked in a pleasant but urgent tone.

"I guess so," Gwen answered.

"Gwen, are we still going to the county fair?" Arty interrupted, showing some frustration that he had not been the center of Gwen's attention.

"Huh…I mean, sure I'm going, Arty," Gwen answered.

"Great," Arty replied with some relief. "I'm sure lookin' forward to it."

"You're coming too, Gill?" Gwen asked.

While Arty tried to signal with his eyes for me to say no, I struggled with how I might be able to make the trip.

"I…don't know," I finally answered. "The cotton should be in by then, but I've promised to work for your brother."

"Nonsense," Guy Peaudane interrupted. "You're only young once. Take the day off and go to the fair."

Gwen smiled, while Arty grimaced, before she turned to Lance and said, "You're coming too, aren't you?"

Lance was caught by surprise, but replied, "I've never been north of Maud before, but the fair sure sounds nice."

"Sure it's nice," Gwen smiled. "Lloyd, Marilee…a whole bunch of us are plannin' to go. It'll be great fun."

"You've talked me into it," Lance smiled.

Arty was sulking at Gwen's mass invitation to the fair, since he had bragged for weeks about taking her—he had assumed alone.

"We've got to go," Guy Peaudane announced firmly and coldly.

He took Gwen by the arm and led her toward the car. After two steps however, Gwen abruptly stopped and turned around. Reaching into her bag, she pulled out a worn piece of felt.

"Thought you might want this back," she said as she handed Lance his old felt hat. "I cleaned it a little."

"Thought I'd lost this forever," Lance smiled as he took the hat from Gwen.

"I kept it for you," she smiled.

"Gwen, we've got to go," Guy stated firmly.

"Bye guys," Gwen said as she spun to follow Guy.

Gwen walked away with our eyes and attention on her.

As the Peaudane car drove into the night with Gwen inside, Lance Carrington teased, "It was nice of you to let us go on your date with Gwen, Arty."

"Shut up," Arty shot back with a perplexed grin on his face.

"No, this will be good for you," Lance continued. "The more of us there are the better chance you'll have of her actually sitting close to you."

"You guys," Arty defended. "You know you could've both said you couldn't come. Heck, I'd have paid your way to go the next weekend."

"That reminds me," Lance smirked. "Could you loan me a dime for the train fare?"

"You don't have the train fare?" Arty replied.

Lance smiled, "No, I got train fare, but I'd still like you to loan me a dime."

"I bet he'll give you the dime not to go on a ride with her," I added.

"Both of you shut up," Arty threatened, although he knew the teasing would last for weeks if not longer.

"I'm confused," Lance joked. "Were you going with Gwen or that skinny sister of yours?"

"Marilee's not going with me," Arty defiantly stated. "I'll see to that."

"Why are you picking on Marilee?" Lance defended. "She may be the only girl besides your mama that'll love you."

Arty just shook his head and decided that any reply he made would only mean more teasing by his two friends.

Lance's tone turned more serious as we prepared to leave and he said, "I really didn't come here to torment you Arty. In fact, I only came tonight to see you."

"What do ya' mean?" Arty asked warily, still stinging from the laughs we had been having at his expense.

"I didn't get a chance to thank you for the other day," Lance continued.

"Thank me for what?" Arty innocently asked.

"In town the other day," Lance clarified. "That wasn't your fight. You could've stayed out of it. Old Haskell would have beat me good for sure, but I'd of still wound up in jail, and you'd have stayed out of trouble with your dad."

Arty looked seriously at Lance for a second and answered, "Don't you know that any fight of yours is a fight of mine? I couldn't stand by if I could help, just like you couldn't stand by if me or Gill were in trouble."

"I guess," Lance shrugged.

"You guess?" Arty scolded. "We've been through a bunch of stuff together…We're brothers of the Cross Timber…ain't nothing ever going to change that. Remember, we're goin' to meet back by the rock on the river every ten years. Wouldn't be much of a reunion if old Haskell killed you before then."

"Sayin' you're a friend and bein' a friend's two different things," Lance said seriously. "I know you two are my friends, and I just wanted to tell you."

"Ain't nothing goin' to come between us," Arty continued. "Not the law, not that cheatin' Haskell Holiday, not moving away…not even Gwen Peaudane!"

"You don't have to worry about that," Lance smiled. "You won't even know I'm at the fair. You'll have Gwen all to yourself. I think Guy Peaudane might not have got me outta' jail if'n I was goin' to talk to his sister anyway."

Lance smiled broadly again as he put on his worn, old hat and said, "I might go dancin' with that skinny little sister of yours, though."

Arty teasingly grabbed Lance and replied, "If you can stand her, you're dumber than I thought."

Lance broke free of Arty's grasp and said, "So, what's at the fair, anyway?"

Arty vividly described the color and pageantry of the Pottawatomie County Fair complete with cooking contest, livestock, the latest machines, newest gadgets, games, rides, and contests offering all kinds of entertainment.

"You know what we can do?" Arty excitedly concluded.

"What?" we asked in unison.

"We need to go to Shawnee, while we're there," Arty revealed. "It's only a couple of miles further and you boys haven't seen anything until you've seen the city."

"Sounds good to me," I replied. Although I had always been fascinated by stories of the city, I had never been there and looked forward to having an experienced guide like Arty.

"Don't know how much more trouble I can find in the city than I can around here, but I'm up for it," Lance quipped.

"Good," Arty said, while rubbing his hands. "You boys ain't seen nothin' yet!"

CHAPTER 10

The early September sun scorched the irregular rows of cotton on our farm and worry etched the sunburned face of my father. I did not fully realize at the time that he farmed out of desperation. Like many in the county, our family came to Oklahoma to escape poverty and find opportunity. Our family survived on poor soil by hard work and stubborn defiance.

My father was not a complicated man, but a person of great contrast. He lived with the constant worry of destitution common to tenant farming, but he also demonstrated a carefree, almost playful attitude, especially around children. This summer something was different, although his slight change in demeanor was a mystery to me. The weeds, however, held no mystery. They mocked us and threatened our cotton. Our cotton was our livelihood so we attacked the weeds daily to protect the crop.

"Saw ya' with that Peaudane girl," Lloyd stoically commented, as he effortlessly passed me on his second row of weeding that day.

"What?" I replied, having not paid attention to his random chatter.

Laughing, he continued, "The Peaudane girl, Gwen. Saw ya' with her. Looked like she was with pretty much every other guy at the church meeting, too."

"What of it?" I asked, tending to be defensive anytime my older brother bothered to take the time to speak to me.

"I was just thinking," he smirked. "That ya' didn't get much for those two packs of Camels."

"What?" I confusingly asked.

"I weeded for you that day so you could go courtin' and looked like every other fella had that girl's attention, besides you," Lloyd mocked.

"Shows how much you know," I desperately defended. "Me and Gwen's going to the fair together!"

Taking a break to lean on his hoe, Lloyd looked surprised as he said, "Well, well, well. Maybe those Camels weren't such a bad investment for you."

"Maybe not," I replied, content to have gotten away with a little lie to stop Lloyd's teasing.

"When?" Lloyd asked.

"After the cotton's in," I boasted. "Takin' the train."

"Old Beck?" Lloyd asked.

Old Beck, a train engine that looked like it had been salvaged from the Civil War, pulled a passenger car and sometimes freight. The ancient engine made daily trips from Tecumseh and Shawnee into the south part of the county. The train was old and looked like it had as much rust as iron, but Old Beck connected the farmers with the rest of the world. Many called the rail line heading south out of Tecumseh the "milk run" since many farmers, including ours, sent fresh milk to the cities for sale. Old Beck would not do more than twenty miles an hour, but special trains were running during the fair to accommodate the extra traffic.

"How did you know?" I asked warily.

Looking casually at the hot sky, Lloyd answered, "I's in Peaudane's store the other day, and Gwen asked me if I'd like to go with the group up to the fair in Benson Park."

Blood flushed to my cheeks as my heart pounded at having Lloyd uncover my exaggeration.

"She said a bunch of people was goin' and said I might as well go too," Lloyd teased.

Overcome with embarrassment, I angrily charged Lloyd. This attack proved to be ill advised when he easily threw me to the ground pinning my arms to the pinkish-brown dirt.

With his easygoing smirk, he said, "Now don't get riled up. For another pack of Camels, I might consider stayin' away from that girl of yours…who you're takin' to the fair."

"You already got a girl!" I shouted.

"I know, but Gwen's getting awful pretty and sweet as candy…I might need to pay her some attention. You know, in case things don't work out with you two."

Straining with all my might to avenge his mocking, I thrashed on the dusty ground trying to get at him. Our ruckus caused enough commotion that Dad trotted over to see what distracted our hoeing of the cotton field.

"What's goin' on?" Dad demanded, as I vainly attempted to free myself from Lloyd.

"We're just talking," Lloyd explained, as he continued to hold me at bay.

"About what?" Dad demanded.

"About that Peaudane girl Gill's goin' to take to the fair," Lloyd grinned.

"Get off of him," Dad instructed.

Lloyd slowly lifted me up as I took a wild swing, which only caused me to lose balance as he easily pushed me away.

"Cut that out!" Dad barked. "Both of you!"

Looking at the fields and wrinkling his forehead, he said in a tone that did not represent his typical, carefree self, "If you boys don't get this field in better shape, neither of ya' will be goin' to the fair."

Lloyd needed no more instruction, as he picked up his hoe and continued down the row. I got back to hoeing, but noticed Dad studying the cotton before walking under the shade of our pecan tree at the end of the field.

Taking my gloves off, I cautiously walked up to him and asked, "Is everything all right?"

"Huh?" Dad replied, obviously lost in thought.

"Is everything okay, Dad?" I asked again.

Smiling in his reassuring way, he said, "Sure. Things'll be fine…they always turn out fine, don't they?"

"Yeah, but…you look worried," I gingerly observed.

Dad grunted a half-hearted laugh and said, "Yeah…things are a little different I guess."

He looked out over the field again without saying more.

After a moment of being ignored, I asked, "Does it have anything to do with me working at the store?"

Changing his gaze from the field to me, he said, "Naw…That store'll be good for you. I'm the one that suggested it to Guy when he said he might be looking for some help."

"Then what is it?" I probed.

Rubbing his chin and his face he said, "Gill, you're a smart kid."

My father usually teased his boys more than complimented them. His more serious and less playful tone ironically caused anxiety.

"Teachers've always said it," he continued. "Heck, I've seen it. Your brother Lloyd can out-work any two men I've ever seen. He was born to do this work, but you…I think you can do more."

"I'll do anything, Pa," I assured. "I'll work hard."

"I know," he continued. "But there's more to it. There ain't ever been a Brooks go to school past sixth grade. I never made it that far. We've always worked and scratched and prayed to the good Lord to make it another year. Things are different now. We've had a couple of good years here. I know this ain't the best land to be had, but we've done real good the past two years. If this crop was looking better, I thought we might make enough to put down on this land and make it ours."

"We're going to buy the farm?" I excitedly asked.

"Well," he groaned. "I wanted to, but you're enough of a farmer to tell this year's crop's not looking that good. I don't know what it is. We got enough rain. You boys have worked it hard. It's just not goin' to be what I thought it was."

Rubbing his forehead as if in agony, he said, "The gin down at Wanette pays a bonus for the first bale in. With you workin' off the bill at Peaudane's, I thought if we got that bonus we might could swing it."

"We can do it!" I urged. "I can start tomorrow. Mr. Peaudane'll let me. I'll work hard—day and night if he'll let me. I don't even have to go to that stupid fair or take the cash."

Dad looked at me, surprised at the enthusiasm and said, "You ain't missing the fair, and Peaudane's store is only open so many days and hours, but you really think we could swing it?"

"Sure," I replied, although I had little real knowledge what the finances would be. "Like you said, Lloyd can help bring in the crop and work better than four of me."

Dad smiled and playfully punched my shoulder before yelling, "Lloyd! Gordon! Come over here!"

My two brothers looked up from their work and slowly meandered to the shade tree.

"Boys," Dad started. "If we get our bales harvested first, maybe we can get that bonus in Wanette. Maybe if we pick this field clean we could make enough to pay down on this place and have a farm that's our own."

Looking anxiously at Lloyd to get his reaction, Dad finally asked, "What'd ya' think, Lloyd?"

Lloyd reached back, scratched behind his ear, and said, "Guess so."

With more vigor than I had witnessed, Dad excitedly said, "I know so. We got three or four weeks until harvest. Gordon, you're going to have to take up some of Gill's slack."

"That'll take about half your day," Lloyd quipped to my younger brother.

Before I could respond, Dad said, "Gill's goin' to work in town, so I'll need both of you to pick up the slack."

Nodding in agreement, the normally easygoing Lloyd understood the challenge of getting the first bales to market. The naïve Gordon seemed happy to be considered more than just a kid.

"You boys'll be farming this land a hundred years from now," Dad boasted. "Who knows, we might be able to buy that back forty and clear those blackjack trees out some day and have a real spread."

With a gleam in his eye, he said, "Yes sir, I don't see nothin' stoppin' us now."

CHAPTER 11

The eagerness to begin working at the Peaudane General Store only grew as I continued in the cotton field the first week of September. Our excitement at the prospect of buying the farm grew with each day, as we diligently attacked the weeds. My father, normally the epitome of calm, had been uncharacteristically tense as he checked his crop daily.

"You boys can head in early and clean up," he declared one afternoon as Lloyd, Gordon, and I sweated in the fields under a hot fall sun. "We'll hit these fields early and get this harvest in. Gill, pick your cotton and put 'em in another bag...separate from the rest."

"What for?" I asked.

"Cause you're slow as molasses in winter," Lloyd factually observed while spitting into the dirt.

Dad smiled and said, "You are as slow as a grandma at pickin', but you pick as clean as anyone I've seen. We'll put yours on top and maybe bump up a grade."

"All ten pounds," Lloyd quipped.

I would have disputed with Lloyd, but Dad's familiar laugh at the observation of my cotton-picking ability made it useless.

"Let's get to the house," Dad concluded. "You're pickin' tomorrow too, Gordon."

Gordon grinned with eager anticipation, but he had never picked cotton before.

We woke at dawn to get our long burlap bags ready for the harvest. Anxious to begin before the heat of the day, we waited for

Dad's signal to start, as he carefully checked the morning dew on the plants. The humidity causing the dew would mean uncomfortable heat in the afternoon. Dad called Lloyd over to look at the boles of cotton. With no fanfare, he nodded to begin, and with all our energy, we attacked the cotton field.

The day seemed to last an eternity. My brain was numb as I pulled bole after bole of cotton to put in my burlap bag. Heat shimmered on the field, and Gordon retreated to the shade of the tree. He would not have come back without Dad's admonishment. Lloyd was like a machine as he dragged the long bag up and down the irregular rows.

At the end of the day, we had a little over two thousand pounds in the back of the wagon. I pulled almost 300 pounds while Gordon added another 200 pounds. Dad picked more than 500 pounds. Lloyd picked almost as much as the three of us combined. My cotton, picked clean of boles, was put on top.

It was a quiet supper as we went to sleep early, exhausted from the day's labor. The next morning Dad, Lloyd, and I traveled to Wanette to sell the cotton with hopes of winning the bonus. The rutted roads made travel slow. It would have been quicker to load the cotton on Old Beck and go to Tecumseh, but the train cost money. The cotton gins in Wanette were offering a bonus, so we made the best time we could. Our horse, Old Betsy, pulled our wagon methodically down a road running roughly along the Salt Creek bottom nearly to Trousdale, before heading south to Wanette.

Wanette, a town in the southern most part of Pottawatomie County close to the spot where the Santa Fe railroad's eastern branch crossed the South Canadian River, was somewhat larger than Romulus with several businesses including a bank, a general merchandise store, a livery stable, a water hauling business, and two cotton gins. We arrived in the early afternoon, and Dad went immediately to Beckner's General Merchandise store to get the town gossip.

After a few moments, Dad came back and hurriedly said, "Come on, we're headin' to Paris & Becotte."

Wanette had two cotton gins in town, Paris & Becotte and The Southland Cotton Gin Company. The Southland Cotton Gin Company was newer and larger, but Paris & Becotte was a fierce competitor. Paris & Becotte offered a fifty-dollar bonus for the first bale of the season with hopes of generating publicity and a larger share of the market.

Dad disappeared into the office while Lloyd and I stayed with our wagon. Lloyd smoked a cigarette, while I took the opportunity to see some of the town. The main street had several two-story brick buildings that showed the prosperity of this railroad town. A hotel was located across the street from the cotton gin and next door to an abandoned saloon.

"Ya' think we'll make enough to stay in the hotel?" I asked.

"I doubt it," Lloyd answered. "It's not cold out."

"Yeah," I agreed, continuing to look down the street.

Dad was still in the office engaged in a lively discussion with the two men inside. The gin was neat and in order, indicating they had not processed any cotton yet.

Across the street, an abandoned building caught my attention. A man loitered outside, with a familiar gait to his walk. I took a couple of steps toward the street to get a better look. The lean man was dressed in a pair of overalls with a flannel shirt underneath. He wore an old black jacket although the temperature was in the mid-eighties. A ruffled, flat cap cast a shadow on his gaunt, almost desperate features.

If Lance Carrington had not walked out of the restaurant next to the abandoned building, I would not have recognized his father, Eli Carrington. Lance's distinctive floppy hat was unmistakable. He handed his father a small package, as Eli Carrington looked at what appeared to be a list.

I started across the street when Lance made eye contact with me. Something in his demeanor caused me to hesitate. Before I took another step, my father hollered at me to get back to the wagon. Lance looked down the street and motioned with his head for me to leave. Stepping back, I saw Lance glance down the street one more time with some concern, as the large form of Haskell Holiday walked menacingly toward them. Before I looked back, Lance and his father disappeared. Haskell Holiday did not appear to see them, but I was surprised when he stepped into the abandoned building where Lance and his father had been standing.

"Get over here, Gill!" Dad commanded.

I obeyed, but taking one more look, I saw the floppy hat of Lance Carrington moving quickly toward the rail bridge across the South Canadian River.

"What are you doing?" Dad asked. "You don't need to be close to that place."

Dad looked concerned and surveyed the old building. I would find out years later the abandoned building was a notorious gambling house and saloon.

"Is this all?" a small man asked as he looked at our wagon.

"That's all we have today," Dad replied as he walked to the wagon. "I expect more in a week or two."

The man reached into the wagon and grabbed a handful of the white fiber. He brought it close to his face to look at it and almost appeared to smell it.

"Decent quality," the man shrugged.

"Decent?" Dad smirked. "That's some of the highest grade cotton I've seen in these parts."

"I've seen better," the man charged.

"Well," Dad cut to the point. "What'll you give?"

"I can give ya' nine-fifty," the man coldly stated.

"Nine-fifty!" Dad exclaimed. "That's less than last year, and this is a better quality."

The man shifted nervously and said, "I don't remember payin' more than ten last year."

"Ten's a lot different than nine-fifty," Dad slyly replied.

"Then we have a deal?" the man said.

"Not at ten we don't. I was plannin' on more like eleven," Dad charged.

"Eleven!" the man screamed nearly matching Dad's indignation. "I won't pay more than ten."

Dad looked at Lloyd, who was sitting in the front of the wagon as calm as a riverboat gambler, and asked, "What do ya' think, Lloyd?"

Lloyd took another drag on his Camel and said, "It won't take no effort to see what that feller down at Southland thinks. He might like to call the papers and report the season's first bale."

Silence followed as Dad surveyed the cotton gin operator.

After a moment, Dad said, "We better get goin' if we wanna get back by dark."

Dad nudged my arm and we both stepped toward the wagon.

"Now, hold on," the man excitedly implored. "Let me think and give me a minute to do some figuring."

The small man quickly stepped back into the office to talk to another man. Dad turned around to where his back was to them while Lloyd stared off in the other direction looking as if he were ready to drive the wagon to the competitor. I was the only one with a view of the office window.

"What're they doing?" Dad whispered.

"Talking," I replied.

"What do you think?" Dad asked Lloyd without looking at him.

"Don't know," Lloyd replied. "We might get a little more than ten."

"I thought you said eleven?" I asked.

Dad smiled at my naivety and said, "It's called bargaining, Gill. It's how the world works."

"Oh," I moaned.

"Only thing," Dad continued. "The rich folk are always better at it."

Before Dad could elaborate, the small man walked out of the office scratching his head.

"My partner's not too happy," the man began. "But we can give ya' ten and a quarter. Not a penny more."

"And the bonus?" Dad asked.

The man grimaced and said, "You're cookin' my grits, but you get the fifty dollar bonus for the first bale."

Dad smiled in relief and said, "You got a deal."

Dad and the man went into the office to conclude their transaction, while Lloyd and I unloaded the wagon. The load produced four bales and with the bonus, we headed home with nearly one hundred dollars.

A couple of miles out of town, Dad said, "Not bad for a day's work, is it boys?"

We were all smiles at the thought of that much money coming to the farm. The fact the money did not represent one day's work but months of weeding did not occur to us in the jubilation of the moment.

"How much more can we glean from that field, Lloyd?" Dad asked.

"It'll take until after the freeze to get it all, but we could get another twenty bales before it's done," Lloyd calculated.

Dad smiled and said, "That's about what I figured."

"Will that be enough?" I asked.

Dad's forehead wrinkled and he said, "Maybe…just maybe. We'll need your money from workin' that job at Peaudane's, but if Lloyd can find another twenty bales in that field, maybe."

It was a warm night. We camped on the fringe of a Cross Timber forest by the banks of the Salt Creek that night. Lloyd could have easily gone to see his girl, but he preferred to stay with us that evening. It was a night filled with laughter, relief, stories, and dreams for the future. Dad took out his harmonica and entertained us with the many songs he had learned through the years. I fell asleep under the stars happy and content, looking forward to getting out of the cotton fields and into my new job in the hardware store.

CHAPTER 12

The excitement of working at the Peaudane General Store intensified with the prospect of helping my family own our farm. Scrubbing floors did nothing to diminish my zeal for the new job.

The store's wood floors needed a remarkable amount of sweeping to give the appearance of cleanliness. Vigorously pushing the broom, which fast became my everyday companion, I heard the back door swing open. Turning around, I saw Gwen Peaudane float into the store to bring Guy his lunch.

"Hello, Gill," she greeted with an intoxicating smile.

Gwen wore a blue gingham dress with a white apron. It was already warm outside but her hair still bounced as if a spring breeze brushed it. Her slightly flushed cheeks, with only a hint of perspiration glistening off them, framed a hint of a smile. Gwen's blue eyes were soulful, searching, and captivating.

"Hi, Gwen," I replied, while raising the broom up to my chin as sweat soaked my white shirt.

The sound of Guy Peaudane coming from his small office to greet his sister caused me instinctively to begin sweeping again.

"Gill," Guy said in a matter of fact tone. "It's broiling in here. The floor looks great, you can stop sweeping."

"Yes, sir," I awkwardly replied in a tone of voice indicating an anxiousness to please my employer.

With a sigh, he said, "Why don't you take a lunch break?"

"Yes, sir," I responded as I reluctantly headed out the back door.

A bench in the back of the store provided a resting place as a refreshing breeze blew through my damp shirt. I closed my eyes and leaned against the back of the wood building to enjoy the light wind.

"You're not eating lunch?" Gwen asked with a slight tone of concern.

Startled and then embarrassed at having been caught daydreaming, I quickly said, "Naw, I ate a big breakfast this morning and we have our big meal in the evening."

"Oh," she replied as she tilted her head slightly.

After an awkward few seconds, she said, "Do you like it here?"

"Sure…It beats sweating in the field," I assured.

"Looks like you were doing plenty of sweating on that floor," she smiled.

"The floors just don't seem to keep swept," I shrugged.

Gwen giggled slightly and said, "You may have more appreciation for what we women do now."

"I do more than sweep," I defended. "Guy has me takin' inventory, and I'm going to organize these back shelves tomorrow so we can actually find something."

Guy Peaudane's previous helper was either lazy or a little slow, because the back room looked like a junkyard with empty crates and boxes intermingled with merchandise. At least twice in the past day, I had nearly thrown out something that could have been sold.

"If you can do that," Gwen smiled. "Guy will probably give you a raise."

I grinned broadly, not at what she said, but in reciprocation of her pleasant demeanor.

"I'll see you tomorrow," Gwen said, as she glided down the back alley and toward her home.

After a few days, I began to get into a rhythm of my new job as Guy gave me fewer instructions and let me use my own initiative to find work to do. One task I found to tackle was sorting and cleaning the back storage room to put it into some kind of order. I invented other jobs inside the store most days, however, waiting for Gwen to appear and have a few moments of pleasant conversation.

"Hi, Gill," she whispered as I was bent over trying to organize nuts and bolts from under the front counter.

"Hi, Gwen," I excitedly replied as she passed by on her way to Guy's office.

My disappointment at her quick exit was short lived because she returned in a few moments carrying a basket.

"I'm sorry," she said softly, as she handed me the basket. "I forgot that I was to bring lunch to the helper the other day. Hope you like fried chicken and canned peaches."

Hardly able to contain my enthusiasm, I beamed as I said, "They're my favorite."

"I've got to run," Gwen said, as she left to finish her chores for the day.

Taking my basket to the bench behind the store, I prepared to enjoy my first lunch in days. Mother offered to fix lunch, but the hassle of toting it all the way into town made it seem impractical. Besides, she had chores to do and needed to prepare the meal for the men left working in the cotton fields. I had been getting along fine with two good meals and an occasional apple at noon.

My mouth watered as I bit into a chicken leg, but the cold piece of chicken was unlike anything I had experienced before. It almost had the consistency of rubber, but was blander tasting. I chewed the first bite for what seemed to be several minutes. More out of curiosity than hunger, I took a second bite and again was amazed at how something could be so bland.

Laugher from Guy Peaudane interrupted my confused expression.

"It's hard to imagine anything tasting like it, isn't it?" he said with a chuckle.

"Oh…It's not that bad," I tactfully tried to assure him, trying not to hurt anyone's feelings.

"Believe me," he shrugged, "it's that bad. Gwen told me the other day you had been skipping lunch. In the past, I've provided a meal for the help."

"That's okay," I replied.

"No," Guy interrupted. "Old Elmer Booze cleans at night and sleeps in the back to watch things. He gets a meal, so I told Gwen to bring an extra plate today."

"Thank you," I politely nodded.

"Thank me for that?" he quipped. "I thought Gwen's mother was cooking today and not Gwen."

"It's not that bad," I lied.

"You're too nice," he bluntly said. "Gwen is a sweetheart of a girl and pretty as a picture, but she's domestically challenged…especially when it comes to cooking. She's pretty handy with a needle and sews her own clothes, but cooking…I usually throw mine out."

While I looked at the two pieces of slightly burnt chicken before me, Guy said, "The peaches will be fine. Her mother canned those."

Sheepishly I put down the drumstick and timidly tasted the peaches. The canned fruit was fine, but it took a minute to get the taste of the chicken out of my mouth.

"Count yourself lucky she burnt the cookies," Guy joked. "She has a way of baking a cookie that looks translucent, tastes like it's been chicken fried, and will mess with your system for days."

I shyly smiled at my employer's good humor while counting myself fortunate Gwen had burnt those cookies.

Looking around, Guy said, "It's slow today. Elmer will be playing dominos down the street. I'll get him up here and take you to lunch."

I feebly tried to protest, but Guy insisted. In a few moments, he came back with Elmer Booze. Elmer was a broken-down old man who did odd jobs for the Peaudane family. He was almost deaf and had only a few teeth, but he was loyal to Guy and willing to watch the store during lunchtime.

Guy took me down the short street to Kelly's Café and ordered me a roast beef sandwich. Being from the country, I had rarely eaten in a restaurant. My initial shyness soon wore off as I enjoyed the meal including a big piece of peach pie. Gwen's chicken had managed to break the ice for me with Guy. He was a charismatic man and energetically explained to me the idiosyncrasies of his business, his ideas about the future development of the county, and some of his family's history.

Particularly interested in anything pertaining to Gwen, I learned that her real father was killed in an accident before she was born. Dr. Peaudane had married her mother when Gwen was small and had been the only father she ever knew. Guy was not sure if Gwen even knew he was not her real father. Dr. Peaudane did not practice medicine any more, but he was content to let Guy oversee the store while he oversaw the small farm on the edge of town. Guy married a woman named Lori a few years earlier, and they lived close to his father's place. I also learned Guy had a sister who had married very young and lived in Tennessee. Guy vaguely explained she had never returned home and did not stay in close touch with the family.

Gwen's mother, significantly younger than Dr. Peaudane, was much more meek and shy than he. A beautiful woman with a graceful presence, she was content to let Dr. Peaudane pretend to be the great overseer of their farm although the farm itself was quite small. Gwen was the baby of the family, and the darling of her aging father. According to Guy, Dr. Peaudane was very watchful of any young man showing his daughter attention.

The day Gwen Peaudane brought me burnt chicken became a turning point in my relationship with her brother Guy. We talked daily about topics from business etiquette to the war in Europe and everything in between. Each day I worked in the Peaudane General

Store convinced me that my future would be away from the farm. I already dreaded the cotton picking that was left to do, but I was still excited about my family finally owning some land.

CHAPTER 13

The back room of the Peaudane General Store was a tangled mess of old crates, packaging, broken merchandise, and trash. I thought it would be a one-day job, but cleaning the back room became my afternoon activity for many days. I still invented jobs close to Guy's office until Gwen brought lunch. Fortunately her mother cooked most days, and Gwen often sat with me on the bench in the back while I ate.

At the bottom of the pile of debris in the back room was an old iron stove that looked as if it had been there for years. With considerable effort, I slid the old stove to the alleyway behind the store before sweeping and cleaning the back room. Dirty from head to toe, I took a moment to enjoy my labor. The once-cluttered room was now a usable space and I felt supreme satisfaction to see the job completed.

The old stove I shoved to the alley represented the last remnant of the back room mess. I had time before the end of the day so decided to see what I could do with the stove. Covered in dust and dirt, the stove did not seem to be broken. After about an hour, the old appliance began to look like it might be of some use.

"How much for the stove?" a voice interrupted my scrubbing.

The farmer wore a patched pair of overalls and looked like he had been in the fields all day.

"My old stove rusted through, and the wife sent me to find one," he explained.

Raising up and looking over my afternoon's work, I said without thinking, "Four dollars."

I had seen Guy sell one that looked only a little better a few days before for that price. It did not occur to me that I did not have the authority to sell something that was not mine.

"Four dollars cash?" the man asked.

"I…I don't know."

"Don't you back out of our deal!" the crusty farmer charged as he handed me four silver coins.

"I…I gotta go check," I rambled as I awkwardly left the man standing at the stove.

It was late, and Guy was preparing to close for the day.

"Mr. Peaudane," I frantically interrupted as he sat behind his desk. "I've done something."

"What is it?" he asked in a tone of concern.

"I…I think you better come here," I said in a voice of resignation.

Guy followed me to the back where the old farmer stood defiantly with his coins in hand.

"Can I help you?" Guy asked.

"Already been helped," the farmer replied. "This boy sold me this stove for four dollars, but he's tryin' to weasel out on the deal."

Turning to me, Guy asked in a stern tone, "Where did you get this stove?"

"It was in the back room," I timidly explained.

Guy looked at the stove a moment before saying to the farmer, "He said, four dollars?"

"Four dollars cash," the man confirmed.

"Sir," Guy graciously said. "He's just a helper back here, and he didn't know the value of this merchandise—"

"Don't matter," the farmer interrupted. "He's an employee of yours, ain't he?"

"Yes," Guy confirmed.

"He said four dollars, and I got four dollars cash," the farmer repeated.

Stroking his chin at the dilemma, Guy said, "Four dollars it is then. Do you have a wagon?"

"Got her right around the corner," the farmer boldly proclaimed as he handed Guy the four dollars.

"Pull around, and we'll help you load," Guy said with a sigh.

The farmer walked quickly to get his wagon with the sly grin of victory on his face. Guy did not say a word to me as he stoically waited for the man. In a few moments, the farmer brought a worn wagon around as Guy and I loaded his stove. The farmer slapped his two mules with the reins as he took his treasure back to his wife.

As soon as the man disappeared behind the corner, Guy put his arm around me and said, "Let's close shop."

"I'm sorry, Guy," I began to plead, certain I would be reprimanded or fired.

Once inside the store, Guy asked, "Why?"

"I…sold your stove," I replied.

Smiling, Guy said, "That's kind of the idea."

"But the price—"

"Yeah, next time you might ask, but I would have sold that stove for three dollars in the store," he reasoned.

Walking to the back of the store, he pointed to an old stove, similar to the one I had cleaned, priced for three dollars and fifty cents.

Sensing my confusion, Guy continued, "It's called negotiating. If I had talked to that gentleman about the stove, he'd have seen my suit and offered me two dollars figuring I could afford it. When he saw a nervous kid, he thought he had won. I tried to tell him about the stove inside, but he was sure he had caught you giving him a bargain. You see, selling is a lot about letting the customer win…even when you're holding the money."

Guy held the four coins in his hand as he walked to the large, brass National Cash Register to deposit his profits.

"Let's go see your back room," he smiled.

Walking to the room I had been cleaning the past days, Guy whistled and said, "Wow, I haven't seen the floor of this place since I cleaned it when I was about your age. This looks great. I forgot about that old stove even being there."

"Thanks," I grinned at his approval.

"You're off tomorrow?" he asked.

"Uh…If that's okay," I replied.

Smiling at me, Guy said, "The county fair only comes once a year. Come back to the office and I'll get you paid for the week."

Following Guy to the office, he counted out the money for my five days worked and then gave me one extra dollar.

"What's this for?" I asked.

"Your commission," he replied.

"You're the one that cleaned up that old stove and sold it. That showed initiative. You're a natural salesman."

"Thanks," I replied.

"I know you're usin' most of your pay for your family, but do me a favor."

"Sure," I said.

"Take that extra dollar and enjoy the fair," he said with a wink.

"I will."

Taking a moment to let me enjoy the satisfaction of earning my first bonus, Guy then added. "Keep an eye on my kid sister, will ya'?"

I enthusiastically nodded, but I needed no encouragement to watch Gwen. The trip to the fair had been on my mind for weeks. With an extra dollar in my pocket, I knew just who to spend it on—Gwen.

CHAPTER 14

Lloyd and I woke early on a brisk September morning to go to the county fair. We walked to the Martin farm to catch a ride to the train station with three of the Martin boys. Lloyd was his normal stoic self, as we approached the front gate. The gate squeaked ever so slightly, as Lloyd and I entered, but loud enough to draw the attention of at least one of the Martins.

"Hey Gilbert," the cheerful voice of Marilee Martin called from the screen door.

"Looks like your girlfriend's here," Lloyd whispered.

Before I could respond and deny Lloyd's assertion, Marilee said, "Hey Lloyd, Ethan's out back getting the team ready."

"Good to see ya' Marilee," Lloyd politely greeted as he headed toward the barn, while giving me a smirking grin.

"It's gonna be a nice day, Gilbert," Marilee enthusiastically noted.

"I guess so," I replied, while straining to see where Arty was.

"Would you like a biscuit…and some sausage?" Marilee asked.

Without giving me a chance to respond, she disappeared into the house. A moment later, Marilee reappeared proudly carrying a plate of biscuits and sausage. She wore a plain, brown plaid dress, with a pink, satin bow nearly as big as her head. Her hair looked as if it had been brushed, but one half of the hairstyle looked like it escaped the braids holding the other half in place as it dangled and frizzed in the morning breeze.

I tore a biscuit in two pieces making a sandwich with the sausage. The biscuit was light and flaky with the sausage seasoned to perfection.

"It's good," I commented.

"Sorry I didn't have any eggs or gravy left, Gilbert," Marilee apologized.

Looking at the awkward girl, I noticed she had smudged some flour and grease on her freckled cheek. As I discreetly motioned with my hand for Marilee to check her face, she blushed with embarrassment.

Desperate for something to say, I asked, "Why do you call me Gilbert? I mean everyone, even my mother calls me Gill."

Sheepishly, she replied, "I…I don't know. I've always liked the way Gilbert sounds I guess…Why, does it bother you?"

"Why don't you leave him alone, you old cow?" Arty Martin good-naturedly teased his sister from behind the screen door.

"Leave me alone!" Marilee shouted back. "Daddy said for you to be nice to me today."

"You shouldn't even be going," Arty charged in a softer voice, obviously not wanting his father to hear the debate.

"Well, I am going," Marilee defiantly stated. "Gwen and me are going to see the sewing exhibits."

Obviously agitated at his younger sister, Arty said in a louder voice, "You're going to ruin everything!"

"What's she going to spoil, Arty?" the firm voice of Mr. Martin rang out from around the corner of the house.

Arty bit his lower lip and quickly replied, "Nothin' Pa…It's just she's too young to be taggin' along to the fair."

"Nonsense," Mr. Martin replied. "Marilee's got more sense than all you boys combined, and I expect you to be a gentleman today."

"Yes sir, "Arty complied.

Noticing me standing on the edge of the porch, Mr. Martin coldly said, "Hello, Gilbert."

"Hello, Mr. Martin," I replied.

He looked as if he would like to say something else, but thankfully, Arty's older brother Ethan pulled the wagon around with Lloyd by his side. Arty, Marilee, Arty's younger brother Floyd, and I quickly boarded the wagon and gladly left the watchful eye of Mr. Martin.

Arty dominated the conversation on the wagon ride into town with his talk about escorting Gwen Peaudane to the fair. I had my own ideas about Gwen today, but was content to let Arty brag while the older boys teased him. Arty's boasting hid the anxiety he felt about having to share Gwen's attention with so many people. His angst grew as we approached the train depot and Gwen attracted the attention of several young men including my older brother Lloyd, who made her laugh with a comment about Arty's boasting.

The county fair was held at Benson Park, between Tecumseh and Shawnee. Arty envisioned taking Gwen Peaudane to the fair for a romantic getaway, but the outing ended up including nearly every young person between twelve and eighteen years old around Romulus. The train would be running until six o'clock in the evening to accommodate the fairgoers, but Arty, Lance, and I planned weeks before to take a bedroll and stay over in Shawnee. Lance, however, was conspicuously absent.

Arty and I managed to isolate Gwen from the others while we attempted to impress her when she suddenly smiled and said, "I see you've been able to keep your hat."

Confused, Arty and I turned around to see Lance Carrington with his floppy hat standing behind us ready to board the train.

"Lance!" Arty exclaimed. "I didn't think you were going to make it."

"Wouldn't miss it," Lance smiled.

While we greeted Lance, Gwen and Marilee boarded the train. The whistle blew signaling the train would leave shortly, as we climbed aboard. Arty glared at his younger sister as she sat on the aisle pinning

Gwen to the window. Taking seats a few rows up, we anxiously quizzed Lance to find out his latest adventure.

CHAPTER 15

The train strained up the slight grade of the Macomb ridge before crossing the Little River. Short blackjack and hickory trees comprising the Cross Timber forest were still green although many fields had turned brown. Some cotton still waited in the fields. Farmers would continue harvesting the county's main cash crop until after the first freeze. We rode the train to Tecumseh and then switched to the interurban, an electric train running between Tecumseh and Shawnee with a stop at Benson Park.

"Where have you been?" Arty asked as he turned in his seat to face Lance.

"Here and there," Lance grinned.

"Saw ya' at Wanette the other day," I added.

"Yeah," Lance shrugged. "Sorry I couldn't talk...I had business."

"What kind of business?" the inquisitive Arty asked.

Lance looked out the window for a moment and said, "Workin' for Dad."

Arty and I looked at each other with a combination of concern and intrigue.

"Doing what?" Arty quizzed.

"Makin' money," Lance replied, as he slowly pulled out a roll of twenty, one-dollar bills.

"Whew—" Arty whistled. "Where'd ya' get that?"

"Like I said, I've been workin' with Dad," Lance repeated.

Looking around to see if he could talk without being heard, Arty leaned over and whispered, "Are you bootlegging?"

Lance grimaced and said, "Like I said, I'm workin' for Dad. I deliver packages, and he gives me money."

"You are bootlegging!" Arty exclaimed in a loud whisper.

Lance nervously looked around to see if anyone noticed the commotion.

"Keep it down," he whispered harshly to Arty.

"Okay, Okay," Arty agreed. "You gotta be careful though. If Leland Holiday caught you, he'd love to throw you in jail."

Lance adjusted his hat on his head and said, "Leland Holiday would do more than that! He's the biggest bootlegger and thief in the county if you ask me. He's slipperier and slimier than a greased tadpole."

"Marshal Holiday?" Arty clarified.

"Him and that rascal Haskell are selling liquor up and down the Rock Island line. That's why they tried to corner me that day in Romulus," Lance explained. "I'm workin' with Dad until we can make enough money to buy back Mom's farm."

"Tell us more," Arty pressed. "I mean, what exactly do you do?"

Looking around to make sure we were not attracting attention Lance answered, "Most of the liquor comes from Texas. There's some stills the Holidays have around, but the good stuff comes from the south. I go around and take orders mainly…I make a list, and Dad fills the orders. There's some old boys in Wanette in the water haulin' business. They get water from a spring by the river and sell it for fifteen cents a barrel to whoever's buying. They'll deliver Dad's stuff for a cut. We slip across the river and bring cases in, but it's risky. There's only one bridge across the river and that's at Wanette. It's the only way across when the river's up. That's where I've been during this wet weather."

"God, that sounds like the life," Arty exclaimed. "We ought to do that, Gill…we'd make a fortune."

"I got a job," I quickly reminded, none too eager to tangle with Leland Holiday.

"You don't want any part of this business," Lance confirmed. "The Holidays patrol the river like it's their own…and they're mean as rattlesnakes. I'm out of it as soon as I make enough to buy the farm."

Lance looked around again and continued, "But I'm goin' to get Haskell Holiday before this thing's over."

"How ya' goin' to do that?" Arty asked.

"Never you mind," Lance smiled, "but I got it all worked out."

Arty occupied the seat in front of Lance and me. He had turned around to face us, but it was now apparent he was looking at the seat where Marilee and Gwen were sitting. Lance noticed this distraction and turned around to look at the two girls.

"I almost forgot," Lance sighed.

"What?" Arty confusingly asked.

"About our talk at the church meeting," Lance smiled.

Convinced Arty did not remember the conversation, Lance explained, "I said I'd leave Gwen for you to have to yourself."

Arty's eyes flashed as he remembered the conversation at the church meeting, before he slumped dejectedly in his seat.

"You see how that's workin' out with that bean pole sister of mine botherin' poor Gwen," Arty moaned.

"I think I can help," Lance suggested. "Do you have anything with writing on it?"

Looking through his pockets Arty pulled out a folded flyer describing the fair.

"Not anything, but this?" Arty shrugged.

Looking at the piece of paper, Lance said, "This will be perfect! Your sister, she's smart, ain't she?"

Arty grudgingly admitted, "She does good in school…but only because she's got no personality."

"Don't matter," Lance smiled. "Give me the paper, and I'll have Gwen up here in two minutes."

Before Arty could ask another question, Lance took the paper and headed toward Gwen. Arty watched with keen interest, while I turned to see Lance better. He leaned over Marilee and whispered something into Gwen's ear. The pretty, young girl's eyes opened wide with surprise, and she looked around nervously. In a moment, she stood up and stepped over a surprised Marilee. After Gwen was in the aisle, Lance slid next to Marilee, leaving Gwen standing bewildered. Lance handed the paper to Marilee, and she looked intently at it before pointing and talking to Lance.

A confused Gwen walked toward Arty and me. Arty beamed with anticipation before his easy smile turned to a frown when Gwen took the seat Lance had vacated next to me.

"Did you guys know?" Gwen asked in a tone of great concern.

"Know what?" Arty asked, before I could get a word out.

"Poor Lance can't read," she answered with a crease of apprehension on her forehead.

Arty and I nearly laughed aloud at her unmerited anxiety.

Gwen turned to me and confessed, "Lance whispered to me that he had never been to the fair and was having trouble reading the advertisement. He asked if Marilee could tutor him."

Looking back at Lance, he was giving an energized Marilee his full attention as she meticulously pointed at words, while he pretended not to understand. Lance Carrington had been a constant troublemaker at school, but Arty and I both knew he could read as well as anyone on the train.

As Arty took the opportunity to console the concerned Gwen, I looked at Lance while he winked from under his felt hat, producing that sly smile so natural to him. Lance continued the ruse as we changed trains in Tecumseh. Arty managed to squeeze Gwen in between the two of us on the interurban electric train. I almost hated for it to stop at Benson Park, fearing I would not get this close to Gwen the rest of the day.

CHAPTER 16

The interurban rail line between Tecumseh and Shawnee stopped at the entrance to Benson Park. The park, built by the Shawnee-Tecumseh Traction Company to attract riders, offered the best entertainment in the county.

Trolley passengers disembarked at a covered depot at the entrance to the park. Baseball teams played on a diamond located east of the tracks and a wooden, arched bridge led across Squirrel Creek into the twenty-acre park. A large picnic area was near the bridge, with a two-story boathouse and skating rink adjacent to a small lake. On the other side of the lake, a botanical garden and bandstand welcomed visitors. As we crossed the bridge, the roar of rattling rails and screams coming from a large roller coaster next to the gardens echoed through the air. The biggest attraction was an indoor swimming pool located inside an old opera house called, "The Plunge" where swimsuits were rented by the hour. It was only ten o'clock in the morning, and people already waited in line for their turn to swim.

"Can you believe this?" I muttered at seeing the park for the first time.

"It's something, ain't it!" Arty excitedly replied. "We're not in the Cross Timber anymore!"

Gwen Peaudane walked between us as we listened to barkers call out from the county fair located on the other side of the roller coaster. Lance disappeared with Marilee and the other Martin children, while

Gwen, Arty, and I tried to decide what to do first. A band blared loudly from the bandstand and the confusion was nearly deafening.

"Ya' wanna swim?" Arty asked.

"Not with you two," Gwen emphatically replied. "It wouldn't be dignified to swim with boys."

Quick to capitalize on Arty's mistake, I added, "We can swim back home anytime."

"Not inside, we can't," Arty defended.

"My mother would not tolerate mixed swimming," Gwen defiantly stated.

"How 'bout a boat ride?" Arty suggested.

"Sounds good to me," I interjected, anxious to be involved in the decision.

Arty glared at me in frustration, while Gwen lazily thought about the idea.

"Okay," she finally said. "I'll let you boys row me around the lake."

Arty fretted at the situation, but he was not about to let me on the lake alone with Gwen. The canoe cost a nickel, and we spent the next half-hour in the boat paddling from one side to the other, with Gwen in between us.

This ritual continued throughout most of the afternoon, as Arty and I competed for Gwen's attention by suggesting activities from sideshows to a ride on the roller coaster. About two o'clock, Arty suggested I check on the price of renting skates for the large indoor skating rink. When I returned, he and Gwen had disappeared into the crowd. With a sigh, I loitered around the grounds taking in the sights and keeping an eye out for Gwen and Arty.

After walking the grounds of Benson Park, I decided to try my luck in the maze of tents erected to house the fair exhibits. The crowd looking at the exhibits tended to be older and the pace more relaxed. I admired the prize-winning pig for a moment and then walked down a row of tents and open displays showing the most modern farm equipment and tractors. Salesmen barked facts and promises like preachers at a revival meeting about the merits of their products. Farmers milled about, ranging from interested to skeptical of the new machines.

In an open field behind the row of tents, a roar and belch of smoke floated into the air as one of the vendors demonstrated his product. A hand-painted sign boldly announced the Bull Tractor Company with the slogan "The Bull with the Pull." The vehicle making the noise and attracting the attention was an iron beast with two steel wheels in the rear, a metal seat atop a flywheel, and a smaller wheel in the front. The salesman could barely shout over the commotion, but when the tractor slipped into gear and started plowing through the ground with ease, he had everyone's attention.

I was not interested in tractors, pigs, or even the baked goods I could smell from the far row of tents. While still searching desperately for Gwen and Arty, I instead heard the distinctive shout of Marilee Martin.

"Hey, Gilbert!" she yelled above the noise of the fair.

Pretending not to hear, I heard her shrill voice again screech, "Gilbert!"

Turning around, I saw Marilee walking quickly toward me with Lance Carrington close behind.

"Where's Gwen?" Marilee asked.

"I don't know," I confessed. "With Arty I suspect."

"Oh," Marilee sighed. "She was going to go with me to see the sewing."

"What'cha been doing?" a happy Lance Carrington asked.

"Not much," I moaned.

Most of my day had involved trying to keep Gwen Peaudane entertained, instead of enjoying the sites.

"That's too bad," Lance shrugged. "Marilee and I have been all over the park."

"We went skating," Marilee boasted. "I nearly fell, but Lance caught me."

"We saw you guys in the boat," Lance added. "But we lost you after that."

"We had ice cream, and I've been showing Lance the baking," Marilee smiled.

"This girl knows her baked goods," Lance politely grinned.

"I can't believe Gwen's not here," Marilee sighed, shaking her head.

"She's with Arty," I grimly replied.

Leaning closer to me, she said in a loud whisper, "She doesn't even like Arty that much."

The hairs on the back of my neck prickled at this news.

"What?" I excitedly asked.

Grinning at Lance and then at me, Marilee mischievously said, "Gwen's just bein' nice to Arty…I can't say more."

"Come on," I pleaded.

"No I can't," Marilee quickly said, "because here they come."

Turning around, Gwen walked gracefully toward our group with Arty trailing behind. It was obvious Arty was none too happy to see us, having worked most of the day to separate Gwen from the herd.

"Marilee!" Gwen shouted.

"Hey, Gwen," Marilee responded.

"Where have you been?" Gwen asked as she walked up to Marilee.

"Oh, you know, I've been around the park," Marilee coyly replied.

"Are you ready to see the sewing?" Gwen asked.

"Sure," Marilee gleefully replied.

"How 'bout you guys?" Gwen asked.

"I think the cookin' display was enough for me," Lance smiled. "I think I'm goin' over to see if I can win some prizes."

Looking at Arty, I could tell he was tired of being well-mannered around Gwen.

"Come on, Gill," Arty proposed. "Let's go with Lance for a while."

I would have been happy to see the sewing with Gwen, even with Arty's little sister hanging around, but Arty knew I could not openly agree to go with the girls.

"Sure," I replied unenthusiastically.

To my distress, Gwen Peaudane did not seem too disappointed in leaving us, as she tilted her head and said, "We'll see you later then."

The girls walked away, as the taller Marilee stooped down to whisper something to Gwen. The girls turned around to look at the three of us and then began to giggle.

"Let's get out of here," a flustered Arty charged.

We walked quickly past the bandstand while a band played a lively tune. A large, rustic platform wrapped around a large pecan tree like a combination spiral staircase and tree house. Many couples loitered around the tree holding hands. Having no one with which to hold hands, we walked back to the amusement area close to the permanent attractions at Benson Park.

"Did ya' have a good time?" Lance asked, looking at Arty.

Arty glared at me, and said, "I did…with what time I had. I spent the last hour looking for Gill. When Gwen couldn't find him, we went looking for Marilee."

My heart nearly burst at the thought of Gwen searching for me, while Lance laughed openly at Arty's romantic struggles.

"Shut up," an agitated Arty demanded, while shaking his head.

Trying to retaliate, Arty continued, "At least I didn't get stuck with that stupid sister of mine."

Lance laughed louder, obviously not affected by the intended insult.

"I'm surprised you didn't jump in the lake and drown yourself, having to listen to her constant chatter all day," Arty said in a more defiant tone.

Lance, still chuckling at Arty's irritation, said, "Marilee's not that bad…You ought to listen to her sometime. She knows more than you think."

"I doubt that!" Arty replied as he headed toward the tents with the games.

"Listen to yourself," Lance reasoned. "You don't know how to take advantage of what's in front of you."

"What do ya' mean?" Arty asked with little real interest.

"Who's Gwen's best friend?" Lance asked.

"Marilee, I guess," Arty responded.

"Exactly," Lance smiled. "And women talk all the time…you might wanna be nicer to Marilee if you want her to talk nicer about you."

Arty stopped in front of one of the games, which involved throwing a ball to knock down lead bottles.

"What do you mean?" Arty asked in a more interested tone.

"I mean Marilee, knows exactly who Gwen likes," he stated, knowing the reaction he would get.

"What?" Arty and I asked at nearly the same time.

"I'm just saying I had an interesting day with Marilee," Lance shrugged.

"Tell me!" Arty demanded.

Lance walked to a man soliciting players for his booth and paid a nickel to play a game. He picked up the ball and hurled it at the bottles, knocking two of the three down.

"Come on," Arty pleaded. "Tell us who Gwen likes."

Throwing his second ball, Lance was only able to make one bottle wobble.

"A gentleman never tells," Lance slyly answered as he prepared for his third throw, while he winked at me.

"Good thing you're no gentleman!" Arty exclaimed.

With the third throw, Lance toppled all three bottles to the astonishment of the carnival worker.

"You gotta good arm, kid," the worker said, while showing Lance the potential prizes.

"I'll take the little bear," Lance said as he pointed at a stuffed bear named after the former president, Teddy Roosevelt.

"What're ya' going to do?" Arty snidely asked. "Give it to Gwen?"

Smiling at Arty's continued irritation, Lance said, "I think I'll give it to Marilee."

Looking disgusted, Arty asked, "What, are you sayin'…you're sweet on my kid sister?"

Lance tucked the bear into his ragged overalls and said with a smirk, "Like I said, a gentleman never tells."

Arty in a more good-natured tone, replied, "I'd actually like to see you show up to call on Marilee. Dad'd have a stroke."

Lance laughed again, and said, "You're probably right, but Marilee's gonna do what she's gonna do."

"So you do like Marilee!" Arty gasped in disbelief.

Shaking his head, Lance smiled, "Like I said, a gentleman never tells…It's just…you ought to listen to your sister every once and awhile."

We continued down the row of games and sideshows, enjoying the rest of our afternoon at Benson Park. Arty directly and myself more subtly tried to glean more information from Lance Carrington about Gwen. We would learn years later that it was less about Gwen Peaudane and more about Arty's sister, Marilee. The only thing we really learned that day was Lance Carrington could keep a secret. This trait would be enduring.

As the day wore on, the rest of the group headed home while the three of us found a place to camp outside of the park. Our conversations evolved away from our trivial infatuations of Gwen Peaudane and toward our hopes for the future. That was a very good night, one of the best memories of my life. Arty's drive and charisma, Lance's easy-going observations, and my practicality were a perfect recipe for friendship. We talked about times we had in the past and dreams we hoped for in the future, while ignoring the significant challenges of the day.

Tomorrow would find us in the city, three young men on the brink of manhood, but still only boys. For two of us, the city eventually would be our destiny and for one a demise. None of that mattered tonight. We were friends and as we planned our future, we again vowed to meet regularly on our special rock on the Salt Creek. Tomorrow would be another day, and our paths were beginning to separate, although we did not sense it at the time.

CHAPTER 17

I awoke with a hint of chill in the air, as Lance stoked the morning fire. Arty, wrapped in his wool blanket, still slept.

"How'd ya' sleep?" Lance asked rubbing his hands over the fire.

"Fine," I replied.

Looking at the pale, blue sky and a pink ribbon of clouds to the east where the sun was rising, Lance said, "The weather's changing…won't be much fun sleeping outside in a month."

"What's our plan today?" I asked.

Lance shrugged and said, "I don't know my way around town…I'm just following Arty."

"Yeah," I agreed, looking at Arty lying peacefully in his nest.

Patches of fog lingered over the river and its banks, outlining the border between south Pottawatomie County and Shawnee. The south side of the river was flat bottomland, and morning fog drifted sporadically over our campsite. Shawnee was situated on a small bluff, higher above the river. In between the breaks in the fog, we could see a large, white building nearly four-stories tall with red letters reading, "Shawnee Milling Company." To the west were several tall smokestacks with gray smoke drifting into the air with a rhythmic pounding of steel on steel already resonating in the quiet morning.

A train whistle moaned in the morning chill, as it crossed the rail bridge not far from our campsite, waking Arty from his slumber.

"What's goin' on?" Arty muttered.

"Not much," I said. "We're just waiting on you."

In fifteen minutes, we stowed our bedrolls and headed to town. Most people crossed a half-mile upstream of our camp at Sweeny Crossing. Arty and Lance were not prone to do the conventional, however, so we headed to the rail bridge, which was closer.

The rail bridge over the North Canadian River stretched three hundred yards. Waiting for a freight train to pass rolling south, the three of us stepped on the bridge to cross. The two minutes across the bridge were filled with anxiety. I watched the river through the cross-timbers knowing we would have to dive into the shallow waters below if another train passed. More cautious than my two friends, I vowed to walk the extra distance to the Sweeny Crossing next time.

We walked toward the center of town, which had a lazy, relaxed tempo this Sunday morning. Some people were stirring, however, and on the north side of the river, a group of rough-looking men camped close to the rail bridge. I walked quickly, eager to avoid the men. I could tell Arty had the same idea as he walked with more pace. Lance, however, stopped suddenly to stare at the haggard-looking group.

Four men raised up as one young man stepped toward Lance with a determined stride. At first, I thought the men were Indian, since they were dark skinned. As the young man approached, he spewed a string of nonsensical words at a rapid rate. Arty and I looked at each other when Lance answered in the same unintelligible manner.

Lance spoke briefly with him. The dark, young man wore a pair of blue jeans and a well-worn, red plaid shirt. He had flashing, nervous eyes and looked to be in his early twenties. The man shook Lance's hand, while patting his shoulder with his left hand, and the two separated on amiable terms.

As soon as Lance stepped toward us, Arty quickly put distance between the group and ourselves.

"Why were you talkin' to those hobos?" Arty asked, as he marched up the train tracks.

"They weren't hobos," Lance sighed. "They work on the rail line."

"They didn't look like railroad men to me," Arty observed.

Shaking his head slightly, Lance said, "Well, they're not exactly railroad men…they just do the work on the railroad. They replace rail, work on trusses, generally on the line from here south."

"Why are they camping out?" Arty asked. "Decent people ought to have a home."

The words came out without Arty thinking, as an awkward silence fell on our group.

"I didn't mean—" Arty began.

"Not everyone has a well painted house and folks to care for 'em," Lance forcefully explained. "Those guys are Mexican and the hardest workin' people you've seen. They probably don't feel that welcomed everywhere they go…so sometimes it's just easier to keep to yourself."

"I…I'm sorry," Arty stammered. "I didn't mean to insult 'em…just seemed funny to me. How do you know those fellas anyway?"

"Like I said, they work up and down the Rock Island line, and I…I'm campin' under their bridges some nights," Lance explained. "Sergio's the man I talked to. He's the only one that speaks much English. The other feller was Juan Alfonzo. I don't know the rest of 'em. They keep to themselves, mostly."

"Ya' seemed friendly," Arty said, looking at Lance from the corner of his eye as we walked.

"Me and Sergio do business, sometimes," Lance matter-of-factly claimed. "Those boys travel all up and down the line…makes it pretty easy to transport…things."

Before Lance could explain more, a sharp blast of a steam whistle startled us from behind, as a freight train lumbered north with its cargo. In the distance, we could see the Santa Fe station. The rock building was round, with a tower that looked like a castle close to the tracks. Even though it was Sunday, a few people milled about the station, with carriages and even a few automobiles parked around.

The bricked Main Street ran just south of the Santa Fe Depot, with a set of rails down the center for the city's trolley car. The city was nothing like Romulus or even Tecumseh. The whole town had a feeling of purpose and importance, as impressive stone, brick, and wood buildings were clustered up and down the commercial district.

Walking west on Main Street, we were amazed at the number and size of the businesses. A couple of blocks north of Main Street, we walked by a white church building with simple stained glass windows and a bell tower over the front entrance. Several nicely dressed people stood outside in the morning sun.

"What time is it?" Lance asked.

Looking at his pocket watch, Arty answered, "About a quarter after ten."

Smiling, Lance Carrington asked, "Are you boys hungry?"

Nodding, neither of us had thought much about food.

"Isn't that the same church you go to?" Lance asked me.

Looking at the sign, I answered, "Yes."

"We're going to church," Lance proclaimed.

"What?" Arty argued. "I ain't goin' to no church, if I don't have to."

"Suit yourself," Lance shrugged. "But Gill and me are goin' and I'm bettin' we get fed too."

I did not know if betting on the Lord's Day was appropriate, but I did not mind going to church and believed Lance might be right about a free meal. Arty, after some persuasion, tagged along. The church building was unlike any I had seen in the country. It had electric lights, which I had rarely seen, gas heat, hot and cold water, and indoor plumbing. I could hardly concentrate on the services while looking over all the modern amenities.

Brother Bell delivered the sermon that morning. He preached twenty minutes longer than Arty could appreciate, but the whole congregation seemed overjoyed to have three young men visiting. As

Lance predicted, the preacher's wife invited us to lunch. We walked across a wooded park in the middle of town to their house. She served fried chicken and mashed potatoes with sweet iced tea. The iced tea was an exceptional treat for us. Shawnee boasted three ice plants, and the Bell's seemed to have an ample supply this day.

After lunch, we quickly excused ourselves and headed back to the empty downtown. Stores were almost all closed, but we were amazed at the variety of goods available in the city. As we walked in front of the J. L. Roebuck's Hardware and Implements Store, we could see the large Rock Island Shops belching smoke on the west end of town. The maintenance shops for the Rock Island Line looked like a city unto themselves. I took a moment to look in the window of the J. L. Roebuck store and compared it to the smaller Peaudane General Store back in Romulus. The Shawnee store was nearly twice the size, with three floors of the latest goods and merchandise.

Turning north, we walked along the city's trolley line past the edge of town until we came to a lonely building at the end of the line.

"That's the Baptist University," Arty explained. "It's opening up this year."

Looking northwest, I spied another tall building rising up from the prairie.

"What's that?" I asked.

"I don't know," Arty had to admit.

The building looked to be about a mile away. It was a large structure made out of red brick, which looked out of place. Shawnee had many impressive structures, but they had all been closely grouped together around the railroads. This oddity seemed to be in the middle of an open field.

"Let's have a look," Arty suggested.

We left the Baptist University, housed in one three-story brick building and headed across the grassy field. The building, which appeared to be less than a mile away, was almost a two-mile walk. As we approached, the massive building continued to appear even larger. The eight-story building was the tallest I had ever seen with four pillars stretching into the sky, making the place appear like a fortress. A man in a dark robe looked at the building, which still had scaffolding on one side. As we approached the man, it became obvious he was a priest.

"Hello, young men," the priest greeted. "I'm Father Zoeller."

"What is this place?" Arty asked.

The priest seemed to admire our interest and said, "It's the Catholic University. We start classes next week. Are you boys interested in attending?"

"Oh, no—" Arty stammered at the idea of more schooling. "We're just looking."

"It's quite a building isn't it?" Father Zoeller observed. "Mr. Victor Klutho from St. Louis…St. Louis, Missouri is the architect. It's a Tutor-Gothic design."

"It's big," Arty agreed.

Laughing, the priest said, "Big indeed."

"Where are you boys from…we're always looking for students?" Father Zoeller asked.

"We're from down south of Romulus," Arty explained, while Lance and I were content to listen.

"From the south part of the county," the Father enthusiastically replied, "from the Cross Timber."

"Yes, sir," Arty acknowledged.

"You know, this school started in the Cross Timber near Sacred Heart," he smiled.

"Sacred Heart!" Arty exclaimed. "We know where that's at."

"The school started there, nearly thirty years ago, before moving to Shawnee," the priest explained. "What's your name? I used to spend time in that part of the county."

"Arty…Arthur Martin," Arty began.

"Your father has a farm on the Salt Creek?" Father Zoeller asked.

"Yep," Arty affirmed.

"And you?" the priest asked looking at me.

"Gilbert Brooks," I answered. "I think I was born at a farm near Sacred Heart."

"Brooks…Brooks," the priest whispered to himself. "I don't think I knew any Brooks. How about you?"

Lance had been trying to be inconspicuous, but now had to answer a direct question.

"Lance," he timidly replied. "Lance Carrington."

The priest looked at Lance carefully before asking, "Was your mother's name Mattie?"

"Yes," a surprised Lance responded. "I mean, I'm pretty sure…She died when I was young."

Looking sadly at him, Father Zoeller said, "Yes, I knew your mother…she was a student at Sacred Heart…she was Potawatomi?"

"I think so," Lance said.

Smiling, Father Zoeller said, "Your mother was a very sweet girl…and very smart. I can see some of her in you…now that I look closely."

Lance looked at the priest and smiled at the attention.

"Father Zoeller!" a man yelled from the scaffolding. "We need you."

"I've got to run," the priest excused himself. "It was good to meet you…You boys should think of going to school here…an education is an investment in your future."

We started the long walk back toward the train station, and Lance seemed to have a renewed energy to him. It was difficult for Arty and me to know what it must have been like to grow up without a mother. Father Zoeller offered some connection for Lance to a mother he never knew.

The Bells invited us to the evening services, but we were ready to head back south. We bought trolley tickets to Tecumseh and then planned to take Old Beck back to Romulus. As we rode the trolley down Shawnee's Main Street and toward the Rock Island Depot, we passed the Western Business College.

"What a town!" Arty exclaimed. "Three colleges...all these businesses...This really is the place we should be, guys."

Arty preached on about the future prospects in this metropolis. I was tired and Lance was introspective as we were content to let Arty lecture. I smiled at my friend's energy as I settled into the wooden train seat for the trip back home. I had looked forward to this weekend for months, and now it was over. I went back to work in earnest the next day, determined to help my family buy the land we had lived on and farmed.

Moving to Shawnee seemed like another world, but I soon found the world was shrinking. The Cross Timber, where the three of us had lived and played, was disappearing. Our way of life was disappearing as well. None of that was on my mind as the train rumbled out of Tecumseh and toward home. Gwen Peaudane dominated my thoughts this evening and the promise I would be seeing her at the store in the morning.

CHAPTER 18

Work at the Peaudane General Store became routine over the next months, but continued to be exciting to me. Lloyd and Gordon handled the field chores, so I devoted more of my time to the store. Working six days a week, the family's account at the store was shrinking, and I was able to contribute to Dad's plans to buy land.

Gwen Peaudane came to the store nearly every day to bring lunch, and our relationship progressed. Guy would take me out to lunch on days Gwen cooked, and although he was over ten years older than I was, we were becoming friends.

Guy liked to talk about county politics and the importance of keeping the county seat in Tecumseh. Guy, much like his younger sister, always demonstrated a pleasant demeanor, but his optimistic and upbeat personality could not hide his concern about the future of Romulus and the Peaudane General Store.

On a Thursday afternoon in late October, Gwen delivered some particularly dreadful meatloaf. After pretending to enjoy it and waiting until she had gone, we ditched the meal and headed to Kelly's restaurant.

Our conversation was typical until Guy ordered pie and asked me in a serious tone, "What do you want to do in life?"

After thinking a few seconds, I gave an insightful shrug and said, "I don't know."

Guy smiled, encouraging me to give a better answer. A future with his sister dominated my thinking, but I did not dare share those plans with anyone.

"We're saving for the farm," I reflected. "I guess I'll keep working to help pay the bills."

"Do you want to be a farmer?" Guy asked bluntly, while placing his index finger on his cheek and thumb on his chin.

"I…I…don't know," I responded. "I hadn't really thought about it."

Looking skeptically at me, he said, "Haven't you? I've watched you the past months, and you seem to like what you're doing. You don't seem to miss picking cotton on the farm."

I had not consciously thought much about a future beyond buying the farm. Although I hated picking cotton, I lived with the assumption my father expected me to be part of the farm.

"You like the store?" Guy asked.

Nodding, I said, "Very much."

Smiling with satisfaction, Guy said, "You're good at it. You learn fast, you're good with customers, and have some initiative."

"Thanks," I bashfully replied.

After taking a bite of his pie, Guy continued, "You ought to think about business…you'd do well."

"I hope to work at Peaudane's as long as you'll have me," I assured.

"You might want to think longer term…maybe have your own business some day."

Looking wide-eyed at him, I said, "I don't know about that…I don't know the first thing—"

"Of course you do," Guy interrupted. "Heck, you could probably run Peaudane's without me."

I shook my head in disagreement, as Guy laughed good-naturedly.

"In fact," Guy continued. "I have a proposition for you."

Straightening in my chair, I listened.

"I've got to go to Oklahoma City for a few days next week," Guy explained. "Dad's not been in the store enough the past year to know where anything is. I think you'd be fine…I've showed you how to make deposits."

Cringing slightly at the possible responsibility, I muttered, "I don't know…I don't think—"

"Nonsense," Guy interjected. "You've got to get 'I don't know…I don't think' out of your vocabulary. I know you can handle things…I'll have Gwen come and watch the register…she shouldn't be too much in the way."

The thought of working alone with Gwen was a strong enticement and provided the courage I needed to accept.

"I guess—" I began.

"Good," Guy blurted out before I could finish. "Go down to Robbins & Newhelm Dry Goods and pick out a shirt and tie. Put it on my account."

Stopping abruptly, Guy hesitated before saying, "I need to ask one more thing."

"Sure," I replied.

"Old Elmer Booze usually sleeps in the back room to kind of watch things. He's got to go to Maud next week to check on his sick sister. Could I get you to sleep over?"

"I guess so," I replied.

"'I guess so' is only slightly better than 'I don't know,'" Guy coached.

"Yes, I can," I smiled. "I'll check with Dad, but he won't care."

"Great," Guy said. "I'll pay you an extra day's wages for sleeping over, and I'll make sure Mrs. Peaudane cooks the dinner, not Gwen."

"That would be great," I said with a grin.

The next week, Guy Peaudane boarded Old Beck to Shawnee and then to Oklahoma City, leaving a set of keys and detailed instructions.

For two days, I would be in charge of the Peaudane General Store. More importantly, I would be working with Gwen.

CHAPTER 19

"I'm here," Gwen Peaudane cheerfully greeted a little before nine o'clock in the morning.

Gwen wore a cream-colored dress with a pink satin sash. Her long, brown hair was pulled back into a ponytail, which dangled over her shoulder. She seemed genuinely excited to be working with me.

"Great," I replied. "I'm glad you could come in today."

In a serious tone, she said, "I'll do almost anything to get out of the house."

I had been at the store since dawn, sweeping before opening the doors and preparing for the day. Guy checked in before catching his train, and I was now in charge.

"Do you have anything for me to do?" Gwen asked.

I had not thought about having to delegate tasks. Having Gwen sweep and clean as I normally would, did not seem right, so I said, "Guy said to watch the cash register."

With a sly grin, she said, "Why? Is it going to run off?"

Slightly flustered, I replied, "When customers come, you'll need to count the money, make change, and make sure it's rung up on the right account."

"I know how to run the cash register," she assured.

Not wanting to risk more awkward conversation, I left Gwen by the cash register and began taking inventory. I was relieved when customers started filtering into the store. I stayed busy most of the morning answering questions and helping customers. Guy's absence seemed to make everything more difficult. It had been easy to ask him questions and let him make decisions. After selling a fifteen-dollar rocking chair, however, I proudly brought the ticket to Gwen and believed Guy would be pleased with our efforts.

At noon, Mrs. Peaudane brought lunch. I enjoyed eating with Gwen and tried not to smirk at the thought of Guy's quips about her inability to cook. Some of the nervousness of the morning began to disappear, as I gained confidence we could make it through the day without major incident.

While reaching to fetch a basket for a customer, I heard Marilee Martin say, "Hey Gilbert."

Marilee stood at the end of the aisle grinning at me, while I tried to finish helping my customer. Looking toward the cash register, I saw Arty leaning over the counter talking to Gwen. I nearly stumbled, when Gwen laughed at something Arty said.

Practically dragging my customer to the front counter to pay for her basket, I said in an almost scolding tone, "Gwen, Mrs. Goodnight needs to check out."

As a confused Mrs. Goodnight fumbled for her pocket book, I motioned for Arty to meet me at the end of the counter.

"What are you doing here?" I asked, trying not to be too sharp tongued.

Since I was responsible for the store, I had no tolerance for any shenanigans Arty had planned.

"I brought Marilee to do some shopping," Arty defended. "Gwen told her you'd be in charge today, so I offered to drive her to town."

"Oh," I muttered back.

As my customer finished her business, I said, "Thank you, Mrs. Goodnight. Hope that basket works for you."

Mrs. Goodnight waved and smiled as she walked out to the street.

"You're good at this," Arty observed. "Maybe we need to start a business."

"With what?" I asked.

"With your brains and my charm, we couldn't miss," Arty smiled.

Shaking my head, I said, "Whatever you say, Arty."

"You're about to miss a sale, though," Arty said, while motioning toward Marilee.

Marilee Martin looked deep in thought as she examined the assortment of ribbons hung overhead.

"When have you ever been so friendly with Marilee?" I asked.

Looking at Gwen, Arty said, "You know what Lance said. I need to get to know my little sister."

Insulted at Arty's blatant stalking of Gwen, I smiled as I whispered to Gwen, "Do you think you could help Marilee find some ribbon?"

Anxious to leave her station behind the cash register, Gwen asked, "Can I?"

"Sure," I said, while glancing at a miffed Arty.

Gwen glided from behind the counter, toward Marilee, and more importantly, away from Arty. He leaned against the counter watching Gwen, as I took her place at the cash register.

"So," I began, trying to distract Arty. "You got out of the fields today."

Nodding, Arty said, "I may be out of the fields for good."

"What?" I asked.

"Dad's buyin' a tractor," Arty boasted. "I imagine I'll be mainly responsible for making sure it runs."

I remembered the demonstration at the fair and thought how useful a tractor would be in my dad's field.

"When are we goin' hunting?" Arty asked.

"I don't know…" I answered before remembering Guy Peaudane's instructions to be more decisive.

"I can go Thanksgiving," I replied. "The store will be closed…the cotton's all in. We can go then. What are we hunting?"

"I thought we'd head south of Salt Creek, into the woods and try to scare up a deer," Arty stated.

"That's pretty far," I noted, thinking we would just hunt the woods closer to home for a turkey or quail.

"It's not that far," Arty assured. "We can set up camp Wednesday and be back in time for dinner."

"You talked me into it," I sighed, as I watched Gwen talking to Marilee by the ribbons.

"Have you seen Lance around?" Arty asked.

"No," I replied. "Haven't seen him in a couple of weeks."

"I saw that Mexican fella come through 'bout a week ago," Arty revealed, "but I ain't seen Lance."

With a shrug, Arty said, "He'll show up…If you see 'em, tell 'em the plan."

As I nodded in agreement, the front door bell rang, which caused me to halt the conversation with Arty. Leland Holiday sauntered into the store, causing all of us to watch silently. He looked at Arty and me with suspicion and then proceeded to walk about the store. His heels jingled, from a pair of worn spurs dangling from his boots. I had never seen Leland on a horse, but the silver spurs were notorious. One of the many stories about Leland Holiday involved those spurs in a fight, when he nearly ripped a man's face off. Although younger than his cousin, Haskell Holiday, Leland possessed a commanding appearance. A combination of charm and intimidation made him a formidable presence.

The store was uncomfortably quiet as the town's marshal walked through, occasionally picking up an item to inspect. As he approached the two girls, he stopped and leered at them as he pretended to look at fabric. Arty started toward the marshal, until I grabbed him by the arm. Nodding for Arty to stay by the register, I swallowed hard and walked toward Leland Holiday.

"Can I help you?" I asked.

Still staring at Gwen, Leland Holiday said, "I'm finding everything just fine."

Sensing Gwen's discomfort with the unwanted attention, I quickly said, "Gwen, I need you back behind the counter."

Without a word, Gwen complied, leaning noticeably away from the marshal as she passed.

Leland Holiday shot me a cold stare and said, "Are you the boss today?"

"Yes…Yes sir, I am," I answered while trying to stand as tall as possible.

He looked at me with some disdain and asked, "Where's Guy?"

"Mr. Peaudane had business out of town and won't be back until tomorrow," I answered.

Looking past me, to the cash register where Gwen was now standing he asked, "Is Booze around?"

"No sir," I answered. "He's got a sick sister over by Maud. Can I help you?"

Leland Holiday took a moment to size me up before focusing his attention once again on Gwen Peaudane and saying, "No, I'm finding everything I need."

Unsure how to handle the marshal, I said, "Let me know if you have questions. I'll be by the counter."

I was too late to comfort Gwen. Arty had already taken the opportunity to stand next to her, and as I stepped closer, I could see Gwen clutching Arty's arm for some feeling of protection. Leland Holiday looked our way for a moment, before continuing to walk about the store randomly picking up items of interest to him. Marilee was left by herself, close to the fabrics and ribbons, but she did not seem to be disturbed by this intruder and continued her shopping in naive contentment.

After a few minutes, Leland Holiday grabbed a box of Roi-Tan cigars and headed to the counter. I waited a moment for Gwen to ring him up, but I soon noticed she was glued to Arty's side.

Stepping to the cash register myself, I asked, "Is there anything else?"

Purposely looking at Gwen, he said with a mischievous smile under his dark mustache, "Not right now...but maybe later."

Trying to ignore his intimidation of Gwen, I completed the transaction and said, "Have a nice day."

Leland stared coldly at me, before turning to Arty and saying, "You seen Carrington around, Martin?"

"Don't know why I'd tell you," Arty shot back without blinking.

The answer did not agree with the marshal and he said, "You don't want to get smart with me, son. Your daddy's not always goin' to be around. Have you seen Carrington?"

A more humble Arty answered, "Not in several weeks."

Surveying Arty for a moment to determine his truthfulness, Leland Holiday added, "Don't expect he wants to see me, but when you see Carrington, tell him I'm looking for him."

Arty nodded slightly.

"You tell him I know all 'bout his Mexican friends," Leland said in a sterner tone of voice.

Turning back to me, Leland Holiday said, "You say Guy's out until tomorrow?"

I managed to nod.

"And Booze is out too?" he asked.

Again, I nodded.

Without another word, Leland Holiday leered one more time at Gwen, causing her to stand even closer to Arty before belching an evil laugh, as he exited the store.

I looked at Arty, as Gwen continued to hold on to his arm.

"Gilbert, do you like this rose ribbon or the green?" Marilee asked as she walked to the front counter, seemingly without a clue about the nonverbal threats by Leland Holiday.

Greeted with silence by the three of us, she insisted again, "What do you think, Gilbert?"

Looking at Gwen, who was still trembling from the perceived advances of Leland Holiday, and seeing she would be of no help, I answered, "The green one Marilee…It'll go with your eyes."

This answer caused Arty to laugh, which helped lighten the mood.

"Rose or green?" Arty teased loudly. "What difference does it make, unless you're going to wear it over your face!"

Only slightly insulted, Marilee shot back, "Gilbert likes the green one…what do you think, Gwen?"

Still unconsciously holding Arty's arm, Gwen said, "The green will look fine...It will complement your eyes."

"Why don't you check Marilee out?" I instructed Gwen, anxious to get her away from Arty.

These instructions seemed to cause Gwen to realize she had been holding on to Arty. She quickly let go of his arm. Taking a second to smooth her dress and straighten her hair, Gwen took Marilee's money. Arty was anxious to stay around and bother Gwen, but Marilee was ready to head home and sew on her newfound prize.

As Arty walked out the door, he shouted back at me, "Don't forget our hunting trip…and keep an eye out for Lance."

I waved in acknowledgment as Arty and Marilee left, leaving Gwen and me alone in the store.

Eager to be Gwen's protector, I asked, "Are you all right?"

"What?" Gwen asked.

"When the marshal was in here…that seemed to bother you," I suggested.

Somewhat embarrassed, she said, "I'm just silly sometimes. It's just the way some men look at me…and he…I…I'm being silly, but he makes me feel funny."

I stepped close, in case Gwen needed an arm to hold, as she continued, "I'll be fine…I'm just funny sometimes."

Seeming to shake off any residual effects of the encounter, she began asking a host of questions unrelated to the incident. We finished the day without saying more about Leland Holiday or Arty Martin. It had been a profitable day. Gwen watched me shut down the store and make the deposit, before asking me to walk her home. In the months I had worked for the Peaudanes, it was the first time Gwen asked to be escorted.

CHAPTER 20

Mrs. Peaudane invited me to supper that evening. Gwen seemed to be back to her pleasant self and did not mention Leland Holiday at dinner. Gwen's mother looked much like Gwen. Her shoulder length hair featured a salt and pepper coloring, but she seemed to have a more youthful vitality than most of the parents I knew.

Dr. Peaudane was considerably older than his wife was. White whiskers gave him a kindly, wise appearance. He was friends with Arty's father, but was much more relaxed and fun-loving than Mr. Martin.

Gwen sat quietly and listened to the evening's conversation without comment. She seemed strangely distant and nervous around her father. I could only assume the encounter with Leland Holiday had traumatized her.

I enjoyed the evening, but eventually headed back to the store to sleep in the back room. Elmer Booze maintained a cot there, complete with a pistol hidden under the bed frame. I read for a short time, but the day left me tired, so I soon dimmed the oil lamp and drifted into a peaceful sleep.

The noise that awoke me was barely noticeable. At first, I wondered if it had been anything at all and even questioned if I was awake or asleep. The second occurrence was more distinct and clear, as I lay wide-awake in the cot hoping it was my imagination or some animal prowling in the night.

The third time, I could tell the ruckus was purposeful and human. The sound definitely came from the front door, which was nearly fifty feet from my bed. Although far from the door, I could hear jingling and scratching in the quiet of the night. Fumbling for a match, I dropped the entire box on the floor. Lying in the dark loneliness of the back room, I hoped the sound was only my active imagination.

I listened in stilled silence for a few minutes and almost determined there was nothing at the door, when I heard the sound of metal on metal again. Someone was trying to force open the door. I tried to cry out, but fear seemed to paralyze my vocal cords. I hoped, as I had never hoped before, the unwanted stranger would go away. Almost by accident, my hand reached under the bed frame and felt the revolver Elmer Booze stashed underneath.

Pulling the pistol from its holster, I sat on the edge of the cot, looking toward the front door. I brought the pistol up to my chest as I quietly prayed the noise would cease. I had no idea if the revolver was loaded or not, but cocked the gun and aimed in the general direction of the door. Guy Peaudane had asked me to sleep in the store, but I had no idea anyone could possibly want to break in. Shaking in the dark, I continued to hope the stranger would leave.

Whoever was at the door now rattled it with more boldness and urgency. I felt as if I should call out, but feared it was too late. When I heard the intruder force the door open, my finger unconsciously pulled the trigger of the pistol. The old revolver recoiled in my hand as I heard the man thud to the ground.

A sickening feeling overcame me. I had shot someone, maybe shot them dead. My mind raced in terror at the thought of killing someone. In the seconds after the shooting, an even more frightening thought overtook my mind. What if I have shot Guy, or Dr. Peaudane? No—I thought to myself, they would have come through the back door, and they would not have come at this time of night.

"What time is it?" I asked myself as I huddled near my cot too frightened to move, but still holding the pistol.

I called out finally, but no one answered. I could hear no one, but even through the darkness, began to sense the front door was open. Soon I heard the most terrifying sound of the night—I distinctly heard blood gurgling from the man I had shot. A sudden burst of energy and courage came over me, as I moved cautiously toward the dead or dying man.

"Who's there?" I called softly.

"Who's there?" I again shouted with more authority.

Stepping closer to the dying man as he slowly bled on the floor of the Peaudane General Store, I suddenly froze, letting out an unmanly screech as my stocking feet stepped into the sticky, freshly spilled blood. Almost crying, I dropped the pistol and retreated to the cot before falling on the floor in despair.

As I clung to the floor, I remembered the matches I had dropped and frantically searched for one. In a moment, I struck a match and with shaking hands lit the oil lamp. Trembling from head to toe, I stepped toward the front of the store to see whom I had killed. A sickening feeling overcame me, and I almost wished it had been me that had been shot.

Peering at the half-opened door, I could see no one there. Assuming the thief had crawled away; I picked up the pistol and cautiously looked out the window. Seeing nothing, I leaned against the doorpost and breathed deeply when I once again heard the blood gurgling onto the floor.

Looking at my damp socks, I noticed they were not stained red with blood. Using the oil lamp to examine closer, I let out a pathetic, relieved sigh of a laugh, as I looked at a barrel of molasses lying on its side with a bullet hole in it. Panic overcame me for a second, as I believed I had invented the whole episode in my mind.

"Guy would never trust me again," I thought to myself.

Looking around, however, I noticed the glass on the floor and could tell someone had tried to break in. Looking at the clock on the wall, I saw it was almost two o'clock. As I stepped away from the door to put on my boots before cleaning up, I heard a clanking sound outside from the corner of the building.

As a match was struck, I could see the round glow of a cigar. My heart began to race as the stranger stood in the smoky shadows. The anxiety I felt did not diminish, when Leland Holiday stepped toward me puffing on his freshly lit cigar.

"Thought I heard a shot," Leland calmly stated.

"It was me," I nervously admitted.

Looking around the broken window, Leland asked, "Did you get a look at him?"

"No," I replied breathlessly. "I was in the back, sleeping."

"You takin' Booze's place?" he asked with a sharp gaze.

"Yes, sir," I admitted.

Taking a long puff on his cigar and blowing the smoke my direction he said, "I'll look around and see what I can find."

Without another word, Leland Holiday stepped off the walkway in front of the store and moved lazily across the street with his spurs jingling rhythmically in the night. The sight of Leland Holiday in the darkness had been nearly as frightening as the thought that I might have killed a man.

Too rattled to go back to bed, I cleaned up the glass and turned the molasses barrel upright so it would not leak anymore. I could not sleep and lay on the cot analyzing every noise in the night. The next morning I tried to clean the floor more thoroughly, but the molasses-stained wood floor, would be a reminder of that night for many months.

Guy Peaudane arrived on the afternoon train the next day. I had practiced telling my story to Gwen but dreaded facing the employer who had trusted his store in my care. Guy listened with great interest, especially the part about Leland Holiday. I expected he would be angry, but after determining that everyone was safe and little damage had been done, Guy showed me a bullet hole he had put in the doorpost years earlier. Gwen, however, told Arty about my misadventure, and for weeks I was known as the "Great Molasses Killer."

CHAPTER 21

Guy Peaudane circulated a petition to remove Leland Holiday as town marshal after the attempted break-in at the store. The clever Leland did not risk being fired and resigned to take a job in the nearby town of Maud. Lance showed up in Romulus a couple of weeks later. I told him about our plan to go hunting and as always, Lance was eager for an adventure. Guy let Lance spend some of the colder nights in the back room where Elmer Booze stayed. There had been no further attempts to break into the store, but people routinely called me "The Molasses Killer."

The Wednesday before Thanksgiving was cold and dreary. Rains earlier in the week left the ground saturated and muddy. Lance, Arty, and I loaded our ragged array of camping gear and headed south. The water was icy as we waded across the Salt Creek into the thickest parts of the Cross Timber.

"What kind of gun is that?" Arty asked Lance as we trudged through the tangled forest.

Lance kept walking, but raised his rifle up for a closer inspection.

"Rusty," Lance said without cracking a smile.

Lance's firearm looked like it was held together with baling wire and nails. The wood stock was weathered gray with a barrel that looked like it had been used as a hammer at some point. The ancient firearm was a muzzleloader, complete with ramrod.

"Where'd you get it?" Arty asked. "The Civil War?"

Lance smiled and said, "I'll only need one shot."

"One shot!" Arty exclaimed.

"I only brought one ball," Lance quipped.

Arty shook his head as he cradled his Winchester '94 lever action repeating rifle. Since I carried a twenty-two gauge rifle Lloyd used to hunt squirrels, Arty had the only real chance of bringing down anything larger than a raccoon.

"You can't get a deer with one shot," Arty charged.

"Well…I brought a little help," Lance said as he pulled back his patched coat and revealed an old pistol.

"Where'd you get that?" Arty excitedly asked, as he stopped to get a closer look at the old revolver.

With a sly smile, Lance quipped, "Let's just say old Elmer promised me it would take down any molasses barrel in the county."

Both laughed at my expense. I had endured weeks of ridicule and jokes about shooting the barrel and the floor of the store was still stained with molasses.

Finding it easier to laugh with people than defend myself, I asked, "Have you heard of any out-of-line molasses barrels since that night?"

"No," Arty laughed. "I think you must have scared 'em off."

The teasing lasted until we set up camp. Lance quickly started a fire with nothing but a flint rock as Arty and I strung a tent between two small trees. We were camping in the Cross Timber, and the sky above was barely visible through the canopy above us. This night, I began to realize we were not really boys anymore. Lance had been on his own for years, and I had a full-time job working in town. Arty was taking more responsibility at the Martin farm, and Mr. Martin had talked of sending him away for more schooling.

The Great War in Europe, which Guy Peaudane and I talked about so much, was also on our minds. We heard stories of adventure and valor in the trenches and in the air. On a trip to Shawnee, we had gone to a picture show to see the war in real life—or at least what we perceived as real life. Things changed more rapidly than we anticipated in the world, but our friendship and commitment to each other remained constant.

It was cold and damp, but I slept peacefully through the night. By early dawn, Lance was up putting logs on the hot fire. We had brought bacon to fry while Marilee sent biscuits and fried pies for us to enjoy. Arty was the last to get up. After devouring the flaky biscuits, we packed our gear and began the hunt.

The heavy frost made tracking simple. About a mile from camp, we came across deer tracks heading deeper into the thick woods. The thick, oak forest comprising the Cross Timber provided only a few yards of visibility, so we decided to track another half mile to find a place to wait for a buck to cross.

Finding a narrow creek, we headed up stream to find a good place to wait. One hundred yards further, we came to a small opening in the canopy of trees. Arty put his rifle down to survey the ground. A strong, pungent odor pervaded the damp air as the ground looked as if it had been crudely plowed, while muddy water collected in a shallow pond. We moved silently in tracking the deer for the past half hour, so we talked with hand signals. Arty stepped toward the edge of the opening, while Lance and I watched.

Suddenly, Arty yelped, "Whoa!"

A frenzy of squeals followed his yell, as four piglets scrambled toward the woods. Arty had time to let out a relieved laugh before an ominous sound rustled in the brush. Without warning, a large boar, nearly four-feet long and weighing nearly three hundred pounds rushed out of the brush and charged Arty.

Arty looked at us helplessly, as his gun leaned against a tree nearly twenty feet away. I took a shot with my rifle, but either missed or the small caliber did not phase the wild boar. Lance's antique musket clicked as he pulled the trigger, but failed to fire. As the boar charged the helpless Arty, Lance tried to fend it off with his malfunctioned rifle. As the pig lowered its head, Lance quickly attacked it with his knife.

The beast squealed savagely as Lance struck the thick back of the black-haired animal with his knife. For a moment, it looked as if the pig would retreat, but without warning, it turned and charged again. Lance tried to fend it off, but the boar's speed and power knocked Lance to the ground. The two inch curved tusk plowed into Lance's ribs and to my horror the boar lowered its head and started driving Lance through the mud.

Screaming, I started to charge the pig myself when an explosion from Arty's Winchester 30/30 jarred the pig off Lance. With a quick click of the lever, Arty put a shot into the boar's head as it dropped only a few feet from a bloodied Lance Carrington. Arty and I ran to Lance, and immediately could tell he was badly hurt. He groaned on the ground with his eyes closed while blood mixed with mud was everywhere.

"Oh God!" Arty cried out. "We gotta do something!"

Arty ripped off his coat and placed it over the wound in the ribs of his friend.

"Can you walk?" I asked in a panic.

Lance was unresponsive.

"We'll have to carry him," Arty frantically determined.

We put him between us and tried to stand him up, but he was as limp as a corpse.

"Pick him up!" Arty demanded.

Reaching under his arms, Arty lifted Lance supporting most of the weight while I carried his feet. We retraced our steps from the morning as fast as possible. When we reached the campsite, Lance was barely conscious and in great pain.

"We gotta get him to a doctor!" a frenzied Arty exclaimed the obvious.

Nodding, I waited for Arty, covered in mud and blood, to tell me how.

"Use the canvas and drag him to the river. I'm running home to get a wagon. Get to the crossing as soon as you can!" Arty screamed as he began running through the woods toward the Salt Creek.

I doubled up the canvas from our tent and gently put Lance on it. He groaned with pain as he now clutched his wound. Pulling back the blood soaked coat Arty had used as a bandage, I could see his side was slit open as if a knife had cut him. Placing the inadequate bandage back on the wound to try to stop the bleeding, I pulled with all my might in sheer panic.

Lance groaned and winced in pain with every step I took. Tears of fear made it difficult to see, but I pressed on as quickly as possible. About a quarter mile from Salt Creek, I heard Arty, his older brother Ethan, and Lloyd running through the woods toward me. I nearly collapsed with my last step as Ethan and Lloyd took over with a new sense of urgency at the sight of the wounded boy. In a few more minutes, we had Lance across Salt Creek, and the Martin's fine team of mules charged off to the only help close by—Dr. Peaudane's home.

CHAPTER 22

The normally amiable Dr. Peaudane appeared grumpy at having his Thanksgiving dinner interrupted, but when he saw Arty covered in blood and a boy laying limply in the wagon, he moved with quickness and energy that defied his age.

"Bring him inside!" Dr. Peaudane shouted to Ethan and Lloyd.

The two older brothers gingerly placed Lance on a board and carried him to a bed in the back of the Peaudane home.

"What happened?" the doctor asked.

"A pig gored him," a breathless Arty answered.

"I'll say," Dr. Peaudane sighed, as he inspected the wound. "Looks like it nearly ripped him apart."

"Guy!" Dr. Peaudane barked. "Get me Doc Sanders. Tell 'em I need him."

Guy, sensing the gravity of the situation, left to saddle his horse. The Peaudanes owned a fine automobile, but Doc Sanders lived far from any decent road. Doc Sanders had not gone to school to be a doctor, but was more of a self-taught herbalist. He had a reputation as a healer, however, and the older Dr. Peaudane knew he needed a set of younger, steadier hands.

"Lance!" Gwen Peaudane shrieked at the sight of a bloodied and unconscious Lance Carrington.

"Gwen!" Dr. Peaudane shouted at the hysterical girl. "Get my kit and boil some water."

Gwen stood wide-eyed and pale white.

"Do it now!" her father sternly ordered.

Coming to her senses, the girl quickly obeyed. For the next hour, Arty and I stood quietly in the front room with Lance Carrington's blood staining our clothes, while Gwen assisted her father in cleaning and bandaging their patient.

Doc Sanders eventually showed up with Guy. He was much younger than Dr. Peaudane was and had a serious demeanor, but his smile reassured us as he stepped into the house. In a few moments, a tired-looking Dr. Peaudane came out to the front room.

"How is he?" I asked.

Shaking his head, the doctor said, "I don't know yet. He's lost a lot of blood. He's cut to the bone and he's broke at least three ribs. The ribs may have saved him. I don't think he's got any organ damage."

"Will he be okay?" Arty anxiously asked.

"I don't know," Dr. Peaudane coldly answered.

"What happened?" Guy Peaudane asked, as he stepped inside the house.

Arty glanced at me, and then said, "We were huntin' south of Salt Creek. I had laid my gun down to look around when I stepped into a hole full of piglets. Out of nowhere, a large boar charged me…Lance jumped in front of me without even thinking…he saved me."

"I took a shot," I added. "But must've missed."

"What were you using?" Guy asked.

"A twenty two…single shot," I answered.

"Even if you hit it, that wouldn't have slowed down an animal that size," Guy stated.

"Lance attacked it with his knife and he tried to protect me, but it just lowered its head and drove him through the mud," Arty added. "The pig just wouldn't let up. I got to my 30/30 and shot him."

"You probably saved him," Dr. Peaudane observed. "That boar'd probably not stopped with piglets around."

"Where's Gwen?" Arty asked, as he looked around the room.

"She's assisting Doc Sanders," Dr. Peaudane explained while giving Arty a sharp look. "Why don't you boys go home? There's nothing you can do here."

"If you don't mind, I'd like to stay around," Arty responded.

"Suit yourself," Dr. Peaudane shrugged as he returned to the back room.

"You boys need to wash up," Guy Peaudane suggested.

In a few minutes, Mrs. Peaudane brought a pail of warm water and towels to the front porch, as Arty and I cleaned the blood and dirt from our faces and arms. Gwen's mother seemed overly distraught and tired, as she walked quietly back into the house, while Gwen stayed by Dr. Peaudane's side. By the time we cleaned up, Doc Sanders came to the front porch.

"How is he?" I asked.

The doctor shrugged his shoulders and said, "We'll know in a day or two."

"What do you mean?" an agitated Arty charged.

In a precise tone, Doc Sanders said, "The boy's lost a lot of blood, but we've stopped the bleeding, and I stitched him up."

Taking a second to rinse his hands, the doctor continued, "He should heal, but he'll be weak for a while. I'm worried about infection now. Dr. Peaudane said he can stay here a few weeks. We'll know more in a few days."

Observing our concern, Doc Sanders said, "You boys go home. You look beat. You'll do no one any good tonight. You did good getting him here. The Peaudanes will watch over him…come back tomorrow."

"You guys go on home," Guy Peaudane added. "He'll be fine. Gill, you look like you've had a day of it. Take tomorrow off and check on him then."

Reluctantly, Arty and I started the long walk home, uncertain if our best friend in the world would be with us in the morning.

CHAPTER 23

Arty and I arrived at the Peaudane house shortly after dawn. It promised to be a bright, sunny day, but the morning was chilly. Mrs. Peaudane answered the door and did not look happy to see visitors at such an early hour after a hectic night. She was shutting the door, when Gwen appeared wearing blood-splattered clothes from the previous night.

"It's okay," a weary Gwen greeted.

"How is he?" Arty asked, as Gwen stood by the door.

"He's sleeping," she said in a lifeless tone. "He's slept all night."

"Can we see him?" Arty asked.

"He's sleeping," Gwen repeated.

"We won't bother him," Arty pleaded.

Seeing no one around, Gwen grudgingly said, "Don't make a sound."

She led us to the back room where Lance lay silently in the half-light of the morning. A chair was pulled next to the bed as his arm dangled limply to the side. After a moment, Gwen ushered us back outside.

"Come back later," she instructed. "Dr. Peaudane will be up then, and he can tell you more."

Neither one of us had the heart to argue with the exhausted girl, so we left. We had abandoned our guns and the rest of our gear south of Salt Creek. Since Arty and I needed to burn off nervous energy, we decided to go retrieve our equipment. Walking back to the Martin farm, we saddled two horses and headed to the creek.

Leaving the horses at the campsite, we walked through the thick brush to the site of the attack. It seemed impossible that we had managed to carry Lance so quickly. Coming to the opening, we stepped cautiously until Arty located his rifle. I searched and found my small rifle, Lance's old musket, and the pistol of Elmer Booze.

We looked at the dead boar lying in the crimson-stained grass. Its fearsome tusk curled around the lifeless snout. Without warning, Arty fired several shots into the carcass before removing Lance's knife from the pig's back and savagely cutting the tusk from the animal. I never asked Arty why, and we walked back to the horses in silence.

We returned to the Peaudane home in the afternoon. There appeared to be more activity, as the house recovered from the drama of the previous night. Lance still slept, but Dr. Peaudane assured us he was doing as well as could be expected.

"Hello guys," a tired Gwen Peaudane greeted as she stepped from the back of the house.

Still wearing the same dress as the night before, she had a faraway, almost lifeless look of a girl who had not slept in a day.

"Gwen," Dr. Peaudane scolded. "I told you to get some sleep. There's nothing more you can do."

She stoically obeyed as she wandered to her room.

"Is she okay?" I asked, concerned about the fragile Gwen.

In a slightly agitated tone, Dr. Peaudane said, "She'll be fine...she just needs to sleep."

After a moment of silence, Arty asked, "Can we see him?"

"There's nothing to see," Dr. Peaudane admonished.

"I know...but I would like to see him," Arty explained in a less demanding tone than was his norm.

Heaving a big sigh, Dr. Peaudane said, "Okay, but do not wake him...and only one of you at a time."

Arty did not hesitate, as he stepped to Lance's room, leaving me with Dr. Peaudane. The doctor soon left me standing alone, so I retreated to the front porch.

As I stared blankly at the door, waiting for Arty to return, I heard a cheerful, "Hey, Gilbert."

Turning around, I came face to face with Marilee Martin carrying a basket of food.

"What are you doing?" I asked, trying to make polite conversation.

"I'm bringing lunch to the Peaudanes," Marilee replied. "I hear they had a long night."

Gently rapping on the door, Mrs. Peaudane greeted Marilee and invited the girl inside. Marilee declined and instead joined me on the porch.

"It's terrible about Lance, isn't it?" Marilee stated the obvious.

"Worse than you can imagine," I sighed. "I thought he was going to die."

"Poor Gwen," Marilee said shaking her head.

"What do you mean?" I asked.

Looking at me strangely and with some frustration, Marilee said, "Boys really are stupid."

"What?" I gasped in defense.

"Surely you know that Gwen loves Lance," she stated in a matter of fact tone.

Silence betrayed my shock and ignorance.

"Arty thinks Gwen is his girl," Marilee explained, "because Daddy and Dr. Peaudane talk about them as a couple all the time, but Gwen's had her eye on Lance for…as long as I can remember."

Not wanting to believe her, I challenged, "You can't know that…you're being silly."

Shaking her head, Marilee calmly said, "A girl knows who she loves…usually before the man does. Like I said, you boys are stupid."

"No," I protested. "I'm not believing this 'girls know all' nonsense."

Looking disapprovingly at me Marilee said, "The day in the store…the day Leland Holiday came to the store."

With a playful smile, Marilee added, "You know the day before you shot the barrel of molasses."

I did not reply but vividly remembered the event. I had been reminded of the molasses barrel many times.

"Gwen was upset," Marilee stated. "She wasn't afraid of Leland Holiday. I mean, Gwen is a nervous girl for some reason, but what was he going to do in broad daylight in front of all of us? Gwen was upset, because she knows Lance has been making money, cutting into the Holidays' bootlegging business. She was planning to meet Lance that afternoon and was afraid he would show up with Leland Holiday in the store. Anybody could see that."

What Marilee was saying made some sense, but I still wanted to deny the obvious.

"I guess not everyone could see that," Marilee replied.

"Does Arty know?" I finally asked.

"He ought to be able to figure it out," she observed. "But he may not be any brighter than you. Poor Gwen's been worried sick. I came by this morning, and she was a mess. Stayed up all night holding Lance's hand trying to will him back to health."

Perceiving I was finally starting to believe her, Marilee added, "Don't tell Arty. Gwen's got enough trouble without having to deal with my scheming brother."

I looked at her in silence before she scolded, "I mean it. Not a word."

Leaving me in a dazed stupor, Marilee turned around at the end of the walk and added, "You need to wake up, Gilbert Brooks, and see the world for what it is."

With that strange piece of advice, Marilee defiantly walked away, stumbling slightly to diminish the force of her scolding.

"Could Marilee be right?" I thought to myself.

In a moment, a cheerful Arty came onto the porch followed by Gwen Peaudane, who had not followed her father's instructions to take a nap. Arty glowed at Gwen's attention as she smiled sweetly to the both of us.

"Your turn," Gwen said in a tired but pleasant voice.

"See you, Gwen," a gleeful Arty said, as she led me to the back room.

A pale Lance rested with a large bandage around his mid-section. After a second, I stole a glance at Gwen and could tell Marilee had been right. Gwen was oblivious to my presence. Gwen's attention was on Lance. I knew immediately Marilee had seen something that had eluded me. Gwen vigilantly watched Lance's every breath, the knuckles of her right hand placed at her lips as if every moment might be the last she would have with him.

"I'm leaving," I finally whispered.

She took her eyes from Lance for a moment, and with a pleasant, intoxicating smile, she waved good-bye before turning her eyes and thoughts back to Lance. Arty was in a good mood, when I returned to the porch. I thought of Marilee scolding me for not seeing the obvious, but I now observed the same ignorance in Arty. I almost felt sorry for the friend who I had long considered my chief rival for the affections of the girl of my dreams.

I walked away from the Peaudane house with a strange feeling of nostalgia. For the first time in my life, I realized Gwen Peaudane might not be mine.

CHAPTER 24

The fate of Lance Carrington remained in fearful uncertainty for three days. On Tuesday of the next week, however, Gwen came to the hardware store with a bubbling smile and news that the fever Lance had from the infection was improving. He was talking coherently again, although he was still weak. Doc Sanders predicted Lance would make a full recovery in time.

After Marilee's observation, I could tell Lance held a special place in Gwen's thoughts. It was amazing how few around her, recognized the attachment. Dr. Peaudane offered to let Lance stay as long as needed, but I wondered if he would have been so hospitable had he known of his daughter's secret infatuation to a young man many would see as unfit.

As weeks passed, Guy Peaudane certainly seemed to be unaware of Gwen's attraction to Lance. Even Arty, who came nearly every day to check on his good friend and flirt with Gwen, appeared to be oblivious to the secret liaison. In watching Mrs. Peaudane, I believed she might have sensed the romance happening under her roof, but I did not really know.

I had other things to occupy my mind besides the relationship between Gwen and Lance as Christmas approached. Dad had been saving for months to make a down payment on the farm. Weeks went by and a few days before Christmas, Dad prepared to take the train to Tecumseh to buy the land. My work helped pay the bill at the Peaudane

General Store, and I added a few dollars for the down payment, but it was Lloyd who brought in the successful harvest.

It was a cold morning, with a blue-gray sky and frost heavy on the ground, as we stood on the platform waiting for the train to Tecumseh. Dad looked like a regular businessman dressed in his new suit with a freshly polished pair of boots. We talked about plans for the farm and how this would be a fresh start for the Brooks family, the first in our memory to own land. Mr. Martin, who owned the acres we farmed, gave Dad a good price and arranged with a banker to carry the mortgage. It was a proud day as I watched the train chug toward Tecumseh, before walking to my job at the hardware store.

Arriving a little before eight o'clock, I was surprised to find the door still locked. Guy Peaudane was usually at the store by seven. He had trusted me with a key, so I let myself in and hastily prepared the store, before unlocking the front door. The weather looked threatening, and traffic was light this morning. Christmas shoppers would be in the store the next few days, so I busied myself with stocking shelves and organizing the layaways for delivery. Guy Peaudane had contracted with Arty Martin to help with deliveries for Christmas Eve, and I looked forward to being Arty's boss for a day.

Nine o'clock passed and I found myself alone in the hardware store listening to several mantel clocks tick in steady rhythm. Mid-morning, Guy Peaudane burst through the back door and headed directly to his office.

"Good morning," I greeted, expecting Guy to acknowledge my labor for the morning and maybe explain his tardiness.

Guy did not respond and shut the door to his office. As the morning wore on, more customers braved the chilly temperatures. By the time I looked at the clock, it was nearly noon, and Guy had still not come out of his office. The back door creaked open again, and I turned around expecting to see Gwen bringing lunch.

"Hello, Gilbert," the precise voice of Mrs. Peaudane greeted instead.

"Good afternoon, Mrs. Peaudane," I replied.

Looking around the store, she asked, "Where's Guy?"

Pointing to his office, I said, "In there."

With a polite nod, she headed to Guy's office shutting the door behind her. Neither was shouting, but they talked loud enough to be heard, although I could determine nothing of their conversation.

After a few minutes, Mrs. Peaudane exited and smiled pleasantly at me as she walked toward the back door.

"How's Lance?" I asked.

Stopping immediately, Mrs. Peaudane stood silently for a moment, before saying, "Better…he's getting around the house some."

With no further explanation, Mrs. Peaudane said, "Have a Merry Christmas, Gilbert."

"Yes ma'am," I replied as she stepped back into the cold winter air.

Surprised that Mrs. Peaudane did not bring lunch, I went back to work preparing for the rush that was sure to come. In a few minutes, Guy Peaudane walked from his office and looked around the store.

"You've done a good job," Guy said with a sigh. "You're a good storekeeper, Gilbert."

"Is everything all right?" I asked.

"I guess my behavior's not been so normal this morning," he answered with a forced smile. "Father…he's had a spell this morning."

"I'm sorry," I replied. "Is there anything I can do?"

"You've done a fine job covering for me this morning," he said before hesitating. "But…there may be something you could do."

"Sure," I offered.

"You and the Carrington boy are good friends, I've gathered?" Guy began.

"The best," I affirmed.

With another forced smile, Guy asked, "I wonder if I might have him stay with you for a few days."

I did not know how to answer. Our home was small, with three boys sharing one small room.

Addressing my indecision, Guy added, "He's doing much better, and I think it would be good for my father if he didn't have the strain of a patient for a few days."

"Arty Martin's a friend of Lance, and his house is much bigger…and closer," I offered.

With a peculiar grimace, Guy replied, "I…don't think…that will be a good solution."

Sensing, Guy's strong desire, I said, "I guess it'll be fine. I'd need to check with Mother, of course."

"Of course," Guy said with more energy to his voice. "Do you need to borrow a wagon?"

"I have Dad's wagon outside," I confessed.

"It's too cold," Guy said, shaking his head. "We'll take him in the car."

"Okay," I said.

"Watch the store for a few minutes, and I'll be back," Guy suggested as he grabbed his coat and headed out the door.

In about thirty minutes, I heard the back door open and Guy walked in with his wife, Lori.

"Let's go," Guy suggested, while a sickly-looking Lori removed her coat, obviously intending to stay at the store.

In the months I had worked for Guy, I had not seen Lori do anything in the store but shop.

"Where?" I asked.

"Your home," Guy answered in a body language that encouraged me to hurry.

Putting on my old coat and a worn scarf, I followed the anxious Guy to his automobile. To my surprise, a pale Lance Carrington was bundled in the backseat. Guy Peaudane smiled as if nothing was out of the ordinary as the car ground into gear and headed down the bumpy road.

Lance did not look well, and he sat in complete silence as did Guy. When we arrived at my house, I quickly went to ask Mother's permission to let Lance stay. Without a fuss, she agreed, and Lloyd helped me walk Lance into the house while mother scurried to make a place for him on an old cot she kept. In a few moments, Lance was resting comfortably, and I returned to the car where Guy had been waiting.

We drove in silence a few minutes, before Guy said, "I'm sorry to have been such an imposition on short notice."

Although Guy Peaudane was my employer, we had developed a relationship during our close contact working in the store.

"What's happened?" I asked.

Taking a moment to choose his words, Guy said, "My sister has…she's grown attached to Mr. Carrington the past weeks. Father came to check on his patient this morning and found Gwen asleep by the boy's side and holding his hand."

I remained silent, not anxious to acknowledge that Marilee Martin had informed me about the relationship weeks earlier.

"I don't know enough about the boy to have much of an opinion, but I guess he's not got much family and…somewhat of a reputation," Guy tactfully explained.

"I've known Lance, a long time," I tried to defend. "He's—"

"You don't have to explain his circumstance to me," Guy quickly assured. "It's my father…he's old-fashioned and…he's got a special attachment to Gwen. I suppose seeing his baby girl in the arms of a boy without much prospects was a shock. He got real excited over it and then became very agitated…words were said."

"I'm sorry," I replied.

Thinking for a moment and talking more like the man I had known the past months, Guy added, "I'm not trying to disrespect your friend. Father is older, and I guess knows he may not be around to see Gwen grow into a woman. He has been…almost desperate since she was young to see her with someone who could provide—he's at least been anxious to keep her away from most boys. He wants her to find someone with family that has some roots…someone like Arthur Martin is what Father has planned for many years."

Adding to his awkward explanation, Guy added, "Father is very protective."

I remained silent, not knowing how to respond.

"I know modern girls think they know what will make them happy, but there's some wisdom in having parents guide the process. Mr. Martin has long felt it would be a good match, too. Since the older boy already has a girl and Arthur is closer in age…they feel it makes sense. That's why I was not able to move the boy to the Martin home."

"I see," I said, somewhat despondent to think my family was only slightly ahead of Lance Carrington's on the county's social ladder.

Guy looked guilty and ashamed that he had revealed so much, as he parked behind the store.

Guy turned off the car and said, "Thanks for your help today. It will be a good thing for my father's peace of mind…and please don't mention any of this to anyone…my family is…just…please don't mention it."

I did not respond, but nodded slightly in acknowledgement.

"You're a fine young man," Guy continued. "I believe you will go far in life…smart, industrious…loyal. I appreciate your loyalty to me. I hope you know that I trust you."

After a brief pause, he added, "And…I admire your loyalty to the Carrington boy."

CHAPTER 25

I finished the day, working at the store before heading back to the train station to meet Dad. I was anxious to get home and find out from Lance his side of the story. I was also eager to hear from Dad. I waited until the arrival of the last train of the day but did not see my father. Determining he had decided to stay the night in Tecumseh, I headed Old Betsy and the rickety wagon toward the house.

Mother had supper waiting on me and did not seem too concerned about Dad's absence. She said he had several things to do in the city and was not surprised the banking had taken longer than expected. Lloyd and Gordon helped in the kitchen as I retreated to the small bedroom to check on Lance.

Lance was awake, but stared blankly at the ceiling under the dim light of an oil lamp. He looked better than he had in weeks, but he was still very pale while his cheeks and eyes had a hollow look.

"How's it going?" I asked.

Turning his head, he said, "Fine."

Waiting a moment to see if Lance would expand on what "fine" meant, I finally asked, "Do you want to talk about what happened?"

He shrugged slightly, which caused him to wince in some pain as he said, "Things didn't turn out like I planned."

"What do you mean?" I pried.

"I knew Gwen was Arty's girl…I've known it for a long time," Lance explained. "I didn't mean to fall for her. It just happened. Dr. Peaudane…he's…well he'll never approve of me."

"Arty can't be mad at you," I reasoned. "Gwen's great…we've all had a thing for her. She's sweet, pretty, easy to talk to—"

"Still," Lance sighed. "I knew she was Arty's girl, and I should've stayed away. What kind of friend am I if I can't be trusted?

"The kind that threw himself in front of a wild boar to save a friend," I quickly replied.

"Maybe," Lance moaned, "but I've made a mess of things now."

"What happened?" I asked.

"I've always got along with Gwen, ever since we was kids," Lance began. "I'd tease her…and she…well she's been better to me than about anybody but you and Arty. You guys don't know what that means. When you got a dad like mine…when you do the things I do to make a dime, there ain't that many people that treat ya' right."

I listened as his forehead wrinkled in thought.

"Arty's saved my bacon more than once," Lance continued. "Given me money when I didn't know what I would do…treated me like a brother. When we went to the fair, I'd determined to stay away from Gwen and out of Arty's way…and your way, 'cause I know you like Gwen too. I decided the best thing I could do was stay away and spend the day with that kid sister of Arty's, but Marilee's pretty smart when you listen to her. She's kind of like that old grandma of Arty's that seems to always tell ya' what's goin' on, she does. Marilee told me Gwen kind of liked me and had for a while.

"You can't imagine how that made me feel to think Gwen Peaudane ever thought of me as anything but a white-trash nuisance. I still tried to stay away, but then that boar got me. When I woke up, it was like from a dream, with Gwen teary eyed and watchin' over me…makin' me feel like I was something special. She came and talked to me every day. She'd come in late at night and come early in the morning. One night she fell asleep, holding my hand with her head layin' next to mine. That was all there was to it."

"Dr. Peaudane came in and threatened to shoot me!" Lance continued. "Gwen cried and told him she loved me and he just had a fit. That kind old man slapped her and started screaming. I tried to get up, but couldn't move…and then he kind of choked or something. They took him out of the room and Mrs. Peaudane locked Gwen in her room. Next thing I know, Gwen's brother's loading me in the car, and I wound up here."

Looking with a degree of astonishment at Lance I said, "Marilee Martin told me Gwen liked you, but I didn't realize Dr. Peaudane wanted to shoot you!"

"I'd just as soon of had the old man shoot me as hurt Arty," Lance lamented. "The only thing is…I don't think I can stay away from her now, and I think that's goin' to be a problem."

Thinking for a moment about how I felt when told that Gwen loved Lance instead of me I said, "Arty'll get over it. Remember, we've pledged to be friends forever…to meet on the rock every ten years no matter what…to be brothers of the Cross Timber. Arty'll do anything for you. He'll forgive you."

Lance smiled for the first time that night. I did not know how much of that encouragement I believed, but it did me some good to see Lance looking more like his old self.

"You better get some sleep," I suggested as I turned down the light.

As I lay in bed, thinking about the events of the day, I knew the first thing I had to do in the morning. Before going to work, I had to see Arty.

CHAPTER 26

Dawn appeared with an azure hue as I hitched Old Betsy to our shaky wagon and stopped by the Martin farm. An amber glow came from the front room, but no activity was apparent. Stepping onto the porch, I knocked timidly to see if I could get someone's attention without disturbing the entire house.

A rustling noise followed by a strange squeaking sound indicated movement inside. In a moment, the door creaked open. At first, it was as if no one was there, but as my eyes scanned down I saw Grandma Nance glaring at me from her wheelchair.

In a demanding whisper, she commanded, "Come in."

"I…I just came to see if—" I began.

"Come in," Grandma Nance harshly insisted. "You're letting the cold air in."

The old woman slowly turned her wheelchair around, while I followed apprehensively.

Once in the room, I asked, "Is Arty here?"

"Sit down," Grandma Nance instructed pointing at a chair close to the fireplace in the front room.

Although I had known Arty for many years, I had rarely been inside the Martin home and preferred to socialize outside or in the barn. While I sat on the soft chair close by the warm fire, the old woman wheeled in a position to look me face to face.

"The Brooks boy," she said with a smile revealing her pointed teeth. "I see you heeded my words."

"What?" I asked in confusion. "Is Arty here?"

"The girl," she explained. "I've seen it before, I'll see it again. Again and again."

"Gwen?" I asked, vaguely remembering my last conversation with the cagey old woman.

With a sparkling of contentment she said, "Yes...the girl. You've done well to heed my words and stay away from her."

"I…I see Gwen nearly every day," I informed.

With her peculiar smile and a strange tilt of the head, Grandma Nance explained, "The girl is not as near your heart. I can see this."

"How do you know…I mean I don't know what you're referring too?" I stammered, unsure of what kind of riddle the old woman was trying to weave.

I looked around the room for some relief while the old woman studied my every motion.

"Gilbert?" the confused voice of Mrs. Martin asked from the doorway to the kitchen. "How long have you been here?"

Standing uncomfortably, I explained, "I just arrived, Mrs. Martin. I was looking for Arty."

"Mother," Mrs. Martin scolded. "Have you been bothering Gilbert?"

Grandma Nance, who had spoken plainly only a moment earlier, appeared unable to speak as she breathed erratically as if in discomfort.

Mrs. Martin sighed at her mother and said, "Let's get you some breakfast."

She walked over to Grandma Nance and gingerly began rolling her to the kitchen. Without Mrs. Martin noticing, Grandma Nance looked back at me with an odd, almost threatening smile.

When Mrs. Martin returned, she handed me a cup of hot coffee and said, "You'll have to forgive my mother…she…doesn't know what she's saying sometimes."

"That's fine," I assured while enjoying the warm cup in my hands.

"Arty's not here," she continued. "Arty, Ethan, Marilee, and Mr. Martin went to Shawnee early this morning…to do some shopping."

"Oh," I said, shifting in my seat and preparing to leave.

"I'm sorry," Mrs. Martin continued.

"It's no problem…I hadn't talked to Arty—" I began to explain.

"Not for that," Mrs. Martin interrupted.

Taking a moment to form her words, she continued, "Mr. Martin is a fair man, but very demanding. He's the kind of man who likes to plan things out…to be prepared."

I nodded in agreement, knowing Mr. Martin to be very strict in his ways.

"He and Dr. Peaudane have known each other a long time. They've both assumed through the years that either Ethan or Arty would be a good match for Gwendolyn. Ethan's going to get married, of course, so the assumption moved to Arty. The thing with Lance I'm sure was innocent enough and was probably just an overreaction…a boy in his condition should be at the Peaudane's house or here until he's well, but things being how they are…I appreciate your mother taking the boy in."

Not knowing exactly how to answer, I mumbled, "It was nothing."

Smiling at me, Mrs. Martin said, "It was the right thing to do, and that's always something."

"I should be getting to work," I muttered.

Mrs. Martin took my cup of coffee and walked me to the door.

As I stepped off the porch, she said, "Arty didn't know…He didn't know they asked Lance to leave. I thought you should know that."

"Thank you," I said as I walked away.

CHAPTER 27

At the store, Guy Peaudane apologized again for the events of the previous day. I believed him to be sincere, but there remained an awkwardness lasting through the day. Mrs. Peaudane brought lunch again. I found out later, Dr. Peaudane had sent Gwen to Shawnee with the Martins.

Throughout the day, I tried to watch the train station to see when Dad would arrive. By five o'clock, the last train made its stop at the station, and there was no sign of my father. Driving back to the house alone, I was anxious to check on Lance and see how Dad's business trip went.

Traveling by, it looked as if the Martin family had returned as all the lights blazed in the night sky. The Peaudane car was parked out front and I assumed Gwen and Dr. Peaudane were inside. As I approached our small house, I noticed a new wagon with a team of two mules outside and an older Model T.

After putting Old Betsy away, I went inside to see my Uncle Horace sitting with Dad, Mom, Lloyd, and Gordon. Mom was serving dinner, while the others laughed and listened to Uncle Horace and Dad tell stories. Uncle Horace was my father's younger brother. He was slightly taller and larger than my father was, and had experienced a little more of life. He was a loud, boisterous man but, like my father, enjoyed a good story and a good time.

"There he is," Dad greeted. "You remember Horace?"

"Sure," I smiled.

"Good to see you," Horace roared.

"You too," I replied, while shaking hands.

"How's Lance?" I asked my mother, who had her hands full getting dinner served.

"He's doin' fine," she said without looking up. "Slept most of the day, but had an appetite. Doc Sanders came by to check on him earlier."

"Is that his team outside?" I asked.

Mother stopped for a second and answered, "No."

"That's a nice-looking team, Uncle Horace," I complimented assuming it must belong to him.

Looking at my dad, Uncle Horace said, "It is a fine looking team, but it ain't mine…it's your pa's."

Dad shrugged sheepishly, while Uncle Horace laughed and took a sip out of a jar he was holding.

"You bought a team and a wagon?" I asked looking at my father.

"He bought that and a whole lot more," Uncle Horace boasted. "Look over there…That's a genuine Victrola music player. Fire that thing up Gordon."

Gordon immediately obeyed the request and in a moment the scratching sound of music came from a megaphone sitting on top a small wooden box.

"Ain't that something?" Uncle Horace bragged.

"Yeah," I answered, noticing Dad did not seem as enthusiastic as my uncle did.

"I better go check on Lance," I said, before slipping away to the small bedroom.

Lance lay in the cot, with the dim glow of an old oil lamp by his side. Awake and with an impish grin on his face, he looked much better than his first night at our home.

"How's it going?" I asked.

"Entertaining," Lance said, referring to the conversation he had been listening to from my uncle.

"I bet," I smiled. "How are you feeling?"

"Better," Lance said. "Doc Sanders came by and said I was doin' fine. Said I'd be up in a couple of more weeks."

"That's good," I replied.

After a hesitation, Lance asked, "Did you see Gwen today?"

"No," I answered. "She…I think she went to Shawnee with the Martins."

Lance did not show much emotion, and before he could say more, my mother brought our supper.

"Thought you boys might like to eat in here tonight," Mother meekly said. "It's probably louder and more crowded in there than Lance needs."

"Thank you, Mrs. Brooks," Lance said.

When she left, I said, "Uncle Horace can be a little loud, I guess you've noticed."

With a muffled laugh, Lance said, "Yeah…I know your Uncle Horace."

"Really," I answered with surprise.

"He's…a customer sometimes," Lance added.

"Oh."

"He's one of the good ones…he's a happy drunk, not mean," Lance quipped.

I laughed quietly, thinking that was probably a good description of Uncle Horace. Mother was a quiet, churchgoing woman, who kept my father away from most vices, but particularly alcohol.

"So, Gwen spent the day with Arty," Lance mused.

"Yeah," I nervously replied.

"That'll be awkward for her, I guess," Lance determined. "Part of me is looking forward to seeing Arty, and the other part's dreadin' it."

Lance and I talked during our supper about his immediate plans for the future, his health, and Gwen. He was concerned about his relationship with Arty, but I could tell Lance intended to pursue Gwen's affections. After about an hour, the door opened and Uncle Horace interrupted our conversation.

"How's this old rascal doing?" he asked, looking at Lance.

"Better than I look, Horace," Lance answered with more familiarity than I would have expected.

"That Mexican kid…Sergio…was askin' about you the other day," Horace said.

"Really?" Lance replied. "Did he know I was laid up?"

"I think everyone up and down the line knows," Horace smiled. "Leland Holiday's been braggin' that he's the one that cut you up."

"That lyin'—" Lance angrily began to reply before remembering he was a guest in someone's house.

In a more serious tone, Horace said, "You need to stay clear of Leland and all the Holidays…They're sneaky and they're mean."

"Tell me somethan' I don't know," Lance defiantly stated.

"Just be careful," Horace repeated. "Leland's getting pretty friendly with some mighty powerful people. I'm afraid someday he'll do what he pleases, when he pleases. I gotta run. Get better kid."

"Will do," Lance said as my uncle exited the room.

"You're pretty involved in being the Holidays' competition," I noted.

"Yeah," Lance answered with a frown. "It's a bad world when you gotta do bad things to beat bad people."

"Are you okay?" I asked.

"Yeah," Lance nonchalantly said. "I'm feeling fine. Doc Sanders says—"

"I don't mean that," I said in a more serious tone. "Are *you* all right?"

Realizing I was talking about his business instead of his health, he stared distantly at the ceiling and said, "I'll be fine…I know how to be careful."

"And Gwen?" I asked, remembering how disturbed she had been when Leland Holiday came into the store.

Taking a moment to answer, Lance said, "That changes everything…doesn't it."

Looking at me, Lance continued, "I'm getting out of it…once I'm well. I've got to tie up some loose ends, and then I got to find somethan' that'll impress Dr. Peaudane. I don't think bootleggin' will do it."

We talked for a while before I let Lance get some rest. Uncle Horace had left at least an hour earlier, and the house was now quiet. Looking out the front window, I saw Dad sitting on our small porch in the cold, smoking a cigar. Putting on my coat, I went out to see him.

"How's it going?" I asked.

"Hey, Gill. What're you doin' out here?" Dad responded.

"Saw ya' out the window," I replied.

"Your mom doesn't like me smokin' in the house," he smiled. "She really don't like me smokin', period."

I smiled and sat down next to him, looking into the cold, dark night.

After a moment of silence, Dad said wistfully, "I couldn't do it. I went to Tecumseh and had the money in hand and couldn't do it."

Having already determined he had not paid down on the farm, I asked with some disappointment, "Why not?"

Hesitating again before answering, he said, "I got to thinking…what if this war continues? What if this land plays out? We had a good harvest this year, but cotton was down all over the county. What if next year the cotton doesn't make? What have I done then?"

I listened, still disillusioned with his choice to buy a wagon and Victrola that he would enjoy in the short-term instead of the farm that might have been a better future for us.

Trying to rationalize the decision, Dad continued, "What does it mean when a fella like Jack Martin is willing to sell this piece of property? If the land were worth anything, he'd hold on to it, right?"

"Maybe Mr. Martin didn't need it," I suggested. "Maybe he wanted the cash to buy a tractor for his place. Maybe he was just trying to help us out."

Shaking his head, Dad sharply responded, "A man like Jack Martin doesn't just help people like us out. You need to learn that boy."

Taking my scolding in silence, Dad said in a more despondent voice, "Truth is Gill, I just got scared…I was afraid."

"Afraid of what?" I asked.

With a half-hearted laugh he said, "Pretty near everything, I guess. I ain't never had nothing, and I guess a man gets pretty used to people having low expectations. I go buy this land…who knows what might have happened. I coulda lost the farm and all we'd worked for…then what?"

"I don't know," I answered, "but we could've tried."

Smiling, Dad said, "We'll still be tryin' every day, son. We got a good wagon now…a Victrola for entertainment anytime we want. I'm gettin' your mother a new washer at Peaudane's tomorrow for Christmas—got each of you boys a decent Christmas for the first time."

I tried to give him a look that would make him feel like he made the right choice, although I did not believe he had.

Putting his arm around my shoulder, Dad continued, "I even got me a banjo."

"You don't even know how to play," I chided.

"No," Dad grinned, "but I'll learn it, I bet."

Smiling at his optimism, even at what I considered a failure, I said reassuringly, "I bet you can too."

Reaching into his coat pocket, he handed me a small book and said, "Got this for you."

"What is it?" I asked.

"It's a bank book," he smiled. "You're the first in our family to have a bank account. I took the money you gave me for the down payment and opened a savings account in Tecumseh…pays interest and everything."

"I gave that to you…for the farm," I insisted.

"We don't need it, besides, if I'da had money on me, your Uncle Horace woulda borrowed it from me tonight, and then we'd probably never seen it again."

"Thanks, Dad," I said, while looking at the bankbook. "It's still yours if you need it."

Rubbing my head, Dad said, "I know that. We Brooks stick together, don't we?"

"That we do," I smiled.

"Get to bed," Dad encouraged. "You've got to sell me a washer tomorrow. I am expecting a good deal."

"I'll make sure you get the best one," I assured.

CHAPTER 28

Christmas Eve was hectic at the Peaudane General Store. Dad came early to enjoy people admiring his team of mules and new wagon. For the first time in his life, he came into a store to make a purchase without worrying about his account.

Arty helped with deliveries this day. Since he was not familiar with the store, he mainly helped customers load, while I stayed inside with Guy. Gwen did not make an appearance at the store.

At five o'clock, customers were still shopping, and it looked like a late night. About seven o'clock, Dr. Peaudane came to the store, which was a rare occurrence, to bring everyone a cash bonus for working the Christmas rush. I pocketed a five-dollar bill, and spent about half of it on gifts for my family. Guy shut down the store a few minutes later and sent us home after wishing everyone a Merry Christmas. Arty had brought the Martin surrey that morning and offered me a ride home.

"Some kind of day, wasn't it?" I noted, as he gently encouraged the horse forward.

"Is it like that every day?" Arty asked.

"No," I assured. "We must have done enough business for two weeks today."

"How much you think the Peaudanes made?" Arty inquired.

Guy had been showing me how to keep books, so I had some insight about the store's profitability.

"I don't know," I hedged. "If we did four hundred dollars in sales, which is possible today, the stored cleared maybe a hundred-fifty profit."

"Whew…" Arty whistled. "Not a bad day's work."

"It's not like that every day," I assured.

"Still…Not a bad little racket," he said smiling.

Arty had the type of personality that put you at ease, but somehow got you excited at the same time. I smiled at his enthusiasm for the business, although he had not been around for any of the hard work required to prepare for such a day.

"I thought Gwen might show up today," Arty said, while glancing at me.

"She's in some days," I responded, somewhat uncomfortably.

"I was with her yesterday," Arty confessed.

"I heard."

"How?"

"Guy told me."

"Oh."

After a moment of silence, I was compelled to ask, "How was she?"

Arty shrugged, "Fine, I guess…she seemed a little distracted, but you know how girls get when they're shopping. She seemed glad to get out of the house. Darn Marilee, never left her side a minute…you know how she is."

Arty talked as if ignorant of Lance's fate, so I felt compelled to ask, "You know Lance is at my house?"

"Yeah," Arty nonchalantly said. "I heard my dad talking about it."

Confused at his concise answer, I had to ask, "Do you know why?"

Smiling mischievously, Arty said, "I heard he got a little too fresh with Gwen."

"Too fresh!" I exclaimed. "Gwen was in his room, just holding his hand and Dr. Peaudane had a conniption."

Looking at me in disbelief, Arty muttered, "What?"

"Gwen likes Lance," I bluntly stated. "Dr. Peaudane was not too happy about it. That's why he sent him away."

"No," Arty protested. "I saw Gwen yesterday—"

"I'm just telling you what I heard from Guy…and Marilee," I interupted.

Arty drove on without displaying any emotion. He did not seem angry but seemed to be calculating events in his head.

Finally smiling, he said, "Lance is a sly dog, he is. Here I've been worried about you all this time and you working with Gwen's brother, and here I should have been watching out for old Lance."

Perplexed, I asked, "You're not upset?"

"At Lance…over a girl?" Arty replied. "That old fox, I bet he got himself gored just so he could move in on my girl."

"Arty!" I protested. "Lance jumped in front of the boar to keep you from getting torn up."

"I'm kidding," Arty said light-heartedly. "I know Lance saved me that day…and I hadn't forgot it."

Still confused at Arty's demeanor, I tried to clarify, "You don't think Gwen's your girl, do you?"

"I don't have a brand on her yet," Arty joked. "But at least I know what the game is now…and don't think I'm not watching you too!"

I did not understand Arty's cavalier attitude, but before I could learn anymore about his trip to Shawnee, we approached my house.

"I heard your dad didn't buy the place," Arty said in a more serious tone.

"Yeah," I said, with a degree of embarrassment.

"How come?" Arty asked.

"I don't know," I lied, knowing Dad had been afraid of the responsibilities of ownership. "Just wasn't sure the land would pay out I guess."

"Well the land's pretty played out, but I thought it'd make a crop enough to make it a good deal," Arty analyzed.

"Maybe," I said, not really wanting to discuss it further.

As Arty stopped the surrey, I asked, somewhat tentatively, "You want to come in and see Lance?"

Without hesitation, Arty said, "That wild boar couldn't keep me away."

CHAPTER 29

Lance was propped up on his small cot, reading a book when Arty and I entered the room. Mother had moved Lloyd and Gordon to the front room so Lance could rest better. Our arrival caused him to move suddenly, almost as if he were trying to escape Arty.

"How's it going?" Arty cheerfully greeted in his typical upbeat tone, which would put anyone at ease.

Looking quickly at me and then back at Arty, Lance said, "Better. Doc Sanders says I'll be up and goin' in a few weeks."

"Good deal," Arty smiled.

"You got everything you need?" Arty asked.

"Yeah," Lance sheepishly answered. "I'm set up real fine here."

Arty looked around the small, sparsely furnished room for a moment before saying, "You know, I never really got to thank you."

"For what?" Lance replied.

With a little laugh, Arty said, "For takin' on that boar with your bare hands, you knuckle-head."

"You'd done the same," Lance stated.

"Maybe," Arty shrugged. "But you actually did it! It meant a lot to me."

"You've got me out of many'a sticky pickle," Lance observed.

Smiling broadly, Arty quipped, "I must be better at it then, 'cause I've never been laid up before."

Lance laughed at Arty's humor causing him to wince in discomfort from his sore ribs.

"What'cha reading?" I asked, noticing the book on his lap.

"Just a book," Lance answered. "It's pretty boring around here, when I take to reading."

All of us laughed, with a little sense of relief at Lance's good humor. I took this as a sign he was on his way to recovery.

Our momentary levity was stifled, however, when Arty said, "I guess the Brooks don't have as many distractions as the Peaudane house."

The room fell so silent at this misfired attempt at humor, that I could hear the flame flicker from the oil lamp by Lance's cot.

"About that," Lance began. "I didn't—"

"Don't think about it," Arty interrupted. "I'm sorry Gwen got you kicked out of the Peaudane's house, but we're okay."

"Really?" Lance said with a tone of suspicion.

"Sure," Arty replied with a sly grin. "I always like a little competition…just don't go poutin' when Gwen and I are engaged."

"But—" Lance tried to explain.

"Really," Arty interrupted again. "We're okay."

Lance did not answer, but I could tell by the exchange between the two friends that Arty did not fully understand the relationship between Lance and Gwen.

Arty broke Lance's skeptical stare by saying, "Hey! I brought you something from Shawnee."

Arty reached into his coat for a canvas sack.

"Here's your knife," Arty smiled. "I took it out of the boar."

Taking the knife, Lance said, "I thought this was gone for good."

"And…I got you a souvenir," Arty slyly said, before producing a leather string with two boar tusks attached.

"Thought you might want these," Arty continued, while handing the boar's tusks to Lance. "I went back and cut these out of the boar that attacked. Thing smelled somethan' awful by the time I got back to it. I cut 'em out with your knife."

Looking at the two tusks, nearly three inches long, Lance said, "Thanks."

"Grandma Nance, heard me tellin' the story about your pig, and said a hunter always needed to take something from the kill," Arty explained.

Looking at his prize a few seconds more, Lance said, "But, these should be yours then. You're the one who killed the boar."

Arty had a confused look on his face, as if he had not considered his role in saving Lance.

"I guess I figured the guy who did most of the fight, deserved the trophy," Arty shrugged. "Tell you what, you keep one and I'll keep the matchin' one."

Arty untied the leather string and slid one of the tusks off to put in his pocket.

"Here's yours," Arty smiled. "I'll keep the matching one."

"Thanks, Arty," Lance said, looking over his prize.

"I gotta go," Arty explained. "Dad'll be looking for me by now. You guys have a good Christmas."

"Merry Christmas," I said to Arty as he left.

"Merry Christmas," Lance added, still in his bed.

Arty urged his horse up the hill, as the scratching music from Dad's Victrola played in the background. It was a good Christmas at the Brooks home that year with more presents than we had ever seen. The family did not mind having Lance Carrington as a guest. We were poor and somehow felt richer taking care of someone worse off than we were.

I had dreaded the potential awkwardness of the meeting between Arty and Lance for days. It was a relief to witness the bond the two friends shared while seeing them laugh with and at each other—a comforting reminder that we were brothers of the Cross Timber. Lance and Arty had friendly competitions for years about almost everything, but now the prize was Gwen. Grandma Nance had warned me about

Gwendolyn Peaudane's destiny to cause heartbreak. I could not have imagined how right the old woman would be and how deep the scars would get.

CHAPTER 30

Christmas Day fell on a Saturday, which meant I enjoyed a long weekend with my family. Lance waited anxiously for any visitors. I could not tell if he expected Gwen, Arty, or his father, but no one came. Dad entertained us with his harmonica and even picked out some tunes on the banjo he had bought, while Gordon played the Victrola repeatedly.

I was back at the store Monday morning, straightening up after the Christmas rush. Gwen came by with lunch around noon. It was the first time I had seen her in days. She had been crying, and it was obvious things were not going peacefully at home.

After a few weeks, I returned to a routine of working, having lunches with Guy, and seeing Gwen nearly every day. Arty came by two or three times that week to check on Lance. The New Year came, and things seemed to be getting back to normal. Even Gwen was more like her old self, though I detected in her an anxiety unnoticeable before.

Mid-January arrived with a few days of mild weather, sunshine, and warmer than normal temperatures. Although spring was weeks away, a hint of spring in the air seemed to lift everyone's spirits and did wonders for my outlook. The days were getting longer and there was still some light from dusk as I arrived home in the evenings. Lance had been out of bed and walking around for a week. He even helped my mother around the house with some chores. This evening the family was waiting on me for supper, and the Victrola was playing a lively tune.

"Hey," I greeted as I walked into the room where everyone was surrounding the dinner table.

Mom had roasted chicken, canned green beans, carrots, and rolls prepared. The feast smelled delicious, and I could tell my brothers were anxious to eat. Mother had not been a particularly good cook for most of my memory, only slightly better than Gwen Peaudane. The past weeks, however, I noticed a difference in her meals. I did not know if having company caused the change, if the extra money was buying better spices, or if Lance had an undiscovered talent in the kitchen, but supper had been worth looking forward to the last few nights.

"That was delicious," I complemented my mother.

Grinning shyly, while looking at Lance, she said, "Thank you, but I'm not the one who cooked it."

Looking at Lance, expecting him to take credit, he shrugged his shoulders as if to say, "Not me."

"Marilee Martin has brought dinner most days the past weeks," Mother revealed. "You're just now noticing a difference?"

"I…I just thought we were putting on a show for our company," I suggested.

"Well, you can thank Marilee next time you see her," she coached. "That sweet girl has come to see Lance nearly every day. She brings him books to read and brings enough dinner for us to share."

"Really," I said almost to myself.

Looking at Lance, he had an impish grin.

Later that night, I asked Lance, "Is something goin' on between you and Marilee?"

Beaming as if he had won some prize, Lance said, "Marilee's right, you're not very observant, are you?"

"You're courting Marilee?" I asked again, remembering the good time they had at the county fair a few months earlier and thinking of how upset Mr. Martin would be.

"No," Lance replied with a sly grin. "Marilee's just being a good friend."

"Oh," I said, feeling somewhat foolish for thinking Lance could change his affections so quickly from the polished Gwen to the quirky Marilee.

Looking at me for a second, Lance said softly, almost in a whisper, "You don't notice details much, do you? Didn't you notice the upgrade in food the past week?"

"I just thought your helping around the house was making Mom a better cook," I defended.

"Your mom's a sweet woman, but she's got little aptitude for cooking," Lance kidded. "Haven't you noticed these books I've been reading?"

"Well, yeah," I stammered. "I just thought you were bored."

"Look here," Lance whispered as he leaned over to show me the book he was reading.

Looking at the book, I saw a handwritten letter stuck between the pages. Lance did not give me an opportunity to read the contents, but I could clearly see the signature of Gwen Peaudane at the bottom.

"Marilee's been bringing you letters from Gwen?" I clarified.

"And takin' notes to Gwen," he smiled.

I set back in the chair and pondered the ramifications of Arty's own sister helping Lance keep in contact with Gwen.

"Marilee's pretty sneaky," I observed.

"More than you know," Lance smirked. "Mrs. Martin felt so bad about me getting kicked out of the Peaudane house; she insisted that Marilee bring food. Marilee sees Gwen most days and started bringing the notes. I'm keeping up with almost everything. I even heard about your run-in with Leland Holiday."

Leland Holiday had come into the hardware store after he had been hired as the constable in Maud. His greeting with Guy Peaudane had been tense, almost threatening. When Leland Holiday spotted me, he quickly walked over and questioned me about Lance in an overly friendly manner. Guy interrupted his interrogation and sent me on an errand. Not wanting to worry Lance, I had not told him about the encounter. Obviously, Gwen found out and wrote Lance about it.

"A guy like Leland Holiday, always has his fingers in everything," I mused. "I guess he was able to work his way in at Maud."

"Yeah," Lance sighed. "Leland Holiday's slippery as a catfish and mean as…he's as mean as that old boar that got a hold of me."

"I didn't want to worry you," I said.

"It's okay," Lance replied. "Gwen's just overly nervous about him for some reason…and…something else's botherin' her…I can tell."

"Maybe she's just nervous about what Leland's said he'd do to you?" I suggested.

Smiling confidently at me, Lance said, "I can take care of myself."

Trying to change the subject from Leland Holiday, Lance said, "Anyway, that skinny old Marilee hangs out here as long as she can in the afternoons waiting to see you."

As I shook my head, Lance continued, "You know she's got her eye on you…'Gilbert.'"

"I know, I know," I said with a grimace. "Marilee's all right, I guess, but she's Arty's sister and she's…she's just pretty darn plain."

Lance laughed at my discomfort from his teasing, but said in defense of Marilee, "She's not that bad…she's been good to me. The days are longer with a hint of spring in the air. Marilee says it's like hope in the air. I think she still holds some hope for you."

"She's the only person under forty that calls me 'Gilbert,'" I fumed.

"She likes the name," Lance coyly replied.

"She told you that!" I exclaimed in embarrassment.

"Marilee talks to me a lot," Lance grinned.

"Better you than me," I quipped.

Our banter continued the rest of the night. It was reassuring to see Lance feeling better and to see his good humor and teasing ways back. Lance was in a constant state of uncertainty, but his confidence and attitude always seemed hopeful. The new year would bring changes to our part of the county, but for tonight, I enjoyed the Lance Carrington I had known since my youth.

CHAPTER 31

As spring transformed to early summer, Dad and Lloyd put the new team of mules to use preparing the fields for planting. Lance Carrington healed and stayed at our house intermittently. Mother became attached to having the fourth boy around the house and began to worry about Lance like one of her own.

My perspective of the world, particularly the world of Romulus, began to change as the gristmill and Robbins & Newhelm Dry Goods store closed. The wooden buildings in Romulus, including the train station, were weathered and in some need of repair. There seemed to be a wait-and-see attitude about further investment in the small town.

Marilee had stopped bringing supper to Lance a few weeks earlier, when it became apparent he was away from our house more than he was there. I still avoided her when possible but missed the cooking. If there was a budding romance between Gwen and Lance, it was secret, although I believed they might be continuing to communicate through Marilee. By the Fourth of July, however, I began to wonder if perhaps I had been mistaken.

Lance disappeared for a couple of weeks during the summer, claiming he had to "clean up some things." Arty had taken Gwen back to Benson Park to see the fireworks show without a chaperone. The Martins purchased a tractor that spring as well as a new Studebaker automobile. Arty had hoped his father would buy a coupe, but proudly drove Gwen around in the sturdy sedan instead.

Guy Peaudane and I had lunch at Kelly's whenever Gwen cooked. I enjoyed our talks. He seemed able to keep up with all the county news and gossip. Leland Holiday was still constable in Maud, and Guy heard he was running a couple of businesses over there, including a domino parlor. Guy continued to talk about the war, but during the summer of 1916, the concern was Pancho Villa's raids across the border. General John "Black Jack" Pershing moved troops into Mexico to track down the rebel. The National Guard was mustered at Fort Sill in anticipation of going to Texas to secure the border, but they were sent home after a few days.

The Mexicans who worked to maintain the rails kept a low profile. I saw Lance's friend Sergio in town one day, but did not speak to him. By August of 1916, I was preparing to pick cotton in the fields. Before the harvest, however, I would get two life-changing surprises.

Sitting on the porch of our small house, I watched heat simmer off the pinkish-brown field. The crackling sound of tires on the hard, hot ground distracted my survey of the cotton fields, as an automobile approached. Arty was usually the only driver we saw, so I was surprised to see Guy Peaudane's car rolling toward the house. I greeted my boss, but he asked to see my father. The two men talked a few minutes before calling for me.

"Gill," Dad began, slowly. "Mr. Peaudane would like to talk to you about something."

"Sure," I replied.

With a look of excitement, Guy Peaudane said, "Gill you've been a good worker, and you're a smart boy…too smart to be working at a store in Romulus."

"What do you mean?" I asked in a concerned tone.

"Your work's been top-notch," Guy said with a smile before looking at my father. "I've contacted a woman in Tecumseh named Ginn. She's kind of a crusty old woman, but she runs one of the best hotels in the county. I was telling her about you and she's looking for a boy…you know to help out around the place."

"I don't understand," I said. "I'm working for you."

Guy shifted uneasily before continuing, "The thing is…I'm not sure how much longer the store's going to need somebody. More people are driving cars, making it easier to get to Tecumseh or even Shawnee to the bigger stores. I've…I've got a lot of accounts that can be collected, and I might be shutting down the store, first of next year."

"Close the store?" I repeated in disbelief, feeling somehow responsible for the failure.

"Maybe," Guy said. "It's a possibility, but what I'm trying to say is I've got an opportunity for you. School's starting next month, and they have a high school in Tecumseh. Ginn told me you could live in the hotel and work mornings for room and board. I know a man who owns a hardware store in Tecumseh, and I'm sure he could use your help."

"Go to school?" I asked, still trying to process this information.

"I've enjoyed having you around the store, Gill, but I know you've talked about going back to school, maybe even to one of those colleges in Shawnee someday," Guy explained. "I talked to your dad…and he thinks it's a good idea."

Looking at my father for guidance, I could sense no excitement, just the stoic look in his eye he got when talking business to someone like Guy Peaudane. My father was a good storyteller and quite personable around his kinfolks, but I always felt he was less sure around someone successful like Guy Peaudane.

Unable to read his thoughts, I asked directly, "What do you think, Dad?"

Looking at Guy Peaudane, almost like he needed permission to talk, he slowly said, "I think Mr. Peaudane makes some sense. Your heart's not in farming, and he's right…you're a smart boy. I got that money for you in Tecumseh that might help you through."

"So I can go?" I clarified.

With a small hitch, he tilted his head and said, "I'm telling you to go."

The thought of going to high school, which had not crossed my mind five minutes earlier, now overwhelmed me with excitement. I spent another half hour going over the details with Guy about my contacts and the school schedule. When Guy drove off, I knew I needed to tell Arty.

It was a brutally hot Sunday afternoon as I walked toward the Martin home. I did not feel the hot sun or my feet touching the ground as I churned over in my head the idea of living in Tecumseh and going to high school. I had not thought at that time, that I would most likely be older than any other freshman starting school. I would be seventeen starting out, which meant I would be almost twenty-one by the time I graduated—if I graduated, I thought. Still, the idea of going to high school, living in a city, and being on my own was exciting.

Approaching the Martin home, the gray Studebaker parked out front indicated Arty was around. Most of the Martin family sat outside on their big porch fanning themselves.

"Hey, Gilbert!" an excited Marilee shouted from the porch.

Looking at the rest of the family, I could not see Arty among them. Mr. Martin gave me a cold, disapproving stare as Marilee bounded to the front gate to meet me.

"Hi, Marilee," I responded still straining to see her brother. "Is Arty around?"

"He's out back churning ice cream with Ethan," Marilee cheerfully informed me.

"Okay," I replied quickly, heading around the house and away from the watchful eye of Mr. Martin.

At the back of the house, Arty perched on the wooden barrel. His muscles bulged as he laboriously turned the crank. With their new car, the Martins could get to the ice plant in Tecumseh and back before the block of ice melted, even in the summer.

"Put a little muscle into it," I chided, as sweat poured off Arty's forehead.

"Why don't you show me how?" he responded good-naturedly. "What are you doing here?"

"Came to see you," I replied.

"You picked a good time, we'll have ice cream ready in a while," he smiled. "What's goin' on?"

"Well," I began, trying to contain my excitement. "I'm movin' to Tecumseh."

"What?" Arty exclaimed. "Hey, Ethan take over."

Arty wiped his face with a towel and asked with some concern, "Is your family moving?"

"No," I answered shaking my head. "We've already got the crop planted. I'm moving. I'm going to school."

"What?" Arty asked again.

"Yeah, Guy Peaudane worked it out for me. Got me a job for room and board…maybe another job to make some money."

With an impish grin, Arty remarked, "Why do you want to go to school?"

"Guy says it's a good opportunity…thinks I'll do well," I defended.

"I have no doubt about that," Arty said with a smile. "It's just…well it's just like you to want to go to school when you don't have to."

"I know," I blushed.

"When are ya' going?" Arty asked.

"School starts in September. I'll probably leave a few days early to get settled in," I reasoned.

"Movin' off to live on your own," Arty said shaking his head. "Before long, you'll be in as much trouble as old Lance. Speakin' of which…have you seen him lately?"

"Not in a couple of weeks," I replied. "Said he had some things to do."

"Sounds like him," Arty sighed. "We gotta get hold of him and celebrate before you go."

"Sounds good," I replied, thinking a night out with my two best friends would be nostalgic.

Looking at me with a sly grin, Arty said, "I can't believe you're leaving the Cross Timber. You're goin' to end up a genuine city boy the way you're going."

"Maybe," I smiled back.

"Your turn," Arty's brother Ethan instructed.

Arty shrugged and mounted the freezer to take his turn cranking the large bucket. We traded insults and stories, while Ethan patiently listened to our nonsense. I always thought Arty had an easier life than I did, but watching him churn through the cream with his strong muscles reminded me the Martins were farmers too, and that Arty was used to hard work. Arty's charismatic demeanor made everything appear effortless.

"Arthur," I heard the stern voice of Mr. Martin call. "I hope you're not wasting time!"

"No sir," Arty barked back. "The cream's about done."

Arty gave a mischievous grin he would not have used in front of his father and whispered, "He ought to come out here and give a crank."

Getting up, Arty challenged me by saying, "Give it a tug, Gill."

With a shrug, I positioned myself to do a little ice cream making. Arty laughed when I tugged at the crank and strained to move it a quarter turn.

"I think it's done," Arty laughed.

Taking the bucket in one hand, Arty carried it to the front porch with Ethan and me following.

"Would you like some ice cream, Gilbert?" Mrs. Martin asked.

"Sure," I replied.

We did not have easy access to ice and did not own a freezer, so ice cream was always a treat.

"This is a new recipe Marilee made," Mrs. Martin revealed with a smile.

"I didn't see Marilee out there turning it," Arty charged.

After a sharp look, from Mr. Martin, Arty refrained from insulting his younger sister further. Mr. Martin received the first bowl, but as company, I was served before Arty or any of the Martin children. The conversation among the Martin family fascinated me. They were respectful of each other, but they did not seem to have as much fun as the Brooks family. Mr. Martin would share tidbits of news and talk about the future of farming, while appearing to continuously correct and mold his children.

The Martins were friendly, but I never felt comfortable around them as a group. Arty, more energetic and playful than the rest, was a different person around his father. After finishing the delicious bowl of ice cream, I excused myself and promised Arty we would get together soon.

About half way home and beyond the view of the Martin farm, I heard a shrill voice yell, "Gilbert!"

Turning around, I saw Marilee Martin running toward me. Her frizzy hair bounced in the breeze, and she had an awkward gait to her trot while her glasses looked as if someone had sat on them before she placed them on her nose.

"Arty says you're leaving?" she asked with a faint tone of distress.

"Yeah," I replied. "I'm going away to school…in Tecumseh."

"You weren't going to tell me?" she said in a near whimper.

"Well…I figured everyone knew. I told Arty," I defended.

"But…I…you should have—" Marilee stammered.

Feeling awkward and confused at Marilee's anxiety, I said, "It wasn't that big a' deal. It's not like I'm going around the world. I'll be back to see my folks."

Regaining some composure Marilee straightened herself and in her more typical tone of voice, she said, "Gilbert Brooks…if you're going to be my guy, we're going to have to communicate. I've got to know what's going through your mind."

I stood speechless at her scolding, having never considered I might be Marilee's guy, having never encouraged her affections.

Before I could say a word, Marilee added, "I'm a patient woman…but I'm warning you, I won't be patient forever."

Without giving me a chance to respond or explain that she had no reason to wait for me, Marilee marched defiantly back to her home. As she turned the bend, there was nothing but the sound of katydids humming in the trees—and my confusion.

Soon forgetting Marilee Martin's outburst, I smiled to myself seeing the more casual Brooks family sitting on our humble porch. A few steps closer I could tell we had a visitor, and it was Lance Carrington.

"Look who showed up," my father smiled while he patted Lance on the back.

"Hey, Lance," I greeted with a warm smile. "What's ya' up to?"

"I came with some news, but sounds like I'm a little late," Lance replied. "Your folks have been tellin' me your news. Congratulations."

"Thanks," I said.

"You're goin' to more schooling," Lance said, shaking his head.

"Yeah," I answered a little bashfully. "What's your news?"

Lance looked at my father and mother, and then said, "I tied up my loose ends and I'm looking for honest work. I'm healed up now and thought I might try cotton picking. I came to ask your folks if I could move in for a while…until I could find a place, and they told me about you movin' out…and…well they offered to let me work for room and board and a percent of the harvest."

This news was surprising and welcomed. I constantly worried about Lance's association with his father's bootlegging. Recent threats by Leland Holiday made Lance's lifestyle seem even more dangerous and uncertain.

"Great!" I said sincerely.

Looking at my easy-going dad, I added, "Can't say I'd wish cotton pickin' on anyone, but the company's good."

After more visiting, Lance took me to the side and said, "I'm thinking about headin' up to Arty's to let him know we'll be neighbors. Want to come?"

Thinking about my recent conversation with Marilee, I begged off and said I would catch them next time. Besides, I had plans to make. School started in less than three weeks.

CHAPTER 32

The next three weeks were a blur of activity. I was genuinely excited at the opportunity for school, although my family harbored unspoken reservations. Arty, Lance, and I made the most of our time. Arty took us all over the county in his family's car. Arty was still seeing Gwen regularly, while Lance appeared to be keeping his distance, which pleased the Peaudane and Martin homes.

My last day at the Peaudane General Store was a bittersweet one. Although I had only worked at the store a little more than a year, the place had a familiarity I would miss. Gwen Peaudane came to the store the last day wearing an indigo plaid dress with a red sash and matching bonnet. She looked like a girl out of a catalog, and there was an unmistakable glow to her. Of all the things I would miss about the store, seeing Gwen Peaudane would be what I missed the most.

Since it was my last day, Gwen stayed to visit and eat lunch. She had cooked, and I had a hard time not laughing at Guy's reaction. The meal, however, was better than I would have thought. Gwen had improved some as a cook, and I began to wonder if maybe we had been too critical of her earlier meals. Gwen took a keen interest in my going to high school and asked numerous questions, insisting I elaborate on my manufactured answers. She confessed her desire to go away to school, too. Gwen left mid-afternoon, and it was as if a fresh breeze had gone away.

Looking at the tidy back room, which had been such a mess on my first day, I felt proud to have left the place a little better than when I came. Guy presented me with a writing kit and five dollars to help get settled in my room in Tecumseh. He let me leave early that afternoon and gave me a firm handshake. Although uncertain about my future, I was excited at the opportunity Guy Peaudane had given me. Feeling nostalgic, I walked around the countryside to see familiar things one last time. Passing in front of Haskell Holiday's place, I remembered the night we swiped a watermelon from his field. It was not much further to our favorite place by Salt Creek on the big flat rock, so I decided to have one more look before heading home.

The early September day was hot, and a gentle breeze barely rustled the leaves of the thick, short Cross Timber forest. I followed a narrow path through the shadowy trail, but just before breaking into the open pasture by the river, I stopped at the edge of the trees.

Something was not right, and the last time I had this feeling of uneasiness a wild boar charged my friend. In a second, I determined what was wrong. Faintly through the trees, I could hear voices and giggling. Cautiously moving forward, I was perplexed to see a woman in an indigo blue dress with a red sash. The matching red bonnet had been carelessly tossed on the flat rock, and Gwen Peaudane stood in the arms of a shirtless man with a scar across his rib cage.

I watched a moment as Lance Carrington held a willing Gwen Peaudane tightly. After the shock of seeing them together, I gingerly stepped back before being seen. The snapping of a dead limb lying on the ground, however, alerted an always-cautious Lance Carrington, and like a panther, he sprinted toward my hiding place.

"Gill?" he asked in surprise.

"Yeah, it's me," I awkwardly replied.

"Are you alone?" Lance asked quickly.

"Yeah," I apologized. "I was just out seeing some of the old places before I left."

In another moment, an uneasy Gwen Peaudane came to Lance's side holding her bonnet in her hand.

"Hey, Gwen," I said, not knowing how to respond to interrupting their liaison.

"Is anybody with you?" a nervous Gwen asked.

"It's just Gill," Lance confirmed.

"Come on down," Lance invited.

"I don't want to interrupt," I confirmed.

With a comforting tone, Lance said, "You're not interrupting. Come on down."

Wanting to leave but not wishing to make Lance and Gwen anymore antsy by declining the invitation, I followed Lance to the big rock. Lance carefully led Gwen by the hand, and it was obvious they were a couple.

"I'm really sorry," I began to apologize again.

"Guess you found our secret spot," Lance sheepishly grinned.

Looking around at the place where Lance, Arty, and I had spent many hours, I said, "I don't think the spot's so secret, but I see the reason for secrecy."

"Yeah," Lance shrugged as he put on his shirt. "I guess this is a little bit of a surprise."

"No," I replied. "Finding Kaiser Wilhelm or Pancho Villa down here would have been a surprise."

Looking at the nervous couple, I explained, "This…this is shocking."

"You won't tell anyone, will you?" Gwen pleaded pathetically.

Faced with the prospect of a beating from Lance Carrington would have been enough of a deterrent, but Gwen and Lance were my friends. Their secret was safe with me.

"No," I assured. "There's nothing to tell…no one's business, I suppose."

"Thanks," Lance said with a smile.

"So how long?" I asked innocently. "I mean, how long have you two been meeting down here?"

Lance looked at Gwen, almost as if to get permission, before he said, "We've been coming here awhile…since the accident anyway. Gwen's folks don't know about this place, and Arty…Arty talks about this place a lot, but there's not a good road down here for a car, and he stays pretty much to the roads these days."

Gwen's fear of being found out had now diminished somewhat, and her anxiety now turned to embarrassment at being discovered in Lance's arms.

"This has always been one of my favorite places," Lance explained. "But…it's a little more special now."

"How long?" I stammered. "I mean, how long will you keep this thing secret?"

Uncharacteristically, Gwen took charge and answered, "My parents haven't learned to appreciate Lance yet, but he's got a job now, and we'll let them know once he's proved himself."

Thinking that it might take some time, I added, "How about Arty? He's thinking and telling everyone that you're his girl."

Gwen had a pained expression on her dimpled brown cheeks.

"I feel bad about Arty," Gwen confessed. "But I've never led him on. It makes Dr. Peaudane happy when we're together, and he doesn't ask where I've been as much. I like Arty, but I think he likes the idea of being with me more than me."

"Arty'll be fine," Lance assured. "I'll let him know when the time's right."

"I guess you know what you're doing," I said with some uncertainty.

"What gave you that idea?" Lance smiled.

"Gill," Gwen quickly added. "It might help you to know that we're…we've promised to be married, once Lance gets established."

"What?" I exploded.

Gwen nearly trembled at my reaction, but Lance calmly added, "We've discussed it and decided we can't live apart. That's why I'm changin' my ways. Gwen here's vowed to make an honest man out of me."

Gwen's eyes sparkled, and she smiled almost uncontrollably at Lance's proclamation before adding, "If he doesn't turn me into an outlaw first."

"Never," a cocky Lance replied. "Your virtue is beyond reproach."

I took an opportunity to leave them alone after a few minutes, but I was surprised when they offered to walk me back to town. Lance said good-bye to Gwen with a kiss as she walked to her home alone. Lance walked back to the Brooks home with me nearly exploding with excitement. I did not know if Lance felt he needed to walk me home to ensure I did not tell anyone about their liaison, or if he was just looking for an opportunity to tell someone about Gwen Peaudane. I tend to believe he was bursting to talk about his secret engagement. By the next morning, I would be on a train out of town. Lance did not take any chances on me telling his secret. He never left my side until the train pulled away from the Romulus station.

PART II

CHAPTER 33

Old Beck, the antique train serving the southern spur of the Rock Island line, screeched to a halt at the station in Tecumseh. The simple wood building, not much bigger than the station in Romulus, was freshly painted white. The unpretentious building represented the practical and orderly nature of the community. The small depot handled traffic coming from the south part of the county traveling to the bigger terminals in Shawnee.

Stepping off the train with all my possessions in a sack, I looked around the near-vacant station before heading toward downtown. Tecumseh, significantly bigger than Romulus, was more relaxed than the bustling city of Shawnee. The main street in town was Broadway, which was a wide dirt street with businesses lining both sides. Many of the businesses were brick, and the Interurban Trolley, which ran all the way north past Benson Park and to Shawnee, continued south to the end of the business district.

The courthouse, a two-story brick building with an awning covering its entire length, sat in the center of town. Across the street from the courthouse stood the two-story Broadway Hotel where I would be staying. I would soon learn that everyone in town called it Ginn's Hotel. Walking into the lobby, I could hear my worn boots rhythmically echo on the wood floors and paneled walls. A plump woman with short graying hair stood behind the counter with an air of authority.

"I'm here to see Mrs. Ginn…I'm Gilbert…Gilbert Brooks," I greeted in an unsure voice.

The woman, who appeared to be dipping snuff stared carefully for a moment before saying, "It's not Mrs. Ginn…It's not Miss Ginn…It's not Madam Ginn…It's just Ginn."

"Yes, ma'am," I timidly replied.

With a look of disgust, the woman reiterated in a stern tone, "Not Mrs., not Miss, not Madam…and for sure not ma'am…just Ginn."

"Yes," I carefully replied. "Is Ginn in?"

"Darlin', who do you think you've been talking to?" she bluntly asked.

Almost afraid to answer, I meekly asked, "Ginn?"

"What can I do for you?" she asked without a smile.

"Guy Peaudane from down at Romulus said you was looking for a boy to work mornings…for room and board," I replied.

"Oh," she answered blankly, as if she could not remember the conversation. "I might've needed someone a month or so ago when Guy was in town, but I don't know…I gotta pretty full crew now."

The blood rushed from my cheeks at the thought of not having a place to stay. The little money I had in the bank would not last two weeks living in town. The prospect of enrolling in school and having to camp out every night was only a little less frightening than the thought of having to go back to Romulus failing to complete school.

The woman bent under the high counter to spit tobacco and continued reading her paper. Of the many things I learned from Guy Peaudane, the most important was to be assertive when talking to people.

"Excuse me," I said with as much courage as I could muster.

The woman looked at me with a combination of scorn and irritation.

"I'm needing a place to stay, and it looks like this place could use some cleaning," I said, trying to keep my voice from trembling. "I'm a good worker and think you might could use my help."

As the woman stared coldly, I continued, "I don't need much. Any place inside'll do and—"

"Shut up," the woman said bluntly. "Guy Peaudane told me about you all right, but he didn't say you liked to talk so much. I've got a room in the back. I won't tolerate no cussing, no loud talk, no liquor of any kind."

Looking at me with a smirk of disdain she added, "No women either. Breakfast starts at 6 o'clock in the dining room. That means I expect your skinny hind-side here at five o'clock, which really means four-thirty, cause if you're late just once, I'll send you back to Guy Peaudane with a stamp on your head 'return to sender.' You'll set up tables and help cook some mornings."

"Yes, ma…Yes Ginn," I replied.

"I'm not kidding," she warned. "I'll take a bite out of you…you won't soon forget if you mess around."

Realizing anything I said would garner a negative response from this woman who obviously was accustomed to getting the last word—I simply nodded.

After staring me down a little longer, she finally said, "Follow me."

Leading me through the dining room and small kitchen, she opened up a room approximately eight feet long and five feet wide with a single bed and no windows.

"There's a privy outback, and a bathroom down the guest hall you can use between three and five in the afternoons, if there aren't guests needing it."

I nodded in agreement.

"You can take your meals in here," she said, referring to my small room. "I can't have someone as skinny as you in my dining room, the guests will think the food's no good. Any questions?"

I shook my head as Ginn gave me one last hard look before leaving me in my new home. Listening to her heavy steps move down the hall, I sunk into the lumpy bed, wondering what I had gotten myself into.

CHAPTER 34

I surveyed the stark surroundings and decided to walk downtown. A block from the hotel was the Exchange Bank of Tecumseh. I timidly entered the lobby and showed the teller my bankbook. When he asked me what I wanted to do, I had no answer. Looking at me, while shaking his head slightly, he updated the bankbook and handed it back to me. I had $57.13 safely tucked away in the bank plus the five dollars Guy had given me still in my pocket. I thanked the teller and headed down the street.

Passing the Cooper Furniture Company, I noticed a sign for used furniture. In the back of the store, there was a dusty collection of used, sometimes worn-out pieces of furniture for sale. For three dollars, I purchased a small two-drawer chest for my things and a used electric lamp.

After wrestling the two-drawer chest to my tiny room, I went back quickly to retrieve my lamp. The electric glow of the lamp made all the difference in my attitude about the dreary room. Even the Martin family did not have electric lights back in Romulus. I drifted to sleep that night with a mixture of anticipation and apprehension about living in the city.

Sleeping restlessly that night, I finally entered a peaceful slumber when a loud bang woke me. In my darkened room, I struggled to gain my bearings in this strange place.

Almost expecting Lloyd to be sleeping next to me, I heard the rough voice of Ginn yell, "You better get your skinny hind-side to work, if you're expecting to stay in that room."

I stumbled for a match, before remembering a turn of a switch would light the room. In five minutes, I entered the kitchen where plates were already clattering and the smell of biscuits filled the air.

"Get those chairs down, wipe the tables good, and then put out salt, pepper, and the silver," Ginn barked.

Not knowing exactly what to do, I attacked the job with great effort while Ginn criticized every movement. By six o'clock, the dining room was ready, and customers started filing in slowly. Ginn was only slightly more hospitable to guests than she had been to me. One gentleman, who dared complain about the eggs, had them dumped in his lap by the temperamental woman. While the guest stared in disbelief, Ginn yelled at me to get a mop and clean up the mess. Later I was ordered to take the man's clothes down the street to a laundry as Ginn had repented of her rash response.

By eight o'clock things were running smoother as I asked Ginn for permission to head to school. With a disapproving shake of the head, she excused me. With barely enough time to run a comb through my hair, I walked quickly to school.

Tecumseh High School was one of the first in the state. The town built a two-story brick building with stately columns at the entrance, but the building burned the previous spring. The structure I approached was a more humble, temporary building that was a large one-level, wood building painted white.

I went to the superintendent's office to enroll. After asking me some scrutinizing questions about my past schooling, he enrolled me as a freshman, even though I was seventeen years old.

The school was nothing like the Unity School we called "Fuss Box" near Romulus. The building had a long hallway with lockers and many classrooms instead of one. There were children of all ages, but they were segregated into separate areas. Almost all students lived in or around the city, meaning I was a stranger. Being the only student in overalls that were patched and about three inches too short, I knew immediately I did not fit in this place.

Most students my age had been in school together for many years and had their own group of friends. I greatly missed having Lance and Arty by my side because I felt extremely lonely although surrounded by people. Arty particularly would have made friends immediately and, in my opinion, would have been one of the most popular kids in this place as he had been back at Fuss Box.

Miss Taylor taught freshman math that day, however, and greatly helped me feel comfortable in my new school. Miss Taylor graduated from Tecumseh High School only nine years earlier, but had worked as a teacher since then. A woman in her mid-twenties, she assured me I could do well in this school.

Immediately after school, I headed to the Walker-Raines Dry Goods store to buy a pair of trousers and cotton shirt, which would more closely match my classmates. The five dollars I had with me was vanishing, as I began to realize city life would be expensive. Passing the train station, I was tempted to leave my tiny room, small chest, and electric lamp behind and head back to Romulus. I decided to face Ginn, instead.

Ginn was in no better mood as she impatiently instructed me about setting up for dinner and then cleaning up for closing. By the time I finished at nine o'clock, my lumpy bed soon had me fast asleep until Ginn banged on the door at four-thirty the next morning to start again.

The second day of school went better. Having new clothes that looked less like the farm, helped me feel more comfortable. The kids pretty much left me alone, but I did meet a girl on my second day of class. Mary Sue McNally was a short, spunky girl with sandy blond hair and green eyes, who never met a stranger. She was the first student to talk to me without telling me to get out of the way. We visited only a minute, but that was all the encouragement I needed to get through the day.

As the days went on, I had less desire to catch the train south as I passed the station. Ginn was still gruff, but as I learned my way around the place, I did my jobs with less instruction. I eventually moved from setting the table to cooking eggs. I cooked eggs by the hundreds and most of them the same way. If a customer wanted sunny side up, we slid it on the plate and if they wanted over easy, they got the same egg flipped over. I did not mind cooking in the morning, and Mary Sue noticed I had "the pleasant smell" of bacon when I came to school in the mornings.

Sunday found me at a church building on South Broadway. Once again, I entered a building without knowing anyone and was only slightly less nervous than my first day at Tecumseh High School. One of the happiest sights of my first days in Tecumseh was seeing Mary Sue McNally at the church I was attending.

After services, the smiling Mary Sue made her way through the congregation to say, "Hello, Gilbert."

"Hi Mary Sue," I greeted. "You can call me Gill."

"I didn't know you were a member here," she cheerfully said.

"Well…I'm just here the first time today. We…my family and me, we go to church in Avoca mainly," I explained.

"Daddy!" Mary Sue said loudly at a distinguished looking man talking to the preacher.

Pulling me by the arm, she said to her father, "This is Gilbert…I mean Gill. I don't know your last name."

"I'm Gill Brooks," I timidly informed.

"Gill's going to high school this year," she beamed. "He's from down around Romulus."

"Good to meet you," Mr. McNally greeted.

Mr. McNally was an attorney with an office down the street from the hotel. He was nicely dressed and had a pleasant demeanor reminding me of Guy Peaudane.

"Will you be graduating with Mary Sue this year?" he asked.

"No," I sighed. "I'm…I'm just starting this year."

In a reassuring tone, he said, "It's an admirable thing to continue a man's education…especially when you have to leave home to do it."

"Gill's working at the hotel, close to you," Mary Sue explained.

"You're workin' at Ginn's place?" he said with a coy smile.

"Yes, sir," I admitted.

"My word, you're going to get more of an education than you bargained for," he laughed. "Don't let her get to you. Ginn's as rough as a cob, but she's got a heart of gold."

"Can we have Gill over for lunch?" Mary Sue asked.

"I don't see why not, but ask your mother," Mr. McNally replied.

In a few minutes, I sat by Mary Sue in the back of the McNally's Maxwell automobile as Mr. McNally drove to their brick home just a few blocks off Broadway. Mary Sue helped her mother with lunch while her two younger brothers played outside.

Talking to Mr. McNally was much like the conversations I had with Guy Peaudane back in Romulus. Mr. McNally was concerned about the Great War in Europe but was more adamant about the United States needing to stay out of the conflict. He questioned President Wilson's resolve to stay neutral while letting American businesses profit by selling war goods.

Mr. McNally took the time to explain that Ginn's husband had run a place called the Maverick Saloon before statehood prohibited all liquor sales or at least the legal ones. He bought the hotel, but when he died, Ginn had to take it over. The hotel had nearly gone bankrupt, but Ginn's stubbornness and hard work had kept it going. He assured me Ginn was a demanding but fair woman.

Mrs. McNally served fried chicken and the creamiest potatoes I had ever tasted. The McNally family was as friendly and optimistic as Mary Sue was. As I walked back to my room that afternoon, I passed the small train station and for the first time did not have the desire to head home.

CHAPTER 35

Arty visited Tecumseh in mid-October. The chill in the air did not dampen his enthusiasm at the number of attractive girls at the school. Arty quipped that maybe he should give his education another shot.

Arty said the cotton harvest had been tough that year. Rains came at the wrong time and yields were down at almost every farm. The war in Europe plus the poor harvest kept prices high, but I began to think my father had shown more prudence than I gave him credit for when he decided not to buy the farm. Arty continued to boast of his future with Gwen Peaudane, even as he ogled some of my classmates, leaving me to believe the relationship between Lance and Gwen remained a secret.

I had not been home since coming to Tecumseh. Besides Arty's visit, the only other connection I had with home was a weekly letter from Marilee Martin. I cringed when receiving the first letter, thinking how awkward our last conversation had been. Marilee's letters, however, did not contain the senseless romance I feared but instead gave a factual account of the activities from home, including some thinly veiled updates about Lance and Gwen. After a few weeks, I actually began looking forward to her weekly newsletter.

Ginn took some getting used to, but after a few weeks, I was accustomed to her blunt ways. As I had at the Peaudane General Store, I soon found my niche at Ginn's Hotel. Although I enjoyed working at the store, the hotel had its share of interesting characters and events. One night, a man from Shawnee rented a room for him and his wife. When his real wife tracked him down about midnight, she created a ruckus. Once Ginn was up, it was hard to tell who was angrier with the man—his mistress, the wife, or Ginn. After the man was unceremoniously booted out of the hotel, Ginn took the time to invite the wife into the dining room for coffee and a chance to settle down before driving back to Shawnee.

Not all days were as exciting, and my life evolved into a routine of work, school, more work, and sleep.

"You're the darnedest employee I've ever seen," Ginn barked at me one day, as I headed to school.

Wondering what I had done wrong, I just grunted, "Huh?"

"You've worked here nearly two months and haven't asked for a day off yet," she charged.

"I…I didn't know—" I stammered.

"It's hard for me to give you a day off, if you never ask for it," she glared. "Are you trying to make me look heartless?"

"No, Ginn," I tried to explain.

"Stop making me look bad and take tonight off," she bluntly commanded. "Go see a movie or something. I'm tired of seeing you around here. Take tomorrow off too."

"Thanks, Ginn," I said while heading out the door.

"Don't thank me!" she shouted back. "Just stop making me look bad."

Although Ginn had given me a job for room and board, she began paying me twenty-five cents a day after a few weeks of work so I would have some spending money. With a night off and a little change in my pocket, I went to school knowing exactly how I wanted to spend the evening.

Since Mary Sue McNally was a senior, I saw her only a few times during the school day. Shortly after lunch, she stood with a group of friends and gave me a reassuring smile as I approached.

"Hi," I said, trying to subdue my grin.

"Hey, Gill," she pleasantly responded.

"I was wondering," I asked. "I have the night off and was wondering if you would like to go to a movie or something tonight?"

Mary Sue did not have a chance to respond, as the gasp from her friends answered the question.

"I…I can't—" she awkwardly replied.

Looking at her giggling friends, I clumsily retreated to my next class. Thankful that most of Mary Sue's friends were seniors, I hunkered down the rest of the day trying to avoid eye contact or any more embarrassment. When school dismissed, I made a beeline out the front gate and toward the sanctuary of my tiny room.

I stopped at the train station for the first time in weeks and sat on a bench calculating the price of a ticket home when Mary Sue walked behind me and said, "Are you all right, Gill?"

Looking up at the bubbly, yet concerned Mary Sue, I casually replied, "Yeah, I was just kidding earlier. I know a girl like you—"

Sitting down beside me, Mary Sue interrupted, "I'm sorry I embarrassed you at school today."

"No, really," I assured. "I wasn't serious."

"It's just everyone around here knows I'm promised to a boy," Mary Sue continued. "Ralph Swan went to school here last year. He's at the University of Oklahoma now. I should have let you know."

"No, it's okay," I replied. "I should have known a girl like you would have a guy."

"No, you shouldn't," Mary Sue corrected. "I didn't say anything about him and you haven't been here before. It's not you. I'm flattered that you asked me."

"Well, I just…You're easy to talk to and—"

"And you haven't made many friends yet?" Mary Sue coached.

"Not everyone's as…outgoing as you," I shrugged.

"It must be hard," she sighed, "to leave home and come to a new place."

"Especially when you're three years older than anyone in your class," I confessed.

"Yeah," she smiled. "I didn't like being around freshman much when I was one."

"A bunch of spoiled kids," I fumed.

After a moment of silence, Mary Sue said, "I really *was* flattered you asked. A group of us seniors are going to the movies tonight. Why don't you come with us?"

"I don't know," I hedged.

"Come on," the personable girl pleaded. "It'll be fun, and I could use an escort. Besides, my friend Laura would love to meet you."

"Laura?" I asked, not recognizing that name.

"Laura's the girl with brown hair...one of the girls that giggled at lunch," Mary Sue coaxed.

Frowning, I said again, "I don't know."

With an unexpected tone of stubbornness, Mary Sue said, "Be at the trolley by six. We're going to Shawnee to see *Pearl of the Army*. I'll be personally offended if you're not there."

With a brash bounce to her step, Mary Sue left me at the station.

A little before six, I timidly approached the trolley. Mary Sue immediately introduced me to a group of five girls. I was surprised to see no boys in the group, but Mary Sue made sure I did not feel awkward. She introduced me to her friend Laura and maneuvered to where I sat by her most of the evening. By the time the trolley arrived in Shawnee, I was feeling quite comfortable with my new group.

At the trolley station in Shawnee, I got a glimpse of Sergio, Lance's Mexican friend who worked on the rail line. He did not recognize me and quickly disappeared to the south of town.

The Becker Theatre was located on the west end of Main Street. The town was much busier and noisier than Tecumseh was as our group walked on the crowded concrete sidewalks toward the theater. The movie portrayed Pearl, the heroine, as an American Joan of Arc thwarting the Kaiser's attempts to attack the United States. Before the feature, a more realistic and harrowing newsreel of fighting planes over the battlefield played. By the end of the newsreel, Laura was so frightened she held onto my arm.

Walking out of the theatre, surrounded by five girls, and with Laura still clinging to my arm, I was surprised to hear a familiar voice shout, "Gill?"

Turning around, I saw an astounded Arty Martin and a nervous Gwen Peaudane. Arty gawked at my group of girls and Laura hanging on my arm. I began introductions, but Mary Sue quickly took over and flirtingly introduced her friends to Arty.

"This is Gwen Peaudane," I added, making sure Arty did not forget.

The animated Mary Sue said, "Good to meet you, Gwen. We've been showing Gill around town tonight."

"I see," Gwen shyly stated.

Gwen was obviously uncomfortable. It would have been easy to think it was because Arty had been so distracted by the other girls, but I knew she feared I might betray her secret. Gwen, as always, was gracious and beautiful. We visited for a few moments. Gwen and Mary Sue would have been friends, I was sure, if they had the opportunity. Arty gave me a hearty good-bye as he winked indicating his approval of my company.

As I returned to my lonely room about eleven o'clock, my head was floating. For the first time since my stay in Tecumseh, I felt like I belonged. Seeing Arty so envious of my group of attractive girls, including the one holding my arm, was just a bonus to my new, euphoric viewpoint. Settling into my lumpy bed, I tried to fall asleep, knowing morning would come early.

CHAPTER 36

Although Ginn had given me the day off, the rattling of dishes in the kitchen made it impossible to sleep past six o'clock, so I dressed to see if I could help. Ginn served me a strong cup of coffee as well as bacon and eggs, as if I were a customer. If I had known Laura's last name, I would have tried to look her up. Instead, I wandered around Tecumseh on my day off. On Sunday, I discovered Laura's last name was Jones from Mary Sue. I also learned from Mary Sue that Laura believed I was a "very nice boy."

By Monday morning, my day off was a memory. I returned to a routine of work and school while Laura Jones occupied all my spare time the next few weeks. With Mary Sue's help, I developed some friends closer to my own age. I smiled knowing my romantic exploits were being reported back home. Marilee's weekly letter made a point to mention Arty had seen me with a girl. The thought of Arty's envy caused me to smile.

By Christmas, however, Laura Jones began taking too much time and effort. Her constant attention and quirky mannerisms lost their appeal. Not knowing how to break up with a girl, I compensated by not being available and taking any odd job Ginn had. After a few weeks, Laura decided I was not worth the effort and informed her friends we were no longer a couple. It was awkward for a while, but Mary Sue continued to be a friend.

I wanted to go home during Christmas, but Ginn convinced me to work during most of the holiday. I caught the train to Romulus on

Christmas Eve to spend the day at home but returned the day after Christmas to resume my ever-expanding responsibilities at the hotel.

I did not see Arty on my trip back, but Lance, who still lived with my parents, told me how jealous he had been of the many girls around me that night at the theatre. Lance confirmed he and Gwen were still a couple, although Arty was becoming more of a concern. According to Lance, Arty insisted on escorting Gwen, and she felt obliged to go to quench any suspicions her father might have about Lance living so close. Lance did a good job as my replacement on the farm and seemed to have left his past associates behind. I told him about seeing Sergio in Shawnee. He was interested in knowing how the Mexican was doing, but appeared to have not seen him in a while.

It was a cold day when I returned to the hotel in Tecumseh. In another week, school resumed, and I was back into my routine. It would be several months before I made it back to Romulus.

CHAPTER 37

January was cold and dreary. My brief trip home only caused me to miss it more. I had made friends in this new place, but they were no substitute for Arty and Lance. Mary Sue McNally continued to impress me with her charm and poise. She loyally defended me several times after my awkward break-up with Laura Jones.

My schoolwork proceeded and by the second semester, the superintendent enrolled me in sophomore courses. Working with Ginn became easier as I began to understand her barking tone of voice was not connected to her attitude toward me.

In mid-January, newspapers reported a telegram from the German Foreign Secretary, Arthur Zimmermann, which stunned the town of Tecumseh and the nation. The secret message, sent by code to the president of Mexico, offered help in returning New Mexico, Arizona, and Texas back to Mexico if that nation would align itself with Germany in the Great War, which the United States was bound to enter eventually. On the heels of the Pancho Villa scare the previous year, talk of war was on everyone's mind, and several of the senior students had already joined the army. Mary Sue became teary-eyed one day saying her college boy had enlisted to be an officer.

Even with the excitement of young men going to war and my improving relationship with Ginn, it was a lonely winter. As the short days seemed to drag on, I found myself daydreaming of home. I imagined the smell of cut hay, the taste of a juicy summer watermelon, and spending time with my two friends under a warm sun on our favorite rock by the Salt Creek. Outside all I could see was the stark, colorless, cold winter.

By April 1917, the United States declared war on Germany. Patriotism ran high throughout the county as many young men volunteered for service before the government had a chance to draft them. I heard from home that Arty attempted to come to Shawnee to enlist, but his father stopped him. A week later, I learned my brother Lloyd enlisted and planned to board a train to Fort Sill in two weeks.

I asked Ginn for an extra day off to see Lloyd before he left for the army. I sent a telegram to Guy Peaudane informing him I would be in town and asked him to tell my folks. It was a brilliant spring day when I boarded the train to Romulus. Dogwoods and redbud trees were in full bloom in some sections of the Cross Timber forest to accent the emerald green of the leafed-out trees.

The small train had just started to slow down, when I looked ahead to the train station in Romulus. The town looked smaller every time I came back and a few more businesses had decided to close since Christmas. I began to wonder if there would be a town at all by the time I graduated.

As I strained to recognize anyone at the station, it was apparent the platform had few people at this stop. Most of the passengers were heading south to Asher. I did not really expect my parents to come to the station, but I looked anyway. It was planting time on the farm, and walking on such a pretty day did not concern me.

Looking out the window, I saw a young woman in a pale yellow dress wearing a blue bonnet and carrying a white basket. At a distance, I could only think it must be Gwen Peaudane as she was the only person in town who regularly dressed so fashionably. I looked forward to seeing Gwen alone to find out what was going on in her life, especially concerning Lance Carrington.

As the train pulled closer, however, I could tell the young woman, though very attractive, was not Gwen. The woman had wavy auburn hair tucked neatly under her bonnet, with high cheekbones and thick, red lips. Grabbing my bag, I stepped off the train and tried not to stare, but it was difficult to be discreet, since we were the only people left on the platform as Old Beck creaked out of the station to make its next stop. As I walked closer to the young woman, I admired her bright, green eyes, which were vaguely familiar. The young woman looked as if she was soaking up the radiance of the spring sunshine.

I could hardly believe it at first, and when the girl did not recognize me, I doubted myself, but hesitantly asked, "Marilee?"

The girl jumped as my voice startled her, and then she squinted for a second. Finally, with some frustration, she reached into her bag, placed the eyeglasses on her nose, and said excitedly, "Hey, Gilbert!"

"What are you doing here?" I asked, as I walked closer to her, while looking around to see we were alone.

"I've come to see you," she factually stated. "Gwen told me you were coming to town today on the train. I just didn't know exactly which one."

"You've been here all day?" I quizzed.

"No," she quickly replied. "Not all day…just most of the day."

"It's nice to see you," I said. "I mean it's great to be back home, and…it's great to see you."

Marilee was normally very serious and had an almost stoic personality, but for the first time I could remember, she smiled in an almost flirtatious manner.

"Did you have a good trip?" she asked.

"Yes," I replied.

After a moment of silence, I said, "You look—"

"Yes?" she eagerly asked.

"You…have you done something with your hair?" I asked.

"No…not really," she said with just a hint of disappointment.

"You're—" I began.

Before I could say anymore, Marilee said, "I look more…filled out?"

Momentarily stunned by her frankness, I said, "Yeah…among other things…I mean your clothes, the hair…If you hadn't put on your glasses, I'm not sure I would have recognized you."

"I hate these glasses," Marilee complained. "But I can't see four feet without them."

"It's okay," I assured. "They look fine…I just…I just can't get over how different you look."

Smiling sweetly, Marilee coyly asked, "Is it a good different?"

Caught off guard, I stumbled trying to answer.

Before I could say anything, Marilee said in a pout, "You wouldn't know. You never paid any attention to me anyhow."

"That's not true," I said, although I knew Marilee was correct.

Desperate to change the direction of the conversation, I said, "I enjoyed your letters."

"Why didn't you ever write back?" Marilee quizzed.

"Well…I was…I had school and work—"

"And time to go to the movies with girls, I've heard," she responded in a huff.

I had no reply, so I decided the best thing to say would be nothing.

After determining I would not volunteer any more information, Marilee asked in an almost sad tone and with the directness I remembered when she was younger, "Do you have a girl in Tecumseh?"

"No!" I said in surprise. "I mean I've made a few friends…and some of them are girls—"

Shaking my head, I confessed, "I work all the time…and trust me…I'm not that great of a catch to those girls from the city."

A more pleasant Marilee looked me in the eye and bluntly asked, "Are you going to ask me?"

"Ask what?" I answered somewhat dejectedly.

"Are you going to ask to walk me to my house on your way home?" she clarified.

Enjoying some of her old frankness, I answered, "Marilee, could I walk you to your house?"

With a big smile, she leaned toward me and whispered, "I wondered if you would ever ask."

CHAPTER 38

Marilee and I walked to the Martin home. Their car was gone, and Marilee explained Arty had probably gone to Maud for the day. Mr. Martin was on the porch, which encouraged me to head home quickly after saying good-bye to Marilee.

Expecting to see the team of mules plowing the field in preparation for the planting, I was surprised to see most of the family on the porch. It was almost time to plant, but coming closer, I saw the field covered in grass with several cows lazily grazing. Gordon was the first to recognize me as he jumped up to wave. My younger brother had grown at least four inches since I had seen him last, and he was taller than I was. Lloyd sat smoking a cigarette and talking to Dad. In a moment, my mother came from the kitchen to meet me in the yard.

It had been several months since I had been home. Everyone asked questions in rapid succession about school, Tecumseh, and even the girl Arty Martin had seen with me. I answered all the questions as fast as possible until I had the opportunity to ask some questions of my own.

"You didn't plant cotton?" I asked my father.

While shaking his head, Dad said, "We struggled to get half the yield we did the year before. Even with prices up, I'm not sure we broke even on cotton. We planted some acres in alfalfa, and I took the seed money and bought a few head of cattle to try that. We put out a little bigger garden plot this year and planted a few acres of corn to see how that might be. It's a good thing too. With Lloyd leaving, I'd have been hard pressed to make cotton go this year."

Turning to Lloyd, I asked, "When are you headin' to the army?"

"I'm leavin' on the train tomorrow," Lloyd replied. "Goin' to Fort Sill to learn soldiering, I guess."

"I'll be headin' back to school tomorrow," I said. "If you're going through Shawnee, I'll ride with you."

"Can't get too far from here without goin' through Shawnee," Lloyd answered, indicating we would depart together.

Lloyd did not elaborate but looked across the field to the tree line. Turning to see what had his attention, I saw Lance Carrington with his floppy hat walk out of the woods with two rabbits hung over his shoulder.

"There's Lance," I stated with a tone of excitement.

I had not heard, but assumed Lance was still living with the family. When he was absent upon my arrival, however, I began to wonder. Knowing Lance for many years, I knew he had the habit of drifting around the county when the weather turned warm.

"Sure is," Dad confirmed. "It looks like we'll be eating rabbit tonight."

"You didn't kill the fatted calf or even a chicken for my return?" I teased.

"You're lucky we didn't find a possum," Lloyd said with a wry grin.

I had eaten possum before, and Mom could make it taste fine, but possum usually only sounded appetizing when there had not been meat for a few days. Eating possum at the Brooks home was a type of family code that indicated times were hard.

"Lance can shoot a squirrel's eye out at fifty yards," Dad noted. "I'm glad to see him with rabbit, though. Hunger's the best sauce, and I like squirrel just fine, but we've eat 'em all winter."

"The squirrels, got into the pecan tree," Gordon added. "Lance took your twenty-two and had at 'em."

"Look who's come back to the country," Lance greeted with a smile as he walked closer.

"I hear you've been puttin' my rifle to work?" I replied.

"Yeah," Lance quipped. "It's a little better on squirrel and rabbit than boar, that's for sure."

"How ya' feeling?" I asked, remembering his weeks of convalescing after our encounter with the boar.

"Fit as a fiddle," Lance boasted. "Doc Sanders says I'm good as new, 'cept for this scar."

Lance lifted up his shirt to reveal his souvenir of the encounter with the wild boar.

"It's good to see you doin' well," I said.

"Good to see you home," Lance replied.

I spent time visiting with my brothers, Dad, and Lance. Lance cut up the rabbit, and Mom cooked it to taste like a feast for us that evening. After supper, Mom produced a pecan pie that was golden brown and smelled as if it came out of a candy store. Mother cut me the first piece, and I had never tasted anything as good.

"I'm glad you kept the family fed in squirrels and kept the squirrels away from the pecans," I joked looking at Lance.

Turning to my mother, I said, "This pie made it worth the train ride down here, Mom."

Mother, smiling shyly replied, "You can thank Lance for keeping the squirrels away from my pecans, but Marilee Martin baked the pie."

"Marilee?" I asked in confusion, almost choking on my bite.

"That sweet girl comes to see me two or three times a week," Mom revealed. "When she found out you was coming home, she insisted on takin' some pecans and making a pie."

Lance looked at me as if he would laugh.

"Well," I stammered trying not to let Lance make me laugh. "It's a good pie, and I'm glad you all ate the squirrels instead of them eating my pie!"

Everyone laughed and we all enjoyed the pecan pie. After dinner, Dad demonstrated the improvement he had made playing the banjo and we even tried to sing along with a song or two we knew. Although he could not read music, Dad had the ability to listen to the Victrola and learn songs. We reminisced about some of our old family stories and especially any involving Lloyd. Dad was his typical, easy-going self, but I sensed he was worried about Lloyd's going to the war in Europe.

I told Lloyd about some of the newsreels I had seen in Shawnee about the war. He and Lance listened intently before sharing what they had heard about the conflict and the plans for the American army. My mother insisted Lloyd walk down and say good-bye to his girl, Neva, although he seemed reluctant. Lloyd looked as if he would have liked to stay, but complied with Mother's suggestion. I stayed up late that night and since it was warm out, Lance and I took a walk under a bright moon.

"It's good to see ya' Gill," Lance said seriously. "You look…well you look content with your world. School seems to agree with you."

"Yeah," I replied. "I've liked it…I guess I've liked getting away a little too."

"Guy Peaudane is trying to send Gwen up to school next year," Lance said.

"Really?" I said. "How does that work with your plans?"

"If she went," Lance shrugged, "your dad's lost another hand, 'cause I'd probably move close by and that may happen. Gwen likes the idea of getting out of Romulus."

"You and Gwen are still…an item?" I asked.

Looking around in the darkness, as if to make sure we were alone, Lance said, "We're goin' to get married. We've talked about it and I'm…working to get some money together."

"You're not back to bootlegging?" I asked.

"Not completely back," Lance shrugged. "But I've been working some with Sergio to make a few extra bucks."

"Does Gwen know?" I scolded.

With a heavy sigh, Lance said, "Gwen don't need to get involved in any of that business or worry about me for that matter. I'm doin' good here. Goin' to church every Sunday. I don't even think the Peaudanes hate me as much as before. As soon as I get a little stake to buy some land or move to town, I'm out of the business."

Seeing I was not completely convinced, Lance continued, "I appreciate your family and what they've done for me. You and Arty have been all the family I ever knew. You two are like brothers to me. When my mother died, my dad…my dad wouldn't work a day even bootleggin' unless he wanted to drink. He's as worthless as they come. You know it… you're just too polite to say it."

"You don't know what it's like to be on your own," Lance shared. "Eatin' whatever you can find…stealin' off people's clothes lines to have somethan' to wear, sleepin' under bridges or houses or any other place just to survive another day. I know what people think 'bout me. I see 'em watch me expecting me to steal anything handy. Except for you and Arty…and of course Gwen, most people don't think much of me. Maybe they shouldn't, but I done what I done to survive. Your folks have been real Christian to me. I want that for me and Gwen. I'll do anything to get it…even if it means I gotta take some from rascals like the Holidays for a while. They's like my dad, 'cept ten times worse."

Lance walked silently for a moment before saying, "That day Leland Holiday threw me in jail…for stealin' Haskell's melon—"

"Yeah," I said, indicating I remembered the event.

"Guy Peaudane came and talked me out of jail…thinking he'd done me a favor. A man like Guy couldn't understand I was in a better place than I was used to. I would've got a meal, a place to sleep, and all it would've cost was the likes of Leland Holiday cursing me for a night.

Guy got me out of jail, but he didn't know I slept with the hobos and Mexicans under the Salt Creek Bridge eating wild onions I found on the way that night.

"The night I came to church to find you…I was lookin' for a meal…but then Gwen gave me back my hat. A few days later, I met Gwen outside of town and we walked down to the flat rock by Salt Creek. She told me she believed in me. She's the first to ever do that besides you and Arty."

"Won't Gwen goin' to school wrinkle your plan?" I asked.

In a less somber tone Lance reasoned, "It would, but I don't have to worry about that. Gwen's mother and Mr. Martin are bound and determined to see Arty and Gwen together, and they're not going to let Guy send her away."

"What does Arty think about you and Gwen?" I asked.

With a hesitation, Lance finally said, "He don't know. He still takes Gwen places and thinks she's his girl, but…even if Gwen was his girl, he don't seem to pay her much mind."

"Is it because her mind's somewhere else?" I teased trying to lighten the conversation.

It took a moment for Lance to appreciate I was referring to him being the distraction.

"Yeah," he laughed. "At least I hope that's where her mind is."

"I saw Arty and Gwen together in Shawnee," I confessed.

"Yeah," Lance shrugged. "Gwen told me about it. She goes to get away from her father…that's all."

"I know," I confirmed. "I could tell she was just there, and Arty…well…Arty scouted out every other girl on Main Street, I think."

"Not what I heard," Lance mockingly replied. "According to Arty, every girl in Shawnee was with you."

With an embarrassed smile, I said, "Arty might have exaggerated the situation, but it was a good laugh to see him so jealous."

"He's a good lookin' guy and used to being picked first by the girls," Lance stated. "What happened with that one girl? Are you still with her?"

I winced at the memory of Laura Jones and my awkwardness in breaking up with her.

"That didn't really work out so well," I confessed.

"Why not?" Lance prodded. "According to Arty she was pretty as a picture."

"She was a pretty girl all right, but she was looking to be more serious, and I was just…looking," I explained. "She was a little too…mature for me I guess."

"Speaking of maturing," Lance said with a coy smile. "Marilee's filled out a little since you've been gone."

"I noticed," I replied. "I saw her at the train station today."

"You're going to wish you'd been nicer to her," Lance teased.

"Marilee's all right, I guess."

"All right?" Lance smiled. "She's got every boy younger than us in this part of the county stirred up. If it weren't for Gwen, I'd probably have an eye on her myself."

I did not know how to respond or even how I felt about Marilee Martin. She looked like a poised young woman earlier in the day, but it was hard to see her as anything more than Arty's bothersome kid sister.

Lance said with a grin, "Besides, Marilee didn't just happen to bake a pecan pie on the day you were coming to town. She comes down to work your mom for information like Mata Hari. That girl's cunning…and she always had her eye on you."

"Maybe," I answered as we stepped up to the porch.

"Trust me. It's a good feeling to know someone's thinking of you no matter what," Lance said while putting his arm around my shoulder.

"Maybe," I replied.

CHAPTER 39

Lloyd and I left the next afternoon on Old Beck heading north toward Tecumseh. Our family came to the station to see us leave. Lance, Arty, Gwen, and Marilee were also there. Marilee wore a simple beige dress with a pale blue scarf on her head and for the first time I could recall, I did not notice what Gwen Peaudane wore.

Though only a couple of years apart in age, Lloyd and I each had a different set of friends. I enjoyed my time with Lloyd on the train. He was nervous about going to war and more anxious about leaving his familiar place on the farm than the possible fighting. As I watched Lloyd's train pull away from the Tecumseh station, I wondered if I would ever see my brother again.

"Gill!" a female voice shouted, as Lloyd's train pulled out of the station.

Turning around, Mary Sue McNally waved vigorously while a man in uniform held her hand. The man was tall with sandy blonde hair, almost the same color as Mary Sue's shoulder-length hair. He had a chiseled, square chin and intelligent green eyes.

Pulling the young man toward me, Mary Sue shouted again to ensure she had my attention, "Gill!"

"Hey, Mary Sue," I replied as she walked closer.

"I wanted to introduce you to someone," Mary Sue said smiling. "Gill Brooks, this is Ralph Swan…my fiancé!"

"Fiancé?" I asked.

"As of last night," she beamed.

"Good to meet you," Ralph greeted with an easy, confident smile.

"Good to meet you," I replied. "Mary Sue talks so much about you, I was beginning to wonder if you were real."

"I don't get back to town enough," he explained.

"When's the date?" I asked.

With a little pout, Mary Sue said, "Ralph's headed to the army—"

"Not just the army," Ralph interjected, "the Signal Corps. I'm headed to Kelly Field near San Antonio to be a flyer."

"We're waiting to get married until Ralph gets back from the war," a worried Mary Sue said with pursed lips.

"It won't be long, darling, once the Americans are over there," Ralph boldly proclaimed.

"It'll be too long," Mary Sue pouted. "Ralph's going to be an officer…a lieutenant."

"Are you signing up?" Ralph asked.

"No," I said meekly. "I just saw my brother off to Fort Sill, and I won't be eighteen until later this year."

"Too bad," Ralph sighed. "I expect you'll miss out on the fight. This thing won't last long with us over there."

A train whistle blew, attracting the attention of Ralph Swan. Dressed in his uniform, he looked as if all his senses were poised for action. If ever a man looked like a hero, Ralph was that man.

Although Ralph's train would not be leaving for a while, I knew Mary Sue was anxious to spend a few moments alone with her fiancé before he boarded the train.

"It was good to meet you," I said as I prepared to head to the hotel.

"Likewise," Ralph said, firmly shaking my hand.

"See you Gill," a proud Mary Sue beamed.

Leaving the two alone, I walked back to Ginn's Hotel. Mary Sue would graduate in less than a month, and Ralph would have graduated from college the next year without the distraction of the war.

Spring was in the air as I returned to class the next Monday at Tecumseh High School to finish my first year. The early mornings in the dining room were easier to tolerate as the days slowly lengthened.

Marilee continued to send her letters, and I actually found time to write her back a few times. Lance had been right: it was reassuring to know someone cared, even if she were far away.

One of Marilee's letters contained the shocking news that Mrs. Peaudane, Gwen's mother, had died suddenly. Marilee thought it might have been pneumonia or maybe some kind of fever. Marilee wrote that Gwen had been nearly crazy with grief and had stayed many nights with the Martins.

When school dismissed for the summer, I arranged to go home for a few days. I had wired Guy Peaudane about working for the summer, but he planned to close the store in Romulus. Through the summer, I arranged to work at Cooper's Furniture Store and keep my morning job at Ginn's Hotel, which meant my summer break would be short. As I packed to go home, I was surprised when the crusty old Ginn hugged me tight and said she would miss me even though I would only be gone a few days.

As the train approached the station in Romulus, I scanned the platform for any sign of Marilee Martin. Spotting her, I frowned to see she was accompanied by Arty.

"How's it going?" Arty greeted energetically.

"Great," I smiled. "Good to be home awhile. What are you doing here?"

"Marilee said somethin' 'bout you coming in today so I said, I'd give my old buddy from the city a ride," Arty explained.

"Lucky for me," I smiled while stealing a glance at Marilee.

Marilee was visibly aggravated at her brother being there. She was wearing the same yellow outfit she wore the last time I came home.

"How are you doin', Marilee?" I asked, as casually as possible.

"I'm sorry to have her taggin' along, but she's as stubborn as a mule and made me bring her to town," Arty complained.

Arty, who always had an eye for any pretty girl in the county, seemed oblivious that his younger sister had blossomed into an attractive young woman and that I might have enjoyed a long walk home with her.

"That's fine," I assured.

"Is that all you got?" Arty asked, looking at my one small bag.

"Yeah," I answered.

Arty grabbed the bag from my hand and headed to the Studebaker car he was fond of driving. Throwing the bag in the back, he held the door open impatiently for Marilee to take the seat next to my scant luggage.

"Get in," he encouraged, as I slid into the front seat. "How long are you here for?"

As Arty put the car in gear, I answered, "Only a few days. I got a job at a furniture store in Tecumseh."

"Oh," Arty groaned. "I thought you'd be back for the summer."

"Guy closed down the store, and I need to work," I explained.

"Yeah," Arty replied. "I was over at the Peaudane's house the other day and heard Guy and Dr. Peaudane talking about it. Sounds like the overhead was outpacing sales, so Guy decided to close up and collect his accounts. Guy's thinking about joining the army."

"What were you doing at the Peaudane's?" Marilee quizzed.

Arty, aggravated at the interruption, said, "I was over there talking some business with Dr. Peaudane that's none of your business."

"Not any business to do with Gwen?" she probed.

Smiling at me, before responding in a condescending tone to Marilee, Arty said, "Like I said…none of your business."

Marilee did not challenge him as Arty raced down the bumpy dirt road toward home. It had been a wet spring, and the roads were more rutted than normal, as the car seemed to slide from one side of the road to the other. Arty drove with reckless abandon before suddenly slowing the automobile.

Across the field, two distant figures distracted Arty from his driving, causing Marilee to shout, "Watch where you're going!"

Arty slammed on the brakes bringing the car to a sliding stop. Walking out of the trees and across a pasture, Lance Carrington wearing his distinctive floppy hat escorted Gwen Peaudane. For a moment, Arty appeared excited to see his friend. It took him a few seconds to notice Gwen and Lance were holding hands. Without a word, Arty quickly exited the car and marched toward them.

I turned to look at a worried Marilee, as she said, "This is going to be bad…Gwen's…I think we better get out there."

Getting out of the car, I hurried to help Marilee navigate some of the mud before we walked toward Arty and Lance, who were already engaged in lively conversation.

"What are you saying?" Arty demanded.

"We've wanted to tell you for a while," Lance tried to explain.

"What! That you've been seeing my girl behind my back!" Arty charged.

"Stop it!" a normally reserved Gwen Peaudane demanded. "Lance didn't do anything behind your back. We're seeing each other behind my father's back!"

Arty stared at them in disbelief, before lunging at Lance and landing a blow to his chin. Lance reacted and pushed Arty off balance before squaring up in position to deliver his own blow. Holding Arty by the collar, Lance refrained from punching back, while Arty pushed him to the ground.

"Get up!" Arty shouted.

"Why?" Lance asked calmly, looking up from the ground. "I'm not going to fight you."

"Get up!" Arty shouted again.

Gwen moved to Lance and bent down on one knee to check the trickle of blood coming from his lip.

A more despondent Arty screamed helplessly, "Get up!"

"Can't do it," Lance said. "I can't fight you Arty. You'll have to keep pounding me."

Arty knew Lance was no stranger to fighting and could have easily defended himself. Not knowing what to do, Arty watched the couple for a moment.

"You don't understand," Arty tried to explain. "Gwen…come on…get up from there."

"No," Gwen answered as she continued to look after Lance.

"Arty," Marilee tried to interject before Arty glared at her.

"You knew?" Arty asked his sister.

Marilee nodded sheepishly.

"I've asked your father—"Arty began, looking at Gwen. "I've asked him for your hand."

The entire group listened in awkward silence as Lance and Gwen looked at each other.

After a moment, Gwen said softly, "You shouldn't have done that."

Arty's eyes darted around the group as he looked desperately for support. Seeing how much he had misjudged the situation, he calmed down changing to a more reasonable demeanor.

"Gwen," Arty pleaded in a composed voice. "Let me take you home."

"No," a determined Gwen said with a slight tremor in her voice.

Arty looked at them for a second and then said, "I see."

Watching them a little longer, Arty walked to Lance and reached his hand down to help him up. Lance took the hand warily as he stood face to face with his friend.

"I couldn't fight you either," Arty stated calmly.

"I didn't want this to happen," Lance said.

Arty looked at them again before saying to Marilee and me, "Let's go."

With little emotion, Arty went back to his car, as Marilee and I tensely followed. Arty started the car and pulled slowly away. There was no conversation as he drove silently to my house.

As I stepped out of the car, Arty leaned over and said with little expression, "It's good to see you Gill. Sorry your homecoming was like this...but we'll go do something to catch up."

"Sure," I replied, as Arty drove away with Marilee still sitting silently in the back seat.

Mom and Dad were home, while Gordon was out milking the cows. My mother mended clothes while letting me hug her neck. Dad optimistically told me about beef prices going up because of the war. I asked about Lloyd, but they had not heard from him and assumed he was still in Fort Sill.

After about thirty minutes, I was anxious to see Marilee and to find out what was happening with Arty. About the time I was ready to excuse myself to go, Lance came walking quickly into the house. While my mother and father continued their routine chores, I followed Lance into the small room he shared with Gordon.

"What's going on?" I asked urgently, while he pulled some things out of a drawer to place in a worn, leather satchel.

"You mean besides Dr. Peaudane trying to marry off Gwen?" Lance answered curtly.

"What else is there?" I replied, while Lance continued to put clothes and other items into his bag.

"Arty must have already talked to the Peaudanes, because Gwen's father was waiting for us by the time we got to town," Lance hurriedly said. "I didn't know if the old man was going to scream or cry. He grabbed Gwen and drug her back to the house."

"What's this?" I asked picking up an old pistol from Lance's drawer.

Grabbing it from me, Lance said, "You ought to recognize it. It's the gun you used to shoot the molasses."

"What are you doing with it?" I asked pointedly.

"Elmer Booze gave it to me," Lance replied. "It makes me feel safer sometimes."

Lance put the pistol in the satchel and continued, "Dr. Peaudane ordered me to stay away from Gwen. When Gwen tried to explain…he just sent her to her room like a child. I never believed that old man could be as angry as he was."

"Where are you going?" I asked.

Before Lance could answer, he was interrupted by the sound of an automobile pulling up to our house. Arty stepped out of the car and headed toward the house. Lance grabbed his bag and headed to the door, before I stopped him.

"Let me talk to Arty," I pleaded.

Lance stopped with a deep breath and said, "No…let's go talk to him together."

Lance put down his bag and walked quickly to the front porch where Arty was standing.

"Hey, Lance," Arty said peacefully.

Lance did not reply.

"I wanted to…I wanted to say I'm sorry for earlier…things caught me by surprise, I guess. I kind of overreacted," Arty said.

"Why did you do it?" Lance charged.

Wide-eyed, Arty asked, "Do what?"

"Why did you go to Dr. Peaudane?"

With a slight gasp of surprise, Arty said, "How did Dr. Peaudane find out?"

With a hesitation, Lance said, "I figured you headed straight there."

Shaking his head, Arty said, "I went driving to figure things out…dang-it…Marilee thinks she knows it all and can't keep her mouth shut. She and Gwen are thick as thieves."

Lance looked carefully at Arty, while I chose to stay out of their brewing feud.

"You didn't tell?" Lance asked.

Without hesitation, Arty said, "I talked to Dad…but all he told me to do was settle down. I guess Dad could have said something…but…oh…I didn't mean to cause no trouble."

Rubbing his forehead before looking at Lance, Arty said, "I just come down here to say I'm sorry. I didn't mean to cause trouble."

Lance looked at him for a moment before saying, "You didn't cause no trouble…I caused it myself…I should've been upfront with everyone…including you."

"It don't matter," Arty shrugged. "That's what girls'll do…make guys a little crazy."

Looking at Lance, Arty stuck out his hand and said, "Friends?"

Lance started to shake Arty's hand before stepping up and hugging him.

"More than friends…brothers," Lance said.

Arty stepped back with a sigh of relief and immediately seemed to be the Arty of old as he took charge of the situation.

"What we need fellas," Arty began, "is a night out."

"A night out where?" Lance asked.

"I've got the car," Arty smiled. "I say anywhere we wanna go. How 'bout you Gill? You're the one's come back to town."

Relieved that my two best friends were not trying to kill each other, I said with a smile, "Sounds good."

After quickly telling my parents I was heading out, we climbed in Arty's car and headed down the road. For the next hour, we talked like old times. The guys asked me about school. They teased me about the city girls. Arty even made a quip about how it would take someone as pretty as Gwen Peaudane to make any of us square up and want to fight. Arty gave me a hard time about the long time crush I had for Gwen and said he figured I lost out with her when I murdered the barrel of molasses in the store. Lance seemed to have a good time but was quiet. Arty, as always, was able to sustain the conversation.

I was so entertained that I paid little attention to where we were heading as dusk turned to darkness. The ride in the car would be the last time things seemed as they were when we were boys. I remembered later how right things seemed with the world when we were together, but the voice of Lance Carrington broke the feeling of contentment.

"What are we doing here?" Lance said in a serious tone of concern as we approached a dark, foreboding building. "I can't be here."

CHAPTER 40

I peered through the front window of Arty's car and saw a large wood building with several cars parked out front. It looked like an old gristmill. Two oil torches dimly lit an entryway with a large man in suspenders sitting out front.

"Where are we?" I asked.

"South of Violet Springs," Arty shrugged casually.

We had driven off the county road and taken a narrow path winding through the thick Cross Timber forest. The ominous building sat in an open pasture surrounded by the emerald wall of trees. A few cars and more horses indicated a fairly large gathering inside.

"It's a saloon," Lance said sharply. "What are we doing here?"

"We're not boys anymore," Arty said assertively. "What did you think we were going to do, steal melons or tip cows?"

Looking at the dark, sinister surroundings, I knew this must be the Potanole speakeasy. The Potanole was a notorious place serving hard liquor, hosting serious card games, and offering other forms of entertainment which I could not imagine at that age. The illegal saloon sat on the border of Pottawatomie County and Seminole County. If a sheriff from one county conducted a raid, the operation would just slide to the other end of the building. Since the rivalry between county governments was nearly as furious as the battles between lawmakers and lawbreakers, the place stayed open although most local residents knew of its existence. The lines between the outlaws and lawmen were sometimes blurry in rural Oklahoma.

"This place is bad news," Lance warned. "I can't be seen here—"

"We'll only go in to see what it's like and drink a beer," Arty coaxed. "It'll be something we can talk about when we're old."

Lance just looked at Arty and I was speechless.

"Come on guys," Arty chided. "We're not kids anymore…I know you can take care of yourself Lance, and Gill…well we can both take care of you."

"I'll go," Lance said, "but don't start any trouble."

"How 'bout you, Gill?" Arty asked.

"Of course," I said, trying not to appear stressed.

"Let's go," Arty said, before I could come to my senses and make an excuse to stay in the car.

Arty got out of the car while Lance looked back to say, "You don't have to go, if you don't want to? Arty's just trying to show off."

"I'll be fine," I assured in a less than sure voice.

"If you say so," Lance smiled anxiously as he took another wary look at the Potanole.

Cautiously getting out of the car, I followed close behind the more confident Lance. I was sure he was no stranger to this kind of place and figured he was my best chance to get out alive if Arty's mouth got us into trouble.

The large man in suspenders glared at us as Arty handed him three silver coins.

"That ought to cover us," Arty smiled.

The man nodded at Arty to enter.

Lance walked by, and the man said, "Watch yourself."

As I walked by, the man just stared and grunted something under his breath. The Potanole smelled of tobacco and sour beer. The place looked like it needed a good scrubbing if not a burning. The interior was nearly as dimly lit as the exterior. The establishment was filled with people that did not want to be noticed as well as people that were looking to be noticed. I was definitely in the party of those wanting to be invisible.

Arty found an empty table in the corner and he sat down as if he owned the place. If I had been at the establishment before, I would have noticed the slight hush that came over the saloon as Lance walked into the room. Lance casually looked around then moved a chair so his back would be against the wall. I sat down as quickly as I could across from Lance, which meant I could not see the larger area. That was fine, as I slouched down trying to stay out of sight. Both of my buddies, however, appeared to be in a contest to see who could make themselves more at home.

After a few minutes, a scantily dressed woman leaned over me and asked, "What's your poison tonight boys?"

"I'll have a beer, Rosie," Arty said immediately.

Looking at Lance, the woman said, "Are you buying or selling tonight?"

"Neither," Lance said. "I'm just watching tonight."

"Watching for what?" the woman asked.

"Watching for trouble," Lance said.

Laughing, the woman said, "You've come to the right place then, 'cause trouble's usually around."

Looking at me, the woman asked, "How 'bout you?"

"I'm not looking for trouble," I assured.

With a hard look, she replied, "What do you want to drink?"

"Nehi?" I asked.

"Beer or whiskey?" she asked sternly. "I don't think you can handle anything else we got."

"Have the beer," Lance said.

The woman returned with beers for us while smiling strangely at Lance. Arty quickly downed his beer and asked for a whiskey, but Lance told the woman to bring him water. I tried sipping my beer, but it was bitter and warm. We had walked into the Potanole and lived to tell the tale. I believed this to be enough for one evening. As I looked at my two companions to suggest we leave, I noticed they both stared across the dimly lit room.

Before I could turn and look, I heard at least two sets of boots walk up behind me and the angry voice of Haskell Holiday, say firmly, "You gotta a lot of nerve coming here. What're you up to?"

It took only a second to determine his question was directed at Lance Carrington.

Coolly taking a sip of water, Lance replied, "Just having a drink before we leave."

Looking meanly at Arty and then me, Haskell said, "You've either got guts or you're a fool to be seen in here. I thought Leland explained things to your dad."

"I'm not here doin' business," Lance calmly said. "Just fixin' to leave."

"You're a liar," Haskell Holiday charged.

Arty began to stand up, but Lance reached out to make sure he stayed seated.

"Your daddy's tryin' to sell brew without payin' no dues," Haskell claimed. "That's like takin' money out of my pocket."

I could tell Lance would have liked to give Haskell a piece of his mind, but he calmly said, "I'm not takin' money out of anyone's pocket…at least not anymore. I'm out of the business."

"That's not what I hear," Haskell said.

"Listen," Lance said coolly. "I've sold some product in the past, but just enough to eat. I'm out now and don't even know where my dad is. You don't have to worry about me."

Slamming his fist on the table, while the entire room went silent, Haskell Holiday shouted, "This is your last warning! If I see you anywhere near this place or any other of our places, you'll be finished. Leland will see to that…if he was here tonight, he'd take care of things now. That goes for your drunken fool of an old man too!"

"That won't be a problem," Lance said without breaking eye contact.

Glaring at him a moment longer, Haskell Holiday and his two younger companions walked away to a table across the room.

When the woman who brought our drinks came by, she said, "You boys better leave."

"Thanks for the advice," Lance said, as Arty left several dollar bills on the table.

We did not make eye contact with anyone as we walked out the door. I felt some relief as I breathed fresh air into my lungs but felt even better when the car door shut. It was not until several miles down the road, when I could tell no one was following us, that I could breathe normally again.

"Don't go back there, Arty," Lance said seriously.

"What do you mean?" Arty asked. "The beer wasn't that bad."

"I know you've been there before," Lance replied.

"What?" Arty answered innocently.

"You knew Rosie's name," Lance observed. "I'm telling you as a friend, that place'll get the best of you. Half the whiskey you get from the Holidays is goin' to be poison. I'm not kidding. You don't want to go blind."

"Okay," Arty shrugged. "I've been there a time or two."

With a sly smile, Arty continued, "But that's the first time I nearly got tangled up with old Haskell. I think we coulda takin' 'em all!"

"What if we had?" Lance scolded. "Then what? Then we'd had to deal with Leland. I'm telling you he's mean and connected. Your daddy can get you out of a lot of trouble, but you don't want him havin' to get you out of that kind of trouble. Trust me; the Holidays are a hard place to get out from under."

"Okay," Arty conceded, "enough of the lecture."

"It's just…I won't always be around to watch out for you," Lance continued.

Arty seemed slightly agitated by this statement and drove on into the night.

"How 'bout you, Gill?" Arty finally asked in a more relaxed tone and a big smirk. "Are you goin' back?"

"I think I'm sticking to the movies," I said. "That's enough excitement for me."

My two friends laughed. It was getting late as Arty drove through the country roads and to my dark house. Mom and Dad were already asleep, but Lance and I stayed outside a while to talk. Although the night was cool, Lance took a cold bath and rinsed the clothes he had worn to the bar that night. Going to bed before Lance, I settled into my bed quickly. I wanted to see Marilee in the morning to see why she might have talked to the Peaudanes about Lance and Gwen. As I drifted to sleep, I feared tomorrow would not be peaceful. Lance was sure to go see Gwen. I was convinced the Peaudanes and maybe the Martins would do everything in their power to stop him.

CHAPTER 41

I woke before dawn. It took a moment to remember I had no responsibilities in Ginn's dining room this morning so I drifted back to sleep. A little after daybreak, I noticed Lance was already out.

Mother was in the kitchen making coffee and eggs. We visited a while, and she told me Lance often left early to hunt. Mother spoke fondly of Lance and his contribution to feeding the family but also voiced concern about his long-term future. I was surprised to find out how much my mother knew about Lance's problems with the Holidays.

According to Mother, Lance's father had a drinking problem for many years. He had worked with the Holidays in their distillery years earlier and learned how to make corn liquor. After statehood, the Holidays had to go underground to keep their customers. The Holidays talked Eli Carrington into signing a mortgage for his wife's farm, but after Lance's mother died, his father's drinking got worse. When he defaulted on the farm, Haskell Holiday bought it from the bank.

After breakfast with the family, Lance was still out. Gordon had milking to do, so I helped him before heading up the hill to the Martin's farm. The clear cool night had turned into an overcast, balmy morning. Rain had been frequent the past few weeks, and the day promised likely thunderstorms. As I approached the Martin home, I noticed the Studebaker was already gone. Grandma Nance napped on the porch, nearly causing me to turn around.

"Hello, Gilbert," the pleasant voice of Mrs. Martin called from her garden.

"Hello, Mrs. Martin," I greeted.

"Arty's out," she said.

"That's…that's okay," I replied, as I kicked the dirt.

Mrs. Martin stood up and looked at me a second as she gently stretched her back before saying, "I think Marilee's cooked some of her biscuits this morning. Let me see."

Before I could respond, Mrs. Martin stepped quickly into the house. In a moment, Marilee came out of the house wearing an apron with smudges of flour on her cheek.

"Hey, Gilbert," Marilee greeted, as her mother discreetly disappeared.

"Hey, Marilee," I replied.

"You want a biscuit?" she asked.

"I'd love one, but I just ate," I smiled.

Ignoring this statement, Marilee disappeared into the house and quickly returned with a fluffy biscuit.

"What did Gwen say?" I asked, while munching on the warm biscuit.

"I haven't talked to her," Marilee answered, as she seemed to be more interested in my reaction to her biscuit.

"How did the Peaudanes find out about Lance?" I inquired.

"What?" Marilee asked in a more serious tone.

"Lance said, by the time Gwen got home, Dr. Peaudane was looking for her and knew about her and Lance," I informed.

"Arty," Marilee said.

"No," I corrected. "Arty came by last night and talked to Lance…he said…he indicated that you might have told."

Looking directly at me, Marilee asked, "Does that sound like me?"

"No," I sheepishly replied.

Softening slightly, Marilee said, "You've still got a lot to learn…about me…and Arty."

"Arty said he talked about it with your dad…maybe he talked to the Dr. Peaudane," I suggested.

"That's possible," Marilee agreed. "Still, Arty has a habit of looking out for his interest."

Before we could discuss it further, a commotion came from the road as the sound of tires banging on the dirt road headed our direction. With Arty behind the wheel, we looked at each other as the Studebaker careened toward the Brooks home with Dr. Peaudane and Guy inside.

"You better go," Marilee suggested.

"Yeah," I agreed.

Marilee took the rest of her biscuits inside as I trotted toward home. Before I was halfway to the house, the car headed back up the hill.

Sliding to a stop next to me, an agitated Dr. Peaudane asked, "Where is he?"

"Who?" I asked.

"The Carrington boy!" Dr. Peaudane clarified forcefully.

"I don't know," I replied. "Mom said he went hunting this morning."

"Don't cover up for him, young man!" Dr. Peaudane demanded.

"Dad," Guy Peaudane said from the back seat. "Settle down."

Stepping out of the car, Guy Peaudane gently guided me from the car and away from his father to ask, "Do you know where Lance Carrington is?"

"Like I said, Mom told me he goes hunting sometimes in the morning."

"When was the last time you saw him?" a serious Guy asked.

"Last night…we went out and then talked," I explained.

"What time?"

"Before midnight," I answered before asking. "What's the matter?"

"Gwen's missing," Guy explained. "She disappeared sometime in the night."

"What!" I exclaimed.

"Father thought she was sleeping late, but after banging on the door, he finally went into her room. Gwen was gone."

"What's that got to do with Lance?" I asked.

"Yesterday, we heard…Dad heard that the Carrington boy had been spending time with Gwen," Guy sighed. "Gwen can be strong-headed, and Dad's afraid Gwen's done something rash. Do you know anything?"

"No," I confessed.

"I believe you," Guy reassured, but did you notice anything peculiar last night…did he say anything about doing something or going somewhere?"

Shaking my head, I said, "No…not anything I can think of…they…I mean I think they go down to the flat rock on Salt Creek sometimes."

"Can you show me?" Guy asked.

I did not want to betray Lance, but I reasoned his secret was already revealed. Nodding in agreement, I climbed into the car and told Arty to head to the flat rock. We left Guy's father in the car as we headed through the thick woods. I tried to make as much noise as possible to alert Lance, in case he had rendezvoused with Gwen. As we came to the opening however, it was apparent no one was at the rock. Water roared restlessly, splashing over the top of the rock as the small river was swollen from the recent rains.

A disappointed Guy asked, "Is there anything else…anything at all?"

"No," I assured, as I thought about the conversation from the previous night.

"How about you, Arty?" Guy asked.

Arty, who had been uncharacteristically quiet, shook his head.

"Wait," I said. "Drive me home. I need to check something."

Walking quickly back through the woods to the car, Arty drove as fast as possible over the muddy roads. When we came to the house, Guy Peaudane and Arty followed me into the small room were Lance was living. Looking in his drawer, I was relieved to find the old pistol Elmer Booze had given him placed there. His clothes were missing, however, even the clothes he had rinsed out the night before. Looking around the room, Guy could tell I noticed something.

"What is it?" he eagerly asked.

Searching the room one more time, I stood up and said, "He packed a leather satchel yesterday. It's gone…along with most of his clothes."

The blood drained out of Guy Peaudane's face as he realized Lance Carrington had gone, possibly with Gwen. Like a condemned man, Guy walked slowly to inform his father.

Guy went to his father and said, "He's gone—"

"What!" the old man exclaimed.

"He's gone…taken most of his stuff," Guy explained.

"What's going on?" Arty asked, sensing the concern.

A pained Dr. Peaudane said, "I'm afraid my Gwen has taken off with that Carrington boy."

"What!" Arty said excitedly.

Ignoring Arty, Guy looked at me seriously and asked, "Do you know where, they've gone Gill? Please tell me the truth."

Shaking my head, I honestly said, "No."

"Marilee'll know!" Arty interjected. "She knows everything that goes on in this county."

Without asking permission, I climbed back inside the car as it backed up the hill to the Martin home.

"Marilee!" a frantic Dr. Peaudane shouted as she stepped outside. "Do you know anything about Gwen and the Carrington boy?"

"I can't say," Marilee replied.

"What do you mean, girl?" Dr. Peaudane exclaimed. "This is of grave importance. My daughter's safety…her very life is in danger!"

Looking unconvinced, Marilee remained tight-lipped. The interrogation continued without success, until Arty fetched his father from the barn.

"What's going on?" the stern Mr. Martin demanded.

"My daughter has run off with that…with that Carrington boy," a flustered Dr. Peaudane informed his friend, Mr. Martin. "And Marilee is being stubborn about giving us information."

"Marilee," her father said in a warning tone. "What do you know?"

Marilee scrunched her nose and pursed her lips before saying, "They've gone to be married."

A collective groan of disbelief greeted Marilee's information. A frantic explosion of conversation and questions followed.

"That can't be!" Dr. Peaudane painfully expressed. "Gwen's a sensible girl. Our argument last night was just a misunderstanding."

"They've been planning it awhile," Marilee factually stated. "They knew this was the only way."

"She's only seventeen," Dr. Peaudane said. "I'll have the law after him…she cannot be married without parental consent…and that will never happen."

The men continued to argue among themselves about the best course of action, while Marilee took the opportunity to head back to her kitchen to cook lunch for the field workers. The group decided to split up between Shawnee and the next large town close by, Ada. The Peaudane's Model T was missing, so Arty and Mr. Martin headed south to Ada in the car, while the Peaudanes headed to Shawnee by train.

The group was about to take off, when Mr. Martin stopped and called Marilee to the porch again.

"Marilee," he asked sternly. "Gwen's a smart girl…and I hear this Carrington character is clever in his own way. They know they can't be married. Is there something you're not telling me?"

A reluctant Marilee looked at her watch and said, "They can't be married in Oklahoma. You're right, they know that."

"Marilee," Mr. Martin encouraged. "Tell me what you know."

With a hint of a reassuring smile, Marilee said, "You only have to be sixteen in Arkansas…and there's no waiting period."

The men all looked shocked. It was approaching noon, and the train from Shawnee or Ada could have left hours ago.

"Where did they leave from?" Mr. Martin asked.

An unfazed Marilee, said, "They didn't tell me."

The men headed their separate directions to search for the Model T and Lance Carrington. They wired the sheriff, but the lawmen had no information about the car or the couple.

I sat on the porch alone with Marilee, after the men had gone.

"When did you know?" I asked.

"They left a little after midnight…Lance didn't tell you?" Marilee asked.

"No," I replied. "I probably should have known something was going on, but I didn't have a clue."

"It's probably for the best," Marilee said. "They should be nearly in Arkansas by now."

"How do you know all of this?" I asked.

"Grandma Nance says the reason people think the Indians have the ability to 'talk to the spirits' and have insight about some things is that they listen. She says if we'd listen more we'd know more, but most people don't take the time to listen to her, 'cause they think she's just an old woman. Grandma Nance listens to everything…and so do I. Besides, every girl knows the marriage laws of her state…and the states close by."

"Pretty clever," I smiled.

"More clever than the men," Marilee confessed. "If they had asked where…they might be sending a telegram to the Justice of the Peace in Russellville instead of Fort Smith."

CHAPTER 42

After two frantic days of searching, Dr. Peaudane found Gwen and Lance in a bungalow near Russellville, Arkansas. Gwen had lied about her age, and a judge annulled the marriage. The scandal was hot gossip the next few days. Mr. Martin had gone with Dr. Peaudane to Arkansas, so I spent most of my free time with Marilee.

Mr. Martin returned to find me sitting next to his daughter on the porch. With a stern, disapproving look, he walked to the house as I prepared to leave.

Marilee stopped him before I could escape and asked, "What's going on?"

A tired and grumpy Mr. Martin, replied, "I'll tell you what's going on young lady…that girl has ruined her life, not to mention her reputation!"

"What happened?" a calm Marilee restated.

"Those two eloped!" Mr. Martin roared as his face turned slightly red. "The blasted state of Arkansas doesn't have a waiting period. Fortunately, Gwendolyn lied about her age. She doesn't turn eighteen for another five months, and you were wrong young lady. A girl does need to be eighteen in Arkansas, unless she has parental approval…for whatever good that does if the blasted state doesn't ask for proof of age. It took some persuading, but the judge annulled the marriage on those grounds."

"So they're not married?" Marilee asked.

Mr. Martin projected an intimidating manner in talking with others, and most people did not question him. Through the years, even Arty maintained a more meek and humble demeanor around his father. Marilee, on the other hand, never seemed to notice her father's boorish ways and continued to cross-examine him—much to my discomfort.

Looking sternly at me, Mr. Martin said, "No. The marriage was annulled…but I'm afraid the damage may be done…to her reputation I mean."

"Where's Gwen?" Marilee asked.

"At home," Mr. Martin explained. "The silly girl is hysterical and talking foolishness. Dr. Peaudane got something at the apothecary in Russellville to calm her nerves, and she's at home resting now. Locked in her room, I hope!"

I desperately wanted to know about Lance but was afraid to question Mr. Martin.

Marilee was not as squeamish, as she bluntly asked, "Where's Lance?"

"Jail," Mr. Martin proclaimed.

"What?" Marilee exclaimed. "Why?"

"Contributing to the delinquency of a minor for one thing, and taking advantage of that poor girl," Mr. Martin replied.

"Gwen Peaudane is not some poor, defenseless girl," Marilee informed. "She knew exactly what she was doing. If anything, she prodded poor Lance into going to Arkansas."

Mr. Martin glared at his daughter for a moment.

Staring at me, he replied, "The boy should have known you don't take an under-aged girl across state lines against the will of her family. It's not done by proper folks."

"I'm just saying, if pressuring someone into marriage puts you in jail, Gwen should be the one behind bars," Marilee frankly said.

Mr. Martin grunted at his daughter's impertinence but did not want to argue with her further. He gave me one more warning glare and disappeared into the house.

"I better go," I said as soon as Mr. Martin left.

"Why?" Marilee asked. "Because my father's home?"

"Yeah," I confessed.

"I don't know why everyone's afraid of Daddy?" Marilee shrugged. "He just sounds grumpy, that's all."

"Maybe," I replied, still taking the opportunity to leave. "Are you going to town tomorrow?"

Marilee smiled and answered, "I'll be in town around ten."

"I'll see you," I said as I quickly looked one more time to make sure Mr. Martin had not heard us.

Walking home, I looked forward to seeing Marilee the next day, but my thoughts quickly turned to Lance Carrington. He told me one time he had been in worse places than jail, but I still worried about him. I decided to visit Mr. McNally in Tecumseh as soon as possible.

CHAPTER 43

The sun shined brightly the next morning, but the air was warm and thick with humidity, while lazy, white clouds boiled skyward in the west. As I walked by the Martin place, Marilee was waiting at the gate to walk with me to town. I told her about my plan to see Mr. McNally in Tecumseh, and she agreed it would be a good idea.

Romulus was a sleepy town, but this morning a group crowded around the train station, where Old Beck had dropped off passengers a few minutes earlier. A ragged Lance Carrington stood in the middle of the crowd. Looking at Marilee, we walked quickly toward the station. The rumors about Gwen Peaudane had been the talk of the town, and the arrival of Lance Carrington drew substantial attention. Lance looked tired and shabby, as if he had slept in his clothes for days.

"Lance!" I shouted, as Marilee and I approached.

Stepping quickly toward me, he asked, "Have you seen Gwen?"

"No," I replied.

"She's at the Peaudane's," Marilee informed.

"Thanks," Lance said, before heading that direction.

"Wait!" I shouted, as Lance stopped and looked impatiently at me. "What's going on?"

"I'll tell you what's going on," Lance huffed. "Gwen and I are married. They literally kidnapped her, and I'm going for her."

"They said the marriage was annulled," I replied.

Lance shook his head and shouted, "On a technicality! Gwen told them she was eighteen…she's seventeen and a half…she just rounded up. I've got to see Gwen!"

"Not like this," Marilee calmly interjected.

"What?" a confused Lance replied.

"Look at yourself," Marilee continued. "You look like you haven't slept in days. Your clothes…your clothes don't smell so fresh. Besides you don't seem to be in much of an attitude to impress in-laws."

Lance stared at her, still out of breath from the excitement.

"You know I'm right," Marilee said softly.

"Maybe," Lance grudgingly admitted.

"Let's get away from these people and talk," I offered.

Lance nodded and we moved from the train platform. With Lance more calm, the crowd lost interest and dispersed.

"This thing…you're marriage," Marilee asked. "Was it Gwen's idea?"

"Well…yeah," Lance confessed. "We've been…we've been getting real close, and Gwen's been talking about getting away from her father for months. When her mother died, we decided to elope when she turned eighteen. When Arty caught us the other day, she said we needed to leave or Dr. Peaudane would lock her away."

"So you went to Arkansas?" Marilee continued.

"Yeah," Lance replied. "Gwen heard you could get married there when you were sixteen. I love her, and we were getting married in a few months, so it sounded like a good idea. Gwen wanted to move away, so I was going to get a job in Russellville and live there…the only thing."

"What?" Marilee coaxed.

"You got to have a parent's consent in Arkansas, if you're under eighteen. Gwen didn't know that so she just…exaggerated her age some," Lance explained.

"We rented a little house, until her father barged in…with the sheriff, and dragged Gwen away like a prisoner. They locked me up and had a judge say the marriage never happened. After the Peaudanes left, the sheriff let me go. I'd spent most of my money renting the house so, I've been catching the freight trains back here."

"You must be exhausted," Marilee compassionately said.

"A little," Lance nodded, now in a more rational state of mind.

"I just want what's best for Gwen," he sighed. "I thought I was doing that, but now I'm not so sure."

"What do you mean?" I asked.

"I don't see her dad ever accepting the likes of me, and…and maybe I deserve that," Lance said dejectedly. "Gwen…Gwen mainly seemed interested in getting away. She wants to get away from here and her father."

"It'll be all right," Marilee assured. "You just need to be patient. It takes time with some folks, but the Peaudanes will settle down…they're reasonable people."

"I hope you're right," I said.

"Huh?" Marilee responded.

"Guy and Doc Peaudane are heading this way," I informed.

Lance, quickly stood up, but seemed to be in a less combative demeanor than a few minutes earlier.

I braced for the inevitable confrontation, but was surprised when Dr. Peaudane asked Lance civilly, "Can I have a word?"

"Yes," Lance tensely replied.

Taking a moment to collect his thoughts, Dr. Peaudane began, "Someday…Someday maybe you'll appreciate my…concern."

Lance listened cautiously.

"Gwendolyn's always been strong willed…and…well she's got some crazy ideas now…I've tried to protect her—"

"I would do nothing to hurt Gwen," Lance defended.

Forcing a smile, Dr. Peaudane continued, "I…I can accept that, I think. I would have liked to have had you wait…to talk to me."

"We thought—" Lance began.

Dr. Peaudane interrupted and said, "I probably haven't made that possible. The important thing now is that we agree that we want what's best for Gwen."

"Lance!" a voice shouted in the distance. "Lance!"

Sergio, Lance's friend who worked on the rail line, ran towards us.

Without acknowledging anyone, the young Mexican frantically said, "You've got to come."

"Come where?" a weary Lance replied, while a disapproving Dr. Peaudane listened.

"Your pa," Sergio said in a heavy accent. "Haskell Holiday's meeting him at the bridge…Juan heard Haskell say they would, 'Fix him good.' I'm afraid…you need to stop your pa from going."

"Where is he?" Lance demanded.

"He's been drinking, but he's headed to the bridge," Sergio revealed.

"Which bridge?" an impatient Lance asked.

"The bridge over Salt Creek," Sergio replied.

Taking a second to look at us, Lance ran with Sergio in the direction of my house and toward the bridge over Salt Creek near the Seminole County border.

As I watched Lance trot off, I looked back at a defeated Dr. Peaudane. He had tried to reconcile with the boy he felt had ruined his daughter's reputation only to have Lance called away to some bootlegging quarrel.

The sky became dark-blue and more threatening as thick clouds blocked out the sunshine. I walked Marilee back home, and we barely made it to her porch before a downpour. Marilee made sweet tea, while I kept a watchful eye out for Mr. Martin. The rain splattered peacefully, as Marilee leaned her head on my shoulder. The tranquility of the summer shower, however, would soon turn into a storm threatening to change our lives forever.

CHAPTER 44

Rain poured down in sheets through the afternoon and into the night, causing a damp cool breeze in my room. I stayed up late for Lance to return, but he never did. The soothing sound of steady rain caused me to doze into a deep sleep. In the dark, stillness of the pre-dawn morning, a nudge on my shoulder interrupted my slumber. After my eyes adjusted to the dark, I looked up at a soaking Lance Carrington, shaking in the room.

"Where have you been?" I asked.

"I think I killed him!" a panicked Lance whispered, trying not to wake the sleeping Gordon.

"What!" I whispered back while looking for my trousers in the dark.

"I think he's dead," Lance repeated.

"Who?" I asked.

"Haskell Holiday," Lance replied. "I think I shot him."

"What happened?" I excitedly asked, as thunder rumbled in the distance.

"Dad was drunk," Lance began. "He'd been selling hooch close to places he shouldn't have…including the Potanole on the border. Haskell's had it in for him a while, but selling whisky so close to his brother's place was the last straw."

"Leland Holiday owns the Potanole?" I clarified.

Lance nodded, as I struck a match and lit the oil lamp by the bed. My watch said it was almost five o'clock in the morning.

"Haskell invited Dad to the bridge to talk business, said he wanted to cut Dad in…but Sergio's friend overheard Haskell talking about getting even. These people think that because someone doesn't speak English they can't understand a word. I ran down to the bridge to try to stop Dad, but by the time I got there, three of 'em was beating him pretty bad."

Lance looked out the dark window as if expecting someone at any minute and continued, "By the time I got in the fray, Dad was in bad shape. I put two of them on the ground and they run off, but Haskell clobbered me with a stick and sent me to the ground. Dad was bleeding, but he was still conscious. I'd come by the house to get that old pistol Elmer gave me. Dad must have seen it in my belt and drew down on Haskell as he came at me again. He missed and Haskell knocked me silly with a board."

Looking closer at Lance, I could see a large gash over his eye and blood soaking his shirt.

"Dad was too drunk to cock the pistol," Lance continued. "Haskell took it from him without much of a fight. He took the pistol and shot Dad in the head. Dad dropped dead right there!"

"Your dad's dead!" I whispered in disbelief.

Lance nodded and said, "I…I kind of lost my mind. Haskell was standing over Dad holding the pistol. I charged him and we wrestled to the ground. He outweighs me but I was mad. We fought over the gun and it went off…next thing I know, Haskell Holiday's fallin' on me with a strange, frozen look to him. I took off running and finally decided to come here for some clothes."

"What are you going to do?" I asked.

"I gotta get out of here," Lance said as he stripped off his blood-soaked shirt. "Leland Holiday'll kill me in a minute as soon as he finds out about Haskell."

Thinking frantically, I said, "Stay here. I'm going for help. I think there's some old clothes of Lloyd's in the bottom drawer."

Lance looked restless, but agreed to wait until I returned. I rapidly finished dressing and ran through the rain toward the Martin house. The house was dark except for a light in the kitchen. Going around to the back of the house, I looked inside to see Marilee starting her day. I knocked on the window startling Marilee for a moment before she recognized me.

Coming to the back door, she whispered, "What are you doing here? And in the rain…come in."

"I can't," I replied. "I need you to get Arty."

Marilee sensed the serious tone and went without questioning me. In a few moments, a confused and sleepy Arty came to the door.

"I need your help," I quickly explained. "Can you drive me to Tecumseh?"

"Sure," Arty said with a yawn. "What time?"

"Now," I said.

"What for?" Marilee asked.

"I can't tell you," I replied as she glared at me. "I mean, it's something you won't want to know right now."

"It's important, Arty," I pleaded.

"Give me a minute," he said as he disappeared back into the house.

Marilee stepped onto the small porch where I was standing and said, "What's going on?"

"I—"

"And don't say you can't tell me," she scolded.

Reluctantly, I said, "Lance…Lance got into a fight…a fight with Haskell Holiday and…Haskell's dead."

"What!" Marilee exclaimed in a loud whisper. "Leland Holiday will kill Lance."

"That's what Lance thinks," I admitted.

"What's he going to do?" she asked.

"I need Arty to take Lance to a man I know in Tecumseh," I replied. "He's a lawyer and he'll know what to do."

With a slight look of admiration, Marilee said, "Well, that sounds sensible."

Arty came down the stairs, and we headed to the car as I left Marilee under the shelter of the back porch. I repeated the story to a concerned Arty, and he agreed to drive to Tecumseh. Half expecting Lance to be gone when I returned to the house, I was relieved to see him waiting—watching the lonely country road for any signs of Leland Holiday.

Arty made good time, even over the dark, muddy roads, as Lance shared the details of his fight with Haskell. Bad blood existed between his father and the Holidays for years. Lance did not have much more to add to the story or the actual fight. It seemed things happened so quickly that even Lance was not sure exactly what transpired. I was surprised, however, to learn Arty knew Leland Holiday owned the Potanole. As dawn made its late appearance through the storm clouds, we approached Tecumseh a little before eight o' clock.

I directed Arty to the McNally home where I had eaten lunch several times. After knocking, Mr. McNally opened the door.

"Gilbert?" Mr. McNally greeted, surprised to see me at his home.

"Hello," I replied. "I need to talk to you…about a legal matter."

"The office opens at nine and I'll be glad to see you then," he offered.

"It's…urgent," I insisted.

Looking outside to see we were alone, he hesitantly said, "Come in…we can talk here."

The three of us followed Mr. McNally into a small study in the front of his house.

"What's so urgent?" he asked in a direct, professional manner.

"My friend—" I began.

Before I could say more, he asked, "Is it you, Gilbert, or is it really a friend?"

Looking at Lance I said, "It's really a friend."

Studying my two companions, Mr. McNally said, "Is that 'friend' here?"

"Yes," I admitted.

"It might be best if I hear it from the friend then," he smiled.

Looking at Lance, as if knowing he was the one in trouble, Mr. McNally asked, "What's your name?"

"Lance, Lance Carrington."

Settling into a large leather chair, Mr. McNally calmly said, "Tell me about your problem."

"I…I think I killed someone," Lance said.

Mr. McNally immediately sat up in his chair and asked, "You think…you killed someone?"

Lance nodded and explained, "My father…you may have heard of him…Eli Carrington."

Mr. McNally did not reveal whether he knew the name or not, but listened carefully as Lance continued, "He's a bootlegger from the south part of the county. He's had a feud with these people called the Holidays."

"Leland Holiday?" Mr. McNally asked.

"He's one of them," Lance confirmed. "But he's not the main one. His cousin Haskell cheated my dad out of a farm, and we've been at it since. It's mainly been threats, but yesterday Haskell asked to see my dad, and I found out from some fellas I know who work the rail line that it weren't going to be friendly. By the time I got there, they was beating him pretty bad. I jumped into the fight, but there was a gun."

"Who's gun?" Mr. McNally asked.

With a heavy sigh, Lance said, "It belongs to a guy named Elmer Booze, but he let me have it and I brung it."

"Did you initiate the meeting? Or did Haskell Holiday?" he asked.

"Haskell did," Lance answered. "I only found out about it from a friend of mine."

"Who's the friend?" Mr. McNally asked as he took notes.

"Sergio," Lance replied. "He's a Mexican fella, and he heard it from one of his Mexican friends that don't speak English so well."

"Do you know the man's name?" Mr. McNally inquired while writing notes.

"Juan," Lance offered. "Juan Alfonzo, I think."

"Continue," a serious Mr. McNally encouraged.

"I get to the place…the bridge over Salt Creek, and they're beating Dad pretty good. Three of 'em. I jumped in and two run off. Dad pulled the gun outta my belt and fired a shot, as Haskell was about to hit me with a board. He missed and Haskell knocked me down."

"Is that where you got the shiner?" Mr. McNally asked, looking at Lance's swollen face and the cut above his eye.

"Probably," Lance shrugged. "I got hit more than once."

"Mary Sue!" Mr. McNally called.

Mary Sue came into the room and cheerfully said, "Hello, Gilbert."

Her friendly demeanor changed to concern when her father said, "Get some ice and a clean rag for Mr. Carrington's eye."

Mary Sue obeyed, quickly disappearing from the room. In a moment, she returned with some ice and a towel for Lance's swollen face.

"Thanks," Lance smiled.

Mary Sue replied, "You're welcome."

"That will be all, Mary Sue," Mr. McNally ordered, as his daughter immediately exited the room.

"Continue," Mr. McNally said while looking intently at Lance.

"Dad missed…he was pretty drunk…he was pretty drunk most of the time. Haskell comes and takes the gun and shot him in the head…I…I didn't know what to do, so I charged him. I—"

Mr. McNally interrupted, "Did he point the gun at you?"

A pained Lance answered hesitantly, "I don't really know. I was still dizzy and not seeing strait. Next thing I know, the pistol goes off and Haskell gets this look in his eyes as he fell on top of me."

"Are you sure he was dead?" Mr. McNally asked.

"I'm pretty sure…I mean you should have seen him," Lance said shaking his head.

"But…did you check for a pulse…was he breathing?" Mr. McNally quizzed.

"I don't know…I just ran," Lance said.

Mr. McNally grimaced, and asked, "Were there any witnesses…the two other men?"

"I didn't see them," Lance answered. "Like I said they run off. I guess they could've hung around, but I wouldn't know."

Mr. McNally looked at his pad and made some additional notes.

After a moment, I asked, "What do you think?"

Mr. McNally looked up and said, "I don't know what to think. We may or may not have a dead man. If this Haskell is really dead, it might be manslaughter. We might say it was self-defense. If they try to prove first degree murder charges, they'll have to show Lance went to the bridge intending in advance to kill the man."

"I didn't mean to kill no one," Lance defended.

Mr. McNally said, "I'm not the one you have to convince, son…I'm on your side."

Looking around, Mr. McNally said, "This thing could be serious. I want you boys to follow me to my office. We'll figure it out there."

In a minute, we followed Mr. McNally out the door and walked toward his office located around the corner from the courthouse. Passing Ginn's Hotel, I thought how wonderful it would be to clean up the morning breakfast dishes instead of sitting in an attorney's office. Mr. McNally took us to a room in the back of his office as he excused himself saying he was going to the courthouse. Lance Carrington sat nervously by Arty Martin as we stared at the wall of the small room.

"What am I going to do?" Lance said, almost helplessly.

"It'll be all right," I tried to reassure. "Maybe he's not dead."

"Yeah," Arty tried to encourage. "As fat as Haskell is…maybe he just passed out."

Lance shook his head and said, "No. He was dead…I'm sure of it."

We hypothesized a few more ideas before Mr. McNally returned, with rain dripping off his fedora hat and a somber look to his face.

"They found two dead bodies this morning," Mr. McNally said gravely, "at the bridge over Salt Creek."

Looking at Lance, I could see the life go out of him as he sunk in the chair.

"We need to find witnesses, to corroborate your story," Mr. McNally replied. "If what you tell me is true…if we can establish that Haskell Holiday initiated the meeting, we could be looking at manslaughter…maybe even self-defense."

Lance continued to look blankly, as Mr. McNally continued, "If it's manslaughter, you're looking at a few years in prison. If they prove murder, you'll be looking at the best, a lifetime in prison."

"I'm sorry," Mr. McNally consoled. "I think we got a shot to prove self-defense…but certainly manslaughter. There's one more thing."

Lance looked at his attorney pitifully.

With a slight sigh, Mr. McNally continued, "Leland Holiday's already contacted the sheriff and he's got a group hunting you right now. He's got enough powerful friends to be trouble. I'm going to the sheriff now to arrange for you to give yourself up. You'll be safer in jail."

Patting Lance on the back, Mr. McNally said, "I know this looks dark now, but sit tight and I'll be back."

As Mr. McNally headed to the sheriff's office, Lance looked like a trapped animal—a condemned man with no hope.

"What have I done?" Lance said almost to himself. "What have I done to Gwen?"

Talking rapidly and almost incoherently, Lance looked at Arty and said, "You got to look out for Gwen…promise me."

Arty nodded and said, "What are you going to do?"

Standing up, Lance said, "I don't know…but I got to get out of here. If the sheriff gets me, Leland Holiday will have me dead by morning."

"You can't do that," I protested. "You heard Mr. McNally. Leland's got people all over the county looking for you. Do what he says. He's a good man."

Lance looked at me blankly, not quite convinced, but seemingly clueless as to what he should do.

"Let's get some air," Arty said as he stood up with Lance. "Things'll be all right. I'll talk to Dad. He has some influence."

Almost pushing Lance out the door, Arty said, "Stay here, Gill. Tell the lawyer fella' we needed some air."

They started toward the door, when Lance stopped and picked up his old, floppy hat.

Looking sadly at me, he said, "See, ya Gill. Thanks for everything."

I should have known what they were up to, but maybe I did not want to know. Lance had lived on his own most of his life and was not about to be caged in the county jail waiting for Leland Holiday's group to lynch him. Lance's greatest concern was Gwen. A few days before, Lance Carrington had enjoyed two days of happiness married to the girl of his dreams. Now, he was on the run, and that happiness must have seemed a fantasy.

When Mr. McNally returned with the sheriff, they asked me where Lance had gone. I could honestly say, "I don't know."

As the sheriff frantically made plans to find Lance before Leland Holiday did, I listened to the rain intensify. I stopped to see Ginn and told her how much I was looking forward to getting back to my room for the summer. Ginn knew something was not right but did not ask. Later in the day, I took the train back to Romulus, hoping I would not see Lance Carrington hanged by the end of the day.

CHAPTER 45

Torrential rains continued as the train approached the station in Romulus. As I stepped on the platform, rumors about the manhunt and stories of the incident with Haskell Holiday buzzed through the small crowd. The sheriff's deputies and Leland Holiday's men had blocked all roads leading out of the county, including the railroads. Leland Holiday had personally offered a reward for Lance's capture.

I waited under the awning of the train station for a while, until deciding the rain was not going to stop. Walking home, I gave up on staying dry and trudged toward the house. A ways out of town, I heard a clamor of people in the distance, as a group gathered near the station. The Martin's Studebaker passed me, and I was surprised to see Mr. Martin driving instead of Arty. Marilee looked helplessly at me as they passed. Immediately, I trotted back to the train station to see what had happened.

A group of men surrounded Arty, and I quickly recognized Leland Holiday as the ringleader.

"I'm telling you," Arty shouted. "He didn't make it."

"What's going on?" I asked Guy Peaudane who stood close by with an umbrella.

"Leland's gang found Arty near the South Canadian River and brought him here to find out where the Carrington boy's hiding," Guy informed as he tried to listen keenly to the conversation.

"What's going on here!" the booming voice of Mr. Martin shouted over the crowd, as he stepped next to Arty.

Marilee crowded close to me, as she tried to stand out of the rain. I moved to make room for her, but I found myself standing under a drip.

"What are you doing here?" I whispered.

"Someone said Leland Holiday had Arty and Lance," she replied.

"I haven't seen Lance," I observed.

Leland Holiday stepped away from Arty to face Mr. Martin and said, "Your boy here's been aidin' and abettin' a murderer."

"There's no proof there's been a murder," Mr. Martin stated.

"Carrington's wanted," Leland bluntly replied. "Your boy here was seen with him last. I found him out in the middle of nowhere on a horse! He'll go to jail if he don't tell me where Carrington's hiding!"

"You know he won't," Mr. Martin said, as he stared at the angry Leland Holiday.

Looking at a soaked Arty, Mr. Martin asked, "Where is he?"

"I tried to tell 'em," Arty said. "He drowned."

A murmur raced through the small crowd, as Mr. Martin asked, "How?"

"We was headin' to the river," Arty explained. "Lance was goin' to Ada."

"So you were helping him?" Mr. Martin asked.

Arty nodded, and said, "We heard there was a lynch mob hunting him, and Lance decided to try his luck in Pontotoc County."

"Where is he now?" Mr. Martin asked, before Leland Holiday could interrupt.

"He started out across the river," Arty explained. "The horse went down, and the water was real high. Lance crashed against a logjam. I guess it knocked him out. He's a good swimmer all right, but I saw him go down until he didn't come up no more."

"He took one of my horses?" Mr. Martin hotly asked.

"No sir," Arty clarified. "He took a horse from the Brooks. A mob was headed to the river, so I went down to warn him…by the time I got there, he was already in the river, and then the horse stumbled."

Turning to Leland Holiday, Mr. Martin said, "I guess your fugitive is downstream."

Glaring at Arty, Leland Holiday said, "We'll see."

With a motion of his arm, Leland Holiday's group of six men headed south on horseback toward the South Canadian River between Pottawatomie and Pontotoc County. The rain started to lighten, but there was less than two hours of daylight left.

An ashen Arty, joined Guy Peaudane, Marilee, and me while Mr. Martin talked to some of the people who were not with Leland Holiday's men.

"What happened?" I asked, hoping Arty's story had been a clever ruse.

"Lance didn't think he had much chance in jail, so he decided to get out of the county when we left you at the lawyer's office. We figured they were watching the roads and bridges so we decided to ride out on horse and forge the river away from the road. Lance took Old Betsy—"

"Old Betsy's not up for that kind of trip," I interrupted.

"I know that now," Arty explained. "The fool horse stepped in a hole, and Lance went into the river. That blow to the head must've knocked him out cause he went down and didn't come up. I…I waded out to help, but the current was too strong. I nearly got swept away myself."

"Lance is really drowned?" I asked in disbelief.

"Haven't you been listening?" an angry Arty replied.

Looking at Guy, Arty said, "Someone'll have to tell Gwen."

Guy Peaudane, obviously shaken said, "Yes…I…I can't believe this."

"Where's my horse?" Marilee asked Arty pointedly.

Arty grimaced, slightly and said, "Your stupid horse got spooked and ran off. That's why we had to take Old Betsy."

"This is terrible," Guy Peaudane lamented. "Yesterday he was going to be a brother-in-law and now he's dead. I fear Gwen will be crushed. She's been so edgy lately."

Marilee and I looked at Guy Peaudane in disbelief.

"Gwen's a stubborn girl," Guy explained. "She had a fight with my father and threatened to run off again…until Dad agreed to let her marry. He was talking to the boy just yesterday, when he ran off and got in this mess."

Arty said, "Lance was worried about Gwen. He wanted to see her before he left, but figured that would've been the first place they'd look."

"He said something this morning about Gwen," I remembered. "He was always thinking of her."

"I better go," Guy Peaudane, said somberly. "She's got to know."

"I'll go with you," Marilee offered.

"Thanks," Guy said.

As they walked away, Arty said, "When Gwen feels up to it, let me know…I…I promised Lance I would look in on her."

"Thanks," Guy said.

I stood on the empty train platform with Arty, who stared strangely at Guy and Marilee as they walked away.

"It's a bad business," Arty finally said.

"Yeah," I replied. "I…I shouldn't of let you guys go. I mean I knew what Lance was thinking and…things might have turned out okay."

"Lance wasn't willing to take that chance," Arty stoically said. "He thought he had lost Gwen. I guess he figured he'd lost everything."

"A bad business," Arty repeated.

We walked home together as we had hundreds of times before. Somehow, it did not seem real, that Lance Carrington would not appear to entertain us with a good story or adventure to tell. I informed my parents about Lance that night. My father could not believe it. In the night, I heard Mother crying softly. The rain ended close to midnight, but her tears continued through the night.

CHAPTER 46

Brilliant sunshine ushered in a fresh morning. As I awoke, the previous day seemed like an ugly dream, but the events were all too real. As my family finished breakfast, the sound of horses and a wagon approaching the house caused my father to get up from the table to investigate. Stepping outside, we saw a group of tired and haggard men coming down the road led by Leland Holiday.

In the back of the wagon, a dead and frightfully disfigured horse was covered in mud.

"Is this your horse?" a curt Leland Holiday asked.

Taking only a moment to look at the animal, Dad affirmed it was.

Looking at me, Leland Holiday threw the worn, floppy hat Lance always wore at my feet asking, "Is that Carringon's?"

I immediately knew it was, as a sense of grief nearly overwhelmed me.

"Yes," I replied. "He never was without it."

As my mother began to cry in front of the unsympathetic Leland Holiday, I worked up the courage to ask, "Did you find…the body?"

"Not yet," Leland Holiday answered. "But if he's out there, we'll find it."

The men with Leland Holiday mercilessly dropped the tailgate on the wagon and dumped Old Betsy in our yard.

"You better do something with that," Leland Holiday gruffly commanded.

Before he and his men rode off, he added, "And be more careful who steals your horse next time."

Gordon and I used the mule team to drag Old Betsy to the corner of the field to burn the carcass. The men searched the banks of the South Canadian River for several days without finding the body of Lance Carrington. Some said he could have washed all the way to the Arkansas River. Still others believed he ended up in one of the many caves by the river's edge or got buried in the river's sandy banks. It had been one of the worst floods on the river anyone could remember, and no one seemed surprised the body was not found. Even Leland Holiday gave up the search after a few days.

Eli Carrington's body was laid to rest without a single person knowing. A bigger funeral for Haskell Holiday happened the next day. Although the body was never found, the Peaudane family provided a memorial service for Lance. A plain stone marker was put by our rock on the banks of the Salt Creek with Lance Carrington's name carved on it. The preacher talked about the temporary nature of life for all of us. People shared stories about Lance Carrington's better qualities, which I had been privileged to witness first-hand through the years.

Mr. McNally and Mary Sue came from Tecumseh. Mr. McNally was particularly distraught. He had continued his investigation and found several men living under the rail bridge who witnessed the incident between Lance and Haskell Holiday, including Juan Alfonso, who had been the boy to warn Sergio. They all confirmed Haskell Holiday had initiated the attack, and Lance's actions had been pure self-defense. I could tell Mr. McNally was frustrated his would-be client never knew the truth that he would not have been charged.

Gwen Peaudane was dressed in black and had a dazed, faraway look. Good to his promise, Arty was with her throughout the day and was very attentive to her. She nearly collapsed one time, but Arty was there to steady her. Marilee stood by me and even held my hand for the first time during the preacher's prayer. I would be leaving for

Tecumseh in a few days to finish my summer, but the events of my trip back to Romulus and even the memorial service for Lance Carrington would haunt me for years. Arty, Lance, and I had been like brothers. Any of us could have done something to prevent this tragic loss, but none of us seemed to be able to do the right things. I could scarcely think of him for several years after without regret for that day.

PART III

CHAPTER 47

The summer heat broiled oppressively, as I prepared to return to Tecumseh. Rains, which had swollen the rivers, washed out several bridges and helped drown Lance Carrington, added a sticky humidity to the warm air. Marilee came to the station to see me and kissed my cheek. Blushing awkwardly, I returned the kiss as she squeezed my hand. Lance once explained how nice it was to have someone thinking of you. I wondered when, if ever, I would stop thinking of him.

Promising Marilee I would be more diligent in letter writing, the train creaked out of the station. Looking through the window until the train turned the bend, she patiently watched. The trip back to Tecumseh presented conflicted emotions. I very much wanted to get back to the hotel and away from the painful memories of the past few days, but unlike the year before, I would be missing Marilee.

Arriving in Tecumseh, I was surprised to see the McNally family, including Mary Sue at the station. Mary Sue, usually bubbly and full of energy, instead sat listlessly on a bench staring blankly, much as Gwen Peaudane had a few days earlier at Lance Carrington's funeral.

Mr. McNally greeted me, while discreetly taking me to the side to explain, "Mary Sue's a little distraught today."

"I see," I replied.

"Ralph, her fiancé, is…was scheduled to leave for Europe this week," he said.

Many soldiers were leaving for Europe to fight in the war. We received a rare letter from Lloyd indicating his division might be leaving by the end of 1917.

"He had an accident," Mr. McNally continued. "A training accident down in Texas. He's been hurt badly, and we're going down to check on him."

"That's terrible," I said.

"Yes," Mr. McNally replied.

"I was sorry about your friend," Mr. McNally continued. "Such a waste…I—"

"Thanks for your help," I interrupted, knowing he had done what he could.

Stepping to Mary Sue, I said, "I'm so sorry."

Looking at me with her kind eyes and forcing her familiar smile, she said, "Thanks, Gill. It'll be okay, I'm sure."

Excusing myself, I headed to Ginn's Hotel. Ginn gruffly greeted me, as was her nature, but gave me a welcome home hug. The next morning, after my duties in the dining room at Ginn's, I started working at the Cooper Furniture Company and soon got back into the routine of work. Letters from Marilee came nearly every day. I tried to write at least once a week but feared my letters did not express how much I missed her.

Two weeks before school began; one of Marilee's letters stunned me. In previous messages, Marilee explained Arty had been looking after Gwen and seemed genuinely attentive to her. To everyone's surprise, Arty and Gwen were now married!

The letter said the couple lived in a small place close to the Martin's house. I eagerly waited to see Marilee again to find out all she really knew. School started, however, and I did not have time to think about Arty, Gwen, or even memories of Lance. My time was filled with school, work, and Marilee's letters.

By late October, days were getting short, and a brisk north wind whipped through town as I walked from school to Ginn's Hotel. Stopping in the small lobby, I spied a letter in my box and quickly opened it. With a smile, I ran to find Ginn.

"Ginn," I greeted, as she scolded one of the new helpers about his inability to scrub floors to her satisfaction.

"What?" she barked back.

"Can I have off this Friday?" I requested.

Stopping to turn her attention away from the boy, Ginn carefully studied me before asking warily, "What for?"

"I…I need to meet someone," I explained.

"You'll have to tell me more," Ginn chided.

"I've got some people from home coming," I said.

Ginn grinned, which caused her nose to wrinkle, as she said, "Is it 'the people' that writes you nearly every single day?"

"Yes."

Ginn stretch her back and said, "I'll let you off…if you bring her by to meet me."

With a sheepish smile, I said, "Sure…but how do you know it's a girl?"

"First," Ginn answered with her hands on her hips, "no man I ever seen writes more than one letter a year…and second, there's something powerful wrong with you if your carrying around and re-reading letters from a man."

"We'll see you Friday," I assured, picking up an apron to start work.

Arty, Gwen, and Marilee arrived Friday afternoon and were at the hotel before I returned from school. I heard Ginn and Marilee laughing while Arty and Gwen patiently waited.

"What's going on?" I greeted as I entered the hotel lobby.

"Not anything," an uncharacteristically cheerful Ginn answered back. "I was just telling your girl here how skinny and worthless you looked your first day here and how you's created more work than you actually did. She's tellin' me it's cuz you don't know what you really want out of life. She's just telling us how she had to nearly make you kiss her when you come back to school."

Arty enjoyed Ginn's assessment of my romantic expertise, while Gwen sat sweetly by his side.

"I'm not saying he wasn't going to kiss me," the factual Marilee corrected. "I just said that sometimes Gilbert needs some guidance."

"Aren't you going to help me out?" I jokingly asked Arty.

"Don't look at me," Arty said putting his hands up as if he were innocent. "I had to live with Marilee for nearly eighteen years."

Putting his arm around Gwen, he added, "I've enjoyed the peace and quiet of being away from her."

Ginn did not need more time to discuss my shortcomings with Marilee, so I said, "Are we ready to go?"

Arty took the hint and helped Gwen with her coat, while I smiled and reached for Marilee's coat.

"Nice to meet you, Miss Ginn," Marilee said as we left.

"Ginn don't like to be called, Miss," I said to Marilee.

"Don't you go bothering that girl," Ginn scolded. "She can call me anything she wants."

"You see what I mean," Marilee whispered to Ginn. "He worries about everything."

Taking Marilee by the arm, I led her away from the hotel and the tormenting grin of Ginn.

"It's good to see you guys," I said, as we walked quickly toward the trolley heading to Shawnee. "I can't believe you're married."

"Well," Arty explained. "I thought it was time to settle down, and Dad pays me a little more now that I'm married. Besides, I was wearing out Dad's Studebaker, driving to Gwen's all the time."

Arty looked genuinely happy, and Gwen looked content. Arty's boisterous personality and tendency to dominate a conversation contrasted nicely with her more reserved nature.

"How 'bout you?" I asked Gwen. "Arty must be a handful to have to take every day."

A blushing Gwen said, "It's…wonderful…Arty's been there for me through good times…and bad. It's nice to be out tonight, though."

"I'm glad you guys came…and especially glad you brought Marilee," I smiled as I held hands with Marilee.

Shaking his head, Arty said, "Still don't know what you see in Marilee—"

Before he could continue, Marilee swatted him with her purse.

"See what I mean," Arty defended. "She's the meanest woman this side of the Cross Timber."

"I hope he's more…respectful of you," I said to Gwen.

With a sweet smile, Gwen said, "He is."

We rode the trolley to Benson Park. A band played cheerfully in the distance at the bandstand as the trolley eased to a stop. People milled about enjoying the brisk, autumn evening. We stayed on the trolley heading to Shawnee to see a movie. Our banter quieted as passengers unloaded while others boarded the trolley for their trip back home. It might have been the extra people around, but I wondered if we were perhaps thinking of the wonderful day we spent at the park with Lance Carrington.

We ate a sandwich at a place in Shawnee close to the train station called Nellie's. Gwen and Arty seemed happy together, and Marilee looked like she belonged in a magazine that night. Arty ran across the street for some gum, and Marilee excused herself to powder her nose, leaving Gwen and me alone for a few minutes.

"How are things really?" I asked.

With a brave smile, Gwen said, "Fine."

After a hesitation, she added, "You must think I'm awful?"

"No," I quickly replied. "I could never think that."

"I cried for a week after Lance died and cried most days after that, but…life goes on. I didn't want to be a burden to…my father. Arty's…well Arty's always been sweet to me and he…he loves me."

"I know," I awkwardly replied. "He has for a long time. I guess we all did in a way."

In a grimaced smile, Gwen said, "I suppose I've always been quite the flirt."

"No," I quickly replied with a smile. "You couldn't help but being you."

"You must think I'm a terrible person for getting married so quickly?" she hesitantly asked.

"No, Gwen," I replied seriously. "No one would ever think you terrible. Are you happy?"

"Yes," Gwen quickly replied. "Very…I enjoy being married. I love making a new home with Arty. I had to—"

"Too late to try to steal this girl," Arty interrupted as he swaggered back to the table. "What are you two talking about?"

Gwen seemed to be in the middle of a thought when Arty rejoined us. She blushed, without having a ready answer, so I quickly said, "We were talking about your favorite subject."

"What?" a puzzled Arty asked.

"You!" I smiled.

Arty shook his head at the insult before saying, "That does sound like interesting conversation."

Recovering her good humor, Gwen added, "I was about to tell Gill about how much you enjoy my cooking."

Arty, temporarily caught off guard on what I guessed had been a topic of discussion with the newlyweds, was sheepishly silent.

Looking at me, Gwen smiled teasingly, "For the complaining he does about Marilee, you would not believe how much he talks about her cooking!"

Arty grinned as he threw his arm around Gwen to give her a hug and said, "But Marilee was never this squeezable!"

"Will you ever, learn to behave in public?" Marilee scolded, as she returned to the table.

"Don't have to," Arty mocked. "We're married now."

After our meal, we headed up the street to see a movie. Arty wanted to see *Cleopatra* with Theda Bara, but Marilee insisted that Theda Bara was too risqué and wanted to see *Rebecca of Sunnybrook Farm* with Mary Pickford. The Mary Pickford film was entertaining, but Arty and I probably were more intrigued by the newsreel about the Great War.

My brother Lloyd almost never wrote, but we assumed he was still scheduled to leave for Europe by the end of the year. Crossing the Atlantic with U-boats prowling would be an adventure to itself. Arty wanted to join the army, but his father prevented it.

"Seeing those newsreels makes you want to get into it, don't it?" an almost gleeful Arty said energetically as we left the theater.

"Arty," Gwen scolded, "don't even think of such a thing."

"I know I can't go now," Arty lamented. "But can't you see me in one of those uniforms, with a chest full of medals?"

Patting him on the shoulders, Gwen smiled and tactfully said, "You don't need any medals to be a hero. You're taking care of me…that should be hero enough."

"Besides," Marilee added. "Your own troops would probably shoot you before the Germans got the chance."

"See what I had to put up with?" Arty good-naturedly said as we walked down the street.

Gwen smiled, while I quipped, "Maybe you should try keeping your mouth shut around her."

Quickly, Arty replied, "Maybe I need to put a cow bell around her neck so I'll know when the old cow's around."

Marilee pushed her glasses up on her nose and dryly said, "Even if I was a cow, I'd still be smarter than you."

"Aren't you going to help me, Gwen?" Arty complained.

Smiling shyly, Gwen put her arm that was not being held by Arty around Marilee and said, "It's hard to choose between my husband and my best friend."

Breaking free of Arty's arm, Gwen playfully hugged Marilee and said, "I'll have to go with Marilee in a battle of wits."

Throwing his hands in the air, Arty said, "See what I'm up against, Gill? I'm telling you…go join the army now before it's too late."

Gwen stepped back to Arty's side and said in a more serious tone, "Don't even kid about the army, Arty."

With a proud smile at Gwen's genuine concern, Arty said, "Don't fret. If you'd choose Marilee for brains, who do you chose for love?"

Embarrassed at Arty's sudden affection, Gwen answered, "You, of course."

Pulling her close, Arty smiled and said, "I thought so."

Marilee and I were able to separate ourselves from our chaperones when they went into a store to look at a Victrola.

"They look happy," I whispered to Marilee.

Nuzzling close, Marilee answered, "Yes, I think maybe they are."

Pushing her away slightly to look her in the eye, I asked, "Tell me what's really going on."

Looking nervously to make sure the couple was still in the shop, Marilee said, "Gwen was devastated when Lance died. She wouldn't eat. Guy was so worried he would not leave her alone. I stayed with her some nights, and Arty…well, for once in his life, Arty wasn't thinking about himself and spent nearly every day with Gwen. Lance affected Arty too, but I guess men and women grieve differently. Arty seemed determined to be better. I know he's been more attentive to Gwen."

"But they got married so soon?" I questioned.

"Grandma Nance says sometimes a girl decides it's time to get married and the man is kind of interchangeable. She told me she was engaged to another man before she met Granddaddy…but Grandma Nance says a lot of other things people ought not to listen to."

"Like what?" I asked.

Smiling at me, Marilee said, "Like some things that don't need repeating. Gwen seems happy, and Arty seems responsible. That should be enough for now."

"You're not going to tell me, are you?" I said with a grin.

Marilee leaned into me and said, "We'll know, then we'll understand. Besides, don't you have better things to talk about besides Gwen and Arty?"

"Like what?"

"Like how great I look in this new dress I bought just to come see you?" she teased.

"I haven't been able to say anything because I can't keep my eyes off it," I smiled.

"You might ought to tell a girl sometime," Marilee pouted. "I'd worry about the city girls more if I thought you had the sense to know how to talk to them."

"You're the only girl I have trouble talking to," I pleaded, before thinking that did not sound quite right.

Marilee smiled at me and in her typical sensible tone said, "You better leave the other girls alone. Like Grandma Nance says, 'Guys are interchangeable.' Besides, your brother Gordon's starting to look better all the time…or I could wait for Lloyd to return."

"Leave Gordon and Lloyd alone," I smirked.

"I'm leaving everyone alone…but you," Marilee smiled.

When we arrived at the hotel, Gwen and Arty climbed into the car while Marilee stood in front of me while they waited.

"I had a good time tonight," I said.

"Are you going to do it?" Marilee asked.

"Do what?"

"Kiss me."

"In front of your brother?"

"Of course."

"Your dad'll find out."

"Eventually."

Leaning toward Marilee, I kissed her on the lips with my eyes closed.

Beaming at me she said, "I had a great time too. Good bye, Gilbert."

With wobbly knees, I watched Marilee walk confidently to the car, while Arty shook his head in mock disgust and Gwen eagerly leaned over the seat to question Marilee. Arty drove into the night, as I watched the car disappear, knowing Marilee was safe inside.

CHAPTER 48

Christmas approached as I prepared to go back to Romulus for the first time since the summer. Ginn gave me a hug and sent me on my way with freshly baked muffins to take on the short trip. Walking to the train station in Tecumseh, I enjoyed the bright and unseasonably pleasant December day. Coming out of the station, I met Mary Sue McNally pushing a man in a wooden wheelchair.

It was hard to recognize the man who had been her dashing fiancé. Ralph Swan was missing his right arm and leg, while he was disfigured almost beyond recognition, with only about a third of his face unaffected by burns received in his airplane accident.

"Hello, Mary Sue," I greeted awkwardly.

"Hello, Gill," she replied.

Mary Sue desperately tried to smile with the same optimism I remembered from my first days at school. She had been my first friend in Tecumseh and the only friendly face for many of those early weeks. She was a special girl with a zest for life that radiated to everyone around her. It was easy to tell she had cried often the past months, although she now put on a brave front in the face of this new adversity.

"You remember Ralph?" she asked with a false tone of cheerfulness, "my fiancé?"

"Of course," I replied, as I instinctively began to reach out my hand before realizing he had no arm.

"Good to see you again," I clumsily greeted.

Ralph Swan looked at me pathetically—only a shell of the man he had been when he left to be the hero. He grunted an unintelligible greeting.

"I'm heading home for Christmas," I said.

Mary Sue smiled kindly and said, "Merry Christmas, Gill."

"Merry Christmas, Mary Sue," I replied as she diligently pushed her fiancé to a waiting car.

Riding the clanking Old Beck toward home, I sat quietly, reflecting on the challenges facing Ralph Swan as well as what Mary Sue must be feeling. My thoughts turned to my brother Lloyd who would soon be in harm's way, fighting in a faraway place.

My melancholy mood evaporated when the train made the last turn into Romulus and I could see Marilee waiting on the platform. The cotton harvest in the area around Romulus had all but failed the year before. The land, which had been carved out of the poor, clay soil of the ancient Cross Timber forest, seemed to be used up, at least for cotton farming. More businesses were shut down, with only Kelly's diner and the deteriorating train depot left.

I came back to Romulus with some anxiety. I looked forward to seeing my parents, but Marilee had invited me to the Martin home for Christmas Eve. It would be the first time I would face Mr. Martin as Marilee's friend instead of Arty's friend. Fighting in the Great War sounded almost more appealing than facing Mr. Martin.

Marilee hugged me tightly and pointed across the road to the Studebaker parked there. Half expecting Arty to be waiting, I was surprised to discover Marilee had learned to drive after her horse disappeared the previous summer. Marilee drove at half the speed as Arty but at twice the rate of excitement as she weaved from one side of the road to the other. As we approached my house, I thought how small it looked every time I returned.

The old place looked neater than I remembered, although the house was badly in need of paint. Everything was tidy, and all the typical clutter had vanished. Dad was on the porch whittling as he yelled inside for Mother to come out. My mother hugged me even tighter than Marilee had. My younger brother Gordon had transformed into a young man who was at least three inches taller than I was and much thicker.

My parents invited Marilee inside and began discussing the family happenings. Lloyd was on a ship, headed to France as part of the 36th Division of what was being called the American Expeditionary Forces. He had not written a single letter but sent a telegram from New York the day before boarding the ship.

Marilee, who was a prolific letter writer, asked what the telegram said. "I'm going tomorrow," was the extent of Lloyd's message. She pressed for more details, but that was about all the family knew of Lloyd's adventures.

The big surprise for Christmas was that the Brooks family was moving. Dad had already moved most of his equipment to a forty-acre farm he rented a few miles south of Salt Creek where he was going to try to grow cotton again. Looking at Marilee, I could tell she was surprised and a little dismayed to think my family was moving away, even though it was only a few miles.

After more visiting, I waved good-bye to Marilee as she drove slowly yet erratically up the hill. I would see her again the next day when I went to the Martins for Christmas Eve.

The small room Gordon and I shared seemed larger than I remembered. I realized after settling into bed, it was the first time only two of us shared the room. Lloyd and later Lance had always been in the room before.

Sleep did not come early for me that night. After visiting with Gordon, I began to dread the upcoming dinner with Mr. Martin. He had always been a very strict man, and I easily believed he would not approve of me.

CHAPTER 49

The sun began to set on what had been a warmer than usual Christmas Eve. The walk toward the Martin home was pleasant, although the prospect of eating dinner with Mr. Martin was terrifying. The house glimmered in the late afternoon sun, and oil lamps already illuminated the rooms in preparation for the evening.

As I stepped into the house, the smell of roasted meats, baked breads, and sweet deserts intoxicated the senses. Marilee came out of the kitchen with an apron around her waist and smudges of flour on her cheeks to greet me. She immediately disappeared back to her cooking, however, leaving me with the Martin men.

Ethan, Arty's older brother, was discussing farm business with his father. Ethan had married the year before Arty and lived on a farm south of the Salt Creek with his wife and their baby. Arty, always more reserved around his father, took the opportunity to leave the conversation between Ethan and Mr. Martin to join me. Arty's two younger brothers picked at each other and were obviously anxious to open their gifts placed under a small evergreen tree in the front room.

Mr. Martin listened intently to Ethan's discussion about the quality of land around his small farm but also looked sternly at me several times. The room was tense, and I assumed my presence was the reason.

Mrs. Martin called us for dinner, interrupting the stiff conversation and continual glares I received from Mr. Martin. Stepping into the dining area adjacent to the kitchen, I nearly stumbled over Grandma Nance sitting in her wooden wheelchair. The old woman glared at me but said nothing. Waiting nervously for Marilee to join me, I nearly gasped seeing Gwen carrying a pan of freshly baked rolls balanced on her protruding belly. Gwen looked a few pounds heavier when I saw her in October, but it was now obvious she was expecting a child.

Gwen blushed as I stared just a bit too long, but fortunately, Marilee joined me, and we all sat down. After a prayer by Mr. Martin, the boys attacked the food as if it would soon disappear. I had never had a meal like this with glazed ham, roast beef, creamy mashed potatoes, sweet yams, and fluffy rolls with desserts including pecan and pumpkin pie.

After dinner, the men retreated to the front room while the women cleaned the kitchen. The group of men seemed to ignore the fact Gwen was pregnant as we started discussing the farming situation, local politics, and the war.

I was content to listen to their conversation when Mr. Martin asked in his stern voice, "You've been seeing Marilee, I understand."

Clearing my voice, I replied, "We've actually been writing more than seeing each other."

Appearing somewhat perturbed at my evasive answer, he restated, "You have feelings for her? I've seen your letters come and suspect she has written you back. I notice I don't see any letters for Arthur."

"Yes, sir," I squirmed. "I have developed an attachment for Marilee."

Looking harshly at me, he said, "I hear your folks are moving…again."

"Yes, sir…they've found a place south of Salt Creek."

"I know the place well," Mr. Martin assured me. "Part of the old Cherry place at the bottom of Cherry Hill…good land."

"I suppose," I answered.

"You'll be going with them to farm?" Mr. Martin asked.

"I…I don't know," I stammered. "I mean I'm going to school, and I don't expect to return to the farm."

"Quit farming!" he roared in a tone of disbelief. "What will you do?"

"I'm working at a furniture store now," I said. "I hope to enter business."

"Gill used to work at the Peaudane's store before it closed," Arty interjected.

"I know that," Mr. Martin stated bluntly. "I also know that store went out of business...seems like farming is more stable. People will always need to eat even if they don't need a new gadget."

"The store in Tecumseh seems to do well," I offered.

"You should see the stores in Shawnee," Arty added.

Staring Arty down, Mr. Martin continued, "So, I assume you're planning to stay in the city...or are you planning to go to war?"

"I...I don't really know," I answered unsurely. "I should graduate a year from this May...and I'm planning on taking some courses at the Western Business College this summer...to learn typing."

"Typing?" Mr. Martin scoffed. "Are you meaning to do secretarial work?"

"No...I...I'm just—"

"Daddy!" Marilee scolded as she entered the room. "Leave Gilbert be. He's my guest, and he's going to be a businessman. Guy Peaudane himself told me Gilbert was a natural."

"And where is Guy Peaudane now!" Mr. Martin barked. "Off to fight in a war he's got no business in, leaving a sick father and—"

Mr. Martin quit his tirade as Mrs. Martin and Gwen entered the room. Mrs. Martin gently guided Gwen to the seat next to Arty.

"I think we've had enough talk of war," Mrs. Martin calmly smiled. "I think it's time to open our gifts."

Mr. Martin did not challenge his wife and started handing out presents to his children. Marilee handed me a package with "Gilbert" carefully printed on the card, and a handsome scarf she knitted. I shyly handed her a package with a small jewelry box I purchased at a store in

Tecumseh. Marilee seemed overjoyed and to my embarrassment proudly showed the small gift to everyone, including her father.

Mr. Martin handed a small box to Arty and Gwen, before saying, "This is something your mother and I are giving you."

Arty, beaming at the gift, quickly opened the box, while Gwen watched.

"What's this?" Arty asked, as he held up a key.

Mr. Martin almost smiled as Mrs. Martin leaned her head on his shoulder while Mr. Martin said, "It's a key to this house."

"I don't understand?" a confused Arty said, shaking his head. "I've already got a key to the house."

"This is *the* key," Mr. Martin explained. "Your family's expanding, and you'll need a bigger place. Your mother and I have bought the Cherry farm south of here, and we'll move in the spring."

"But Dad," Arty began.

"There's no buts…you cannot enlist in the army and abandon your family!" Mr. Martin explained. "This is a fine house, and I need someone to look over the farm here. This is a good opportunity for you."

Looking at me, Mr. Martin added, "With the Brooks family moving on, we can run some cattle on that land."

Arty had not planned to be a farmer, but I sensed there were many things about married life that an adventuresome spirit like Arty did not foresee.

"Thanks, Dad," Arty finally said while grabbing Gwen's hand.

"Thank you," a more sincere Gwen replied.

"We're moving?" a surprised Marilee asked.

"In the spring," Mr. Martin explained.

"But," she began to protest.

"Don't 'but' me, Marilee. This is a big house, and I'm sure Arthur will be glad for you to come visit and…cook. Your mother and I have discussed it, and you can stay until the baby comes in May.

"Don't you think you should ask Gwen?" Marilee bluntly observed.

Looking as if the idea had not crossed his mind, Mr. Martin stared at his outspoken daughter.

"That'll be fine," Gwen quickly said. "Thank you, Mr. Martin…and Marilee. It would be wonderful if you could stay with me."

The younger boys were getting restless, and I was looking for any excuse to leave the watchful eye of Mr. Martin.

Leaning close to Marilee, I whispered, "Would you like to go for a walk…to try out my new shawl?"

"It's a scarf," Marilee corrected with a giggle. "I'll meet you on the porch."

As discreetly as possible, I left the Martin family to their various discussions and met Marilee outside. The afternoon had been pleasant, but the clear winter sky was now chilly as I wrapped the thick scarf around my neck. Marilee soon appeared with her wool coat and mittens.

"Nice shawl," she teased as she took my hand.

Blushing, I replied, "It keeps we warm."

Walking under the moonlight, my attention was drawn to how the soft light radiated on Marilee's cheeks while making her eyes sparkle.

"What do you think?" Marilee asked.

"About what?"

"Christmas at the Martins."

"I like the walk after," I replied. "How come you didn't tell me about Gwen?"

"What? You didn't notice on our trip to Shawnee?"

"No," I emphatically replied.

Marilee said with a mischievous grin, "You don't notice much."

"I guess not," I smiled. "I have a hard time thinking of Arty as a father."

Shrugging, Marilee answered, "It makes some sense why they married so quickly. You know Arty enlisted in the army…or tried, until Dad found out."

"When?"

"A few weeks before we came to Shawnee…a few weeks before he knew he was going to be a father. Arty feels like he's missing out," Marilee explained.

"He's got a lot on his plate now," I suggested. "A wife…a family…now a farm to be responsible for."

"I think it's Dad's way of helping him grow up," Marilee sighed. "Arty's always been kind of the wild child…doin' pretty much what he wanted. I think Dad sees a lot of himself in Arty."

"Really?" I replied, not seeing much connection at all between the free-spirited Arty and the stern Mr. Martin.

"Daddy hasn't always been old," Marilee smiled. "He rode through this country on the eastern Chisholm Trail before meeting my mother. I've heard him tell stories to old friends who used to come around…when he didn't think I was listening."

"Really?" I said again, having a hard time thinking of Mr. Martin as a roaming cowboy.

Marilee nodded her head.

"So what have you heard him say about me…when he didn't know you were listening?" I asked.

"Not that much," Marilee factually replied. "I don't think he's made his mind up about you yet. I know he was surprised when your dad didn't buy that land, but it sounds like the Martins and Brooks are going to be neighbors again on Cherry Hill."

"Where?"

"That's what the place is called, where Daddy's moving…you'll be close by," Marilee replied.

Stopping for a moment and looking at her, I said, "You know I'm not moving with them?"

I could tell by her expression, that Marilee had not completely thought of that possibility.

After thinking a moment, she smiled and said, "That's okay…I know where to find you."

We walked for a little longer, until Marilee began to shiver. I kissed her on the back porch, under the moonlight and said good-bye. It would be the last time I made the walk down the hill from the Martin farm to my home.

CHAPTER 50

The war in Europe dominated everyone's thoughts during the first, cold months of 1918. Lloyd was in France, but we had not heard from him since the brief telegram from New York. Marilee continued to write me through the spring, while her family prepared to move south of Salt Creek.

Gwen Martin had a difficult winter. Besides being an expectant mother for the first time, her father, Dr. Peaudane died of some ailment. With Guy off to fight in Europe, Gwen was the only remnant of the Peaudane family in the county. Grandma Nance also died that winter. Marilee said she passed peacefully in her sleep.

I continued to work at Ginn's Hotel and the Cooper Furniture Company. My typical day started around five o'clock, before I headed to school. Friends like Mary Sue McNally and even acquaintances like Laura Jones were gone, and I was older than everyone in my class, including some of the grammar school teachers. Work and school did not allow much time for socializing, but I had letters from Marilee, and she even came to visit about once a month.

My family moved a few weeks after Christmas. Mr. and Mrs. Martin expected to move close to Easter, but Gwen's baby arrived early so Mrs. Martin stayed at their old home for a few weeks to help with the baby.

About a week after Easter, I took advantage of the longer, warmer days to walk around town to an arched bridge north of the high school.

Trees bloomed along the creek banks as I spotted a familiar person staring blankly over the side of the small bridge.

"Mary Sue?" I asked, walking closer.

"Hey, Gill," she replied while wiping tears from her eyes.

"Are you okay?" I asked.

Putting on a brave smile, with a hint of the optimism I had known the year before, Mary Sue said, "I'm fine."

Looking at her puffy eyes, I observed, "You don't look fine."

Crying, she turned away, as I awkwardly said, "I'm sorry…I didn't—"

"It's not your fault," she quickly said, as she wiped her eyes and turned back around. "It's me being silly."

Seeing that we were alone, I responded, "You're not a person I've ever seen as silly. You want to talk about it?"

With a heavy sigh, she said, "I don't think talking will help."

"Could it hurt?"

With a faint smile, she said, "No…I guess it can't. Will you walk me back to town?"

"Sure."

After walking silently for a few yards, Mary Sue said, "Ralph's…Ralph's not…Things are different than I thought they would be."

Listening silently, I remembered how horrific Ralph Swan looked after coming back from his airplane accident.

"Ralph's…Ralph's—" she tried to say.

"How is Ralph?" I finally asked.

Grimacing, she cried in despair, "He's not well…you've seen him—"

"What do the doctors say?"

Shaking her head, Mary Sue said, "It's not that he's…disfigured…I…I think I could get over that…but he's not the same. He's not the same in the head since he's come back."

"It's tragic…for such an accident to happen," I tried to comfort.

"Do you think I'm a bad person?" Mary Sue blurted out.

"Of course not," I quickly replied.

Mary Sue looked at me as if she was not convinced and walked in silence.

"I think I may be a bad person," she finally said, as she lowered her head to look at her feet while continuing to walk listlessly.

"Why would you say that?" I exclaimed in disbelief.

"When Ralph was handsome and captain of the football team and wearing that striking uniform, I couldn't help but think how lucky I was to be his future wife. I had all these plans in my head about how our life would be, and now—"

Mary Sue continued to walk but did not talk for a few seconds.

"Now all I see is his burnt face, his missing limbs, and I wonder what I'll have to do to support him," she confessed. "I…I was perfectly willing to be his wife, but now…now I'm dreading everything."

Mary Sue, who had always been poised, controlled, and encouraging to everyone broke down in uncontrollable tears, as we approached the train station.

"What does your father say?" I asked.

Shaking her head, she said, "I don't know. He'll expect me to follow through with my commitment, I suppose. It would be the honorable thing to do."

Stopping on the sidewalk, I turned Mary Sue toward me and said, "Talk with your parents. I don't see that anyone would expect you—"

"Marriage is for better or worse," she cried.

"But you're not married," I reminded her. "You've promised to marry. You've considered it, but you're not married."

Collapsing into my arms, Mary Sue cried tears of sorrow and regret for a happiness lost that seemed sure only months earlier. I let her cry, while gently patting her back.

"Let's get you home," I suggested, as she buried her head in my shoulder.

"Gilbert?" the confused voice of Marilee whispered from behind me.

Turning around, with a distraught Mary Sue still clinging to my neck, I tried to say something to the wide-eyed Marilee. Before I could, Marilee turned and headed down the street. Mary Sue had not seen the encounter and continued to cry.

Wanting to chase after Marilee, I could not abandon the anguished Mary Sue in the middle of town. Taking her by the arm, I gently moved the teary-eyed girl toward her home, four or five blocks away. Before I could cross the street, the Martin's Studebaker sped by with Marilee behind the wheel glaring at me.

CHAPTER 51

It took half an hour to coax the crying Mary Sue back to her house. With every step, I envisioned Marilee driving further away from town. Marilee was a strong, independent young woman, but she was not a good driver, and I worried about her being on the road in a flustered state of mind.

"Would you like to come in?" Mary Sue politely asked, as she wiped her eyes with a lace handkerchief.

"Not tonight," I replied. "I've got to run."

"Thanks, Gill," she smiled. "I think I just needed someone to talk to."

"Things will work out," I tried to assure, as I left her at the door.

Trotting back toward the center of town, I wondered if I could catch the last train out of town, when I heard a female voice yell, "Gill!"

Turning around, Laura Jones, who lived a few houses from Mary Sue, came outside.

"What'cha doing?" the overly flirty girl asked.

Trying to be polite, I said, "I'm headed to town."

Smiling, Laura walked toward me to pull her skirt up slightly, showing her shoes.

"I bought some new shoes…for dancing," she playfully said.

"They look nice," I said, as I started to walk away.

"Gill!" she demanded, as I came to stop.

"Yes," I said impatiently.

In a superficially sweet voice, Laura Jones said, "Why don't you take me dancing tonight?"

"What?" I exclaimed.

"Take me dancing," she repeated. "We could go to Benson Park's pavilion or…if you could find a car, we could go to a place I know called the Potanole."

"The Potanole?" I replied.

"It's a place—" she began.

"I know where the Potanole is," I replied impatiently.

"There aren't that many boys around these days, and I thought—"

"I don't dance," I abruptly informed her. "And I've got to go."

"Gill—" she began.

Turning around, while still walking I shouted, "And you should not go to the Potanole!"

Running, to make up the time Laura Jones had wasted; I arrived at an empty train station with no more trains running south for the evening. Thinking for a moment, I headed up the street to the Cooper Furniture Company. Mr. Cooper was reluctant, but after telling my story, he let me borrow his delivery truck. Although not much more experienced at driving than Marilee, I headed to Romulus.

CHAPTER 52

The rough and bumpy road running toward the south part of the county caused the borrowed truck to bounce all the way to Romulus. A thirty-minute trip on Old Beck took almost an hour before arriving at the Martin home. I breathed a sigh of relief to see the Studebaker parked in front, meaning Marilee made it home safely. Marilee sat alone on the front porch with her ankles crossed looking more like the little girl I used to ignore than the young woman I had courted the past year.

Marilee squinted into the setting sun, not recognizing the truck I had borrowed. Her confusion turned to a pathetic frown when she saw me.

"Marilee—" I began.

"What are you doing here?" she asked angrily.

Walking to her, I said, "I came to see you."

"What for?" she sarcastically replied.

Looking at her angry eyes, I hesitated before saying, "I was…worried about you."

Coldly staring at me, Marilee cocked her head and adjusted her glasses uncomfortably before saying, "You didn't come to explain about…your girl."

Sitting down beside her, I said, "You're my girl."

"Didn't look like it back in town."

"What were you doing in Tecumseh?" I asked.

"I was going to surprise you," she replied. "Boy did I!"

After a moment of silence, Marilee said, "She's pretty…do you like that girl?"

"Mary Sue's a friend," I explained. "She's going through a tough time, and I was helping out."

"Is that what they call it now? Is that why you were hugging on her?" a concerned Marilee quizzed.

"Mary Sue's fiancé…he was hurt real bad in an accident…in the Army, learning to fly airplanes. He's lost an arm and a leg and is burned over most of his face. He was a…he was a good looking fellow, but now…it's been very hard on Mary Sue…she's usually very in control…kind of like you."

Marilee showed a hint of a smile as she continued to listen.

"I guess she held things in as long as she could, but kind of broke down. I just happened to be a shoulder to cry on," I explained. "I couldn't just leave her like that, and then you ran off…and I was more worried about you. I borrowed this truck and got here as quick as I could."

"So…she's not your girl?" Marilee asked anxiously.

With a smile, I said, "You're my girl."

"It's hard to tell sometimes," Marilee complained. "Seems like I make you do everything. I saw you with a pretty city girl, and I…well, I wonder if maybe I haven't just made up in my head how you feel about me."

Seeing a rare tear in Marilee's eye, I said something I had thought about, but had not had the courage to say.

"I want to marry you," I proclaimed. "I've wanted that for a while now."

"Gilbert?" Mrs. Martin greeted from the screen door. "I'm surprised to see you. I guess you've come to see the baby?"

Leaning into me, Marilee whispered, "Yes."

Smiling more than Mrs. Martin would have expected, I said to her, "I came to see Marilee, but I'd love to see the baby, too."

"Why are you keeping Gilbert out here?" Mrs. Martin asked.

"Just trying to see what's on his mind," Marilee smiled.

As I followed Mrs. Martin inside, she asked Marilee, "I thought you were going to Tecumseh this afternoon?"

"I didn't have to," she said while squeezing my hand.

Gwen cuddled the infant in a rocking chair. Only a few weeks old, the baby made cute, gurgling noises as he rested peacefully in Gwen's arms.

"Hey, Gill," Gwen cheerfully greeted. "Look what I've got!"

"I see," I replied smiling at her happiness. "He's a little thing."

"Yes," Gwen agreed, "Do you want to hold him?"

"No," I replied. "I'll just watch, if it's okay?"

"His name is Jackie," Gwen said.

"Was that your father's name?" I inquired.

"No," Gwen coldly replied. "He's named after Mr. Martin."

"I was sorry to hear about your father," I consoled.

Gwen did not reply and returned to nurturing her small child.

"Where's Arty?" I finally asked.

"He's out," Gwen pleasantly replied. "He's got a truck now and went down to the place by Cherry Hill to help Mr. Martin with some plowing today. Can you stay a while? He'll want to see you."

Looking at the clock and seeing the shadows lengthening outside, I said, "No…I really need to get back. I just came to see Marilee…and the baby."

"Come back when you can stay longer," Gwen smiled. "I'll tell Arty you came by."

On the front porch, Marilee said, "Thanks for coming. I'm sorry I overreacted…earlier."

"I'm just glad you made it home safe," I smiled.

"When are you going to ask?" Marilee grinned.

Thinking for a moment, I finally realized Marilee was talking about my earlier impromptu proposal.

"I thought I already asked," I replied with a smug smile.

With a flirtatious tilt of her head, Marilee said, "No…when are you going to ask Daddy?"

CHAPTER 53

Except for a ring and permission from Mr. Martin, I was now engaged to Marilee, although the proposal came out of my mouth so fast I hardly knew what I was saying. The thought of being with Marilee excited and frightened me at the same time. I was glad to be in school, which gave me a good excuse to put off having to talk to Mr. Martin.

Arriving at the hotel the next evening, I felt the need to check on Mary Sue McNally. It was a warm, breezy afternoon as I walked quickly toward the McNally home.

"Did you change your mind?" Laura Jones asked, as I passed by her house on the way to the McNally home.

"What?" I asked, surprised to see the attractive young woman sitting on a porch swing.

"Did you change your mind about taking me dancing?" she mockingly asked.

"Uh...No…I…like I said, I'm not a dancer," I stammered, as I was caught off guard by her playful banter.

Shaking her head, she said, "Too bad…I might have been able to show you a thing or two."

Walking quickly to avoid awkward conversation, I noticed Mary Sue standing on the porch a few houses away watching me. When Laura Jones saw Mary Sue, she retreated into her house without teasing me further.

"Hey, Gill," Mary Sue greeted when she could tell I was headed to her house. "Is Laura giving you a hard time?"

"I think so," I said bashfully.

"She disappears when she sees me now," Mary Sue said listlessly.

"How come?"

Motioning me to sit by her on the porch, Mary Sue said, "It might be that she doesn't want to be reminded of Ralph. We used to be competitors for him. He was so handsome and older."

I listened quietly, not sure how to respond. Laura was a beautiful young woman but did not have the common sense or pleasant personality of Mary Sue.

"She's seeing someone now," Mary Sue continued. "I don't think she wants anybody to know, because I see her sneak away from her mother. I don't think she wants to think about Ralph, either. We used to be friends, but now she just disappears whenever she sees me."

"How are you doing?" I finally asked.

With a brave smile, Mary Sue said, "I'm fine…I'm so sorry for making such a scene yesterday. I needed someone to talk to and…I'm glad it was you."

After a few seconds of awkward silence, I said, "I better get going. I just wanted to see if you were okay."

Before I could leave, Mary Sue said, "I've decided."

As I stopped to listen, she continued, "I've decided to stay with Ralph, no matter how long it takes for him to get well."

Sensing I was not going to say anything, she added, "He needs me now, and it will be the right thing to do. I'll feel better. It just wouldn't be right to abandon him now."

"Have you talked to him…have you talked to Ralph about the future…about his future?" I tactfully asked.

Turning away for a moment, she said, "No…not so directly I haven't, but he's so depressed right now. I'm sure everything seems hopeless compared to what he expected, but…I suppose I should talk with him."

Smiling at her, I said, "I'm sure you'll do the right thing, and…I hope everything works out."

"What's life without a little seasoning to make us appreciate the good things," Mary Sue smiled.

I left the optimistic Mary Sue and walked quickly past Laura Jones's house, hoping more than believing my friend would find happiness.

CHAPTER 54

By the summer of 1918, war still raged. The Russians were out of the conflict in the east, while the Americans started arriving in the west. The German army had driven within 75 miles of Paris, but the allied forces pushed them back. We still had no word from Lloyd. While anxiously waiting to hear of his whereabouts, we also dreaded any telegram, which might bring bad news. I watched newsreels with great interest and found myself searching the multitude of grimy faces to maybe see him. After a while, all the sad soldiers began looking alike.

I saw Mary Sue McNally a few times, as she bravely cared for Ralph Swan with a gallantry that would have matched any soldier's bravery. The increasingly quirky Laura Jones occasionally engaged me in conversation, as if she held some secret of which I was oblivious.

By the end of the school year, I completed my junior course work and planned to graduate the next year. Ginn and Mr. Cooper arranged for me to have a weeklong break in June to go visit my folks. Although anxious to see their new place and Marilee, I dreaded the trip back to the country, because I had promised to speak with Mr. Martin.

Pulling into the station at Romulus, the town had all but vanished. The train station had only one stop a day. Almost all of the stores and even the post office were closed. The cotton fields had played out in the area, and most of the farming moved south of Salt Creek. I decided to walk to the old Martin place where Gwen, Arty, and their son Jackie were living, to see if I could catch a ride to my family's new home.

Deciding to take a detour, I walked by Haskell Holiday's old place, which was rundown and grown over with weeds, on my way to the rock by Salt Creek. Emerging from the Cross Timber, I spotted the flat rock, where we had played as boys, and the small marker placed there for Lance Carrington.

I stood on the rock watching the muddy water flow gently within the banks, while the sun warmly shone on my face. I fondly remembered the many adventures I had as a boy on the banks of the river and surrounding woods. It seemed like it must have been longer than two years since I went away, and something about that day reminded me I was not a boy any longer. Water gurgled softly while a light breeze moved through the trees.

Kneeling for a moment to look at the small, stone marker, I heard a sound rustling from the trail. Squinting in the afternoon sun, I was surprised to see someone familiar emerge from the trees carrying a small bundle.

"Gwen?" I greeted from a distance, trying not to alarm her.

"Gill?" Gwen replied with a degree of surprise. "What are you doing here?"

"I came from Tecumseh today to see the folks, and thought I would take a little walk," I smiled. "I'm actually heading to your house to see if I could catch a ride down to my parent's place."

Now standing by me and looking at the marker, Gwen said, "You miss him too, I guess."

"Yeah," I replied. "I used to think about him every day, but now…well, I still miss him, but I stay busy with school."

Gwen reached to pluck a blossom from a nearby mimosa tree, before kneeling down to place the delicate, pink flower, beside the marker.

With a sigh she said, "I don't even have a picture of him. I wonder if I'll ever forget what Lance looked like?"

I watched her look at the marker while holding her small son.

"I like to go for walks sometimes, and I…I usually wind up here," Gwen smiled pleasantly. "I see why you guys always liked this place."

"We planned a lot of adventures down here," I smiled. "The mimosa tree has sure gotten big."

"The blooms are beautiful this year. I always loved mimosa trees," Gwen said.

"I see you've got a walking partner," I smiled.

Gwen held the baby so I could see him better and said, "We've been walking when the days are warm. Doc Sanders said it's good to get him out in the sun a little. It's been a lonely time, but he's good company, don't you think?"

Enjoying how much Gwen admired her small prize, I replied, "Looks like it…he must be a good listener."

"He is," Gwen laughed.

Looking closer at the baby, I said, "He's got the prettiest eyes."

"They always look sleepy don't they?" Gwen noted.

"And his little ears," I smiled.

"He's a good baby," Gwen assured.

"I can see you're proud," I replied.

Seeming to want to change the subject, Gwen asked, "So what are you doing home?"

"I hadn't been down to see the new place and wanted to see Mom and Dad," I stated.

"And Marilee?" Gwen smiled.

"Well, of course, I want to see Marilee," I stammered.

"She's at the house today," Gwen teased.

"Your house?" I questioned.

Nodding her head playfully, Gwen said, "She thought you might be through here in a day or two."

With a mischievous grin, Gwen said, "Congratulations."

Looking at her with a puzzled expression, it took me a second to understand her meaning.

"Marilee told me," Gwen said with raised eyebrows.

"I guess Marilee would tell you," I surmised.

"And," Gwen smiled. "What I know Arty knows."

Shaking my head, I said, "Maybe he's talked to Mr. Martin for me. That's what I'm really here to do."

"Arty's pretty good at keeping secrets," Gwen stated. "I don't know what he's up to half the time. I think your secret's safe, and…I think you'll find that Mr. Martin's not that bad. He's been very good to me and Arty."

"How is Arty?" I asked.

With a shrug of her shoulders, Gwen said, "Fine, I guess. He's…well I think he's a little bored at the farm. If you noticed Romulus on the way in, there's not much left. You know Arty; he likes a little more social life than we have around here."

I nodded, thinking how Arty always seemed to be so comfortable in the city.

"Would you like to hold the baby?" Gwen asked, changing the subject.

"Oh…I don't—"

"Go ahead," Gwen laughed. "He won't break."

Taking the small infant, I held him gingerly in my arms. He squirmed gently as I admired his small features, flat little nose, and droopy eyes. Baby Jackie seemed content to stare at me and stick his little tongue out.

"He's a handsome boy," I complemented.

"Thanks," Gwen beamed. "He's a wonderful baby."

After a few moments, I carefully handed him back to his mother. Gwen cradled him securely in her arms, and I could tell she was a natural at being a mother.

"Do you want to walk me home and see Marilee?" Gwen asked.

I nodded as we headed toward the old Martin home. As we approached, Marilee straightened her apron before running to hug me.

Arty drove up in a truck before dinner. While Gwen tended to the baby, Arty and I sipped sweet tea on the porch enjoying the last beams of sunshine from the summer day.

"It's good to see you, Gill," Arty sighed while the women worked inside.

"It's good to be back," I assured. "Things look like they're going pretty good for you."

"I guess," Arty shrugged. "Got a truck to get back and forth from this place to the new farm. It's nice having Dad down there. The soil's not near played out, so he's planting cotton down there, and I'm running cows up on this place."

"I never thought I'd see the Martins running cattle," I observed.

"Dad's pretty good at figurin' out farming, and he figured it'd be best to give these fields a rest. Don't matter to me much. I'd rather not tend to cotton."

"So you like runnin' cows?"

With a sly smile, Arty said, "It's only a little better than cotton, in my book."

Arty had always been a reluctant farmer. He worked hard enough to pacify his father, but never had the passion for farming that the rest of the Martins possessed.

"How's school?" he asked.

"Fine. I'll be finished this time next year."

"Still workin' in that store?"

"Yeah."

Shaking his head, he said, "You're the smart one. Don't think I'd leave city living if I had a set-up like you."

Smiling, I had a hard time imagining Arty getting up at five o'clock each morning to cook and clean up after other people.

"Why don't you go back to school?" I asked.

"No…I'm too old, got a family now…and Dad'd never allow it…besides, I'm still a fair bit smarter than you."

Shaking my head at his good-natured kidding, I replied, "I'll never convince you otherwise."

"Seriously though, what're you goin' to do after school?" he asked.

"I don't exactly know," I replied. "I like working in business. I figure I'll get a job as a clerk…maybe even a salesman someday."

"How 'bout ownin' a store?"

"Own a business?" I asked. "That'd be my dream, I guess…but I'd have to work for years."

"Maybe not years," Arty replied with a familiar glimmer in his eye.

Arty Martin had always been a master of thinking up ideas and then convincing me to go along. Many of his schemes required a lot more work and inconvenience on my part than his. Not every idea was a bad one, but I'd been involved in enough of Arty's shenanigans to be wary.

"Arty, I've seen that look in your eye before…and it generally means trouble," I tried to defend.

"Not this time!" Arty said in a whisper, as he leaned close to me. "I've got some deals workin' and saving a little cash…you're marryin' Marilee, I hear."

As I blushed awkwardly at Arty knowing of my unofficial proposal, he added, "Oh yeah, I know all about that. I told you, I'm smart."

"Smart nothing," I chided Arty. "I know Marilee told Gwen and Gwen told you."

"Like I said, smart. You're not giving me credit. I'm the one married Gwen, wasn't I?"

I shrugged pretending to be indifferent and asked in a low whisper, "Speaking of which, how is married life? I mean really?"

With a frown, Arty said, "It's definitely got its advantages…if you know what I mean. Gwen…well Gwen's great…never talks back…thinks the best of everyone…but I got to tell you, it ain't all roses and candy. She can get a mood and cry for no reason at all.

Sometimes I just have to leave the house till she gets out of it. And since the baby…I mean I love having the little tyke around, but he wakes me up in the night and takes all Gwen's time. I'm mean *all* of Gwen's time."

Arty stopped abruptly from discussing his family life and grinned, "Don't think I don't know what you're doing. You're getting' me off the subject of you wantin' to marry that ornery sister of mine. I know she's not quite as ugly as she used to be, but you have no idea what you're getting into my friend. You think it's goin' to be huggin' and kissin,' which with me thinkin' of Marilee, is disgusting!"

I had to laugh at the way Arty was taking control of the conversation to tease me.

"But," he continued, "I believe that Marilee has cast a spell on you like a witch or something…and you're not getting away. Dad has money set aside for his kids…you know to help 'em get a start. He had money for Ethan and me…and I figure he's got some for Marilee too. I figure I take what I got, keep tryin' to put a little more back and we take what you and Marilee are goin' to get and wham! We've got a little stake to get a store on our own."

"You don't know the first thing about running a store," I tried to explain.

Arty smiled, strangely and said, "Why do you think I need you?"

"Besides," I continued. "I don't know how excited your dad's goin' to be to find out Marilee's marrying the son of one of his renters?"

Asking tentatively, I added, "Does Mr. Martin know?"

"Heck no," Arty said emphatically. "Do you think he'd let Marilee out of his sight and let me chaperone if he thought it was serious?"

"So he won't approve?" I replied dejectedly.

"No," Arty bluntly answered, and then in his likable way he added, "but his precious little Marilee always gets what she wants from him, and she wants you."

"Supper!" Marilee announced from the screen door.

"We're coming," Arty said in the resentful tone he had used with Marilee since she was old enough to bother him.

"Think about what I said," Arty whispered as we headed toward the door.

As I entered behind Arty, Marilee gently tugged my arm to stop me at the door and said with a big smile, "Don't worry Gilbert. My brother might be right for once. I do usually get what I want…and I want you."

CHAPTER 55

The next morning, Marilee and I drove to my parent's new home. After dropping me off, Marilee went to her father's house, and I promised to come later for supper. Dad waved at Gordon to come in from the fields when he saw me, and Mother waddled out of the house to hug me tight. It was the first time in months we had been together, and it was a sobering reminder that Lloyd was far away.

Lloyd, they supposed, was still in Europe, but he had not written a single time since his arrival. Mother diligently wrote and was hopeful of receiving a reply.

The new house looked a lot like the old places we had before, and Dad already talked about trying to make a go of it somewhere else, if this harvest did not work out.

By late afternoon, I started the walk up Cherry Hill to see the new Martin home. The excitement of seeing Marilee was subordinate to the dread and terror I felt at the prospect of talking with Mr. Martin. The Martin home sat on the very pinnacle of the small hill. Like the old place by Romulus, the Martin farm looked organized and prosperous.

Supper was delicious, but without Arty at the table, conversation was sparse. In the past, Arty added entertainment and Grandma Nance provided awkward tension. Both were now absent as I painfully tried to maintain a dialogue with the rest of the Martin family. Even Marilee was unable to help, as any topic I chose brought a systematic disagreement from Mr. Martin.

After dinner, the boys went to finish chores in the barn while Marilee and her mother cleaned the kitchen. With a look and a nod, Marilee reminded me to speak to her father this evening.

"Did you plant cotton in all the fields?" I asked, trying to find something with which Mr. Martin might agree.

"Of course not," Mr. Martin sharply responded. "It would be foolish to put all your eggs in one basket. Diversification is the secret. You make your best bet on what crops will be in demand, but always hedge your bets, when possible."

"I see. So, the land here is good?"

With a frown at having to explain the basics of agriculture to a novice, he answered, "The land's not much different, but hasn't been planted in cotton…yet. Cotton's hard on land. That's why I'm giving the place near Romulus a rest. If Arty will focus, he can make good raising cattle until we can plant again."

"Sounds like a good plan," I said, forcing a smile.

"Planning's important," Mr. Martin lectured. "It gives a person a direction, establishes purpose. Life may take you a lot of directions, but if a man has a plan, he can always get back on track."

I listened, struggling with what to say next.

In his stern, commanding voice, Mr. Martin asked, "Do you have a plan, Mr. Brooks?"

"I…I…think I'm working towards being in business of some kind," I stammered before remembering from earlier conversations that Mr. Martin did not think much about businessmen.

"There's more to life than a man's occupation," Mr. Martin snarled. "Did you have a purpose this evening?"

"Yes…I…Yes, Mr. Martin," I said, trying to find the courage to speak openly. "I've come to ask about Marilee."

"What about Marilee?" Mr. Martin replied. "Are you going to ask my permission to call on her…formally?"

Surprised at the question, my eyebrows wrinkled as I continued, "No...we've been...I mean we've been writing...and seeing each other for a while now."

"I see," he stared coldly.

"I came to ask your permission to marry Marilee," I finally admitted.

The request was greeted with silence and an unbelieving stare.

"You're asking me...you're saying you would like to marry my Marilee?" he said with a degree of uncertainty.

"Yes sir," I meekly replied.

"You've discussed this with Marilee?" he asked pointedly.

"Yes, sir," I confirmed. "In fact, she's the one who suggested it was time for me to talk to you."

"Marilee!" Mr. Martin shouted, while continuing to stare at me.

In a moment, Marilee walked casually into the room with a dishcloth in her hand.

"Yes?" she asked.

In a tense tone, Mr. Martin said, "This...boy tells me he has feelings for you...and...I need to know if you've been up to something I should know about."

"Daddy," Marilee replied stoically. "Gilbert and I have known each other since...well, as long as I can remember. If you haven't noticed, I've had him to dinner several times, and he's been around the house regularly. We're in love and we're going to be married."

"I...I won't permit that...you're too young—"

"I'm older than mother was when you married her," Marilee informed.

An agitated Mr. Martin, quickly replied, "She was too young."

With a calming smile, Marilee added, "Gilbert's asking, Daddy...I'm not. I've made up my mind."

Mr. Martin was rarely at a loss for words, but his eyes darted from one side of the room to the other as he searched for something to say to his daughter.

Marilee walked to him, placed her hand on his shoulder, and said, "You know me, Daddy. Don't you trust me?"

"I trust you, but—"

"Gilbert has always been honorable towards me," Marilee frankly assured.

"Mrs. Martin!" Mr. Martin shouted.

In a rush, Mrs. Martin entered the room quickly, asking frantically, "What is it?"

"Your daughter!" he replied. "She's gotten this young man to propose…He's—"

With a giggle and a slight squeal, Mrs. Martin, said, "Oh! Marilee, I'm so happy for you."

"What?" Mr. Martin roared.

Looking at her husband, Mrs. Martin said, "Surely this cannot be a surprise to you?"

"Surely it is!" Mr. Martin responded.

Looking at her husband with a sly smile, Mrs. Martin said, "If you were as observant about people as you are about your fields, Marilee's engagement would not be a surprise to you."

Mrs. Martin then looked at the corner where I had been standing and said, "Congratulations, Gilbert. I'm so happy. I know you and Marilee will be happy together."

"Wait a minute!" Mr. Martin shouted. "I have not given my consent!"

"Well," Marilee coaxed, while smiling at her mother, "give your permission."

Mr. Martin, realizing his women outnumbered him, decided to take the opportunity to put his mark on this relationship.

"I will give my consent, but there are some terms," he began.

"Daddy—" Marilee interrupted.

Without paying attention to Marliee's protest, he continued, "Marilee's too young, so you will wait until she's eighteen."

"Yes, sir," I agreed. "We were planning to wait until after I graduate next spring."

Irritated at my comment, Mr. Martin went on to say, "Not only that, you must have a steady job and the ability to support my girl."

"Yes, sir."

"I won't have no rushed-up wedding like Arty had," he firmly stated.

"Jack!" Mrs. Martin protested.

"I want my girl married in a church, and I expect you to be a gentleman," he scolded.

"Yes, sir," I contritely agreed.

"Marilee," he said pointing his finger. "I'll expect you to only go courting with a proper chaperone."

"Thanks, Daddy," Marilee smiled, while hugging her father's neck.

After hugging her mother, Marilee turned to me and said, "Let's go for a walk, Gilbert."

Mr. Martin wanted to protest, but Mrs. Martin gave him a look he would not challenge. We went on our walk on this warm, summer evening, as I held her hand. Marilee looked radiant in the glimmering moonlight. Feeling a tremendous sense of relief, to have spoken to Mr. Martin, I walked back to my parent's small home to tell them the news. My summer break would be short, but I now anticipated returning to school in a few days with a renewed sense of purpose—to find a job that would support a wife.

CHAPTER 56

The realities of the war in Europe tempered my feelings of good fortunes about being engaged in the summer of 1918. A German offensive in the spring had driven to within seventy-five miles of Paris, and there was genuine fear the continent would fall before General Pershing could fully deploy the American Expeditionary Force in the trenches.

The day before returning to Tecumseh, I saw my mother cry as she held a single piece of paper in her hand. Fearing the worst, I was quickly relieved when she handed me a short one-page letter from Lloyd.

The brief note explained he was in France near the town of Toul. While setting up artillery, he encountered mustard gas. Lloyd was fine, but he had stayed in the sick tent for a few days and talked a nurse into writing his letter. Lloyd said he would return to duty in a few days and asked Mother not to worry. The handwriting was obviously not Lloyd's, but the brief, concise tone was definitely his way of talking. Mother fixed chicken that night, and Dad played tunes on his banjo while Gordon kept rhythm on an old washboard. It had been nearly a year since we had heard from Lloyd, and all the Brooks family was in a festive mood to hear he was alive and out of danger—at least for a few days.

Marilee traveled back with me to Gwen and Arty's place, where she was going to help with the baby. Walking up to the house, we could tell Gwen had been crying. She held a telegram about Guy Peaudane in her shaking hand. Shrapnel from an artillery shell bursting nearby had hit Guy, who was serving as an officer with a supply detachment. He survived but was wounded badly and had been moved to a hospital near Paris. The message said nothing else.

Marilee and I tried to convince Gwen things would be fine. I did not have any basis for such optimism but hoped for a speedy recovery for Guy. Arty came to the house after dark, as Gwen was beginning to count her blessings that at least Guy was in a hospital and being looked after. Arty did not have much to say that evening. He and Gwen went to bed early, while I spent most of the night on the porch, planning my future with Marilee. In the morning, I caught the train back to Tecumseh.

Although Ginn had never met my brother Lloyd, she listened attentively to my stories about my brother and Guy Peaudane. I tried to be hopeful but had difficulty getting the image of Ralph Swan out of my thoughts when thinking about Guy's wounds.

As summer closed I continued to work at the Cooper Furniture Company when a familiar face walked by the store one day with a renewed bounce in her step.

"Mary Sue!" I yelled as I stepped outside.

Turning on her heels, Mary Sue McNally smiled and walked toward me.

"How are you doing?" I asked, as she looked more like her old self.

"Great," Mary Sue replied. "I've been talking to Ralph, and we've decided to wait to be married until…well until he's better and I finish school."

"What school?" I asked.

"I've decided to go to the Normal School in Edmond and learn to teach. It'll take two years, but I think it'll be wise for me to have a profession…at least for a while."

"That's great," I said. "I know you'll be a terrific teacher."

"I hope so," she smiled.

"I know so," I replied.

Mary Sue was off to shop for some things for school, which started in less than a week.

By September, the world seemed to be making sense. The Allies stopped the German push toward Paris and began an offensive of their own. American forces were in the field, and the new men and energy seemed to make a difference. We learned Lloyd made a full recovery and Guy Peaudane was also healing, although still in a hospital in Paris. The Americans were heavily involved in the Battle of Saint-Mihiel in France. Looking on the map, I saw the battle was only a few miles from the town of Toul, where Lloyd had been staying. I waited every day hoping a telegram would not come.

The war, which seemed like it might last forever in the spring, ended abruptly on November 11, 1918. School let out, and the whole town celebrated the victory and the news that our troops would be coming home. Later that month, however, a single shot rang out in the still of the night that turned the celebration into mourning for a few citizens in Tecumseh.

Ralph Swan never recovered from the serious injuries received during flight training in Texas. Mary Sue McNally pledged to stay by his side, but Ralph died that November night with a bullet in his head. The official report said it was an accident while he was cleaning a hunting rifle. Whatever the true cause and whatever those left behind needed to believe, Ralph Swan was finally out of the misery his life had become since leaving for the war.

Mary Sue McNally sobbed at the funeral. Since Thanksgiving was the next week, she stayed in town a few days. I went to see her several nights, and she appeared to be coping as well as possible. She had decided to stay in school and planned to return to Edmond after Thanksgiving. Mary Sue McNally was an extraordinary person with an inner strength I admired. I said good-bye to her on the porch of her family's home the night before she returned to school. It was a cold, clear night as I walked back toward my room at Ginn's Hotel.

A truck parked in front of Laura Jones's house caused me to move to the other side of the street when I noticed two people inside the fogging windows. I was almost past the vehicle when the door suddenly opened, and a slightly intoxicated Arty Martin stumbled out. Perplexed and confused, I looked inside expecting to see Gwen, but was shocked to see a ruffled Laura Jones.

"Hey, Gilbert," she said flirtatiously, as she had obviously been drinking.

Arty, more shocked to see me than I was to see him, said sternly to her, "You need to go inside now."

"Arty—" she began to whine.

"Right now!" he demanded, as she shrugged before stumbling toward the house.

After a moment of silence, Arty said, "I know this looks bad—"

"What are you doing?" I demanded.

"I'm just dropping Laura—"

"No excuses, Arty!" I replied sternly. "What are you doing?"

"Hey," Arty defended. "I met Laura after seeing her with you. She likes to dance. I like to dance...we're...we're just friends who like to dance."

"Where? At the Potanole?"

"Sometimes."

Looking at the stars above and trying to think, I finally said, "Are you crazy?"

Arty did not respond.

"You've got a wife and baby at home," I scolded. "You've got Gwen...and she's three times the woman that Laura Jones is!"

"Gill—" Arty tried to defend.

"We all loved her, Arty," I interrupted. "Me. Lance...how could you do this to poor Lance? You're out at this time of night with Laura Jones? How can you do this to Gwen?"

"I'm tired of hearing about poor Lance," Arty tersely replied. "I'm the one that's having to take care of everything."

His comment about Lance temporarily stunned me, as I stared blankly at him.

Recovering his composure somewhat, Arty said more assertively, "What have I done to Gwen? Give her a nice home? Take her in when even her old man knew her reputation was ruined?"

Shaking his head and walking closer to me Arty continued by pointing a finger into my chest and saying, "You don't know as much as you think, buddy boy. I'm not doing nothing with Laura Jones but having a good time. She likes to dance, and I like to dance. Gwen doesn't have time. You don't know what it's like to have a woman and have her spend all her time with a baby and no time for me."

Almost shouting, Arty continued, "I'm just having some fun, and I'm not doing nothing to Gwen!"

Taking a deep breath to give Arty time to settle down, I hesitated before finally asking, "Do you really believe that?"

Looking me in the eye, Arty said, "I was breaking it off tonight. It's not like I've cheated on Gwen or nothing. It's kind of like you being engaged to my little sister, and I hear from a good source—"

Arty pointed up to Laura Jones's house and continued, "That you've got a little friend, too. You wouldn't want Marilee to find out about her would you?"

"That's completely different," I sharply defended.

With a friendly smile, Arty said, "Is it really? The girl's awfully pretty, and I hear from Marilee you've already been caught with her once. What do you think Marilee would think if I told her how many times you've been here for that pretty little girl...a girl who don't have a fiancé anymore?"

"You wouldn't—"

"You're right," Arty smiled. "I wouldn't think of telling Marilee about something that would do you no good, and you're not going to mention anything to Gwen…and particularly not anything to Marilee about Laura Jones."

I glared angrily at Arty Martin as he calmly looked at me.

After a moment, Arty put his arm around me and said, "Listen. You're right to be upset…and I'm wrong. I don't know what I was thinking. A girl like Laura Jones is bad news…I…I really was going to break it off…tonight. I'm glad you saw me. It's the jolt I needed to get back to my senses. Gwen's the greatest, and she deserves the best in me."

Looking me over, Arty shook me gently and said, "Are we friends?"

Unable to stay angry at Arty for any length of time, I said, "Of course, we're friends."

"You agree no good can come from our girls finding out about my stupidity," he reasoned.

Reluctantly, I nodded my head. I could see no reason for Gwen to have to endure my suspicions over such a silly girl as Laura Jones.

"I'm a changed man," Arty smiled. "I could always count on you to keep me on the straight and narrow."

"God knows you need someone," I grudgingly admitted.

"Well, that job is now Mrs. Gwen Martin's," Arty proclaimed. "I think she's the only one that makes me whole."

"She's got her work cut out," I quipped.

"I got to get home," Arty lamented. "It's getting late."

"Are you okay to drive?" I asked, since Arty had obviously been drinking some.

"Absolutely," he replied. "This old truck knows these ruts so well that I hardly have to steer."

"Are you sure?" I asked again. "You can sleep in my room."

"And leave Gwen alone…with that inquisitive sister of mine? I don't think so," he smiled. "I've already made enough mistakes for one night."

Seeing I was not totally convinced, Arty added in a serious tone, "I'll be fine."

Climbing into his truck, Arty rolled down the window and said, "Thanks, Gill. You're the best."

I did not feel like the best, as I watched Arty drive down the dark road.

It was a few weeks before I saw Arty over Christmas break. He seemed to be back to his senses and very attentive to his family. Arty had the ability to make people believe in him and even with his faults; one always hoped the best for Arty. Thinking of Arty's family responsibilities was sobering for me. As I returned to Tecumseh to finish my last semester of high school, I was beginning to feel the pressure of finding a job and making my way in the world to support a family of my own.

CHAPTER 57

One constant during my time in Tecumseh had been the early mornings in Ginn's dining room. The smell of brewed coffee, sizzling bacon, fried eggs, fresh baked biscuits, and simmering grits greeted me every morning. There was also the constant clattering of dishes and the buzz of gossip in the air adding to the dining room's hectic atmosphere. These sights and sounds had become so familiar that I paid them little attention.

The day Leland Holiday showed up for breakfast at Ginn's dining room, however, was the exception. Leland had traded in his silver spurs and broad-brimmed hat for a suit and shiny shoes. The memory of his threats against Lance Carrington still made my blood run cold, as he ate casually with a small group of nicely dressed men. Trying to avoid his attention, I shuddered when his menacing eyes met mine. I could immediately tell he recognized me.

Staying in the back as much as possible to evade Leland Holiday, I fried eggs while letting one of the other boys work out front. After fifteen minutes, however, Ginn summoned me as she sat next to Leland Holiday. Shuffling across the floor, while trying not to look fearful, I obeyed Ginn's request.

"Gill, I'd like you to meet Mr. Holiday," Ginn smiled.

Nodding awkwardly, I shook Leland Holiday's hand when he extended it.

"I know this boy," Leland announced cordially.

"Really!" a surprised Ginn replied.

"Yeah," I muttered unenthusiastically.

"You're the Brooks boy, aren't you?" he asked.

"Yes…sir," I acknowledged.

"Yeah, I know this boy," Leland smiled under his thick mustache.

Looking back at Ginn, Leland continued, "His folks had a horse stole that drowned down in the South Canadian. Bad business, it was. I believe the thief drowned as well."

I listened silently to Leland Holiday talk about my friend who he had all but chased into the river.

"You used to work for Guy Peaudane, didn't you?" Leland questioned, although he had to have known the answer.

I nodded in affirmation.

With an artificial laugh, Leland Holiday continued, "This boy's the great molasses killer of Romulus."

"What?" Ginn smiled.

"He got spooked by the wind and shot up the Peaudane General Store," Leland mocked. "Put a bullet in a perfectly good barrel of molasses."

Laughing, Ginn warily asked, "You didn't?"

Continuing, Leland said, "Thought he heard a burglar, but I looked around and didn't see anything but the wind."

"Someone broke the window," I defended, before receiving a sharp stare from Leland.

"The thieving and debauchery that goes on in this county," Ginn sighed. "I hope there's something you can do about it if you're sheriff."

Cutting his eyes away from me to smile graciously at Ginn, he said, "With your help and your vote, I think we can."

I excused myself before being tempted further to explain that Guy Peaudane always suspected Leland himself of the attempted break in.

As I walked away, Leland said, "What happened to that Peaudane girl?"

Turning around, I said, "She's married now."

"That's right," he smirked wickedly. "She married old Arty Martin, didn't she?"

"Yes."

"You ever make it back down to Romulus?" Leland asked.

"Yes."

"Tell her I still think about her sometimes," Leland said with a cold hard stare.

Walking away without answering his innuendo, my heart sank at the thought of Leland Holiday as sheriff of the county.

"What a nice man," Ginn said, after Leland left. "He's thinking of running for sheriff next year."

"He's not so nice," I stoically said.

"What?" Ginn replied.

"I've known him a long time, and he's not all that he seems," I tried to convince without saying more.

"He seemed very likable," Ginn stated.

"You ever heard of the Potanole?" I said.

Ginn looked sternly at me and asked, "What do you know about the Potanole?"

"I've been there," I bashfully admitted.

"To the Potanole?" Ginn gasped. "I didn't even think it was a real place! Were the women…were they—"

"I don't know anything about the women," I assured. "But I know Leland Holiday owns part of the place."

"The man thinking of running for sheriff is a bootlegger?" Ginn asked in disbelief.

"I think so," I confirmed.

"Well," she sighed in a tone of indignation. "I guess you can't always go on appearances."

"I guess not," I agreed.

Ginn was a wise old woman. It would take me years to learn the lesson that it is more valuable to be trusted than to be liked.

CHAPTER 58

Most men of influence ate breakfast at least occasionally at Ginn's dining room. Located across the street from the courthouse, it was the perfect place to have a meal, rest your feet, and listen to the town's gossip. I was too busy to pay attention to much of the town talk, but I could not help but notice Ginn actively spreading the truth about Leland Holiday's past to her patrons.

Leland Holiday's chances for public office diminished with his reputation for operating in the gray areas of the law, but his good fortunes continued. With his smooth tongue and veneer of confidence, the Rock Island Railroad employed Leland as their chief of security, giving him opportunity to move products freely around the county.

By March, American troops began coming home from the war. Mother received a telegram that Lloyd arrived safely in New Orleans. After traveling to Memphis, he would be decommissioned and then take the train to Shawnee.

The Monday before Easter, the Brooks family arrived at the large Rock Island Depot in Shawnee to meet Lloyd's train. The depot, built with native red brick and sand-colored stone archways, hummed with activity.

Lloyd stepped off the train wearing a wrinkled olive-drab uniform with half a cigarette in his mouth. He looked older and thinner than before. His eyes had a hollow gaze to them, and his high cheekbones appeared more chiseled. Otherwise, he looked like the same easy-going Lloyd as he smiled broadly when seeing us.

My brother always had an effortless way of walking which made him appear to be conserving his energy. At the sight of his mother, however, Lloyd dropped his bags and ran to hug her. Dad grinned broadly, as he patted Lloyd on the back before embracing him.

After greeting us, Lloyd asked, "Where's Gordon?"

"He's here," Mother explained. "He just went down the street for a minute."

"You'll be surprised when you see him," I cheerfully informed.

"Why?" Lloyd asked with a look of some puzzlement.

"He's bigger than both of us," I replied.

"Naw," Lloyd disagreed.

"Yip," Dad smiled, still holding on to Lloyd's shoulder.

"Well," Lloyd smiled. "I'm a trained fighter now, and I can still take the both of you. I'm still number one around here."

"I don't know," I smiled.

"Tell us where you been," Dad said eagerly.

"Been all over France, settin' up field artillery," Lloyd explained. "Don't know all the places, but I got into some mustard gas near Toul that put me in the hospital."

"Sounds rough," I observed.

"Not as bad as those poor devils in the trenches," Lloyd shrugged. "I got to sleep inside most nights. The artillery was usually several miles from that mess. Thing is, when they'd find out where the guns were, they'd start shelling us and we'd have to move again. That's pretty much all I done was set up guns and break 'em down."

"At least you're back safe, now," Mother beamed.

About that time, Gordon returned to our group.

"Who's this?" Lloyd gasped, looking at our younger brother Gordon.

Gordon, the youngest of the Brooks brothers, was only fourteen years old, but was taller and heavier than Lloyd or I. He still had a hint of a baby face, but he'd been shaving for months.

"Hey, Lloyd," Gordon greeted.

Looking at me, Lloyd grinned and said, "Looks like you're the number three brother now."

Walking up to Gordon, Lloyd placed both hands on Gordon's shoulders and said, "You've grown."

"A little," Gordon shyly grinned.

"Tell us more about France," Dad insisted.

"It's pretty country…the part that ain't been torn up by the war. Don't think it's warm enough for cotton, but they had all kinds of grains…and grapes…you can buy wine there nearly as cheap as water."

"How 'bout that nurse, that wrote us?" Dad teased.

"She was nice, to write my letter and all," Lloyd blushed. "There's some pretty French girls all right, but there's forty soldiers for any pretty girl…I'm sorry I didn't write more…but…I stayed busy."

Lloyd was a good farmer and good with his hands, but reading and writing were subjects he tried to avoid.

"It's okay," Mother smiled. "You're back home now."

With a big smile, Lloyd said, "It's great to be back."

As if remembering something, Lloyd said, "I saw Lance, once…at least I think it was him."

All of us went silent, realizing Lloyd had not read any of our letters or at least had not heard about Lance.

"That can't be, son," Mother replied. "I thought you knew. Lance died a few weeks after you left."

"Huh?" Lloyd responded.

"He drowned," Dad explained. "Got in some trouble with the Holidays and killed Haskell."

"It was self defense," I quickly added.

"He was headin' across the river tryin' to get to Ada on Old Betsy. The river was high and swept 'em both away," Dad continued, with a hint of sadness in his voice.

"Guess that's why that feller' didn't look when I hollered," Lloyd reasoned. "Sorry to hear about that. Lance was a good guy. I was worried 'bout 'em. Those boys got in a tight spot in the Argonne, but I guess Lance already found his tight spot."

"You probably don't know we've moved either?" Dad questioned.

"What?" a surprised Lloyd answered.

"We left the old place last year…the fields just give out, so we've moved south close to Cherry Hill," Dad replied.

"Is it good land?" Lloyd asked.

"Pretty good," Dad shrugged. "Mr. Martin bought a place nearby, so we're still neighbors. Did you read any of our letters?"

Lloyd kicked his feet on the ground and said, "I didn't have much time, I kept meaning to."

It did not occur to me before that Lloyd had not written us because he could not write or read more than an advertising sign. He had been in Europe, truly alone, not knowing anything happening from home except what he heard from others.

"You better tell him," Dad smiled while looking at me.

"What?" Lloyd asked.

"I'm engaged," I beamed. "I'm going to marry Marilee."

"That skinny little Martin girl?" Lloyd teasingly smiled.

"Well, yeah," I responded. "Anyway, she's not so skinny anymore…she kind of grew up."

Rubbing me on the head, Lloyd quipped, "She's always been better lookin' than you…and at least she knows how to fry pies! Where's Gwen at? I guess if you're sweet on Marilee, Gwen must be lonesome?"

"She married Arty Martin," I replied.

"Huh?" Lloyd shrugged. "I wouldn't have thought that."

We spent another half hour on the train platform, getting Lloyd caught up on all the local news. He seemed surprised about Arty and Gwen, but seemed almost pleased to find out Ethan Martin was married to one of his old girlfriends and living close to Cherry Hill. We told him about Guy Peaudane being hurt and questioned Lloyd if he had seen him. Lloyd explained there were millions of soldiers everywhere, and he had not been aware that Guy Peaudane was even in Europe, much less wounded. Lloyd showed us his medal for being wounded but did not want to talk much about the actual fighting.

By the afternoon, we took the train back south. I learned Gordon had an interest in going to high school. Dad did not seem thrilled with the idea, but Mother asked me to check with Ginn to see if Gordon could possibly work at the hotel for room and board. I got off the train in Tecumseh while the family traveled south to the home Lloyd had never seen.

CHAPTER 59

By May 1919, warm weather already created several thunderstorms, one of which forced the graduation at Tecumseh High School into the gymnasium. Marilee planned for weeks to come to the graduation, but I was surprised to see my father, mother, and Gordon with her. Dad wore the same suit he had bought when he went to Tecumseh to buy land. Lloyd stayed at home, and Mother explained he did not like being in crowded places.

I finished high school in three years and took a couple of classes at Western Business College in Shawnee. At nearly twenty years old, I was looking forward to putting my education to good use.

Mr. Cooper wrote a letter of introduction to Mr. Kib Warren of the Warren & Smith Hardware Store in Shawnee. Mr. Warren, a former county commissioner and postmaster in Shawnee, had once lived in Tecumseh and now was part owner of the store. The Warren & Smith Hardware Store sold everything, including tools, hardware, furniture, and even appliances. Mr. Warren's partner bought a posting machine to keep accounts and was having trouble finding someone to operate it. His secretary quit in frustration at trying to tame the large piece of office equipment. Although I had never operated such a machine, I had learned to type and had taken a course in bookkeeping.

Mr. Warren offered me thirty dollars a week to start, and I had my first full-time job. The Warren & Smith Hardware Store was located on Main Street three blocks from the Santa Fe Depot and in the middle of the busy business district. With trains arriving daily and roads improving, many people in the county made weekly trips to Shawnee to do their shopping. The Shawnee Milling Company, a large flourmill, operated close to the Rock Island Depot while the Rock Island and Santa Fe railroads housed large shops to maintain the many trains traveling throughout the country. The Rock Island shops were the largest in the southwest, employing over one thousand men. Shawnee even had a garment company that made overalls for the many men working in the railroad shops.

Using most of the money left from my bank account in Tecumseh, I rented a room two blocks south of Main Street and bought two new suits of clothes. Scheduled to start work on Monday, I bought a train ticket back to Romulus to tell Marilee about my good fortunes and spend a few days with my family.

On the brief stopover at Tecumseh, I ran into Mary Sue McNally. She wore a white dress with an emerald green trimming and looked like the energetic young woman I had met on one of my first days in Tecumseh.

"Hello stranger," I greeted, while walking up behind her.

"Hey, Gill!" the spunky Mary Sue replied. "What are you doing here?"

"Just passing through," I smiled.

"Passing through?" Mary Sue asked, while cocking her head slightly.

"I'm not living in Tecumseh anymore," I informed.

"What?" she screeched in surprise.

"I got a job in Shawnee at the Warren & Smith Hardware Store," I boasted. "I rented a place today and start work Monday."

"You're moving to Shawnee?" Mary Sue said, while shaking her head in mock disapproval.

Citizens of Tecumseh were sensitive about their neighbors in Shawnee. Many Tecumseh residents believed "the rascals" in Shawnee had stolen their railroad by manipulating the rail lines to run through

Shawnee when they should have run through the county seat. More hard feelings festered when Shawnee used the same enticement of free land to ramrod a petition that would move the courthouse. Shawnee won the election, but a court in Oklahoma City prevented the move by ruling the land gift a bribe. People in Tecumseh viewed the business community in Shawnee as too aggressive, but they traveled to the larger town weekly to shop. Citizens of Shawnee rarely mentioned the smaller town except to complain about having to make the trip to the courthouse and mocking Tecumseh's little train, the Lillian Russell.

"A man's got to go where the opportunity is," I playfully defended.

"Well," Mary Sue smiled. "I guess you'll be the one businessman I can trust in that rabble over there."

I laughed at her teasing and thought how pleasant it was to see Mary Sue as she had been before Ralph Swan's unfortunate accident.

"I'm moving from Tecumseh too," Mary Sue said gleefully. "I'm taking a job at Unity School down south."

"You're teaching at 'Fuss Box!'" I exclaimed.

"No," a confused Mary Sue replied. "I'm teaching at Unity."

"That's it!" I said excitedly. "That's where I went to school. We ran off three teachers one year, and people said the place was nothing but a 'Fuss Box.'"

"Oh," a slightly dejected Mary Sue replied.

"Don't worry," I tried to console. "You'll do fine."

In a more serious tone, Mary Sue asked, "Do you really think so?"

"Sure I do," I replied. "Tell you what; I'll take you down there sometime so you can meet some folks and see the place."

"You would do that?" Mary Sue sweetly smiled.

"Sure."

"When?"

"Any Sunday, I can probably go," I said. "I'll be working otherwise. We can go to church down there, and you can meet Marilee."

"Your girl?" Mary Sue asked.

"Yeah," I bashfully replied. "I'm engaged now."

As the words left my mouth, I wanted them back. Mary Sue had lost her fiancé, and I feared my statement would cause her painful memories.

Unaffected, an appreciative Mary Sue said, "That would be great, Gill."

"How about in three weeks?" I asked.

"That's great," she confirmed. "Here's my phone number."

"You have a phone?"

Nodding her head, Mary Sue said, "Yes. Daddy put it in for business, but he doesn't mind me taking calls, and I know he won't mind you calling."

Taking the three-digit number she scribbled, I put the paper in my jacket pocket.

"I'll give you a call," I assured.

The whistle blew signaling Old Beck was about to depart.

"I got to run," I hastily said. "Good to see you."

"You too, Gill. When I find a place to live, I'll have to come buy some furniture from you."

"I'm not a salesman yet," I apologized.

"I'll come by anyway," she assured.

I quickly boarded the passenger car, and the small train chugged out of town before I could sit down.

CHAPTER 60

Trains running on the Rock Island spur to Asher were now sparse. Even Old Beck made the trip only once a day. The Santa Fe Railway ran the Doodlebug, a combination engine and passenger car, which looked like a bus on rails, to the western part of Pottawatomie County over the South Canadian River at Wanette. The Santa Fe line continued through Pauls Valley where it connected to the main line to Fort Worth, Texas. The Missouri, Kansas & Texas Railway ran through Maud and to Ada serving the eastern side of the county.

The train pulled into the run-down depot at Romulus, and it looked as if future trips home might involve taking the Missouri, Kansas & Texas line to Maud. The post office in Romulus had closed down after the end of the World War. The closing of the post office was the end to the town of Romulus, which had no stores and only a few farmers and churches left in the area. Farmers, like Arty Martin, used their vehicles to get to larger towns for supplies, making smaller communities like Romulus obsolete.

When the train slowly pulled away from the station, I looked around the lonely platform, while the wind howled through the few vacant buildings still standing. Walking to the old Martin house, I did not pass a single wagon or car on the way, adding to the lonely feeling. Gwen was working in the small garden beside the house when I arrived while baby Jackie lay on a blanket nearby.

"Hey, Gwen!" I yelled as I approached the front gate.

Gwen nearly jumped into the air as her arms came across her shoulders in a protective motion while she let out a muffled scream.

"Sorry," I quickly added. "I didn't mean to scare you."

Gwen sighed in relief and said, "I'm glad it was you."

Taking a second to catch her breath and regain her composure, Gwen looked about, as if to see if anyone else was around, and said, "What are you doing here?"

"I got a job starting Monday and thought I'd come see the folks," I smiled.

"Great," Gwen replied. "Where's the job?"

"Warren & Smith Hardware Store, as a bookkeeper," I boasted.

Putting her hands on her hips, Gwen said, "You're back in business. Guy would be so proud."

"How is Guy?"

With a gleam of excitement, Gwen answered, "He's been in a hospital near Washington, but he's coming home in a couple of weeks."

Thinking of Ralph Swan, I felt compelled to ask, "So he's all right?"

Nodding, Gwen said, "He's doing well…Martha, Guy's sister is coming with him to visit."

I had never met Guy's sister. He had talked about her occasionally, but she had married and left home at a young age.

"That's great," I replied.

"They'll be going to Ada where Lori is, but they'll be coming through Shawnee on the way," Gwen informed.

"Maybe I can see him," I suggested.

"He would like that," Gwen affirmed.

Looking around at the empty barns and house, I asked, "Where's Arty?"

With a slight frown, Gwen shrugged, "I'd be the last to know."

Looking awkwardly at her, Gwen continued in a more upbeat voice, "He's off doing business…selling cows I suppose. We've about sold them all, and there's not much left here for Arty to do but watch grass grow."

"He could help you with the garden," I playfully suggested.

In a lower tone of voice, Gwen said with a smirk, "I don't think Arty likes getting his hands dirty, which is not good for a farmer."

Walking over to the baby, I watched the small child lay listlessly on the small blanket Gwen had spread out under an umbrella. I had only looked at the small child for a moment when I heard Gwen crying behind me.

Spinning around, I asked urgently, "What's the matter?"

Tears flowed down Gwen's cheeks as she stepped to the blanket and carefully picked up Jackie.

"Haven't you noticed?" she sniffled.

"Noticed what?"

"The baby," she tried to explain while lovingly picking up the child and trying to control her emotions. "He's almost two, and he can't walk. Something's not right."

"What!" I exclaimed.

Marilee had mentioned something about the baby having some health issues, but I did not know the details and was not expecting Gwen to be so upset.

Wiping her tears, while holding the child, she explained, "He's been such a wonderful baby, but he doesn't seem to grow right. He can't hold himself up. Arty thought it was because I held him all the time. We would get into fights, and then I took him to Doc Sanders. Doc Sanders said he has some kind of palsy that's affected his muscles. It's been hard on Arty. He seems to find things to do away from home when he can."

Stepping to Gwen empathetically, I asked, "Can I hold him?"

Looking at me with teary eyes, she replied, "If you want to, but be careful...he's like a rag doll."

Taking the baby in my arms, I noticed what Gwen tried to explain. His eyes looked alert, but it was as if he could not move. Gwen and I walked around the yard, under the shade of the trees surrounding the house for a while, and she seemed to appreciate the company.

"How are you doing?" I finally asked.

"I don't know," Gwen confessed. "It's a big shock…Doc Sanders has tried to tell me what to expect, but I'm afraid Jackie's never going to be right…I mean the way other people think 'right' is. Arty wants to put him in a home."

"What do you want?"

"I don't know. He's a sweet child, but I'm afraid he may never be more than a child. Doc Sanders said there's a special home in Oklahoma City, but I don't know what to do."

Seeing Gwen was desperate for answers, all I could manage to say was, "You'll work it out."

"You didn't come to hear my troubles," Gwen said, trying to change the topic. "What are you really doing down here?"

"I came to see Marilee," I confessed. "I was actually hoping she would be here."

"Marilee's been a doll through everything," Gwen replied. "She's here with me more than not, but she's home for a few days. I'm sorry."

"That's okay," I assured.

After a moment of silence, I added, "It's been good seeing you. I was in the hardware store in Shawnee this morning and thinking of all those lunches you brought me at Guy's store."

With a mischievous smile, Gwen said, "Yeah. You and Guy fed a lot of cats on my lunches."

"What?"

"I know you and Guy used to throw my cooking out and go to Kelly's. I'm not as stupid as people think."

"No one thinks you're stupid," I assured.

"I'm not sure about that," Gwen replied. "I feel like all I've done is cause problems. I don't deserve Arty and…I'm afraid Arty's about figured that out."

"Arty knows how lucky he is," I tried to convince. "You've got to know you're the girl we were all crazy about."

"Maybe, I'm crazy," she smiled.

"I was hoping to catch a ride to Cherry Hill tonight. When do you think Arty will be back?" I asked.

With a pained expression, Gwen said, "I don't know. Sometimes he's back for supper, but sometimes he's gone on business late. I wish I could tell you."

Feeling uncomfortable for asking the question as I remembered my encounter with Arty and Laura Jones, I awkwardly asked, "Can I wait here?"

"Of course," Gwen replied while she looked around at the silent countryside. "I don't think my reputation will suffer if yours can stand it."

"Your reputation's first rate with me," I smiled.

"I'll even cook you dinner," Gwen teased.

I helped Gwen in the garden until she cleaned up to cook dinner. Baby Jackie was obviously different from other children, but I entertained him while giving his mother a break. By eight o'clock, dusk was approaching, and there was still no sign of Arty. I wanted to ask Gwen how often Arty was out so late but did not feel comfortable asking. My anxiety grew as darkness approached, and I faced the prospect of being alone with a married woman for the night.

While sitting on the porch enjoying the peace and quiet of the country, Gwen came to sit with me and said, "Jackie's asleep."

"Thanks for supper," I replied. "It was good."

"Not up to Marilee's standards, though?" Gwen teased.

"I don't know if anyone measures up to Marilee," I smiled. "I'm sorry to bother you tonight…I…I would've walked if I'd known Arty was going to be so late. It's not that far."

"It's fine," Gwen assured. "I know you're anxious to tell Marilee the news, but it's been nice having you to myself today."

Before I could reply, I noticed Gwen staring into the moonlit night as if looking at something. Following her eyes to the edge of the woods, I detected nothing extraordinary.

"Do you see it?" she whispered.

"What?" I replied.

"In the edge of the woods…there's a faint glow," she pointed.

I looked in the direction she indicated but could see nothing unusual.

"He's gone," Gwen whispered uneasily.

"Who's gone?"

Looking at me with a pained look on her face, Gwen said, "You'll think I'm crazy now."

"What is it?"

"I think someone's watching me…or maybe watching over me," she answered.

"Who?"

"There was a man there…at the edge of the woods. You didn't see him?"

"No."

Laughing almost to herself, she said, "I *am* starting to think I'm crazy."

"Gwen, you're not making sense."

"I've had the feeling the past weeks someone…or something has been watching me. I broke a shovel in the garden about a week ago, and then a few days later someone had put a new handle on," she claimed.

"It was probably Arty," I shrugged.

Shaking her head, Gwen said, "It wasn't Arty. A few days ago, Arty and I had a fight, here on the porch. He was going to do some business, and I had asked him to mend the rail here on the porch. He was agitated and shouted he didn't have the time. The next day the rail was fixed, and Arty said he was sorry that I had to do it on my own! Gill I didn't do anything but go to sleep."

"How long have you noticed this?" I asked with more concern.

"Like I said, I've sensed someone out there for several weeks, and tonight I was sure I saw a faint glow and the silhouette of someone, but…you didn't see anything, so I'm afraid I am losing my mind."

"Do you have a lamp?" I asked.

"Yes, what for?" Gwen replied.

"I'm going to look for your ghost," I smiled.

"We've got a flashlight."

"Get it," I said.

In a few moments, I headed into the dark where Gwen had pointed. I did not expect to find anything but felt the need to calm Gwen's fears. The moon was bright enough that I walked without the light as I silently approached the spot. A sudden rustling sound in the thick woods caused me to jump, as I turned on the flashlight and came face to face with the glowing eyes of a bandit-faced raccoon. The large raccoon stared at me a moment before heading deeper into the woods.

Catching my breath, I surveyed the area with my light, but could see no one was around. As I turned to walk back to the house, I noticed something white on the ground. Picking the small piece up, I headed back to Gwen.

"Did you see anything?" she asked anxiously.

"Just a coon and this," I replied. "Has Arty started smoking?"

Handing her the remains of a smoked cigarette, I said, "I found this where you saw the glow. It looks fresh."

Gwen's face turned ashen as she said, "So someone *has* been watching me."

CHAPTER 61

Car lights shined from the road a little before nine o'clock, as Gwen and I sat on the porch, talking about her intruder. I breathed a sigh of relief as Arty's truck slid to a stop in front of the house.

"There he is," a worried Gwen stated as Arty slammed the truck door shut.

"Gill?" Arty greeted in a surprised tone.

"Hey, Arty," I answered.

"What're you doin' here?" he asked in a strange combination of welcoming and anxiousness.

"I got a job starting next Monday and came back to see the folks. I took the train to Romulus and was hoping to catch a ride."

Looking uncomfortably at Gwen, Arty asked, "How long have you been here?"

"Since about three," I answered.

"Sorry to keep you waiting," he apologized. "I was over at Maud selling a few head of cattle and…it took longer than I thought."

"No problem," I assured. "I didn't leave word with anyone I'd be down. You didn't see anyone when you drove up, did you?"

A puzzled Arty answered, "No."

I explained about Gwen's fears and finding the cigarette butt in the edge of the trees. Arty seemed concerned and went with me to the spot to search for more signs. Finding no other evidence of anyone around, we headed back to the house in a few minutes.

Convinced no one was stalking his residence, at least at the moment, Arty said, "Tell me about the job."

"I'm working at the Warren & Smith Hardware Store."

"The big store in Shawnee?" Arty excitedly asked.

"That's the one."

"What are you making?"

"Thirty a week."

"Thirty a week!" Arty exclaimed. "You might as well be pickin' cotton."

"It's just to start," I defended.

"At least you're in the city," Arty sighed. "What do you think, Gwenny? Think maybe I need to move to town for thirty a week?"

Gwen did not answer directly, but nodded slightly in agreement. The night air was beginning to chill, as Gwen moved back into the house.

"If we're going to get you to Cherry Hill tonight, we better leave," Arty suggested.

"It's late," I protested. "I can stay here until morning."

"Nonsense," Arty chirped. "It won't take but a minute. Gwen, you don't mind?"

"Have you had supper?" she asked.

"I got a bite while I waited to settle up on the cattle," Arty claimed.

"I don't have to go tonight," I offered. "I don't think we should leave Gwen alone at night."

Arty looked strangely at me, as if perturbed that I might suggest his wife needed protecting.

"I don't mind," Gwen replied. "Will you be late?"

"No," Arty assured. "I'll just drop Gill off and be back."

Walking over to his wife, Arty gave her a kiss on the forehead and headed out the door.

"Maybe we'll see you in Shawnee when Guy comes through town," Gwen said, as I headed out the door.

"Sure," I replied. "I hope to be seeing you guys before I head back to Shawnee."

"I hope so," Gwen smiled.

Arty cranked up his pickup and tore down the road past my old home. The house had been vacant since my family had moved. Although it needed some repairs, it looked to be in reasonable shape.

"Stop!" I demanded as we passed the old place. "Shine your lights on the house."

Arty backed up his truck and positioned the headlights on the abandoned house. Jumping out of the car, I headed for the front door with Arty following close behind.

"What are you doing?" Arty asked.

"I got to see something," I replied.

The house looked vacant, but entering my old bedroom, I noticed a mat on the floor and evidence someone had camped in the place recently.

"What are you looking for?" Arty asked.

"Gwen thinks someone has been watching her," I explained. "Have you noticed anyone around here?"

"No."

"Have you been around enough to notice?" I asked pointedly.

"What do you mean?" an irritated Arty answered.

"Never mind," I said, while pushing past him to the truck.

In an angry tone, Arty charged, "What are you trying to say?"

"I'm saying you got a wife and child that are left alone an awful lot."

"You don't know anything!" Arty defended.

"I know I walked up on Gwen today, and she was alone. She was scared to death, Arty. I walked up on her and…and it could have been anyone."

In a more contrite tone, Arty said, "You don't understand…Jackie—"

"I know the baby's not right, Arty. I know things must be tough...but Gwen needs you."

With his characteristic smile of confidence, Arty said, "I know. Did you see anyone?"

"Well...no," I replied. "But I went to the woods and found an old cigarette, and this house...you can tell someone's been camping here."

"Maybe," Arty shrugged. "But, you don't know all Gwen's been through. I didn't know."

"So you're not worried about her being alone with someone shacked up so close?"

"Sure," Arty affirmed. "But standing out in the dark lookin' at an old house ain't getting me home any earlier. Let's go."

I followed Arty back to the truck. Arty still had his old swagger and confidence, but the burdens of family responsibility seemed to have aged him more than school had matured me.

Driving into the darkness, Arty said, "I got to get out of here."

"Out of where?" I asked.

"Out of here...this place," he explained. "I need to get to town. I just haven't been able to convince Dad yet."

"How about Gwen and the baby?"

Arty shrugged, "Gwen'll do fine in the city. Might help her relax and get out of crying all the time. The baby...we'll have to send him away, I'm sure, but Gwen can't come to admit that."

"I was sorry to hear about Jackie," I said seriously.

"Yeah," Arty stoically replied. "That was a surprise we didn't count on."

Arty seemed to be almost perturbed to be reminded that his child was not normal.

"How are you doing?" I asked.

With his easy smile, Arty said, "I'm fine...we'll be fine. Gwen thinks she can keep him at home, but...I don't know. Gwen's great with him now, but it takes all her attention."

"She looked fine to me," I tactfully suggested.

"Well, maybe, but you can tell she's not herself. I think I need to get her out of here and to town," Arty restated.

"You'll have to talk to your dad," I reminded.

"I shouldn't have to," Arty shot back. "But he keeps all the money. That's why I think we need to go into business…you know, make it on our own."

"Maybe someday," I agreed.

"Maybe sooner than you think," Arty smiled.

I listened as he excitedly explained, "I know you probably think I'm out late horsin' around, especially after that night with Laura Jones, but I ain't been running around on Gwen. I've been workin'—makin' contacts and tryin' to get some cash out of these cattle we've been running."

Stopping for a moment, Arty asked in a more serious, almost ominous demeanor, "You didn't say nothin' to Gwen, did you? I mean about Laura."

Remembering how disappointed I had been when I discovered Arty with another woman, I dejectedly replied, "No."

Looking at me with his pleasant grin, he said, "Good. Trust me, that night straightened me out good. I've been on the straight and narrow ever since."

"Good."

Arty drove on through the darkness, full of energy and ideas as he schemed how we would start a store that would be the talk of the county. He admonished me to pay attention at Warren & Smith's to see what I could learn. I did not really take Arty too seriously, but a part of me enjoyed being around his rapid-fire ideas and contagious enthusiasm. Soon, we arrived at the Brooks home.

CHAPTER 62

The hour was late, but Dad lounged on the porch picking out a tune on his banjo while Gordon puffed on the harmonica. Thanking Arty for the ride, I watched him drive into the night hoping he headed straight to Gwen.

"My, oh my!" Dad exclaimed. "Look at what's come down to this hootenanny."

"Hey, Dad," I greeted with a smile as I sat down next to Gordon.

"What brings you down here this time of night?" Dad asked.

"I meant to come sooner, but got caught up at Arty's place," I explained.

"So, why do we have the pleasure of your company?" Dad restated.

"I got a job," I beamed.

"You've always had a job," he replied.

"This is a real job," I explained. "Workin' full time at the Warren & Smith Hardware Store…in Shawnee."

Gordon started to say something, before Dad said, "A city job, you say…in Shawnee?"

I nodded.

Looking over at Gordon, Dad smiled and said, "Well, we're nearly goin' to be neighbors then."

"What?" I asked.

Dad nodded and said, "We're moving this summer west of Shawnee to eighty acres already planted in cotton and alfalfa. A widow lady has it. She made me a good offer to farm it for her. I won't even be out seed money this year."

"What about your crop here?" I inquired.

"Lloyd's volunteered to stick around and harvest it," Dad explained. "Gordon's goin' to a new high school they're openin' up at Bethel. He'll be able to go to school and live at home. It's only about five miles from Shawnee. Good bottomland this lady has."

"That sounds great," I said. "How's Mom feel about it?"

"I'll dig her cellar, and she'll love it," Dad claimed.

We visited a little longer about the move and Gordon going to school, before I asked, "Where's Lloyd?"

"He's out walking," Dad explained. "Lloyd likes to go out by himself in the evenings when folks aren't so likely to be around."

"Why?" I asked.

Dad looked at Gordon and said, "He don't like being around people so much since he got back from the war. That's why he didn't come to your graduation…and, his girl from before the war…the one down at Asher. She's married and moved off. Lloyd's just trying to find himself, I think."

"But Lloyd's okay?"

"Sure," Dad replied. "He just likes to be alone sometimes."

"And Mom's okay leaving him behind?" I quizzed.

"Yeah," Dad assured. "Mom's fine with the move."

Mom was so accustomed to moving that she would not know what to do without packing and unpacking. We talked longer, before Lloyd stepped out of the night and onto the porch.

"Look who's come calling?" Dad cheerfully greeted Lloyd.

Lloyd looked at me and nodded his head.

"Hey Lloyd," I said.

"What's you doin' here so late?" Lloyd asked.

"I came down to tell you guys I got a job, but I kind of got caught up at Arty and Gwen's."

"Really?" Lloyd shrugged. "That's a long walk in the dark."

"Would've been," I agreed. "If Arty hadn't given me a ride."

"Arty'd know about night driving, I suppose," Lloyd grinned.

"I guess."

"Gwen doin' all right?" Lloyd asked.

"Seemed fine," I replied.

"Too bad about the boy," Lloyd continued. "I hate to see a girl like her have to go through that."

"Yeah," I agreed. "That'd be tough."

I talked a little longer with my brothers before making a bed on the floor in Lloyd and Gordon's room. It had been a long day traveling back into the Cross Timber, and soon I slept soundly.

CHAPTER 63

A blood-curdling scream awakened my peaceful sleep, as I peered into the darkness while Gordon fumbled for a match. A soft amber glow of an oil lamp soon lit the small room. In horror, I watched Lloyd sitting up in bed, alternating between high-pitched yells and a pathetic whimper.

"Lloyd!" Gordon urged. "Lloyd! Wake up!"

With a gentle tug, Gordon awakened Lloyd, as our older brother sat shaking and sweating, unaware he had been screaming in his sleep.

"Are you having the dreams again?" Gordon asked urgently.

Lloyd appeared unable to answer for a moment before he looked strangely at Gordon and nodded, almost like a small child. Mother entered the room and quickly went to Lloyd's side, assuring him it was just a dream. Lloyd regained his bearings in a short time and fell back into his bed. Gordon also returned to his pillow as if nothing unusual had occurred. I followed Mother out of the room to get answers.

"What was that?" I asked.

"Nothing," Mother assured. "It's the first time he's had them in a while."

"That didn't seem like nothing," I frantically replied. "He scared me to death."

"Lloyd's been through a lot," Mother reasoned. "Since he came back from the war, he's had terrible dreams and sometimes he shakes for no reason at all, until he snaps out of it."

"Is he okay?"

Putting her hand to my cheek, Mother said, "Lloyd will be fine. War's a terrible thing. Lloyd won't talk about it, but I'm afraid a part of him's still there. Time heals all wounds—for those who want to get well and Lloyd's a strong person. We just have to give him time."

I had difficulty falling back asleep after Lloyd's episode, but Gordon and Lloyd soon snored rhythmically. Gordon explained the next morning that Lloyd had the dreams regularly when he first returned. According to Gordon, Lloyd was having fewer dreams, but Gordon confessed he looked forward to moving into a room without Lloyd for a while.

After breakfast, I headed up the hill to the pristine Martin place. The fields were plowed in neat rows with pinkish dirt already hosting the seed that had been planted just weeks earlier. There was some activity around the farm, and I noticed Mr. Martin down by the barn with two of his sons. Carefully moving to the back of the house to avoid Mr. Martin's line of sight, I knew where to find Marilee.

I knocked gently on the screen door to the kitchen. Marilee squealed when she saw me. I quickly repeated the story about having a job, as she flung her arms around my neck and squeezed tightly. I spent most of the day with Marilee, and she talked about marriage plans. I did not want to speak with Mr. Martin until I had kept my job and saved some money, but Marilee decided we needed a picnic to celebrate. I could not spoil Marilee's excitement but did not look forward to confronting Mr. Martin with the news.

CHAPTER 64

The afternoon was hot, as Dad fussed about having to leave the fields early to attend Marilee's gathering. What began as a simple picnic turned into an engagement party by the time Marilee finished organizing. If my father was upset about leaving the fields early for a party, I could only imagine Mr. Martin's attitude.

The Martin and Brooks families gathered for the picnic, and though our families were close together geographically, we were far apart in prosperity. The Martin farm was large, efficient, and profitable, while our place seemed in constant threat of failure. Arty greeted my family with personality and charm, but I worried about the sharp contrast of Mr. Martin's organization versus my father's more casual attitude toward success.

My concerns were unfounded. Dad proved to be sociable in any setting, including conversation with Mr. Martin. Marilee's stern father did not laugh as much as my father, but he seemed tolerant of the idea that his only daughter was marrying into a family of tenant farmers.

"It's going well, isn't it?" Marilee smiled as we walked around the corner of the house and out of sight.

"Your dad hasn't shot any of us, if that's what you mean," I quipped.

Giving me a teasing punch, Marilee defended, "Daddy's not that bad!"

"No, he's been very gracious," I admitted. "I still don't think he's so keen on the idea of us getting married."

Hugging me tight, Marilee said, "At least I'm keen on the idea."

After a moment of nuzzling me, Marilee stepped back, holding a slip of paper, which came from my jacket pocket.

In a serious tone, Marilee asked, "What's this?"

"What's what?" I smiled innocently.

Handing me the paper, she replied, "Who's Mary Sue and why do you have her phone number?"

Looking at the phone number Mary Sue McNally had slipped in my jacket pocket, I hesitated long enough to give the appearance of guilt as I said, "It's…It's just a friend from Tecumseh. She's moving this way and needed some furniture and…well she's asked me to take her down here in a few weeks and meet some folks…she's going to teach school at the old Fuss Box."

Studying my fumbled response, Marilee asked candidly, "It's not the same girl I saw you hugging at the train station?"

Every instinct told me to lie and that being a liar would be better than hurting Marilee's feelings, but looking at her, I answered, "It…well…it does happen to be that girl, but we're just friends."

Taking a few steps back to the group, Marilee stopped suddenly and said with an uncharacteristic teary eye, "Gilbert Brooks! Are you sure you want to marry me?"

Stepping quickly to her, I frantically said, "Marilee, you're the only girl for me."

Taking the note from her hand, I continued, "This girl is a good person. She was a friend when I needed one, and she's had some tough luck."

Looking pitifully at me, Marilee did not respond.

With a hint of frustration, I added, "I love you, Marilee…and I can't believe you could think anything else."

Having regained some of her composure, Marilee looked at me as if trying to reveal some truth about my character.

Finally, she stated bluntly, "Gilbert, I do love you. I've loved you a long time, but trust is more important than love…and I do trust you. I'm sorry to be so silly sometimes, it's just…it's just, I've seen how some men can be."

"I won't be like some men," I promised. "I'm going to be your man…and I hope to be the man you think I can be."

Marilee studied me a little longer before smiling and stepping to my side to say, "I think you're going to be a great man, Gilbert Brooks. When are you bringing this girl to Fuss Box?"

"I don't know," I confessed. "She's starting in the fall and said something about two or three weeks."

"Will you bring her to see me?" she asked.

"Sure."

"If you think so highly of her, I'm sure we'll get along fine," Marilee reasoned. "Besides, if I'm going to have this girl always pestering you, I'd better find out what I'm up against."

Smiling at her sly analysis, I replied, "I wouldn't want to be up against you."

Reaching out to hug her, Marilee seemed to melt into my arms. After a few moments, I said, "We better get back to the others, before your dad comes looking for me."

"I think you may be wise about that," she smiled.

Walking back to the group, I noticed my dad trying to entertain the stoic Mr. Martin. I was thankful Mr. Martin did not notice Marilee and me hugging not far from his sight. Gwen, Mrs. Martin, and my mother talked to Ethan and his wife as they watched their little boy play while Gwen sadly held the helpless Jackie.

At the edge of the yard, Arty and Lloyd talked alone. The two had known each other for years but never seemed to be particularly close. Marilee had some snacks to serve, so I joined Arty and Lloyd. Before I could get there, Arty yelled and waved for Gwen to come over.

"What's going on?" I greeted.

Arty, always quick to take charge of a conversation, said, "Just doin' a little business."

"What kind of business?" I asked.

Before I could get an answer, Gwen arrived to ask, "What do you need, Arty?"

Arty looked at both of us and explained, "I've got a solution to your worries about being alone all the time. Lloyd here's willing to move into the old Brooks house and maybe do some work around our place. I told him the land's pretty played out, but maybe he could do some work for me. It'd mean someone around all the time, and Lloyd said he'd be willing to do work for the rent...do what he could do farming that forty acres."

"Is that what you want to do, Lloyd?" Gwen asked.

"If you don't mind," Lloyd replied. "Mom and Dad are moving, and I know that land pretty good."

"Then it's settled," Arty proclaimed.

Lloyd shook Arty's hand, confirming the deal. Lloyd would be doing much of the work at the old farms near Romulus. Lloyd had always been a good farmer, and I had no doubt he was up to the task. I also wondered if he might feel more comfortable in the place he lived before the war. After the previous night, I was certain Gwen would enjoy having someone familiar around.

The party ran out of steam before dark. Arty invited Marilee and me to his place for the evening. Mr. Martin did not like the idea, but after a scolding look from Mrs. Martin, he gave Marilee permission. To my surprise, Lloyd accepted an invitation from Gwen to come and start getting the old house ready. I told Lloyd that it looked like someone had been camping there, but he did not seem concerned. Before dark, we were loaded in the car and headed back toward Arty's place.

CHAPTER 65

Arty borrowed the Studebaker to drive the group back to his house. Gwen held little Jackie in the front with Arty, while Marilee squeezed between Lloyd and me in the back. The drive only took about fifteen minutes, and as we approached the old house where my family once lived, dusk was approaching. Lloyd asked to be dropped off at the house so he could get things organized before it was completely dark.

"You're welcome to stay at the house," Gwen offered. "There's plenty of room."

Lloyd smiled and said, "I've been sleepin' in trenches so long, this old house looks pretty plush."

"Come up if you change your mind," Gwen said, as Lloyd shut the door.

We left Lloyd, as Arty started the short drive to his house. It was getting darker, although the road was still visible without the headlights.

"Did you see him?" Gwen shrieked suddenly from the front seat.

Screeching to a halt, Arty said, "I saw something."

"What is it?" I asked, not able to see as clearly from the back seat.

"Something just bolted into the woods," Arty answered. "Let's go see who it is?"

"Did it look like the person we saw last night?" I asked Gwen.

Gwen, noticeably shaken at seeing a stranger dart into the woods, said, "I…I don't know…maybe."

"Come on," Arty admonished as he jumped over the drainage ditch and looked into the thick woods.

Following Arty's lead, I hopped out of the car and helped him search the thick woods, while the girls and baby stayed behind.

"Stop," Arty commanded in a whisper. "Do you hear anything?"

Listening intently, I shook my head to acknowledge that I could hear nothing out of the ordinary.

"Me either," he replied in a more normal tone of voice.

"Who do you think it was?" I asked as we headed back to the car.

"Don't know," Arty confessed. "I'm not really sure what it was...could have been a deer maybe. I just heard Gwen scream and got a glimpse of something dashing into the woods. I can't believe a man could run through this mess without making a noise or leaving some kind of trail."

"So you didn't see anybody?" I asked.

"I don't know," Arty confessed. "But I saw something."

"Who was it?" Gwen demanded, as Arty and I climbed back into the car.

"Don't know," Arty replied. "We didn't see anybody."

"Are you sure?" Marilee questioned.

"I didn't see anything," I replied.

"Let's get to the house," Arty said, as he put the car in gear.

"You don't believe someone is out there!" an agitated Gwen charged.

"I believe you," Arty calmly tried to reassure. "I just didn't see anybody."

"You don't believe me!" Gwen shouted. "You leave me and the baby alone nearly every night then think I'm crazy because I think someone's prowling around."

Arty glanced back at Marilee and me before looking at Gwen to say, "I believe you. Gill told me he saw someone around here. It's just that I didn't see anyone right now, and I think you need to settle down."

Gwen shook in anger but did not respond as Arty pulled up to the house in a car filled with awkward silence. Arty quickly opened the car door to help Gwen with the baby as Marilee and I stared at each other for a second. We all entered the house without saying a word.

"Marilee," Arty asked in a tone of voice that was more pleasant than he normally used with his sister. "Could you take the baby for a minute?"

Marilee nodded and took the baby in her arms as Arty guided the distraught Gwen to a chair. Arty then went to a cabinet and poured Gwen a drink from a flask.

"Arthur Martin, do you have liquor in this house!" a shocked Marilee scolded.

"Something the doctor from the city prescribed for her nerves," Arty defended.

"A doctor, nothing," Marilee continued. "That's no medicine bottle you have there!"

Gwen took the small glass anyway and quickly drank it before handing the glass back for a refill.

"Gwen!" Marilee gasped. "Are you drinking?"

A stoic Gwen answered, "I'm just trying to calm my nerves."

"Daddy will not—" Marilee began to say.

"Daddy doesn't live here," Arty stated. "This is my house, and I make the decisions here."

A stubborn Marilee replied, "It's against the law, and…it's not right."

Finishing her second glass, Gwen said, "Settle down, Marilee. You may need something to calm your nerves after you're married."

A dumbfounded Marilee looked at me for support, but I had nothing to add to this family dispute.

"I'm sorry," Gwen apologized. "I shouldn't have said that."

Rubbing her head, Gwen asked, "If you'll watch Jackie for a minute, I need some air."

Putting down her glass, a listless Gwen walked slowly out the door.

"Aren't you going to go with her?" I asked Arty.

Looking somewhat uncomfortable, Arty replied, "No. She just needs some time to herself. I'm sorry you two had to see that. It is just Gwen's had a hard time since the baby. She just gets crazy sometimes, but she'll be fine."

"And you think giving her alcohol's going to help?" a still-agitated Marilee asked.

"You don't know as much as you think—" Arty responded.

Arty was about to lecture his sister more, when Gwen screamed from outside.

Gwen stumbled through the door and ran into Arty's arms shrieking, "I've seen his ghost!"

CHAPTER 66

The bizarre antics of Gwen Martin were impossible to explain, but her terror was real. Hesitating for only a second, we headed out the door to investigate. Marilee stepped on the porch behind me, still holding the baby, and we watched a fight in the moonlight of the front yard.

Lloyd was holding his own, but the uniformed man with short, dark hair was about to break his grasp. Running to help Lloyd, I grabbed the strong man and tried to subdue him. Lloyd and I were barely able to hold the stranger, but we finally threw him to the ground and held him there.

"Lance?" a puzzled Marilee exclaimed.

At Marilee's voice, the man ceased struggling. His hair was shorter, and he looked older, but to my astonishment, I stood looking at Lance Carrington.

"Lance?" I whispered in disbelief.

"Hey, Gill," Lance Carrington answered with his easy grin.

Lloyd let Lance stand. Lance dressed in an Army uniform, quickly brushed himself off.

Before anyone could say anything else, a loud sound thudded by the open screen door, as Gwen fainted. Without hesitation, Lance leaped onto the porch to help Gwen. Marilee handed Lloyd the baby as she too assisted Gwen.

"I never believed you were dead," Marilee smiled, as she stood close to Lance. "They all said you drowned, but you took Little Blackie, didn't you?"

"Gwen?" Lance pleaded while ignoring Marilee's question. "Are you okay?"

Gwen leaned into Lance's arms, as beads of sweat glistened off her pale forehead.

"How?" she asked in confusion. "You're dead."

"No," Lance smiled. "I'm not dead. I ran away."

Seeming to regain her composure, Gwen shook off Lance's help and stood on her own by balancing herself on the doorpost.

"But," Gwen tried to reason, "it can't be you."

Lifting up his shirt to show the scar left in his side by the boar attack, Lance said, "It's me."

"But—" Gwen began in a more agitated tone.

"Hush now," Lance suggested. "I'll explain later."

"No!" Gwen said in a harsher voice. "Explain now."

Laughing to himself, as if he were an old man telling a funny story, Lance said, "I ran off when I knew Leland Holiday was after me. I knew I couldn't get any kind of trial in this county, at least not with the Holidays involved, so I went to Texas. Didn't know what else to do, so I joined the army. I've been in Europe the past two years fighting Germans and just got back today."

"Did you fight in the Argonne?" Lloyd asked as he held the baby.

"Yeah," Lance replied. "How did you know?"

"I saw you," Lloyd claimed. "They told me when I got back you'd died, but I knew I'd seen you."

"Maybe," Lance said. "It was some fight. Do you have a baby, Lloyd?"

"No," Lloyd answered. "The baby's…the baby is—"

"The baby's mine," Gwen stoically stated.

Lance's eyes shifted nervously at the news, as he made no response.

"Why didn't you take me?" Gwen cried. "I needed you, and you left without a word. And worse than that, you let me believe you were dead!"

"But Gwen," Lance tried to defend. "Arty—"

"Arty and I are married," Gwen stated flatly.

The color left Lance's face as he stared silently at the group now surrounding him.

In a defeated tone, Lance said, "But Arty—"

"Hey, Lance," Arty Martin said from the doorway. "I thought that might have been you. I don't know anyone else that could have moved through the Cross Timber like that."

"Arty?" Lance asked. "What's going on?"

"You shouldn't be here," Arty said flatly. "Leland Holiday's still around, and he won't be too glad to see you around here."

"You said you'd take care of things," Lance muttered.

"You're still alive," Arty said. "And you're not in jail."

"That's true," Lance meekly replied.

Without warning, Gwen stepped to Lance and slapped him.

As a surprised Lance rubbed his face, Gwen said, "You left me! Without even saying good-bye. You left me!"

"Arty said he'd take care of things," Lance defended.

Arty Martin looked sheepishly, as Gwen glared at him. Leaning toward Lance, she said, "He's taken care of things, no thanks to you. Now you're not welcomed here, so quit sneaking around and leave me be!"

Lance looked at her like a hurt puppy, as Gwen took the baby from Lloyd and turned to Arty to say, "Let's go inside. Marilee, you and Gill are welcomed…and you too Lloyd."

Glaring one more time at Lance, Gwen disappeared into the house with Arty close behind. Marilee, Lloyd, and I, however, were not about to leave Lance and his tale alone for the night.

CHAPTER 67

"Tell me what happened," Marilee assertively demanded.

"I think I better get away from here before Gwen shoots me or goes for the law," Lance replied.

"Don't worry about that," Marilee replied. "What's going on?"

Walking toward the front gate and away from the house, Lance said, "After I shot Horace, I decided to make a run for it. Arty said Leland would follow me wherever I went, so we decided the only way to keep him off my trail was if I were dead. We took Big Blackie and Little Blackie, but took Old Betsy as well.

"Sorry about your horse, Marilee, but I knew Old Betsy couldn't make it across the South Canadian in flood waters, Little Blackie barely did. Arty said he'd handle things…and I guess he did, 'cause Leland never came after me."

"Lance," I interrupted. "Mr. McNally found the men living near the bridge, and they confirmed your story that it was self defense."

Lance looked at me warily.

"You didn't have to run," I explained. "You were innocent."

Shaking his head, Lance said, "Leland would have never let that be."

"Arty knew you were alive?" Marilee asked.

Lance nodded his head and said, "Arty knew. It was his idea. He said he'd let me know when things were all right to come back, but I hadn't heard from him. I got out of the army and couldn't wait. I just got in this afternoon. I went back to the house, but it didn't look like anyone's living there."

"Mom and Dad moved south of Salt Creek during the war," Lloyd explained.

"So it *was* you Gwen saw this afternoon?" I asked.

"I heard a car this evening and hid in the woods, but didn't know it was you guys," Lance confirmed.

"And last night, sneaking in the woods?" I continued.

"Couldn't have been me. I didn't get here until this afternoon."

"I can't believe it," I exclaimed. "You've been alive all this time, and no one knew it."

"Arty did," Lance corrected. "He said he would take care of things. I guess he did. Are he and Gwen really married?"

"They got married just a few weeks after you…I mean, after we thought you had died," I explained.

Laughing to himself and shaking his head, Lance continued, "Arty said he would take care of things."

"I can't believe you guys ever listen to Arty," Marilee charged. "Don't you know he always takes care of himself?"

"Maybe," Lance agreed. "But he got me out of town when I needed him to."

"Don't you see that he got you out of town to get what he wanted?" Marilee said.

"What are you going to do?" I asked.

"Hadn't thought about it," Lance shrugged. "I only came back for Gwen."

"Aren't you angry?" Marilee asked.

Lance smiled at her, and said, "Guess I should be, but—"

"But what!" Marilee said. "He set you up and stole your girl."

"Naw," Lance replied. "He didn't take anything from me. I made the mistakes. I shouldn't have been bootlegging; I shouldn't have been on that bridge. I shouldn't have killed Horace Holiday, even if it weren't my fault."

Thinking for a second, Lance added, "I didn't deserve Gwen, and…I couldn't have made her happy. What was she going to do? Be on the run with me? That'd be no life. Arty knew what he wanted, and…well Arty knows how to take opportunities."

"Gwen loved you," Marilee said.

"Maybe," Lance shrugged, "but I don't know…I think Gwen was always more in love with the idea of getting married than with me. It don't matter now."

"You're going to walk away?" Marilee asked.

Nodding, Lance replied, "I think that'd be best. I don't got nothing to offer her, and Leland Holiday'll be after me when he knows I'm back."

"What are you going to do?" I asked.

"I'm going away," Lance said. "I met some guys in the army that said they'd have some work for me. I think I need to stay away. Don't see no good coming from me being here."

Walking to him, Marilee gave Lance a teary hug and said, "You belong here. We'll miss you…I mean, now we know you're alive."

"I'll be back someday," Lance smiled while patting her on the head. "Can I bunk with you tonight, Lloyd?"

"Sure," Lloyd replied.

"I'll camp with you guys too," I said. "That'll make Marilee's dad feel better anyway."

"I'll get you some blankets and an oil lamp," Marilee said.

Looking coyly, Lance asked, "What's going on with you two?"

"We're getting married," Marilee beamed.

"Really?" Lance replied gleefully.

"Really," I smiled.

"When?" Lance asked.

"September," Marilee replied. "At least that's what we're planning now."

"I've got to keep my job and save some money," I explained.

"Congratulations," Lance smiled.

Looking at Marilee, Lance said, "You always told me you were going to marry this guy. I guess you knew what you were talking about!"

"When did you have this conversation?" I asked.

"That day at Benson Park," Lance replied.

Looking at Marilee, I teasingly said, "Really?"

With a smug grin, Marilee said, "I'm going to get you some blankets."

When Marilee left, Lance said, "Sorry I won't be at your wedding."

"Especially since I attended your funeral," I joked.

"What?" Lance asked.

"Yeah," I replied. "We had a marker and everything down by the flat rock on Salt Creek…It was very touching."

"Sorry to disappoint everyone," Lance quipped.

Marilee brought blankets and some pillows for our stay in our old house. Armed with an oil lamp and many stories to share, we headed down the hill to spend one more night together.

CHAPTER 68

Lance entertained us with stories of his escape through Texas and his first days in the army. Lloyd and Lance shared frightening stories about the war, and I could tell they shared an experience I would never fully understand.

A little past midnight, we prepared to extinguish the flickering flame of the oil lamp, when Arty Martin said from the shadows, "Is there room for one more?"

A strange quietness overcame the room as Arty stood in the doorway looking at us. Arty and Lance had been the best of friends, but Lloyd and I were not sure how this confrontation would unfold.

"Come in," Lance Carrington finally invited.

Cautiously, Arty entered the room, carrying the flask he had given Gwen earlier.

"You boys look like you could use a drink," Arty smiled.

"I don't drink anymore," Lance said. "Not since the war."

"I don't drink any less since the war," Lloyd quipped as he took the flask from Arty.

Taking a swig, Lloyd gasped, "What is this, gasoline?"

Arty smiled and said, "Not far from it…A little goes a long way."

"I think I will have a taste," Lance said.

Lloyd handed Lance the flask, as Lance carefully took a small sip.

"How 'bout you, Gill?" Arty offered.

"You heard Marilee, tonight," I replied. "I want her wrath aimed at you…not me."

"How 'bout you, Lance?" Arty asked cautiously. "Where's your wrath aimed at tonight?"

"Have a seat," Lance replied. "Don't think I have much wrath left after the war. Didn't seem that wrath did anyone any good."

"Amen to that," Lloyd added.

"This moonshine?" Lance asked. "It tastes a lot like Leland Holiday's brew."

"I don't know," Arty innocently answered.

"You know alcohol's not going to cure your guilt," Lance said.

"I sleep pretty well," Arty replied.

More pointedly, Lance asked, "How could you do it? How could you marry Gwen when you knew I loved her and knew we'd lied to her? Knew you were lying to her?"

With a pained expression, Arty answered, "I didn't mean for it to go that way at first. I honestly thought you needed to get away from Leland Holiday…and the law. I'd go check on Gwen when she thought you was dead. One thing led to another, and before long she's ready to get married. Dr. Peaudane was willing and Gwen…no disrespect, Gwen was eager."

"You didn't think to tell me," Lance quizzed. "Didn't think you needed to tell me the girl I was dreamin' about in the trenches had a child?"

"Things ain't been a honeymoon the whole time," Arty shot back. "The baby…the baby's got problems, and Gwen…well, Gwen's not exactly the same."

Laughing sarcastically, Lance said, "I'll have to hand it to you Arty Martin, you never cease to amaze me at your ability to explain away the most extraordinary just like everything was normal as could be."

"So," Arty sighed. "What are you going to do? Try to take Gwen back from me?"

Lance looked away for a moment, before saying, "Can't change that. Don't see where it'd do Gwen any good…or me. One thing I learned in the war was to live in the moment, and my moment with Gwen is gone…I know that. I'm headin' out of here, Arty. It'll be best for Gwen, and I suspect it'll be best for you…but you need to know, I'm doin' it for Gwen and not you."

Arty took his scolding in silence before, Lance said, "I loved you…I love you like a brother Arty, but I can't trust you anymore. I wish I could, but I think that may be gone forever. You're going to think I'm mad and think I'm just tryin' to hurt you, but I got to say this. In the war, there were two kinds of men. The ones that looked after themselves and the ones that looked after each other. The ones of us that learned to look after each other…well, some of 'em died, but they knew they were never alone or forgotten. You're one of those guys always lookin' out for himself, and there's no good going to come from it Arty…not for you and not for Gwen. You're as likable a fellow as I've ever met…and that makes it all the worse when you let people down."

"You don't know as much about Gwen as you think," Arty defended.

"You're right, Arty. I never got the opportunity, but I know you, and I'm just telling you the way I feel," Lance sighed. "I'd done anything for you, Arty, but now I'm gone from here, and I hope you learn to be one of those guys who's lookin' out for other people at least some of the time."

"Guess I deserve that," Arty admitted.

"You don't get it," Lance disagreed. "I'm not tryin' to give you what you deserve. I'm tryin' to tell you that you got to change."

"It's getting late," Arty said. "I got to get back. It was good to see you, and I was tryin' to work things out so your homecoming would be more hospitable. I am sorry."

Arty turned with his flask in hand to leave, when Lance said, "I don't like you so much right now, but you're still my friend. Stay away from Leland Holiday, though. No good can come from that stuff you got in the flask."

With his inextinguishable smile, Arty said, "Jeez, Lance. You're starting to sound like Marilee."

"I told you years ago, you needed to listen to her," Lance replied.

"I'll take it under consideration," Arty said, as he headed out the door and back up the hill to his house.

Lloyd, Lance, and I turned in for the night. By the time I woke, Lance Carrington was gone. Lloyd said he left a little before sunrise. Lance never was big on farewells. Gwen came with Marilee to apologize to Lance for her outburst, but he was already gone. Gwen seemed only slightly disappointed and looked as if she had expected him to disappear again.

I asked Marilee later, what Gwen was really thinking, but Marilee confessed she had no idea. I was leaving the Cross Timber later that day wondering if or when I might see Lance Carrington again. In talking with him the night before, I began to realize how he and Lloyd had suffered in the war. Lance also carried the burden of killing a man and leaving a girl he loved. Inadvertently, Lance also knew he had caused hardships for Gwen. Unfortunately, I feared Lance would have to pay more penance in his own mind before he could ever come home.

CHAPTER 69

Two weeks after beginning my new job, I received a telegram from Gwen and Arty saying they would be in town Saturday afternoon to meet Guy Peaudane's train. Since they were not scheduled to arrive until late in the afternoon, I planned to meet them at the train station.

After work, I hurried to the station hoping to get there before the afternoon train arrived. More importantly to me, Marilee would be at the station. The depot was crowded, but I quickly saw the tall profile of Arty Martin standing out in the crowd. Gwen stood by him as well as Lori Peaudane, Guy's wife. Searching the crowd around them, I could not see Marilee.

"Looking for someone, stranger?" Marilee asked from behind me.

"There you are," I replied. "I didn't see you."

"Obviously," Marilee pouted. "You walked right by me and headed for Arty and Gwen."

"Arty's a little taller and easy to spot," I defended.

With a shrug of her shoulders, Marilee said, "He does seem to stand out in a crowd."

Taking Marilee in my arms, I playfully said, "But you've got my attention now."

"How have things been?" I asked hesitantly. "I mean between Gwen and Arty."

"Actually better," Marilee said. "Arty seems to have straightened up, and Lloyd's been a big help. You must have had a talk with him."

"Not me," I confessed. "Lance did."

"Oh," Marilee chirped, "maybe Arty listened for once."

Walking hand in hand toward the rest of the group, we waited for the train to arrive. No one dared mention Lance Carrington, and it seemed in a strange way as if he were still dead, at least in our conversations. Lori Peaudane looked pale, as if she had endured many worried days. In the distance the whistle blew, signaling the train would soon make the final turn into town.

Guy Peaudane exited the train with a crutch to steady himself, but otherwise appeared to be in good health. He looked thin, but flashed a broad smile as he spotted his wife in the crowd. Behind Guy was a plain-looking woman wearing a grey dress, with straight brown hair and sad eyes. The woman looked around nervously, but it was obvious she was with Guy.

"There's Martha, I think," Gwen stated. "I've never really met her."

Guy's sister, Martha had married at a young age and left without returning to the Peaudane family. Gwen had been very young when her mother married Dr. Peaudane and had only seen Martha in a few pictures.

As Lori Peaudane ran to embrace her husband, Gwen suggested to Arty, "Why don't you check on their baggage? Guy looks like he'll be occupied for a while."

Arty agreed and sauntered off to the baggage area where nicely dressed porters loaded luggage onto carts for passengers. While Guy enjoyed his reunion with his wife, Martha walked toward Gwen, Marilee, and me.

"Gwen?" Martha asked, uncertainly.

"Yes," Gwen answered.

Looking straight at Gwen, Martha said, "I was so worried about you after your mother died. Are you all right?"

Gwen looked nearly panicked as she replied, "Yes…Yes I'm fine."

In a serious tone and seemingly oblivious to the presence of others, Martha said, "He was a despicable man, I tried to tell Guy he needed to get you out of that house, but I was so glad when I learned you had married."

"Yes," Gwen meekly replied.

Putting her hands on Gwen's face, the older Martha said, "Don't worry about anything that might have happened. He can't hurt you anymore."

Surprisingly to me, Gwen began to sob as Martha continued to hold her cheeks gently.

Marilee, never one to let an issue rest, said, "That's a terrible thing to say about your father."

Martha with equal bluntness replied, "He was a terrible man that couldn't keep his hands off of any woman…including his own daughter."

Looking at Gwen, we could tell she knew firsthand about Martha's indignation toward her father. Now openly crying, Gwen put her head into Martha's shoulder, while the stepsister she had never met kindly patted her head.

"It's not your fault," Martha consoled. "It's not your fault…It's mine. I tried to tell Guy, but he couldn't bring himself to listen. He believed I was the crazy one and believed my father when he said I was unstable. I should have come for you, but I couldn't face him…but it's all right now."

As Marilee and I stood in disbelief at what Martha was insinuating, the woman looked at us and said, "Why don't you help Guy? I need to talk more with Gwen."

I walked away awkwardly with Marilee as the two stepsisters continued to talk. Guy wanted to spend the night in the old Peaudane home, but his sister flatly refused and asked Gwen if she could stay with her and Arty. Gwen seemed to appreciate her stepsister's visit. Arty and Guy would never understand why. Marilee, who was accustomed to reading people, seemed upset at herself for not understanding her best friend's desperate desire to get married.

The unspoken belief by many was that Gwen was expecting before she and Arty were married, possibly with Lance Carrington's child. Whether there was validity to that rumor or not did not matter anymore. Gwen had been desperate to marry, and Arty had been her way to escape. Watching the group board the train to head to Maud and back to the heart of the Cross Timber, I noticed Gwen holding tightly to Arty's arm and firmly to her hopes of happiness.

CHAPTER 70

Work at the Warren & Smith Hardware Store differed greatly from my previous jobs. Guy Peaudane had been friendly and encouraging. Although I only worked for Mr. Cooper a short time, he also had been relaxed in his management style. Ginn had been the hardest person I had worked for, but even she turned out to have a soft spot in her heart for a lonely high school boy.

Mr. Warren was all business. The level of traffic and the amount of business was beyond anything I experienced in my other jobs. Salesmen were at the top rung of the ladder in this operation, and everybody's job was to support their efforts. When I was hired, I wondered what I would do with the extra time, since my only duties were keeping the records and running the posting machine. I soon learned the meaning of the term full-time employment as I stayed at the store until nearly ten o'clock one night correcting an entry to the accounts.

One particularly hectic day, I did not notice a friendly face until Mr. Warren said in his precise manner of speaking, "Mr. Brooks, you have a customer."

Looking up in surprise at hearing Mr. Warren say those words to me for the first time, I saw Mary Sue McNally and her father standing at the end of the counter. Mary Sue looked full of energy, and she was smiling sweetly.

"I didn't know if you were going to ever call, so I decided to become a customer," Mary Sue playfully teased.

Out of the corner of my eye, I could tell Mr. Warren watched with a critical eye.

"Hello, Gilbert," Mr. McNally greeted. "Mary Sue needs a few things for her home, and she suggested we start here."

Mr. Warren almost smiled, once he understood this was a business instead of a social call.

"I've got a place picked out Gill, but I'm going to need a bed and chest of drawers and a chair to start out," Mary Sue explained.

"So you're really going into the Cross Timber to teach school?" I asked.

"The Cross Timber?" she replied while crinkling her nose. "What's that?"

"Brother. You are from the city. That's what we call the thick woods down around Unity School…The Cross Timber."

"I guess I'll be a Cross Timber girl then," she smiled.

I was only vaguely more familiar with the showroom floor than a customer was, but I helped the McNallys find what they needed.

"You'll need one of these, too," Mr. McNally said, as we walked by the oil lamps. "There's no electricity down there, is there Gilbert?"

"No electricity," I agreed. "You'll probably want two of those."

I could tell Mary Sue had not completely calculated the inconvenience of living in the country.

As she went to the drapery department to look for some blinds, I asked Mr. McNally, "Does she know what she's in for?"

"I don't think so, but she's been so excited I haven't bothered her with the details," Mr. McNally answered.

"What do you think about her living on her own?" I continued.

With a smile, he replied, "Mary Sue's a very independent girl. She'll do fine. This teaching thing has helped her get her mind off of…well, it's gotten her mind off the past."

"I've got a surprise for you," I said to Mr. McNally. "Do you remember my friend, Lance Carrington?"

In a sober voice, Mr. McNally said, "Yes, the boy who drowned."

"That's the news," I excitedly explained. "He showed up a couple of weeks ago. He's been in the war all this time."

"What?" Mr. McNally said. "He's alive?"

"Yes," I smiled.

"That's great news," Mr. McNally said. "Did you tell him what a wonderful funeral we had?"

"I did."

"You might want to have him come by the office sometime, to straighten out the death certificate," Mr. McNally added.

"He's not here anymore," I explained.

"Oh," Mr. McNally replied. "Well, if he ever does show up, I'd like to meet him. I've never had a dead client resurrect before."

"I'll tell him," I assured.

Walking up to us, Mary Sue asked, "Are you still going to take me down to…the Cross Timber…to introduce me to some people?"

"Sure," I confirmed. "When do you want to go?"

Looking at her father, she said, "How about this Sunday?"

"It works for me," I replied.

"Can we borrow the car?" she asked her father.

Mr. McNally agreed, and we arranged to meet at the McNally home early Sunday morning. I rang up the sale and walked Mary Sue to the door, confirming our trip to the south part of the county. Sending a telegram to Marilee, I told her to expect a surprise on Sunday.

CHAPTER 71

Church members frantically fanned the stale air to keep pesky flies away at morning services at the church building in Avoca. A wary Marilee had been cordial to Mary Sue McNally, but strategically positioned herself in the pew between the visitor and her fiancé.

Marilee invited Mary Sue to the Martin home for lunch, and the only apprehension came from Mr. Martin's disapproving stare directed at me. After lunch, the younger Martin boys wrestled the ice cream freezer as Marilee and Mary Sue began forging a friendship.

I was content to let the boys churn the ice cream I was soon to enjoy when I heard the boisterous voice of Arty Martin say, "Put your back into it, boys. I like my cream frozen thick."

"Hey, Arty," I greeted. "What's going on?"

"I heard they were having ice cream and came running," Arty smiled.

"Is Gwen with you?" I asked.

"She's with Marilee," he replied before barking at his brothers. "Come on, boys, use your muscles."

"We are," Arty's younger brother, Floyd, defended. "I'd like to see you do better."

With his mischievous grin, Arty quickly rolled up his sleeves and said, "Move over."

The skinny Floyd vacated his spot on top of the freezer, while Arty replaced him. Arty's muscular arms turned the crank at twice the rate the other boys had managed. There was no real need to churn the ice cream with that much effort, but it was Arty's good-natured way of challenging his younger brothers.

After a few minutes, Arty pretending not to be tired, got up and said, "Now that's how you do it."

Another younger brother, Elmo Martin, took over and I could not help but smile at his feeble attempts to match his older brother's pace.

"So, what are you doin' here?" Arty asked, as he struggled to hide that he was nearly out of breath.

"I brought the new school teacher down to introduce her around," I explained.

"There's going to be another teacher at Fuss Box?" Arty smiled. "She must be an old battle ax like old Miss Long."

"No," I corrected. "She's actually our age and attractive."

With a wry smile, Arty said, "Let's go meet her."

Shaking my head, I smiled at Arty's enthusiasm to meet a pretty girl. His excitement vanished, however, as we entered the house. With a quick tug, Arty pulled me back out of the room before the women noticed us.

"Why did you bring her here?" a frantic Arty whispered.

"You know Mary Sue?" I asked in confusion.

Giving me a harsh look, Arty explained, "She's the girl that lived down the street from Laura Jones. How could you bring her here?"

"She's the new teacher," I defended. "She was coming here with or without me. How indiscreet have you been?"

"That's not the issue," Arty responded. "I can't believe you brought her here to meet Marilee! Are you crazy?"

With a deep sigh, I said, "I don't have anything to hide. She was coming here whether I invited her or not."

"Gilbert, is that you?" Marilee asked from the other room.

While looking at Arty, I answered, "Yes, I'm on my way."

Arty followed me while the women vigorously fanned themselves and sipped iced tea. Marilee sat close to Mary Sue while Mrs. Martin and Gwen were across the room.

"There you are," Marilee smiled. "Do you know where Mary Sue is going to live?"

"Not really," I replied.

"She's going to be at the bottom of Cherry Hill, where your family used to live," Marilee revealed.

"Really," I said. "That will be a little ways from the schoolhouse."

"It's okay," the energetic Mary Sue confirmed. "Daddy's letting me have his car to drive so it will be no problem at all."

Seeing that Mary Sue was tactfully trying to see Arty, who was standing behind me, I said, "Don't know if you remember my friend Arty? I think you met him at the movies one time."

Arty glared at me while smiling superficially at the guest.

"Yes, I remember," Mary Sue sweetly said. "I was talking to Gwen about that night just a while ago. It's good to see you, again. Gwen tells me you have a son?"

Arty, convinced Mary Sue did not recognize him from his trips to see Laura Jones, said, "Yes…yes we do."

"I can't wait to meet him," Mary Sue smiled.

Quickly looking at Gwen to confirm his secret was safe, Arty said, "Well, he's—"

"I know," Mary Sue interrupted. "Gwen told me he was special, but all children are special, don't you think?"

"I suppose so," Arty muttered.

"Mary Sue was telling me about a school in Oklahoma City," Gwen added, "that might be able to help Jackie with his condition when he's older."

Determining the women's conversation had been about children and not his indiscretion, Arty said, "I appreciate your concern. I know

Gwen has struggled with what to do. I'm sure she's enjoyed your suggestions."

"Good to meet you," Mary Sue restated.

Looking around the room, Mary Sue added, "It's been wonderful meeting all of you. I'll have to confess, I've been a little nervous about coming to a strange place for my first teaching job, but you have certainly made me feel welcome."

"I'm looking forward to having you so close," Marilee smiled. "It will be like having a sister around."

We ate ice cream and visited more during the afternoon. Arty seemed relieved that Mary Sue did not notice his trips to see Laura Jones, but he kept his distance from her just the same. Marilee and I took Mary Sue to meet a few families with children enrolled in school, before Mary Sue and I headed back north.

It would take me several months to learn the real reason for Arty Martin's anxiety about the attractive, young schoolteacher coming to the Cross Timber.

PART IV

CHAPTER 72

The second Saturday of September 1920, was warm, with only a hint of fall in the air. It was the first Saturday I had asked to be off since June, and it was a special day as I traveled to the Martin home for my wedding. As Mr. Martin had requested, we were married in the church building with many of our friends and family attending the simple ceremony.

Mr. Martin handed Marilee an envelope on our wedding day, and to my astonishment, it contained a check for $2,000. Mr. Martin never seemed happy or impressed with Marilee's choice in a husband, but we gladly accepted the dowry.

Arty warned me about the challenges of matrimony, but Marilee was superbly organized and took immediate charge of our household. With a portion of Marilee's wedding money, we moved from my cramped one-room apartment to a small house south of Main Street in Shawnee, near Franklin School. We stashed most of the money in the bank for rainy days, although at our young age, it seemed nothing but prosperity was on the horizon. Marilee, who had been accustomed to cooking for large groups, bought a fifty-pound bag of flour from the milling company. It took several weeks to transition to making smaller meals, and she looked for every opportunity to invite friends or family to our house to eat.

By Christmas, my job, marriage, and living in the city had become normal, as Marilee and I settled into our life together. By the time our first anniversary approached, however, things started to change. The

Great War in Europe had sustained prices and created a boom, as material and, unfortunately, men were consumed in the effort. By 1921, the war boom was over, as prices for crops fell and business began to slow down.

Compounding the problems in Shawnee, 800 Rock Island Railroad employees went on strike, threatening to shutdown the entire Rock Island line. The strike was settled in a couple of days with no disruption to workers or freight, but the action had a poor affect on business at the hardware store.

It was a pitiful October day in 1921, when Mr. Warren called me into his office to explain the slow business meant he was going to reduce his staff. Being the newest employee, I left my place of employment with a small severance for the week's work. I faced a long walk home to tell Marilee our rainy day had come.

Walking to the house, I noticed a slick, new Oldsmobile parked in front. Taking a moment to admire the automobile, one I was now sure I could never afford, I headed into the house to find Arty and Gwen sitting in our small front room.

"There he is," an energetic Arty proclaimed as I dejectedly walked through the door.

"Hey," I replied, nodding slightly to our two guests.

"Arty and Gwen are moving to Shawnee," Marilee informed, as she wore a flour-splattered apron and was obviously baking pies from the aroma coming from her kitchen.

"Really," I replied. "What about the farm?"

"The weeds can have the farm," Arty replied. "At the price of everything, it's not worth the effort."

"What does your dad say?" I asked suspiciously.

Arty adjusted the collar on his starched white shirt and said, "He wasn't excited about the proposition, but…well, that's why I've come to see you."

"What do I have to do with anything?" I warily asked.

"You'll see," Arty said excitedly. "Let's go for a drive. You too, Marilee."

"I've got pies in the oven," Marilee protested.

"Well…how long will they be?" Arty asked in an agitated tone.

"About a half an hour," she replied.

"We'll wait," Arty said. "But hurry up, will you."

Marilee frowned at her charismatic brother and returned to her kitchen. Gwen, dressed in a stylish black dress that came up nearly to the knees, followed her friend into the kitchen.

"What's up?" I asked, as I studied Arty.

"Opportunity," he smiled. "Lots of opportunity."

"There's a depression going on, if you haven't noticed," I said, still stinging from losing my job earlier in the afternoon. "The stock market's down, business is bad…and you know what commodity prices are."

"There's nothing like a little downturn for opportunity," Arty boldly proclaimed.

"I don't see it," I complained.

"You will," Arty grinned. "You will."

"So, where are you moving to?" I asked.

"We've found a house on North Park," Arty boasted.

North Park was an area of some of the biggest and finest homes in town. It contrasted greatly with the modest home where Marilee and I lived.

"What did you do, sell the farm?" I asked.

"Naw," Arty claimed. "Just paid down on a house. The farm still belongs to Dad."

"How's the baby?" I asked.

Baby Jackie had been taken to a home in Oklahoma City shortly after Marilee and I married. Gwen and Arty fought for months about what to do with the child. Gwen had always wanted to keep him at home, while Arty was convinced the child needed more care. Arty's main concern was the drain the child seemed to have on Gwen.

With a frown, Arty said, "He's doing great. Gwen goes at least once a month, and I think she's beginning to see he's getting the care he needs there."

"How's Lloyd?" I asked.

"Lloyd's a good worker," Arty shrugged. "I don't see much future in farming, but I hear your dad's done well farming that widow lady's land west of town."

"I think he has," I agreed.

"Does Lloyd have a girl or anything?" I asked.

"Not that I can tell," Arty replied. "He spends most his time 'round our place…I think it hurt him as much as Gwen to see Jackie go off. He seemed to take a liking to the boy. Your friend, Mary Sue, tried to get his eye, but Lloyd didn't seem too interested."

Hesitating slightly, I asked, "Have you heard from Lance?"

"Naw," Arty grimaced. "Not since he left the last time. How 'bout you?"

"I got a letter a couple of months ago," I confessed. "Said he was doing well, but…didn't really say much at all."

"I guess that's Lance," Arty reasoned, seemingly ignoring the fact that he was one of the main causes for Lance staying away. "I thought we might see him at your wedding, but who knows."

"Yeah," I nodded.

After a moment of silence, Arty said, "I miss him. I wished I'd handled things different, but—"

Leaning over to whisper he said, "Gwen was goin' to get married, didn't matter to her. She finally told me some of the stuff happenin' at her house…I had no idea."

"How is she?" I asked, having heard some of the past traumas of Gwen's home life from Marilee.

"She's fine," Arty said. "I think moving to town and away from that place will help."

Leaning over to whisper again, he said, "Since the baby's away, we're finally getting to act like a couple again."

"What are you two gossiping about?" Marilee asked, as she and Gwen came from the kitchen.

"Just talking about how much we love our wives," Arty playfully answered.

"I bet," Marilee answered her brother suspiciously.

"Are you finally ready to go?" Arty asked.

"I don't look as dressed up as you, but you said we were just going for a drive?" Marilee confirmed.

Looking at Gwen, Arty said, "You look fine."

Arty's Oldsmobile was a black coupe with leather seats and whitewall tires. Although Marilee asked several times, Arty would not tell us what he was up to as he headed the car toward town. Turning on Main Street he drove west up the slight rise past the Santa Fe Depot. As he continued west, I concluded Arty was heading to Park Street to show off his new home.

Before coming to Park Street, however, Arty parked the car on Main Street in front of the old J. L. Roebuck Hardware store. The large hardware store was next to the Cozy Theater, where various shows stopped to perform. The vacant store was also located close to the Rock Island Shops where several hundred men worked, maintaining the trains that rumbled across the southwest.

"Are we going to a show?" I asked, assuming we were headed to the theater.

"No, we're going here," Arty claimed, pointing at the J. L. Roebuck store.

"This place has been out of business for over a year," I explained.

"Not anymore," Arty smiled. "It's ours!"

"I don't understand," I said in confusion.

"I want you to be my partner," Arty explained. "I've got a silent partner to put the money up, but I need someone who knows the business. When I told Dad, he said he would only support me moving to town if you'd be my partner."

Looking at Marilee, I asked, "Your dad said that?"

Arty nodded.

"Mr. Roebuck left the building in good condition, all we need is a sign and merchandise, and we're in business," Arty gleamed. "You still have the two thousand from your wedding, don't you?"

"Most of it, but that's Marilee's money," I noted.

"What do you say, Marilee?" Arty pressed.

"I don't know," she sighed. "I was cooking pies a few minutes ago."

"You better let us talk about it," I surmised.

Arty, frowning at the delay, said, "Okay, but don't take too long. I've already put down a deposit on this place that I can't get back. Dad won't support me being here, if you don't come in on the deal. I've got train tickets to Chicago next week to attend the market."

"What kind of business are you thinking about?" I asked.

"We're going into the furniture business," Arty stated flatly.

CHAPTER 73

Arty drove by a beautiful two-story house on Park Street. A sculpted hedge in front was accented by fluted columns framing a large porch. An eager Arty dropped Marilee and me off at our house, and we promised to give him an answer in two days.

As Arty and Gwen's Oldsmobile turned the corner, Marilee asked, "What do you think?"

"I don't know what to think," I sighed.

"Daddy must think it's a good idea," Marilee supposed.

With a blank stare, I said, "Doesn't sound much like your father, does it?"

"Dad has a lot of confidence in you, Gilbert," Marilee claimed.

Looking at her suspiciously, I said, "Your father? The man who once said, 'No share cropper's goin' to marry my daughter.' The same man who still stares me down to this day?"

Laughing, Marilee smirked, "I said he had confidence in you…I didn't say he was happy about you marrying his daughter."

I smiled at Marilee's assessment, as she leaned her head on my shoulder.

As I stood reflecting on the day, Marilee asked, "What's wrong?"

"Huh?"

"Gilbert, I've known you long enough to tell when something's bothering you," Marilee reasoned. "Are you going to tell me?"

"I lost my job today," I confessed.

"Why?" a concerned Marilee asked.

Shrugging my shoulders, I said, "Business is soft, I guess. They've figured out how to run the posting machine, and I'm the last man they hired."

"I'm sorry," Marilee said.

"I've been dreading telling you all afternoon, and then Arty shows up with his big car, a big house, and big plans. How much confidence would your father have in me now?"

"I believe in you," Marilee smiled, "and obviously Daddy does too."

"Thanks."

"I guess it's a good thing Arty asked you to be a partner," Marilee said.

Looking at her, I replied with a raised eyebrow, "You think it would be a good idea?"

"Of course," Marilee said. "We've got the money to buy in. Arty's got some harebrained ideas, but he knows how to promote. You've got good business sense. I've heard Guy Peaudane say so himself."

"But if business is slow at an established store like Warren & Smith, what could we expect?" I explained.

"Things are never as good or bad as they seem," Marilee said. "I think that knuckleheaded brother of mine might be right. This is a good opportunity to get in business. Sometimes you have to throw your hat over the fence and try something new."

"You think so?" I asked.

"I know so," Marilee affirmed. "It'll be the store confidence built."

Looking at Marilee, I said, "I guess we're in the furniture business."

CHAPTER 74

With Marilee's savings, the Brooks & Martin Furniture Company opened in the spring of 1922. Arty ordered a sign saying Martin & Brooks, but Marilee was dogmatic that Brooks & Martin sounded better.

Arty and I caught the train to Chicago to buy merchandise. Chicago was like another world for someone who had never been out of Pottawatomie County. Arty adapted quickly to the pace of the city. For some reason, his accent and drawl sounded charming while mine felt like I had just arrived from the farm.

Arty and I were well-matched partners, although we had different personalities. He let me conduct the daily business, while he attended meetings and promoted the store in the community. Arty was a natural salesman when he happened to be in the store, and within a month, the store made a small profit.

Gwen and Marilee were also learning they had some differences. Gwen lived in the big house on Park Street, joined every club possible, and socialized with a more fashionable crowd. Marilee seemed content with our modest house, keeping a garden, and maintaining a home. Gwen had changed to where I barely recognized the girl I had known back in the Cross Timber. More conscious of her appearance, Gwen was also increasingly concerned with her acquaintances.

The growing conflict between Gwen and Marilee almost boiled over in the store one day, when Gwen suggested Marilee might want to buy some of her old dresses. Marilee was about to explain that she did not need a hand-me-down from her brother's wife, when the front door bell dinged indicating a customer had come to shop. It was my turn to wait on the customer, but Arty nearly knocked me down to greet the man coming in the front door. I did not pay much attention to the man or who he was, as I went back to make sure Marilee did not do bodily harm to Gwen.

As I approached, the always-observant Marilee said in a strange whisper, "Do you know who that is?"

Shaking my head, I turned to see a man in an expensive suit talking to Arty Martin in the front of the store. At first, I believed my eyes were deceiving me, as the two men appeared to be having a cordial almost jovial conversation.

Looking at Marilee, I said, "It looks like Leland Holiday!"

As I moved to the office to be less conspicuous, Marilee followed close behind. We looked at each other in disbelief, as Arty carried on a lively and friendly conversation with Leland Holiday. Leland was a distinguished-looking man in his early forties. He had a touch of gray in his temples, but the mustache was still black and thick. Although looking like a respectable businessman, he still had a hardness to him that seemed to dare anyone to cross him.

Arty and Leland walked casually about the store looking at merchandise. As they moved toward Gwen, I shuddered thinking how uneasy he had made her feel not so many years ago at the Peaudane General Store.

I heard Marilee audibly gasp, when Leland approached and Gwen greeted him with a kiss on the cheek. As Gwen flirtingly followed the two men around, they eventually meandered to the office.

Trying to appear busy and avoid eye contact, I cringed when I heard Arty say, "Gill, I need you to write up a ticket."

Marilee glared at Arty, not because he was selling furniture to Leland Holiday, but because of the tone of voice he used with me. She tugged gently on my sleeve to stay, but I went to serve the customer.

"You remember Leland Holiday, don't you?" Arty introduced, as if he were an old friend.

I nodded in acknowledgement as Leland carefully studied me.

"Leland's been working security for the Rock Island line, but tells me he's taken a new position as head of the craft union of the shop," Arty informed.

"Good to see you," I muttered.

Leland Holiday looked suspiciously at me, before saying, "I've got an office across the street and thought it was time to furnish it."

I wanted to ask about all the other side businesses, like bootlegging and running the Potanole speakeasy, but politely nodded instead.

"Leland's, goin' to order one of those fancy leather chairs," Arty smiled.

Pointing to a catalog, Arty showed a stylish leather chair costing almost seven hundred dollars. I nearly gasped. A sale like that represented weeks of business. With a total inventory of less than four thousand dollars, this was a huge sale for us.

"How much would you like to pay down?" I asked.

Looking at Arty, Leland replied, "I'll catch you when it gets here."

Somewhat flustered, I said, "I'm sorry we require at least ten percent down on special orders."

Leland Holiday cut his eyes at my business partner, and Arty quickly said, "That won't be a problem. You can take care of it later."

Speechless, I just glared at Arty. We spent many hours writing store policies before we opened, and it had been Arty who demanded we require down payments on all special orders. Trying to hide my anger at Arty's tone, I slid the sales slip to him and retreated to do some office work while he continued to talk to Leland Holiday.

While Arty and Leland stood at the counter, Gwen sauntered up to join them.

Leland, admiring her low-cut dress with a high hemline, said, "You two need to come to a party I'm having this Saturday for Frank

Watson, the state representative. It should be quite a time. Everyone will be there, and I know Frank would love to meet you two."

"Sure," Arty smiled. "We'd love to come."

"Do we need to bring anything?" Gwen asked.

Laughing, Leland Holiday said, "Just your checkbook! That'll guarantee the representative will be glad to see you."

Arty and Gwen laughed superficially at his comment as Leland continued to ogle Gwen. Writing down the address and time, Leland Holiday excused himself and headed out the door.

Before leaving, Leland said to Arty, "You want to go see my new office?"

Arty enthusiastically accepted the invitation, and the two men headed out the front door.

"What's going on?" an agitated Marilee asked Gwen, who was still loitering at the front counter.

"What do you mean?" Gwen answered in an innocent tone that only infuriated Marilee.

"What do I mean?" Marilee replied. "Arty's buddy-buddy with Leland Holiday like he's some long lost friend!"

"Arty's just promoting the store," Gwen replied, while batting her painted eyelids.

"Arty's promoting himself," Marilee charged.

Trying to avoid the fight brewing between the two women, I said, "I think we're just surprised Arty would seem so friendly to someone like Leland Holiday."

Looking at me as if I did not understand the situation, Gwen said, "Leland Holiday's a very important and influential man in this town and in the county now. He's worked his way up to some considerable influence with many people at the rail yard. You two need to learn how the world works."

"How the world works!" Marilee angrily interjected. "Have you forgotten what the Holidays did to poor Lance?"

Gwen grimaced at the question and said, "That was a long time ago."

Talking sternly to her, Marilee said, "I know you don't like to be reminded that you were once married to riff-raff like Lance Carrington, but I clearly remember how you used to tell me how much you loved him…and I know for a fact he loved you."

In an angry tone, Gwen pointedly said, "You're right! I don't like to be reminded. You know nothing, Marilee. If I did love Lance, that love vanished when he left me alone with my stepfather without saying good-bye! Arty was there for me, and he's taken care of me. He's trying to take care of you two now with this store and neither of you appreciate all he's done for this place!"

Gwen was on the verge of tears, when Marilee said in a kinder voice, "You're right, Gwen. I don't know what all you've been through and won't pretend to know, but I know you're my sister-in-law now, and I'm afraid we were closer when we were just friends."

Gwen cried as she walked out the back door and whimpered, "I'm still your friend, Marilee, but you just don't know."

A bewildered Marilee stood at the counter with me and said meekly, "That didn't go well."

"No," I agreed.

Looking at me as if I should have a more comforting answer, Marilee said, "How can you stand the way Arty's treating you? You're a partner in this business, and Arty orders you around worse than Guy Peaudane ever did."

"I don't take it personal," I tried to explain. "Arty's got his strengths, and I have mine. I'm glad he's good at drumming up business and just never thought it would be with the likes of Leland Holiday."

"You've got that right," Marilee replied. "I'm worried about Gwen."

"She seems fine to me," I observed. "Maybe a little too full of herself, but I guess the city does that to some people."

"I've known Gwen since we were girls," Marilee said. "This is not the girl I knew. Something's bothering her, and I don't know what it is. Maybe it was Lance, maybe it's what happened before, or maybe it's the baby, but she's hurting, and I don't like the medicine she's using for the pain."

"She'll be all right," I reasoned.

"Maybe," Marilee sighed. "I need to try to be more supportive, I guess."

Arty walked in front of the store window on his way in when Marilee said, "This is the one I want to straighten out."

As Arty walked in, I decided to spare him some of Marilee's wrath by pointedly asking, "What was that about?"

"What?" he answered innocently.

"Leland Holiday comes in here and instead of throwing him out on his ear, you're treating him like he's some long lost friend," I charged.

"Relax," Arty said. "He's a customer now."

"One that's ordered a chair without a down payment," I hotly replied. "A chair that will break us if he doesn't come through and buy it. It'll take three months to get that piece, and if he doesn't take it I don't know who we'd sell it to."

"He'll come through," Arty calmly assured. "I'll guarantee it."

"With what," I asked. "We've got everything we own in this store and not much room for mistakes. You're spending money like it grows in the warehouse, and I'm worried."

"Don't worry," Arty smiled. "Just manage the business, and we'll be fine. Do you think it's easy drumming up business for this place?"

"No," I said shaking my head. "I appreciate your efforts, but Leland Holiday? Have you forgotten what he did to Lance?"

"That was a long time ago," Arty curtly explained. "Do you think I would jeopardize one of the best business contacts in town about a squabble over stealing watermelons?"

"It was more than that," I replied. "A man got killed, and you helped send Lance running away. It wasn't that long ago, either."

In a stern voice, Arty said, "That was Lance's mistake, not mine. Leland Holiday's in a position to help me out…to help the store, and I've got to play his game."

Giving me a condescending look, he added, "You need to grow up and forget about childhood mischief."

As I stood dumbfounded, Marilee said, "You better straighten up, Arty Martin."

"Or what?" Arty replied. "Are you going to run home and tell Father?"

"Daddy's part owner of the operation too," Marilee noted. "I think he might have an interest in how you're running things. I know he wouldn't like how you're treating Gwen."

"What do you know about Gwen?" Arty sharply replied. "She's living in a fine house, being driven in a new car, and wearing the best of everything. I would think your daddy would be more appalled that you don't have those things."

In a more rational tone, Marilee said, "You're not going to be able to buy Gwen out of the pain she's in. She needs you Arty, not your fancy friends and expectations."

"Marilee," Arty said impatiently. "If you want to give me advice on how to bake a casserole, I'll listen, but you're not the person I depend on to coach me on how to live life. You need to get out sometime."

Marilee fumed as Arty put on his hat to leave early for the day.

"You mind closing tonight, Gill?" Arty said in a mocking tone. "Marilee says I need to see to my wife."

Marilee did not respond as Arty headed to the back door before stopping to say, "And don't worry about bothering Father. He's not our silent partner…Leland Holiday is."

CHAPTER 75

Arty came to work the next day, as if revealing Leland Holiday as our partner was of no consequence. When I tried to discuss the situation with him, he turned surly and found other distractions to occupy his time.

The business was doing well, thanks in part to Arty's efforts to promote the store and himself in town. We joined the Shawnee Commercial Club, which included many of the business and professional men in the city. Arty was immediately appointed to a committee.

By the summer of 1922, however, events threatened our fledgling business. First, boll weevils infested the county's cotton crop, causing worry to farmers like Mr. Martin and near ruin to men of lesser means like my dad and brother Lloyd. Besides the plight of boll weevils, a national strike was called for all railroad shop workers on July 1, 1922. With the Rock Island Shops located so close to Brooks and Martin, any labor dispute was bad for business.

During the war, the Railroad Labor Board made sure the nation's transportation system ran smoothly, but by 1922, the post-war business doldrums caused the board to reduce the wages of shop workers by seven cents. The shop workers organized a nationwide walkout on all rail companies, but the operator's union did not join the strike, meaning the railways were still open for business. The railroad companies believed the labor could be easily replaced in the slow economic times, and the Rock Island Shop in Shawnee quickly hired replacement workers to cross the lines. One of the men desperate for a job was my brother Lloyd.

The strike appeared to be a short inconvenience to our business, but events escalated as angry workers demonstrated daily in front of the gate to the Rock Island Shop. Business suffered. Eight hundred workers were without a paycheck at the Rock Island Shop, and another three hundred were off work at the Santa Fe Shop. By the end of the month, the situation was critical enough that President Warren Harding mediated the conflict. Harding's proposal offered little to the workers on strike except a provision to ensure they would retain any seniority achieved before the walkout.

Temporary workers, like Lloyd, bought a few items at the store, but their futures were uncertain, and railroads hired only enough men to get the most essential work done. Lloyd made enough money to rent a small house, but he was grateful to come to supper to enjoy Marilee's cooking on the last Friday night of July.

"You outdid yourself, Marilee," the lean Lloyd said, as he stretched his back and patted his flat stomach.

With a pleasant smile, Marilee replied, "I'd take that complement more seriously if it weren't coming from a bachelor."

Lloyd laughed and said, "I'll have to admit my cooking's not so good, but I'm not that picky. That was a great meal, though, and I appreciate it."

Marilee grinned. "You're welcome here any time."

"That's good to know," Lloyd stoically said. "I'm not welcome everywhere."

"What do you mean?" a naïve Marilee asked.

I worked close enough to the rail yard to know the anger and hostility spewed at the workers. Men like Lloyd were cursed daily, spit on, and often pelted with rocks. The strike caused a steep division in the business community with merchants not wanting to take sides.

"Lots of people don't have no use for a scab," Lloyd explained.

Never afraid to ask a question, Marilee inquired, "What's a scab?"

"That's what they call us," Lloyd replied. "That and other names I prefer not to repeat in your company."

"That's terrible!" Marilee exclaimed. "You're just trying to make a living."

"I feel that way, but I see where the other fellas are coming from. I'd be none too happy to see some farmer taking my job," Lloyd reasoned. "It don't matter much anyway. President Harding settled the thing, and from what I hear, the union boys are happy to be back to work."

"Did they tell you anything today?" I asked.

"Naw," Lloyd shrugged. "The foreman didn't say nothing, I've just heard things. I'll keep showing up until they tell me not to come. The foreman likes my work. I got used to fixin' things in the artillery during the war. It's not a lot different."

"Things'll work out," Marilee encouraged. "They always do."

"I hope," Lloyd replied. "Do you see Gwen or Arty much?"

Trying to conceal a frown, I said, "I see Arty most days. He stays busy outside the store. Gwen I don't' see so much."

"Gwen's not got much time for common folks like us," Marilee pouted, still stinging from the information that Arty and Gwen had befriended Leland Holiday.

"She was always nice to me," Lloyd said. "Arty'd leave her alone all the time back home, and I'd come check on things around the house. She was always eager for company."

"She's got new company now," Marilee complained.

"Sending the boy away was tough on her," Lloyd reasoned. "She hated it, but Arty insisted. You don't know how a thing like that'll work on you."

"Maybe you're right," Marilee politely agreed. "But it don't mean you got to go putting on airs."

Lloyd thought for a moment and said, "I knew a fella in the army whose family was some muckity-muck from back east. I'd never been around anyone so hateful. But we's both soldiers, and in the fight, none of that mattered much. I got to know him, and we became friends. Found out his carrying on was just coverin' up the fact he didn't want people to know he was scared just like the rest of us. His father sent him to war to toughen him up. He turned out to be a good fella after you got past the things he's afraid of."

"Where's he from?" I asked, seizing on the opportunity to question Lloyd about his war experience.

"Providence, Rhode Island," Lloyd said quietly.

Lloyd was always hesitant to discuss his war buddies so I asked. "What's he doing now?"

With a slight tilt of the head and pained expression, Lloyd answered, "He's dead. Got blown up not more than twenty yards away. I ran to help him, but there was nothing left. We'd talked five minutes earlier; then he was gone. I miss that fella."

After an awkward silence, Lloyd added, "Anyway, I figure I can handle about any abuse the strikers throw at me. It's just words."

"I'm sorry," I apologized, for asking about his friend.

With his easy, reassuring smile, Lloyd said, "Not your fault. You didn't know."

Anxious to redirect the conversation, Marilee said, "When are you going to settle down, Lloyd, and get married?"

With a bashful smile, Lloyd said, "I'll get around to it one of these days. My brother here has married up the best cook and seems like all the good women are already taken."

We talked a little longer about some of his war experiences. Lloyd explained he had been shy around people upon coming back from the war, but said he was feeling more comfortable. He said the old home place became lonely when Gwen and Arty moved away. Lloyd left after dark, and I empathized with his uncertainty about his future. Lloyd, however, was much less concerned than I was about his outlook, and he seemed fairly content with his life. None of us could have expected that warm July night how crazy our world could get.

CHAPTER 76

The rumbling of the crowd could be heard on Main Street early Monday morning as angry workers lined the street around the entrance to the Rock Island Shops. President Harding had suggested a resolution to the nationwide rail workers strike, which appeared to settle the issue only a few days before.

Harding outlined three points. The railway managers and workers were to agree to recognize the authority of the Railroad Labor Board in all disputes. The railroad carriers would withdraw all lawsuits growing out of the month long strike. The third point allowed employees on strike to return to work at their former positions. Wages and benefits were not discussed. The striking workers were not excited about the outcome but were eager to get back to work and collect their pay.

In the Sunday *New York Times*, however, the Association of Railway Executives replied to the President's decision in a letter published in the newspaper, which said they would agree to the first two parts of the president's plan but explained they could not agree to the third, since commitments had been made to replacement workers. The executives reasoned the union violated the Railroad Labor Board's original orders by going on strike forcing the companies to hire replacement workers. In their opinion, they were obligated to fulfill commitments made to their new workforce. The executives agreed to let workers return to the shops, but they would not assure workers their former positions. The response caused anger and division among the shop craft workers.

"I don't know why those fools won't shut up and go back to work," Arty lamented, as he looked out the store window at the rowdy crowd. "They're bad for business and not doing anybody any good."

"They've definitely hurt traffic this morning," I replied. "We haven't made a sale today. It's bad business and bad for business, but I don't see this thing ending soon."

"I was at the Shawnee Commercial Club meeting the other day, and something's going to give," Arty said flatly. "A lot of the businessmen understand this constant harassment and threat of riot on the streets is hurting commerce."

"I think we better stay out of it," I admonished. "It don't matter how this thing turns out, there's going to be some bitter people on both sides. Guy Peaudane always told me business and politics were bad partners."

"Maybe," Arty admitted. "But something's got to give."

Sidewalks were crowded as men wandered about the downtown area, some carrying signs, some meeting in small groups, and some with a desperate look I had seen so many times on the farm. The constant motion of people this morning, including police, blocked my view of Leland Holiday walking to the front door. With the hundreds of people outside looking as if they might storm the front gate of the Rock Island Shop, Leland Holiday stepped into the store with a relaxed demeanor and seemed to ignore the rowdy workers outside. He had an attractive young woman on his arm with a mischievous look and the kind of appearance hard to ignore.

"Leland?" Arty greeted.

"I'd like to introduce you to someone," Leland politely explained. "This is Veronica Willis. Veronica, this is Arty Martin and Gilbert Brooks."

Never shy about meeting a pretty girl, Arty enthusiastically said in a low-pitched voice, "Good to meet you, Veronica."

In a more formal tone, I said, "Hello."

"Nice to meet you," she replied, while chomping her gum.

"Didn't expect to see you here today," Arty cordially said to Leland as he continued to glance at the girl. "Figured you'd be busy policing this mess."

Leland smiled under his handlebar mustache and said, "I left that dead cat on someone else's door this morning."

"What do you mean?" an interested Arty asked.

"I resigned my position as chief of security," Leland said.

"Wow," Arty whistled. "That's a surprise."

Leland shrugged, "This thing's gone on too long, and I'm tired of guarding those scabs crossing the line."

I grimaced to think of Lloyd in harm's way but kept quiet and listened.

"Besides," Leland continued. "This thing with the union is bad politics. Frank Watson and I figure these union boys are going to be aggravated enough to vote with a vengeance come November. Frank's thinking about giving up his representative's seat to run for the senate. We can't be seen as standing against the union."

"Are you goin' to run for Frank's seat?" Arty asked.

With an insincere laugh, Leland said, "Not me. I learned long ago there's no real power in getting elected. The trick is to work with the bunch getting the guy elected. Once your man's in, you can profit a whole lot more behind the scenes than being up front. I'll leave it to the pretty boys like Frank to run, and I'll stay in the background finding out where the roads are goin' and who's deciding the bids. Heck, we might put you in old Frank's place."

Arty could barely contain his excitement at this prospect.

"Anyway," Leland asked. "How's business?"

"Been slow," Arty confessed. "People are either out of work or distracted. I'm ready for this mess to end."

"It'll end, I'm going to make sure of that soon enough," Leland assured. "Speaking of which, I may need a favor. You're part of that Shawnee Commercial Club, right?"

"Yeah," Arty answered.

"Good," Leland smiled. "I'm not sure they're going to back the union on this one, and I may need your help to explain to 'em that these workers being out of a job is bad for business."

"Sure," Arty eagerly accepted. "But I don't know how much influence I got."

Laughing at his new protégé, Leland said, "I'll give you some pointers, besides, what we need more than anything, are some eyes and ears in that group. You tell me what's going on, and I'll make sure it makes the paper in the right way. I need another favor too. Veronica needs a job, and I think she would be perfect as the secretary here. What do you think?"

Before I could explain we were barely keeping the doors open and could not afford a secretary, Arty cheerfully said, "Sure. Gill and I were just talking about needing someone."

Looking at me, as if daring me to speak, Arty added, "Veronica will liven the place up. Right, Gill?"

"I think we should maybe talk about—" I began.

"No need," Arty interrupted. "When can you start?"

Veronica looked at Leland Holiday, as he said, "She can start tomorrow."

"Great," Arty replied.

"I appreciate it," Leland said. "Veronica's father is one of the union leaders, and he'll consider it a favor."

"Anything I can do," Arty smiled.

Looking at his watch, Leland said, "I've got people to see. I got to go."

Before stepping out the door, Leland addressed me and said, "You haven't killed no molasses barrels in this place have you?"

Arty laughed as I stammered to answer. Leland walked out the door and through the crowd, while Arty continued to chuckle at my expense.

"Did you hear that?" Arty boasted. "Could you see me as a state representative?"

"No," I flatly replied. "And what are you doing hiring someone without consulting me! We can't afford a girl in the office!"

"Don't sweat it," Arty chided. "It'll be good business to keep Leland happy and…even you'll have to admit a cute little thing like her will brighten the place up."

Shaking my head, I said, "I don't have a good feeling about you bein' close to Leland Holiday like that."

"Listen," Arty explained. "A man like Leland Holiday knows how things work, and it wouldn't hurt you to be a little more respectful when he comes in. I know how to handle him."

"He asked you to spy for him," I charged. "Sounds like he's handling you."

"I know what I'm doing," Arty responded. "I know Leland pushes the envelope of ethics sometimes, but I can handle him. I plan to ride this pony as far as it'll take me."

A skirmish between groups of men broke out in front of the store, interrupting our conversation. The near riots settled down in a day or two, but there were strong feelings on both sides of the strike, and it was getting harder to stay neutral. I studied our books and it was clear we were barely breaking even. If the strike did not end soon, we would be broke.

Veronica Willis started her job at Brooks & Martin the next day as I struggled to discover what her job would be. She could answer the few calls we received on the telephone, and as best I could tell, she had abilities in filing her fingernails. The girl was attractive and pleasant at times, but she seemed to have no experience in bookkeeping or other business functions and appeared to have little interest in learning those skills. She did lure Arty into the store more as he took on the job of training her, although he appeared to take her to lunch as much as anything.

The violence over the railroad strike only increased as autumn approached. When the Association of Railway Executives ignored President Harding's suggestion and agreed to follow the original Railroad Labor Board ruling, the hostilities escalated. The Attorney General of the United States, Harry Daugherty, agreed with the railway executives, and in September, a federal judge issued an injunction against striking, assembling, and picketing on railroad property while ordering the striking workers back to work. Only a fraction crossed the line, but the frustration and anger of the striking workers grew. In August, several men fired random shots into the Rock Island roundhouse. Ricocheting bullets injured two men, but fortunately, no one was killed.

As October came, the strike continued and both sides were getting testy. A meeting was held in the convention hall to discuss the problem, and over 1,500 shop workers, businessmen, and citizens were on hand. Over 300 business and professional people signed a resolution pledging to cooperate with national, state, and local authorities in enforcing the law and opening the shop gates to allow the workers now employed access to the facility.

The meeting grew tense when Frank Watson, now the chief spokesperson for the shop craft union, claimed the businessmen in town had been hoodwinked by the Rock Island Railroad into believing the company would leave town if the strikers were supported. Many businessmen were sympathetic to the strike, but all believed it was past time for some law and order. Noticeably absent from the meeting was Leland Holiday, who left Frank Watson to face the crowd alone. The meeting did little but anger people on both sides of the strike. Few, if any, issues were resolved. Soon the Great Railroad Strike of 1922, as it was already being called, would become even more personal.

CHAPTER 77

"What time's Lloyd coming over?" Marilee asked.

Marilee and I were traveling south in the morning for a noonday meal at the Martin's on Thanksgiving Day, so my family agreed to have our dinner the evening before. The Brooks family always celebrated holidays modestly, while the Martins made them a production. Mom, Dad, and Gordon arrived early, but Lloyd was running late, causing some stress for Marilee as she tried to keep everything hot and fresh.

"He worked today, so maybe he got caught late," I reasoned.

Lloyd had moved from the Rock Island Shops to the Santa Fe Shops, which seemed to be less volatile than the situation at the Rock Island where the strike affected many more men. Over eight hundred men had walked off the job in July. By Thanksgiving, more than three hundred had crossed the line and returned to work. Angry shouts and threats were now common in town as the holidays approached.

Marilee stewed around, while my family ignored her impatience at the Brooks tendency to run a little late. Dad had fought the boll weevils and brought in a decent harvest. With prices depressed, however, he did little more than survive. Gordon was doing well in school at Bethel and had met a girl. Mother expressed her concern about Lloyd—not so much his work situation, but the fact he was not married.

About seven o'clock, we finally heard Lloyd shuffling up the front steps of our porch. As I got up to open the door, we heard a crash. Dashing to the porch, we found a beaten and bloodied Lloyd had fallen before getting to the door.

"Lloyd!" I shouted, as I ran toward my brother.

"Hey, Gill," he lazily replied.

Blood showed through his teeth, and his left eye was cut open. His calm demeanor and tone of voice did not match his pummeled appearance.

"What happened?" I urgently asked, as Dad and Gordon immediately joined me to help Lloyd to his feet.

"I ran into some fellas that didn't think much of me working on Thanksgiving Eve, I think," Lloyd said as he walked gingerly inside with our help.

"Oh my!" Marilee shrieked at the sight of Lloyd in the light of the room. "I'll get some water. Put him on the sofa."

As Marilee rushed to find her first aid supplies, we wrestled Lloyd to a seat.

"Who did this?" Gordon angrily demanded in a tone indicating he was ready to take revenge.

"Settle down," Lloyd warned. "I couldn't recognize all of them, but there were several. They jumped me a block from the gate and took my pay."

"We need to get 'em!" exclaimed the rash Gordon, who was now big and strong enough to think he could fight anyone.

With a sarcastic laugh that caused him to wince in pain, Lloyd said, "Hadn't you heard of turning the other cheek?"

"Turn the other cheek?" Gordon asked confusingly. "That don't apply to those animals that attacked you!"

"Here, Lloyd," Marilee interrupted. "Wash up. Are you okay?"

"I'm fine," Lloyd assured.

Looking at Gordon, he smiled showing the blood still between his teeth and said, "I turned the other cheek, then turned it again."

Letting Gordon see his bruised and bloodied fist, he added, "The good book don't say what to do after that, so I had at some of 'em.

Thing is, my fist hurts nearly as bad as my face now, so I don't know if I accomplished much."

"Let me see," Marilee said calmly as she proceeded to clean and bandage Lloyd's hands.

"Wasn't a total loss," Lloyd said. "After last time, I learned to put most of my money in my boot, so at least I didn't lose all of it."

"This has happened before?" I asked.

"Down at the Rock Island Shop," Lloyd calmly confessed. "That's why I switched to the Santa Fe. John Allen, the blacksmith at the shop, told me things were a little better, but I guess not much."

The houses of three railroad employees opposed to the union had been burned in Shawnee since the attorney general's ruling allowing the railroads to replace workers. Several men had been beaten and robbed as Lloyd had been. The men on strike considered them fair game, while workers like Lloyd counted it as part of the price of having a job. Some people had begun to leave town to find other careers. As the strike went on, business continued to be slow.

Lloyd, now cleaned up, stood slowly and said to Marilee, "Sorry to keep supper waiting. I've been looking forward to your turkey and dressing all day."

"Oh, Lloyd," Marilee said as she put her bandages and towels away. "I hope it's worth the wait."

Marilee's meal was perfect, and after a while, we forgot about Lloyd's adventures even though his eye continued to swell throughout the evening. When it was time to go however, Dad, Gordon, and I decided to walk him back to his house, which was a few blocks south of mine. Lloyd protested, but we all felt better when he was inside without any incident.

The next day, Marilee and I traveled to the Martins to enjoy Thanksgiving. Without Marilee in the kitchen, however, the meal was not as grand as previous Martin feasts had been. We rode with Arty and Gwen in their Oldsmobile. Marilee looked at me and nearly made me laugh when she saw Gwen and Arty. Gwen looked as if she had gone into the attic to find a dress two or three years old, which would appear more modest than her contemporary wardrobe. Her attire was so different from the slinky dresses we were accustomed to, that it made Marilee smirk. I personally enjoyed seeing the sweeter-looking Gwen, who looked younger in her more modest wardrobe.

Arty filled us in on all the town gossip and about the strike. We told him about Lloyd, but he had the flippant attitude that the replacement workers were taking their chances. He did not have to see Lloyd or clean him up like his sister Marilee had done.

Leland Holiday, Arty confessed, had been giving advice to the strikers hoping to leverage his expertise for intimidation for their votes in the fall, but Frank Watson had lost badly in his attempt at state senator. Arty had been willing to be Leland's eyes and ears at the Shawnee Commercial Club and said Leland was not concerned about the outcome of the election. When Leland could not get the votes needed to get his man elected, however, he quickly lost interest in helping the working men of the union or the strike.

Arty was boastful to his family about our business in Shawnee, although I knew the store was barely surviving. I had several paychecks locked in the safe because it was not convenient to cash them without overdrawing the account. Gwen was pleasant but distant. I tried to have a conversation with her a couple of times during the day, but got the feeling she was afraid the conversation might evolve to talk about her and Arty's new friends. We had a good Thanksgiving at the Martins, but the trip reaffirmed the broadening gap in lifestyles between my business partner and me.

CHAPTER 78

A loud boom rocked our small house the night after Thanksgiving, as the windows shook from the shockwaves in the darkness of the night.

"What was that?" a panicked Marilee asked.

"Something blew up south of here!" I whispered frantically.

My first thoughts were of Lloyd and the trouble happening in town with the railroad strike. Three houses had been burned to the ground the past month.

Jumping out of bed to put on my trousers, I hastily said, "I'm going to check."

"Be careful," Marilee pleaded.

About six blocks south, smoke bellowed into the sky as orange flames danced in the air. A sickening feeling caused me to run through the darkness as the fire glowed in the direction of Lloyd's house. With each block, anxiety grew as I became more convinced the explosion must have involved Lloyd. As I got to within a block of the house, smoke clearly spewed into the dark sky from Lloyd's side of the street. A few more steps, however, I breathed a sigh of relief to see the charred and splintered remains of the house two doors down from Lloyd's small place. Standing across the street, Lloyd leaned safely against a car.

"Lloyd!" I shouted above the hectic confusion of the firefighters.

Looking up at me as casually as if he were in the fields, Lloyd said, "Hey, Gill."

"Are you okay?" I asked hurriedly.

"Fine," Lloyd confirmed.

"Do you know what happened?" I asked.

"They dynamited a house," Lloyd explained. "It belonged to John Allen, the blacksmith that talked me into coming to work at the Santa Fe Shop last week."

"Was anyone hurt?" I inquired.

"Naw," Lloyd said. "John went to Oklahoma City tonight to see his mother."

"Do you know who did it?"

"Sure," Lloyd said. "The same bunch that hung around Leland Holiday. This is the third house they've blown up this month. Someone knows how to use dynamite or they'd blown themselves up by now. They're usin' sticks they've stolen from the train yard."

"Who are they?" I asked frantically.

"I don't know the particular people," Lloyd replied. "There's a gang of 'em, I hear, that decided to take matters into their own hands. John crossed over two weeks ago, and they've been after 'em ever since. The man busts steel all day and has forearms as thick as most men's thighs, so I guess they figured jumpin' him wouldn't be a good idea. John had to work 'cause his mom's sick. He tried to explain, but there ain't a whole lot of rational thought goin' on right now…in fact, there's just a whole lot of hate. I hear Leland Holiday was helping 'em."

"You want to sleep with us tonight?" I asked.

"Heck no!" Lloyd emphatically said. "Don't want no one botherin' you and Marilee. I've seen worse than this. I'll be okay."

"Are you going to quit?" I asked.

"Probably ought to, but I'm stubborn enough to stick it out to show I can," Lloyd smiled.

Lloyd assured me he was fine, as I walked back through the dark street to Marilee and my home. The bombing was the talk of the town for several days. There was speculation about some of the men involved, but no one knew for sure. I was certain my silent business partner, Leland Holiday, probably knew, but he had tired of the strike. He showed up in Shawnee less often, and I assumed he was down south looking after his more clandestine business operations. Arty swore Leland was interested only in legal businesses now, but I could never trust that man.

Christmas was grim with strike tensions still thick and many out of work. We managed to keep the doors open, but things were getting tight at the store. The uncertain economic times did not keep Gwen and Arty from throwing an extravagant Christmas party with some of the more socially active people in town including Leland Holiday. The former state representative, Frank Watson was not invited. It seemed his usefulness to Leland Holiday's group was over and Arty did not see him as a good investment at his party. Marilee and I were also not invited, although I helped deliver a mahogany dining room table to their house for the occasion.

Another outbreak of fighting, fires, and near rioting in the streets caused the city commission to finally act. In January, the city placed a ban on all outdoor meetings and gatherings in an attempt to curb the violence. Three houses in the city had been dynamited, and men were being routinely attacked on the city's streets. The Shawnee Commercial Club had called for action months earlier, as the city seemed to be spiraling into chaos. Noticeably absent from the meeting was Frank Watson. The once outspoken politician supported by Leland Holiday had not been seen in weeks.

To help the city deal with the violence, United States Marshal Alva McDonald arrived from Oklahoma City to set up an office to investigate the bombings. Marshal McDonald was a bookish looking man with a thin nose that looked as if it had been broken at one time. Although his appearance was less than intimidating, his speech was forceful, as he vowed to track down the people responsible for the lawlessness. He assured the crowd that he had the full force of the

United States government behind him and he would call for troops to come in and establish martial law if necessary. His rhetoric would have seemed extreme a year ago, but people were now desperate for some order from the chaos the strike had produced.

CHAPTER 79

With the arrival of Marshal McDonald, the violence subsided somewhat as groups of men were routinely dispersed under his direction. The marshal set up an office and after a month, the town slowly began returning to normal.

Some complained the marshal was more talk than action, as his officers methodically went about their business. On the last day of February, however, the marshal and his squad, grabbed headlines across the state by arresting seven men suspected of dynamiting area homes and firing shots into the Rock Island roundhouse.

In the coming days, thirteen men were arrested for planning and committing bombings of homes, railroad bridges, and other facilities, including six homes in Shawnee. Warrants were issued for two other men, including Frank Watson. The gang had organized in August in a barn south of town with the intent of intimidating the replacement workers. The Shawnee group was responsible for bombings throughout Oklahoma and Texas.

Confessions from the arrested men showed a connection with the shop craft union, and all indicated that Frank Watson had direct knowledge of the activities of the terror squad. I wondered if Leland Holiday would ever show back up in town, since many believed he would surely be implicated in the plot.

After the bombers were arrested, people gradually began feeling safe again. The strike ended, and most of the union workers returned to work, but the animosity between the railroads and the workers lasted for years. The Rock Island kept the roundhouse open, but it would never again employ as many people as it had before the strike. The tumultuous walkout was the beginning of a slow death for the facility.

By the summer of 1923, the nation, as well as Shawnee, began recovering from the post-war depression with rampant optimism. Farmers learned to fight the dreaded boll weevils as the outlook for crop production and prices improved. I thought Lloyd would return to the farm, but he took a job maintaining equipment for the milling company. Lloyd's ability to work in the fields translated well into his work. Still single and affable, Lloyd bought the small home he had been renting.

More importantly to me, people began to buy furniture again. I was able to cash the checks I had been holding and was beginning to believe the furniture store would prosper as Arty had projected. Arty was as active in the community as ever, while Gwen still acted erratically and did not socialize much with Marilee or me.

By September, the Great Railroad Strike was a memory, and I was involved in the business night and day. One Saturday afternoon, I poured over the books to see if there was any way to reduce expenses, increase sales, or manage the inventory better. Arty had given Veronica the day off, and as usual, my partner was also absent on the busiest day of the week.

Deep in thought, I heard a familiar voice say, "Can't a girl get any service around here?"

"Mary Sue McNally!" I greeted. "How in the world are you doing?"

"I'm doing great," Mary Sue smiled. "But it's not going to be Mary Sue McNally much longer. I'm getting married!"

"Congratulations," I smiled. "I guess teaching in the Fuss Box would make marriage look more attractive. I even thought you might hook up with my brother Lloyd."

"I actually thought Lloyd was quite charming," Mary Sue confessed in a whisper. "He was so handsome and laid-back, but he never had much interest in me. I always got the feeling he had a girl somewhere."

"Lloyd knows nothing about love," I joked. "Tell me all about your guy."

"He'll be here in a minute, but he's just the best," Mary Sue beamed. "He bought a farm not too far from the school and was so helpful. I fell for him immediately."

"Where's the farm?" I asked. "I know that area pretty well."

"It's south of the old Romulus station about a half mile from the Salt Creek," Mary Sue explained.

"East or west of the old Martin place?" I quizzed.

"East," Mary Sue replied. "You can walk down through the trees on a narrow trail, and there's a big rock overlooking the river."

"That's the old Haskell Holiday place," I smiled nostalgically, thinking of the many summer days spent on the banks of the Salt Creek.

As far as I knew, no one had lived there since Haskell Holiday had died.

I began to ask more questions when Mary Sue shrieked, "Come over here, honey! There's someone you have to meet."

Turning around, Lance Carrington walked slowly up the aisle and said, "You're a few years too late to introduce us, Mary Sue. I can't remember when I didn't know this guy."

"Lance!" I said in a surprised tone. "When did you get back?"

"You know him?" Mary Sue asked with a look of bewilderment.

"He's like my brother," Lance smiled.

"I can't believe you're back," I said. "And you've bought the farm?"

"Gill?" Mary Sue asked. "How do you know Lance, and why didn't I know?"

As Lance walked up to hug me, I answered, "Actually Mary Sue, I introduced you to Lance years ago…You just…don't remember."

With a suspicious grin she asked, "What do you mean?"

"When you came to the funeral of my friend…with your father—" I began.

"The boy who drowned?" Mary Sue interrupted.

"You're looking at him," I smiled.

"You're the boy my father always talked about?" Mary Sue said with some confusion. "I bandaged you one time!"

"That was you?" Lance grinned. "That was a bad day. I don't remember much."

"Glad I made such an impression," Mary Sue teased.

With a grimace, Lance said, "One of the reasons I've put off meeting your folks as long as possible is trying to figure out how to explain my…resurrection."

"This will be interesting," Mary Sue said coyly as she grabbed hold of Lance Carrington's arm. "I wonder if he'll recognize a dead man?"

"I may have ruined that surprise," I confessed. "I talked to Mr. McNally a while back and told him about Lance…being alive."

"That's a relief," Lance sighed before smiling broadly. "I do have another interesting surprise, though."

Lance gazed at Mary Sue a moment, before looking at me. "I'm going to ask Brother Cotham to marry us."

I could not help but laugh aloud at his information.

"What's so funny?" Mary Sue demanded.

Lance grinned, while I said to Mary Sue, "Brother Cotham's the man who preached Lance's funeral! That young preacher did everything but lie that day to make Lance sound good. I wonder if he's ever preached a man's funeral, then preached his wedding!"

"We'll find out," Lance shrugged.

I was about to ask Mary Sue and Lance to come by the house for dinner when I heard a rustling in the back room. Stepping back to investigate, I yelled, "Is that you Arty?"

"Yeah," Arty replied, as he had his head stuck in a pile of boxes. "I'm looking for a box that Gwen needs at home."

Since Arty did not notice I was with a customer, I asked, "Do you remember Mary Sue? That girl I knew from high school."

"Sure," Arty replied without looking up. "She's the one I thought was trying to marry you and mess things up with Marilee."

I nearly died of embarrassment, but the good-natured Mary Sue had a difficult time restraining her laughter as she looked at a calm Lance.

"Well, she's here," I flatly said.

Arty shot straight up and said, "Why didn't you say something?"

Putting on his most polished professional demeanor and quickly straightening his clothes, Arty marched out to meet the customer, as he was accustomed to doing. Arty had the ability to take charge of almost any situation, but he stopped in his tracks with a bewildered look, as Lance said, "How are you, Arty?"

"Lance?" a puzzled Arty groaned, as he looked at Mary Sue holding Lance's arm.

"In the flesh," Lance replied.

Regaining a measure of his composure, Arty managed to say, "Hello Mary Sue, it's good to see you again."

"Good to see you," Mary Sue said quietly as she sensed the tenseness between Arty and Lance.

After an awkward couple of seconds, Lance said, "It looks like you're doing good…the store looks great…you look well."

"Thanks, Gill does most of the work keeping the stock up to date," Arty replied with uncharacteristic humility. "You look good."

"Thanks," Lance said. "I bought the old place and met Mary Sue. We're going to be married."

"Great," Arty said sincerely.

After an awkward break in the conversation, Lance stepped toward Arty and hugged him. Arty put his arms around his old friend's shoulder as Lance said, "It's good to see you, Arty."

An emotional Arty said, "It's good to see you again."

The two stepped back, and I said, "I was about to ask you guys to come to dinner tonight."

Lance looked at Mary Sue for approval before saying, "We'd love to."

"How 'bout you, Arty? You and Gwen want to come?" I asked.

Arty thought for a second, before saying, "Sure…we'd love to come…but why don't you come to my house. I've got more room and everything."

With his disarming smile, Lance said, "Thanks Arty, but if it's all the same to you, I'd rather go to Gill's house."

A confused Arty said, "Sure…but why?"

With a laugh, Lance whispered, "Cooking! If I go to Gill's house, Marilee will be cooking. If I go to your house…well, Marilee won't be cooking."

Patting my slightly protruding stomach, Lance playfully said, "See what I mean!"

In one of the few genuine laughs I had heard Arty let out in a long time, he smiled broadly and said, "I see your point."

CHAPTER 80

Marilee was thrilled when I called to say Lance was coming for dinner. I believed she was even more excited to learn he was engaged to Mary Sue. Even though I invited the couple on short notice, I knew Marilee would have plenty of food. After I gave Lance directions to the house, the couple left while I finished work for the day. By the time I arrived home, the girls were busy in the kitchen, while Lance sat in the front room reading the paper.

"There he is!" Lance shouted as I walked in.

Marilee bounced out to the front room to kiss me cheerfully on the cheek. I had to smile as my wife had flour smeared on her forehead and her glasses were somewhat askew. Marilee loved to cook and enjoyed entertaining, especially with an old friend like Lance Carrington.

As the girls retreated to the kitchen, I asked Lance, "Tell me what you've been doing."

"I went round the world," Lance explained.

Noticing my shock and interest, he continued, "I made a couple of friends in the army, and one happened to be from a well-to-do family back east. I had a reputation for being able to take care of myself with the boys, and this fellow hired me to be his personal bodyguard, but in truth, all we really did was pal around. He decided to take a long vacation, so we traveled around the world…sailed to England. He taught me to play golf and we went to Scotland to play for a few days until I started beating him."

"Golf!" I laughed.

I had seen the golf course in Shawnee, and the men in knickers swatting at the ball but had never played.

"Yeah," Lance smiled. "It's fun…I'll have to teach you sometime."

"I hope you can play in the dark," I quipped. "I seem to be at the store during any daylight hours."

"How about your partner?" Lance asked. "Don't tell me Arty's got you in this deal doing all the work."

"Not all," I replied. "Just most."

"Same old Arty," Lance observed.

"He's got his strengths," I explained. "He's real active in the community and brings in a lot of business."

"He's real active when your secretary's around too," Marilee curtly interjected as she set the table in the front room.

"You have a secretary?" Lance asked.

Before I could answer, Marilee said, "That's what they call her, but I've never seen her do anything but polish her nails and primp her hair."

Marilee retreated to the kitchen after giving her blunt opinion, and I said in a lower voice, "The secretary's real cute and…I don't think Marilee always responds well to cute."

Lance laughed loud enough that Marilee stuck her head around the corner to investigate.

"Just man talk," I explained.

Marilee gave me a scolding look but returned to the kitchen with Mary Sue.

"Same old Marilee," Lance smiled. "And sounds like the same old Arty."

"Pretty much," I agreed. "So what happened after the golf?"

"We traveled through Germany," Lance said sadly. "It's pathetic what's going on there. We crossed the Alps, headed down into Italy, and stopped a few days in Florence. Met a girl from Oklahoma there.

Real cute. Her name was Lydie and she was from Ponca City. I thought I'd like to get to know her better, but we traveled on down through Rome and caught a ship to Egypt to see the Pyramids."

"Sounds like you saw everything," I gasped.

"Almost," Lance agreed. "My friend wanted to retrace the Exodus, so we rode camels across the desert to Jerusalem before traveling east. It took months, but we eventually ended up in Tibet to see the Himalayas. It was an awesome sight…and life changing. We spent a few weeks with Hindu monks in the mountains before traveling through India and back to the sea. After that, we spent a few more months hopping islands through the Pacific before coming to San Francisco and taking the train back to New York City."

"Wow," I exclaimed. "You really did go around the world. Why did you give up the job?"

"My friend paid me a thousand dollars for the trip," Lance replied. "Never thought I'd see that much money ever. This is home, and I got a little homesick. I've always wanted to buy Mom's old home place, so when I got the money together; I came and made a down payment. I didn't really expect to stay, but I fixed up the house a little and then…well, then I met Mary Sue."

"I was crazy about her from the start," Lance smiled. "And…well, I just stuck around. It took me a couple of weeks to figure out she knew you, but I didn't let on we were acquainted cause I knew she was planning to introduce us. Mary Sue thinks a lot of you, but I didn't know she had been at my funeral 'til today."

"Not every guy gets to resurrect," I quipped.

In a more serious tone, Lance said, "Everyone gets a second chance, Gill. That's God's great gift. We get power from belief, we're responsible for the choices we make, but we always have the opportunity to change. I'm sure of that now. When I went away…I was always looking out for myself. I figured the world hadn't treated me so good, and I was due to take some back. When I went away, I grew up some and saw how taking care of yourself didn't get you too far."

"I'm not like I used to be," Lance said seriously. "A monk told me the secret to life is to be more selfless and less selfish. He explained the physical man is enslaved to the physical things we see, feel, and experience, but he said the enlightened man strives for the inner strength. He said it's in the spirit of man to find out that it's all about what you do for others. I thought it was life changing until I realized I'd heard that for years at church. I just wasn't ready to pay attention, I guess. You could call it religion, but to me it's more of a change in how I look at the world. I still feel bad about what happened with Gwen and how that worked out, but Mary Sue. Well...Mary Sue's just the best."

Sensing Lance's sincerity, I had to say, "She's a great person, and you two will be perfect together."

"The old monk in the mountains said love is fine, if you can find it, but to have trust in another human being is supreme. 'To be trusted is a greater complement, than love,' he preached. I trust Mary Sue and I'm determined to earn her trust."

With a hesitation, I said, "Has Mary Sue told you much about—"

"I know all about Ralph and what that did to her," Lance interrupted. "We talk about everything, Gill. She knows about my past, she knows about Gwen. Mary Sue understands me better than I think I understand myself."

After a moment, Lance asked, "How is Gwen? I mean, how is she really?"

"Gwen's changed," I shrugged. "She's still beautiful...in fact, she's stunning, but in a different way. I feel Gwen's lost somehow."

"What do you mean?" Lance asked with some concern.

"Her and Arty got different kinds of friends now. Me and Marilee don't see so much of them anymore. They're more...social. And I'm not just talking about Arty. Gwen seems more interested in her things and how people think about her…you know having the right clothes, the fancy house. She's just different."

With a grimace, Lance said, "It must be difficult living up to Arty's expectations."

"Maybe," I sighed.

"Walk with me outside for a moment," Lance asked.

As we walked out to the porch, Lance asked pointedly and with a pained expression, "Do you think…Do you think Gwen's child could be mine?"

The idea of Gwen having Lance's child was not a fresh idea to anyone familiar to the elopement, but it was a topic that was never discussed openly.

"She married Arty right after I left, and…well I've done the math and it could be. We were married for two days," Lance reasoned.

Thinking a moment to choose my words, I said, "I don't know. She's never said anything to me or Marilee. Arty's never acted like that could've been a possibility. They put the child in a home, you know."

"I heard," Lance admitted.

"I think that tore Gwen up some…she seemed to change once Arty sent the child away," I frowned. "There's something you may not know about Gwen."

"Huh?" Lance groaned.

"After the war, when Guy Peaudane came back home, he brought Gwen's step-sister with him," I began to explain.

"I don't really remember her," Lance said.

"She married young, moved away, and never came back," I continued. "When Gwen's step-sister came back she was concerned about Gwen…about Gwen living alone with Dr. Peaudane."

With a stunned look, Lance began to calculate what I was saying.

"Marilee told me, some things might have gone on that weren't…that weren't right," I concluded.

With a heavy sigh, Lance said, "That's why she was so desperate to run away. I was crazy about Gwen, but I didn't understand her insistence on running away…but…but I should have known."

"You couldn't know that," I defended. "No one knew."

"Poor Gwen," Lance said. "She didn't deserve that…I guess I really messed up for everyone. She needed me, and I let her down. No wonder she was so angry last time I saw her."

Sticking her head out the door, Marilee said, "There you are. Guess who's not coming to dinner? Arty called and said Gwen has a headache. Said he might come over later, but said to go ahead and eat."

"Typical Gwen," Marilee added with disgust. "She's probably drunk! Are you ready to eat?"

"We'll be there in just a minute," I explained.

After Marilee went back inside, I said to Lance, "A lot of things have gone on between Gwen and Marilee since we moved to town. Marilee's really not bitter. She just gets frustrated at what she sees as selfishness."

"Gwen's drinking?" a concerned Lance asked.

"I'm afraid so," I admitted. "It's one of those changes I was telling you about. We better go eat before Marilee comes and gets me."

I did not have the courage to tell Lance that Arty and Gwen now socialized with Leland Holiday or that Leland was a partner in the furniture store. Marilee prepared a wonderful meal, and I enjoyed watching Lance and Mary Sue together. We learned Lance and Mary Sue were going to wait until next summer to be married so that Mary Sue could complete her school year. Lance said they would probably move to town after that although he did not know exactly what he would do. They stayed late, as Lance waited to see if Arty would come to visit, but by nine o'clock they headed out the door.

"It was good seeing you, Lance," I said as they headed toward their car. "You too, Mary Sue. Hope to be seeing more of you."

"You will," Lance smiled. "We may even move to Shawnee."

Just before opening the door, car lights flashed on the couple as an automobile sped straight for them. Slamming on the breaks and sliding to a stop a few yards from their car, Arty Martin jumped out and said, "You're not leaving now, are you? The party just got here."

Arty was in a jovial mood. I looked at Marilee, and we wondered if he had a little social lubricant before heading over.

"We're just leaving," Lance pleasantly replied. "It's late for us country folks that have to get home."

"Oh, Lance," Arty said. "You got to move to town where the excitement is."

"Are you alone?" Lance asked.

Walking to his old friend, Arty said in a more serious tone, "I'm sorry we didn't make it tonight. Gwen had one of her headaches and just couldn't get out."

"Does she have these headaches often?" a concerned Lance asked.

"Only occasionally," Arty replied. "She took her medicine, and now she's out like a light."

"You're not drinking that stuff Leland Holiday makes, are you?" Lance pointedly asked.

Marilee and I knew the correct answer so I was shocked to hear Arty say boldly, "I don't drink! Of course, I take a little remedy for the cough…and I haven't coughed in years so it must be working!"

Arty laughed proudly at his own joke, but the rest of us were not joining him. Gwen's behavior had become increasingly erratic, and Marilee believed she was intoxicated much of the time when she had her headaches.

Putting a hand on Arty's shoulder Lance said, "Arty, you got to be careful with that stuff. You don't know what they put in it."

"I don't drink that much," Arty claimed. "I'm just teasing you…you used to like a good joke."

"Still do," Lance smiled. "I just worry about you."

"I know," Arty replied. "You always did worry about me…but I'm a big boy now."

"Listen, Arty," Lance said pleasantly. "It was great to see you, and I can't wait to catch up on things, but I can't have the school teacher out late…even if it's not a school night. You know how people talk in the country."

With an exaggerated nod, Arty said, "Believe me, I remember. Why do you think I'm up here now?"

Lance laughed at Arty's quick wit and said, "Old Leland Holiday don't seem to care much about what I do these days, so I'll be up to see you guys. Remember, we still got to meet at the flat rock on Salt Creek in a year or so…our ten-year reunion."

With a nostalgic smile, Arty said, "You remembered. After all these years, you remembered."

"I can't ever forget those days…even if I try sometimes," Lance replied. "We are after all, brothers of the Cross Timber."

"Lance, you don't have to worry about Leland," Arty assured.

I flinched nervously, afraid of what my partner might say next but breathed a sigh of relief when Arty said, "He stays kind of scarce since that railroad business last year. He's got some things going in Oklahoma City, I think, and a few interests in the county."

"Like the Potanole?" Lance slyly smiled.

"Just like the Potanole," Arty grinned.

"You need to stay away from there too," Lance preached.

"There you go again," Arty said shaking his head. "Always worryin' 'bout me. I swear you're worse than Gwen and my mother…and even Marilee about giving me advice to keep me out of trouble."

"Someone has to," Lance laughed. "Great to see you, but we got to go."

Lance and Mary Sue headed out of town. Arty loitered for a few moments, but then he too, drove into the late, dark night—in a direction that would not lead home.

CHAPTER 81

Lance and Mary Sue married in the summer of 1924 with a large church wedding in Tecumseh. Mary Sue had been very popular in school, and the McNallys were well known in the town. The death of Ralph Shaw delayed her starting a family and friends were genuinely excited about her happiness. Mr. McNally had been surprised to find out Lance was alive, and he was even more shocked to learn the young man wished to marry his daughter. It took time, but as Mr. McNally knew Lance and the changes he had made in his life, he gave his blessing to the marriage.

The war, the post-war depression, boll weevils, and the railroad strike took their toll on the county and Shawnee. In the country, once-active farmland went untended, and many houses were simply abandoned, causing land valuations to slump in the once-fast growing area. Optimism and hope began to infect most of the nation, but the challenges in the wake of the rail strike lingered as local businesses tried to recover. Employment in the rail yards continued to shrink, meaning fewer customers and fewer sales.

Lance farmed, with some success, but Mary Sue kept her teaching position to make ends meet. They talked of moving to Shawnee, and Mary Sue even looked at taking a position at Horace Mann Elementary School. Lance did not know exactly what he wanted to do in town, but he had some money left over from his exotic work after the war, and the couple seemed happy together.

The day before August 19, 1925, I reminded Arty about our appointment to go to the flat rock by the Salt Creek. I had been excited for weeks to meet up with my old friends at the place where we invented so many boyhood adventures, but Arty had forgotten and made other plans. He said the rock in the Cross Timber was a long time ago, and he had too many important things to do that day. Arty assured me he would get together with us soon to do something fun, but he could not see the point in driving all the way to the south part of the county in the August heat.

August 19th fell on a Wednesday, which was not a good day to be out of the store. We had hired a man who had moved to the area from north Tulsa a couple of years earlier named Wesley Brown. Wesley was a tall black man that had once owned his own business, before it burned down. Wesley had good business sense and had once owned his own cafe. Veronica Willis was still on the payroll, although she struggled with the simplest tasks. I could not count on Arty to be at the store, but on this Wednesday, I took a rare afternoon off and trusted Wesley and Veronica to watch things.

On the drive to south Pottawatomie County, I began to believe Arty might have been right about the trip. It did seem foolish, but I needed a break from the grind of managing the business. An afternoon drive to my old stomping grounds sounded like a good diversion. When I arrived at Lance's house, I was disappointed to find it empty. A crew of men worked in the corner of the field erecting some kind of tower, while bulldozers leveled an area about the size of a baseball infield.

The men had leased mineral rights to drill for oil, but the men were busy with their project and had not seen Lance. A large oil field had been discovered in Seminole County a couple of years earlier, but wells in Pottawatomie County had been expensive failures for the most part.

I walked around looking for the old trail to the flat rock. The Cross Timber around Salt Creek had changed little since I was a boy, but the path had overgrown somewhat. I picked my way through the trees and brush trying to keep from tearing my cotton shirt on the way. As I walked into the clearing, a smile emerged on my face while looking at a regal Lance Carrington standing on the rock as if it were his throne.

"You remembered!" I yelled, as Lance turned around and waved.

"Of course," Lance replied. "I wouldn't miss it. Where's Arty?"

Trying to mask my disappointment, I said Arty had an important business meeting. I did not have the heart to tell Lance that Arty thought the trip childish. According to Arty, he was constantly promoting the store, so I believed this to be only a small exaggeration.

"Oh," a deflated Lance moaned. "And it was his idea too."

"I know. He just couldn't make it, I guess."

"I'm glad you came," Lance said with a smile.

"Like you said, I wouldn't have missed it," I grinned. "How are things?"

"Things are great," Lance answered. "Mary Sue's giving up teaching next fall."

"Really," I said with surprise. "I thought she liked it."

"Oh, she does," Lance coyly grinned. "It's just going to be hard with the baby and all."

"A baby!" I shouted.

"Doc Sanders thinks it'll be around the New Year," Lance bragged.

"That's great," I congratulated.

"We think so."

Seeing how proud he was, I said, "Marilee and I are trying to have a baby, but it hasn't worked out for us yet."

With his easy smile, Lance said as seriously as he could, "You keep trying…because tryin's most the fun."

I shyly grinned at his teasing.

"It's really great to see you, Gill," Lance said. "I've been thinking about this day for a long time."

"Really," I said.

I had been looking forward to coming to the rock since Lance mentioned it about a year ago, but I certainly had many distractions since the night we stole the watermelon from Haskell Holiday.

"When I was in the war," Lance explained, "things were just terrible. It was either too hot or too cold. Mud everywhere and the stink…well you can't believe it…and to see men slaughtered like hogs nearly every day, I can't really describe how horrible it all was, but this place…I always thought about this place, and I always dreamed of being back here…back before I ran away…back before the bootlegging. I just remembered being here with you and Arty and…well; this place got me through a lot of stuff."

"I see some fellas are drilling for oil," I said. "You may be a rich man before long."

"Not likely," Lance said. "They paid me twenty bucks to tear up my field and said they'd pay me a percent in royalty if they found something, but all I've heard about is salt water in this part of the country. At least I got the twenty dollars."

"How's farming?" I asked.

"It's tough," Lance admitted. "I still got a little money from my work after the war, but I may have to be a better farmer. You know, I always admired your dad."

"My dad?" I said with surprise.

"Yeah, your dad," Lance repeated. "I lived with 'em when you went to school and knew things was tough, but nothing seemed to get your father down. He had to be up against the wall a lot of times, but always made the best of things and treated me good…and you know your dad treats pretty much everyone well, including an old grouch like Mr. Martin. What's it like havin' him for a father-in-law?"

"It's okay," I sighed. "I'm the only son-in-law, and I think he still checks the obituaries hoping maybe I've died, but other than that he's great."

Lance laughed at my assessment.

"The Martins do think highly of themselves," Lance smiled.

"They've been successful," I agreed. "But they can brag like Texans sometimes. Thank goodness Marilee's content to be in her kitchen and away from them."

"Marilee's great," Lance smiled. "She always has been, and she's always been crazy about you. I can tell she still is!"

"Marilee believes in me," I confessed. "Sometimes more than I believe in myself, but I can't imagine me without her. It's like Gill and Marilee are one person anymore."

"That's the way it should be," Lance smiled.

"I guess."

Lance and I agreed on many things that afternoon. It was the longest talk we had since he had returned, and I was impressed with how content he seemed with his life. A deep inner strength seemed to keep Lance centered. I headed back to Shawnee in time to get to the store before closing, but I thought how much Arty had missed out by not making the trip home.

CHAPTER 82

Driving past the train yard on the way back from seeing Lance, I noticed the Rock Island roundhouse seemed peaceful in contrast to the bitter confrontations from the previous year. Some work had moved to El Reno, and many believed the violence from the strike in Shawnee was the reason. Although most workers had returned to the shops, business had been flat since the strike.

As I turned the corner, I looked at the Brooks & Martin Furniture store. Things seemed quiet with few cars parked outside. Since it was near closing time, I parked in front. The store was dead, without a single customer in sight.

"Did you drive all the customers away?" I good-naturedly asked Wesley, as he stood in the front, dusting.

"No sir," he quickly replied, in a nervous tone. "It's been quiet all day."

Seeing the store empty affected me strangely. It was depressing to think business had been slow, but I felt less guilty for spending the afternoon away from the store.

"It'll pick up by the weekend," I assured.

"Yes sir," Wesley agreed.

Looking around and seeing Wesley alone, I asked, "Where's Veronica?"

Wesley's eyes looked away without saying a word.

"Did she go home?" I asked, somewhat agitated at the girl's lack of work ethic.

"No sir," Wesley sighed. "She's in the back."

Before I could ask why, Arty's office door quickly opened and then shut.

"I thought I heard the door bell," Arty energetically commented. "Thought it was a customer."

"Didn't think you were going to be here," I answered. "You told me you had meetings."

"Thought I needed to put a little time in at the store," Arty explained calmly. "Especially since you took off today."

Out of the corner of my eye, I saw Veronica Willis stepping out of Arty's office with hair and clothes ruffled and her make-up smeared.

"Did you find those customer files?" Arty asked, as I now noticed he was without a tie.

"Huh?" a bewildered Veronica asked.

"The customer files," Arty repeated. "Let me help you."

Arty disappeared into his office to avoid further questioning, followed by our disheveled secretary.

Walking back to Wesley, I asked seriously, "How long has this been going on?"

"They've been back there most of the afternoon," Wesley confessed.

"Is this the first time?" I quizzed.

"As far as I know," Wesley replied. "You're usually here, but Mr. Martin talks to her and pats her when you're not looking."

Trying to remain calm, I said, "Thanks for watching things today, Wesley. You can go on home."

"I'm awful sorry, Mr. Brooks," Wesley said.

"Not anything you could do." I assured as he walked to the back door to leave.

It was not quite time to close, but I locked the front door in preparation for my conversation with Arty. Before I could get to the back, Veronica Willis had left, and Arty was feverishly trying to get out the back door while tying his necktie.

"Are you crazy?" I shouted sternly in the empty store.

"What's your problem?" Arty angrily shot back.

"What do you think we're running here?" I asked pointedly. "A furniture store or a dance hall?"

"Just relax," Arty assured in his commanding voice. "Nothing's going on, but your imagination."

"And what should I imagine when I find you in the back with the hired help!"

"Okay," Arty confessed. "Maybe I got a little fresh with my hands, but nothing was going on. We're just friends."

"But you're married!" I shouted.

Arty scratched his neck and said, ""Well about that. I'm not so sure Gwen and I are cut out for each other. We've had our problems."

"What are you saying?" I asked.

"I'm saying, I'm divorcing Gwen," Arty said flatly.

"What?" I whimpered in disbelief.

"Gwen's not been the same since we sent the boy away. She drinks…a lot. Acts crazy. I didn't bargain for all this," Arty revealed with irritating self-piety.

"Divorce?" I said.

"It happens sometimes," Arty casually stated.

"On what grounds?" I demanded.

"What grounds?" Arty laughed insincerely. "She's a drunk. She's got this crazy kid…and who knows who it belongs to. Lance…her step-father? Let's face it…Gwen was damaged goods before I married her."

"You're not being fair," I protested.

"Maybe not," Arty shrugged. "But I didn't sign up for all this."

"Who started her drinking? Who made her send the child away?" I demanded.

"Don't pin Gwen's problems on me," Arty sternly warned.

"You would leave Gwen for Veronica Willis?" I asked.

"Maybe," Arty stoically replied.

After looking blankly at him for a moment, I said, "You better think about what you're doing. What it'll do to Gwen? What it would do to you? If you give up on Gwen now, I wonder what else you'll give up on?"

"Don't worry about me," Arty replied. "It's my problem, but don't go making things impossible by blabbing to Marilee. I'll see you, partner."

As if he had no concerns or guilt in the world, Arty Martin put on his hat and left me in the empty store.

CHAPTER 83

In my years of knowing Arty Martin, many things became apparent about his personality. He had the ability to be eloquent in a variety of social settings, people naturally liked him, and he was a take-charge person, instilling a "can-do" attitude in whomever he decided to charm.

Arty's most distinctive characteristic, however, was his ability to put up a brave front regardless of the circumstances. I had not completely decided if his aptitude for ignoring what people might think was a strength or weakness—an endearing virtue to be optimistic no matter what faced him or a fatal flaw in his character.

The weeks after the Veronica Willis incident should have been tense and filled with conflict, as I morally cringed at his treatment and attitude toward Gwen. Veronica Willis felt guilty. I could see in the way she avoided eye contact with me in the following days. Arty, however, went about talking of grandiose plans to expand our still fragile business as if nothing had ever happened.

Brooks & Martin had survived the trauma of the railroad strike, and not all businesses had. There still was not a lot of cash in the operation, but we had grown our inventory and customer list. Prospects looked bright for our partnership, as we prepared for the upcoming market trip to Chicago.

Two days before our trip, I was surprised to see Arty and Gwen at the store. Gwen looked thin and pale, but as always dressed as if she were heading to a party.

"What are you two doing here?" I asked cheerfully since it was a rare occurrence to see Gwen at the store or with Arty.

Veronica Willis was still employed as the secretary, against my wishes, and she glared at Gwen as the couple sat in Arty's office. I could not determine if Gwen was ignorant about Arty and Veronica or if she had grown as calloused as her husband about their marriage. Gwen's once soulful, searching eyes now looked lifeless and cold—neither joyful, hopeful, or even sad.

"We had some business," Arty said nervously as his eyes darted around the store.

"Really," I smiled. "Are you ready for the trip?"

"What?" Arty asked.

"We leave Friday for Chicago," I reminded.

Arty sighed, strangely. "That's part of the business I came to discuss."

"I'm very disappointed in you, Gilbert Brooks," Gwen hotly blurted.

I was too flabbergasted to respond as she continued, "I've heard rumors about Arty and that girl you hired all around town. I can't believe you would be so jealous as to ruin Arty's reputation and after all he's done for this place. I'm ashamed for these slanders to have come from you."

"Gwen," I struggled to explain.

Before I could say more, Arty interrupted and said, "Gwen dear, why don't you wait in the car. This won't take long."

An agitated Gwen fumbled for a cigarette to light as she glared at me. Finally, without a word she stomped out the back exit.

When Gwen had gone, I asked, "What's going on?"

"Sorry, buddy," Arty explained calmly. "Gwen heard some talk about our secretary and had some suspicions about me being out late doing business. I had to distract her, so I said you had spread the gossip about our hot little secretary and me."

"That's a lie," I protested.

"That's not really the point," Arty said, as if nothing were out of the ordinary.

"Arty," I said tersely. "I like you, and you're my brother-in-law, but we've got to get some things straight about this partnership's—"

Before I could finish the sentence, the front doorbell dinged as Leland Holiday walked into the store. Leland had been scarce in Shawnee since the railroad strike. He was never officially implicated, but there were plenty of rumors floating around about his involvement. Marshal Alva McDonald, the United States Marshal, had suspicions and even some witnesses, but they all disappeared before Leland could be charged.

"And we've got to talk about him!" I demanded.

"That's the business I want to discuss with you," Arty replied, "the partnership."

Looking at Leland Holiday, who had now joined us, Arty said, "Are you ready to do this thing?"

"Sure," Leland nodded.

"What's going on?" I asked nervously.

Leland began, "This business has done well, but we think it can do better with the right leadership and a new direction."

"What do you mean?" I asked again.

"It's not personal, Gill," Arty explained. "It's just business. We're going to buy out your share. You're going to do okay, but you'll be out of the store."

"But Arty," I protested. "This is my business too. I've put my sweat and effort into it…in ways that will never show up on a balance sheet. I won't sell!"

Leland Holiday said sternly, "You don't understand. It's not your choice. We went into this thing equal partners. I figure this place has got to be worth $18,000 by now with the inventory and accounts."

"But that's not counting other things like customer relationships and the work I've done every day while you never work and Arty works only occasionally," I explained.

"That may be," Leland Holiday calmly conceded. "But according to the law, a partnership is an option to buy or sell. Your partners are willing to buy you out for $6,000, and unless you're willing to pay us $12,000, you have no choice."

"I don't have that kind of money," I muttered.

"Then you're walking away with some cash," Leland remarked. "You can thank your friend Arty for that. I've brought the papers to sign. Arty has a cashier's check in the safe."

"I've got to talk to my wife," I said meekly, as I looked at Arty Martin's calculating stare.

"That's fine," Leland smiled. "You've got two days or the offer goes down to $5,000."

"We can manage things today," Arty said sympathetically. "Go talk to Marilee and...take the offer, Gill. It's a good one."

As I slowly put on my hat to walk out the back door, I could hear my former partners making expansion plans excitedly without me. I walked by Arty's car and heard Gwen sobbing.

"I'm sorry, Gill," Gwen said sincerely.

I just looked at her without a response.

"I don't know how things got this messed up," she said in a shaky voice. "I just need to know you're okay."

"You knew, didn't you?" I asked pointedly.

Gwen nodded.

"And you know I didn't start any rumors about Arty?" I quizzed.

"I know more," she said. "Arty said he'd leave me if I didn't help. I sold my part of the land near Romulus to put in the business. Arty and Leland were talking about getting you out and leaving you with nothing...I insisted he pay a fair price."

"You've made some fine friends," I coldly said. "You're smoking, drinking…I remember when you couldn't stand the smell of cigarettes. And the drinking, Gwen?"

"You don't know," she defended.

"What don't I know?"

"What I need to get through the day," she cried.

Looking unsympathetically at her, I said, "You need to find something else. I've got to go now. I've got to tell Marilee…who used to be your friend, that we're out of work and out of the store."

"Gill," Gwen started to defend through her tears.

I did not respond, as I headed to the house to break the bad news to Marilee.

CHAPTER 84

"They can't do that!" Marilee exclaimed in disbelief.

"I'm afraid they have," I confessed.

"But you're the one who knew the business. You're the one that put in the hours," Marilee reasoned.

"Maybe," I replied. "But we had a partnership, and I either have to sell or come up with $12,000."

"How much money do we have?" Marilee asked.

"Maybe $200 in savings," I answered. "Everything we got is in that store. I guess $6,000 isn't the worst that could happen, but it still hurts. Business is just starting to take off, and $6,000 won't be enough to open a new store."

Marilee twisted her lips strangely and adjusted her glasses to say, "I bet Leland Holiday wants a speakeasy in that place...probably in the basement."

"What?"

"Why else would those two want you out," Marilee calculated. "You do all their work. You're the one bringing in the profit. You're so naïve sometimes, Gilbert. It makes perfect sense. Leland Holiday owns that despicable place on the county line called the Potanole. Why wouldn't he want a place in town, close to the rail yards? It's perfect. A respectable business would be the perfect front."

"Do you really think—" I began to reply.

"Do I think my brother would sell out his best friend for some easy money?" Marilee interrupted. "You better bet it! He knew you would never go along."

"You mean our name is going to be on front of a saloon?" I groaned dejectedly.

"Maybe not," Marilee said energetically. "Go to the store tomorrow and bring back your books. Tell Arty you're considering another investor, but you'll need a couple of days."

"What investors?" I protested.

"Don't worry about that," Marilee said. "But I want you to talk to somebody."

Marilee, as expected, was compassionate and encouraging. With so much on my mind, I decided to take a walk. The October evening was brisk, as darkness had overtaken the dusk. After walking aimlessly for half an hour, I found myself strolling by Lloyd's small house. It had been several weeks since I had seen Lloyd, so I decided to knock on his door.

"Hey, Gill," Lloyd greeted. "Come on in."

Lloyd's small front room was scarcely furnished but neat. A lone lamp sat on a table by a single chair with a book sitting on top of the daily newspaper. Lloyd retrieved a chair from his dining table for me. Although the room was sparsely furnished, it was spotlessly clean and even smelled fresh.

"You've quit smoking," I observed, as I sat down.

"Yeah," Lloyd shrugged. "I quit when I was living close to Gwen. I was up there a lot. Gwen never liked smoke, and I didn't think it was good for the baby."

I thought of how much Gwen had changed, since coming to the city and how much Lloyd had once liked his Camels before saying, "It must have been tough."

With a smile, Lloyd said, "I shook for a week, but the baby didn't cough as much when I was around."

"I wonder how the kid's doing?" I asked.

"I went to see him a few weeks ago," Lloyd replied.

"Really?"

"I spent a lot of time with him before Arty moved 'em," Lloyd explained. "He's almost seven now and can talk as plain as me. The little guy can sit in a chair now too."

"That must be a relief to Gwen," I said.

"Don't think she visits much. He gets lonely, doesn't understand," Lloyd noted. "That was hard on her when Arty sent the boy off."

"Arty has a way of getting what's good for him without thinking about who it hurts," I replied sharply.

Lloyd looked surprised and said, "That's kind of a harsh tone comin' from you."

"Sorry," I said. "It's been a bad day."

"Don't be sorry," Lloyd smiled. "Somebody should've thrashed Arty years ago."

"Arty's forcing me out of the store," I revealed.

"He can't do that," Lloyd said.

"I'm afraid he can," I sighed. "And he has."

"He and Leland forced you out, did they?"

"How did you know about Leland Holiday?" I asked.

With a sarcastic laugh, Lloyd said, "I'm not quite as stupid as people think. I haven't trusted Arty since he began to walk! He can talk smooth and be as likable as the devil, but nothing he does surprises me."

"No one thinks you're stupid," I said. "At least you were smart enough to see Arty for what he is."

Leaning forward in his chair, Lloyd said, "Gill, you trust everyone. You always have. That makes you a nice guy. I wish I could think the best in everyone. You need to temper that trust with some reality. In the war, guys didn't get killed so much when we were afraid, but when they relaxed…when they felt comfortable…that's when they got it. I like that you're so trusting. It's one of your best traits, but it makes you vulnerable to a snake like Arty."

"Marilee said the same thing," I admitted.

"Marilee's a smart girl," Lloyd smiled. "Now she's a Martin you can trust. What are you goin' to do?"

"I don't know," I confessed. "Be a little wiser…a little less trusting next time."

Lloyd laughed and said, "Don't go changin' too much. Remember, the cream always rises to the top. You keep seein' the best in people. Don't give up on anyone…miracles happen all the time."

"If I don't come up with $12,000 I'm out," I sighed.

"Whew!" Lloyd whistled. "I got a little saved back, but nothing like that."

"It's okay," I replied. "I'll be getting some cash. I'll figure something out. How about you? What are you going to do?"

"What do you mean?" Lloyd replied.

"You got a girl? Are you planning on settling down?" I quizzed.

"Naw," Lloyd shrugged. "I'm settled down, but there's no girl."

Looking at the table by his chair, I asked, "Looks like you're doing some reading?"

With a bashful grin, Lloyd said, "Yeah. I guess you're never too old to learn. Mary Sue tutored me some when she was teaching. She told me to do a little reading each day. It's amazing what goes on in the world."

"That's great, Lloyd," I encouraged.

"Yeah," he shrugged.

We talked a little longer before I walked back to my home. Lloyd seemed to be doing well. His nightmares from the war had stopped, and he liked his work. My brother seemed satisfied with his life, but I sensed loneliness in him, as if he were missing or searching for something.

As I walked out the door, I said, "Thanks, Lloyd."

With a reassuring smile, Lloyd said, "You're goin' to be fine…you just needed someone to remind you. Don't sound like you're eatin' possum any time soon."

"Count our blessings," I smiled.

Lloyd wryly said, "Count our blessings."

CHAPTER 85

The next day, I arrived at the store, to see Arty leaning over Veronica Willis. It was one of the few times Arty had been in the store early.

Straightening up, Arty said compassionately, "Hey, Gill. Are you ready to sign?"

"Not yet," I replied, hurt that Arty would sound so patronizing. "I'm taking the books home to see about my options."

"Options?" Arty quizzed. "You don't have that kind of money."

"I could find investors," I defended.

"Investors!" Arty smirked. "Come on Gill. Don't embarrass yourself. Who are you going to ask? Your dad? Lloyd? Take the offer today before it costs you more."

"Why?" I asked tersely. "So you can run a saloon in the basement?"

Arty's silence confirmed Marilee's speculation.

"I'll see you," I said while walking out the back door with the balance sheet and income statement tucked under my arm.

For the next few hours, I talked to every banker in town about borrowing money to buy out Arty and Leland. Most bankers listened, but all passed because I lacked collateral to back the loan. A couple of bankers, I felt, seemed to be in Leland's sphere of influence as they encouraged me to sell.

Walking into the house, I was shocked to see Mr. Martin sitting stoically in the front room.

"Hello," I timidly greeted.

"Marilee!" Mr. Martin yelled. "He's here."

Marilee came from the kitchen and asked, "Did you bring your papers?"

"I got the books," I confirmed.

"I told Daddy about our dilemma, and he's offered to come listen," an excited Marilee began.

"Gilbert," Mr. Martin interrupted. "I'll have to say I'm disappointed in you."

"That's not fair, Daddy," Marilee scolded.

"I'm sorry," I meekly confessed.

"I thought with your involvement in the business, you could make a go of it and keep Arty in line," Mr. Martin explained. "I've loaned Arty over $3,000 to keep things going during the strike, but now I'm concerned your business may not make a return."

Looking at Marilee before responding, I said, "The store is making money. That's one of the reasons Arty wants to buy me out."

"What?" Mr. Martin asked.

Looking at Marilee, he said, "I thought you needed to borrow money?"

"Daddy!" Marilee replied. "You never listen. I told you I had an opportunity."

"Arty hasn't put any money into the business except our initial investment," I said.

"What!" Mr. Martin barked again. "Show me your books."

Laying the balance sheet and general journal in front of him, I showed the changes in the value of the business from the incomes generated.

Mr. Martin carefully evaluated each entry before saying, "You're right. The loans don't show up on your balance sheet or the checkbook."

"Arty never said anything to me about the money," I explained. "We had some tight months during the strike, but we made ends meet."

"*You* made ends meet," Marilee corrected.

"It looks like the net worth is nearly $19,000, isn't it?" Mr. Martin asked.

"My partners have rounded that to $18,000 and said if I don't make up my mind today they're offering me $5,000."

"Who's this third partner?" Mr. Martin asked.

"Leland Holiday," I answered in a tone of confusion, assuming Mr. Martin already knew.

"Leland Holiday!" Mr. Martin gasped. "Good lord, Gilbert. What were you thinking, asking that man to be a partner in anything?"

"I didn't know," I defended. "Not at first."

"How's that possible?" he asked.

"Arty brought him in as a silent partner when we opened," I replied. "I always assumed he had you as his partner."

Mr. Martin's ears turned bright pink, and he looked as if he might explode. Shifting and fidgeting in his seat, Mr. Martin asked, "You're telling me Arthur is running with Leland Holiday?"

"That's exactly what Arty's done," Marilee interrupted. "Gill's done almost all the work. I think you know that…and Arty thinks he can make some quick money forcing Gill out."

"How?" Mr. Martin asked.

"I think they want to open a saloon in the basement," Marilee factually replied.

While Mr. Martin studied me, I added, "I think Marilee's right."

Mr. Martin got up and began walking around the front room while rubbing the back of his neck. I looked nervously at Marilee as his silence and pacing continued another five minutes.

Finally, Mr. Martin looked at me and said, "They gave you an option to sell or buy them out for $10,000?"

"They offered $6,000 per share," I corrected.

"They offered $6,000 per share yesterday, but they told you they would pay $5,000 tomorrow?" he asked.

"Yes," I replied.

"That means you can buy them for $5,000 a piece or $10,000 for the deal," Mr. Martin asserted.

"I guess so," I reasoned.

Mr. Martin then said in a more consolatory tone than I had ever heard, "Gilbert, someday maybe you'll have a son and understand what I go through. Arthur's as likable a boy as I've ever known and I…well I love him, and that'll never change. Maybe I should've raised him different. I've tried to keep a reign on him, but he's cursed with having the ability to find the easy way too many times."

Looking at Marilee and then back at me, he continued, "Marilee's my only daughter, and I guess it's been hard for me to let go of her sometimes. Why Marilee's like she is and Arthur does what he does, I don't know. I love Marilee, too, but more importantly I trust her. She seems to trust you…and…I trust you too."

Taking a moment to rub his forehead, Mr. Martin said, "I can loan you about $3,000, do you think you can raise the rest?"

Shaking my head, I said, "Lloyd's got a couple of hundred he'd let me have, but I've already been to the banks, and they've all passed…said I didn't have enough collateral.

Looking almost kindly at me, Mr. Martin said, "Grab your hat, Gilbert. We'll fix this."

CHAPTER 86

Mr. Martin co-signed a loan to help me—his son-in-law—buy out his son. The blood rushed out of Arty's cheeks when he saw his father walk into the store.

"Dad?" Arty asked with a puzzled expression.

Arty Martin had the ability to take charge of almost any situation with his strong, personal charm and a boisterous confidence bordering on arrogance. Facing his father was the one exception to this trait. Ever since he was a boy, Arty had a different demeanor around his father, and this day was no exception.

"Hello, Arthur," the stoic Mr. Martin greeted.

"What are you doing here?" Arty asked timidly.

"I've come to do business," Mr. Martin informed.

Mr. Martin did not have much formal education, but he had a reputation for shrewd business dealings. In the past, Arty often bragged about his father's prowess with money, but today he listened to the words with foreboding.

Looking at me, Mr. Martin said with a forced smile, "Let's get to it, Gilbert."

Before I could say a word, Leland Holiday emerged from the stairway leading from the basement.

Unable to see his partner's expression, Leland Holiday smiled broadly under his thick mustache and said to me, "I see you've come to claim your check."

Reaching out to shake Mr. Martin's hand, Leland continued, "I guess you've come to help your boy celebrate."

"Gilbert," Mr. Martin urged with a slight nod.

"I've actually come to take your offer to buy," I said.

Leland stared blankly at me for a second before looking at his partner's pale expression.

"I've brought cashiers' checks and papers for both of you to sign," I explained while handing Leland one check and then putting the other in Arty's hand.

"What's this?" Leland asked pointedly. "We're not selling."

"What are you doing, Gill?" Arty pleaded.

Mr. Martin wanted to take over the negotiation, but refrained as I said, "I'm taking your offer to buy. You said I had to either sell or buy at your price…I'm buying."

"Can I talk to you, Dad?" Arty asked.

Looking at Leland Holiday, Mr. Martin asked, "Could you excuse us?"

"Not now," Leland stated flatly. "Our offer was for $6,000, and this check is only for $5,000. That's not the deal."

Now drawn into the negotiations, Mr. Martin said, "My new partner said the offer was for $6,000, but the offer depreciated to $5,000 today. I can only assume the business has lost some value, because surely the boy's two partners wouldn't try to pressure him into a decision."

Leland Holiday laughed uneasily and said, "I'm not selling, not at this price."

"Wasn't that the offer?" Mr. Martin quizzed.

Looking at me hatefully and then back to Mr. Martin, Leland said, "You have no idea who you're messing with."

"Don't I," Mr. Martin said calmly. "Maybe you've forgot who you're dealing with? Remember Hookie Miller and Frank Starr?"

Leland Holiday looked at Mr. Martin nervously before saying, "I'll burn this place, before I'd sell."

In a lower tone of voice, Mr. Martin said, "I wouldn't do that. You have two options. You can take the offer, and we'll give you some time to move the liquor I suspect you've already moved into the basement, or I'll get Marshal McDonald down here to investigate right now. I would prefer the second option if I wasn't afraid my boy might go to jail."

Looking at Arty, Mr. Martin said, "Of course, that might do him some good."

Leland Holiday had the look of a trapped animal for a moment, before swallowing hard and saying, "Looks like you just bought yourself a furniture store. I'll send some men down to clear out my personal possessions in the basement. I guess making $5,000 off a $2,000 investment wasn't a total waste of time."

"I'm glad you see things that way," Mr. Martin said without breaking eye contact.

"If you'll excuse me, I've got other business to attend to," Leland said.

Putting on his hat, Leland Holiday walked out the front door and down the street without another word.

"I'm glad we managed to finally get him out of this operation," Arty said, as if it had been his idea to buy out Leland Holiday.

"We didn't manage anything," Mr. Martin coolly assessed. "You have a check for $2,000. I've taken the liberty of deducting the amount of the loan you told me you needed for the store."

Looking pathetically at his father, Arty said, "You'd send me away with nothing? You'd help *him* buy out your own son?"

"I'm not sending you away with nothing," Mr. Martin corrected. "You're leaving with your investment, and I expect that's more than you've earned. The day's still early. I suggest you clear out your things and begin looking for a job. I don't think Gilbert will want to hire you. It's his store now."

Arty spent the next half hour clearing out his personal property from the office under the watchful eye of his father. In the mean time, I took the opportunity to fire Veronica Willis, which should have been done months before. As a defeated Arty walked out the door, I looked around the neatly displayed store and could not help but think that it now belonged to me without the distractions of Leland Holiday looming as a partner.

Looking at Mr. Martin, who appeared as defeated as Arty had a short time earlier, I asked, "Are you all right, Mr. Martin?"

"Yes," he answered. "That was a hard thing to do…but it was the right thing to do. Arty needs to make some improvements in his life in many areas, or times will be hard on him I'm afraid."

"Who were Hookie Miller and Frank Starr?" I asked, remembering the exchange between Mr. Martin and Leland Holiday.

With a sly smile I had never witnessed, Mr. Martin said, "I haven't always been so respectable. Hookie Miller and Frank Starr were gunfighters from the old town of Corner. The worst place you can imagine; three saloons where the owners fought all the time and blood stained the floors. I rode with Marshal Gus Bobbitt as a deputy when he cleaned out the place. There were six of us that rode with Marshal Bobbit. We charged Hookie and Frank and horseback. They fired a couple of rounds, but when we closed in…they ran. Hookie was killed a year ago in Three Sands. Leland's old enough to have heard the stories about…my role."

"I had no idea," I said in amazement.

"You know something my children don't know…and I wouldn't mind keeping it that way," he smiled with a wink.

"Your secret's safe," I said. "Thank you…for everything."

Speaking plainly to me he said, "I don't know I've done you any great favor. You have a store now, but you also have debt and all the responsibility. Plus, I don't think I made a very good friend of your former partner."

"Thanks anyway," I said.

"You should know by now," he smiled, "that my Marilee typically gets what she wants."

PART V

CHAPTER 87

The euphoria of buying out Arty Martin and Leland Holiday was short lived, as the responsibility of ownership and the associated debt weighed heavily on my mind. Arty, for all his faults, was personable and effective in promoting the business. That burden was now mine. I hoped more than believed past conflicts with Leland Holiday were history, but uneasy feelings of dread persisted.

Marilee and I decided to keep the store name, Brooks & Martin. We had spent several years developing recognition for the store, and since Marilee's maiden name was Martin, it made sense. The real reason for keeping the name, however, was the cost of painting a new sign. Business was steady, but barely good enough to make the bank payments. I had worked hard the past years, but the hours and effort increased with the departure of Arty from the partnership.

A few weeks before Christmas, I headed home one evening to report the day's activities to Marilee. We were depending on a good Christmas selling season to get us through the lean months of winter, and I was beginning to have a perpetual crease along my forehead from constantly thinking of ways to increase sales or reduce expenses. Approaching the house, I noticed an unfamiliar car parked in front. It was already dark, and the lights in the front room indicated we had company.

"There he is," Lance Carrington greeted, as I walked into the room.

"This is a good surprise," I smiled.

I had not seen Lance since the summer, and he was dressed in a new suit, complete with shiny shoes and a felt hat. Mary Sue sat next to Lance, and her smile was radiant this evening. Typically, Mary Sue would have assisted in the kitchen, but she was expecting a child in a couple of months, and Marilee insisted she sit comfortably in the front room.

"Look at the both of you," I said.

Mary Sue smiled broadly and said, "I know. I'm big as a house."

"You look great," I assured.

"There you are," Marilee said, while sticking her head out of the kitchen with a bit of flour attached to her cheek and a smile on her face. "I've been waiting dinner on you."

Marilee had the ability to cook a feast on short notice without seeming to exert extra effort.

"I'm surprised you're not as big as Mary Sue," Lance quipped.

"Not yet," I replied as I patted my slightly swollen mid-section. "It looks like you're doing well."

Looking at Mary Sue for a moment, Lance said, "We're planning on making some changes. The McNally's gave us their old car, and I got a suit today 'cause I'm looking for a job…in town."

"That's great," I said. "So you'll be moving to Shawnee?"

"If I can find work," Lance replied.

"I figured you'd be a rich oil tycoon by now," I said teasingly, remembering the drilling crew on his place in the summer.

"Me too," Lance said. "Those fellows drilled a well, and it spewed enough oil to ruin most of my cotton, but the foreman said they just hit a pocket of gas, and they left after a few days. Hey, I got the twenty dollars anyway."

"They didn't pay for damaging your crops?" I asked.

In a more serious tone, Lance said, "No. I asked, but before I could settle anything, someone put a torch to the field and burned the whole crop. The foreman said he wasn't payin' for a burned field."

"That doesn't seem fair," I replied.

Shaking his head, Lance said, "Not to me either, but that's the breaks I guess."

Looking at Mary Sue, I could tell the subject was upsetting to her. A younger Lance Carrington would never have let an injustice like this take place without a fight, but I could only guess the responsibilities of family had tempered him somewhat.

"What're you going to do?" Marilee asked.

"We're moving to town," Mary Sue said pointedly. "Things have changed in that part of the county."

"What do you mean?" Marilee inquired.

We had not lived near the old Romulus town site for years, and Marilee's parents now lived several miles away from there.

Mary Sue seemed hesitant to answer, but Lance finally said, "Leland Holiday, I think."

"No!" I said, with a distraught tone remembering the man's threats against me only a few weeks earlier.

"He found out I bought the old place when they began checking the records for the oil leases," Lance explained. "He came by one day and wanted me to sign some papers saying the mineral rights were excluded from the property. When I wouldn't sign, he made some threats and claimed he would have me thrown in prison for killing Haskell. It threw him off when he found out my father-in-law was an attorney."

"They fired shots into the house last week!" an emotional Mary Sue added.

"That's terrible!" Marilee exclaimed.

"There have been coon hunters coming on the place the past months," Lance said. "Their dogs were tearing up the fields, and I asked them to stop. They've been a little testy and fired a couple of rounds into the roof, but I'm pretty sure they're some of Holiday's friends. Knowing Leland like I do, I figured it would be better to be in town."

"Are you going to sell the place?" I asked.

Looking at Mary Sue, Lance said, "Don't want to, but we don't plan to live there either. Besides, I'd rather be closer to a doctor in town."

"Gill had problems with Leland Holiday, too," Marilee revealed.

"Really?" Lance questioned.

Feeling embarrassed at my association with Leland Holiday, I did not respond immediately.

"What kind of problems?" Lance asked.

"Leland tried to take Gill's store," Marilee explained.

After Marilee's abbreviated version of the story, I confessed, "When we started the store, Arty had a silent partner that invested in the business. Marilee and I assumed it was her father, but after being open a few months, I learned it was Leland Holiday."

Lance looked at me with no sign of emotion and without comment.

"He wasn't involved in the business until a few months ago," I continued. "I caught Arty in his office with the secretary the day I went to see you at the rock. A few weeks later, he and Leland tried to force me out. Mr. Martin helped me get the financing to buy them out. Leland wasn't happy about the deal, but Mr. Martin threatened to get the U. S. Marshal involved if they didn't sell."

"What were their plans?" Lance asked.

"They were going to open a speakeasy in the basement," Marilee blurted out.

"And you didn't know Leland was the partner, Marilee?" Lance inquired.

"It was a surprise to me," Marilee confessed. "But I wouldn't put anything by that man…or my brother for that matter."

"I'm sorry," I said to Lance.

"About what?" Lance replied.

"About being partners with Leland Holiday," I winced.

Finally, Lance reached out to pat my shoulder and said, "I'd expect you to be trusting of Arty, but I'd thought Marilee would have figured out what her brother was up to."

"I don't get surprised too often," Marilee quipped.

"You're not mad?" I asked.

"At you?" Lance shrugged. "Gill, you trusted Arty. I'd have done the same. I don't have a problem with anyone taking Leland's money, but…have things gone okay?"

"I've had a few windows broken and some random vandalism, but nothing too serious. I suspect Leland might have some kids harassing me, but I might just be paranoid."

With a smile, Lance said, "Is it paranoia, if it's true?"

With a half-hearted laugh, I said, "Maybe not."

"This is terrible," Mary Sue protested. "How can this man get away with such nonsense?"

"Mary Sue's nearly as naïve as you, Gill," Lance quipped while taking his wife's hand. "Leland gets away with it, 'cause he's helped elect half the officials in this county at one time or another and he's smart. He never really breaks the law as much as operates at the very fringes of it."

Looking at me, Lance said, "I doubt he'll give you too much trouble over the store. He's working with a fellow out of Tulsa trying to get his hands on any oil lease he can lay claim to…Leland figures that's where the big money is now."

"But he didn't get yours," I commented.

"He tried," Lance said. "I know he's helped his new friends swindle at least three families out of their land rights in the area. He's got this fellow from Tulsa that's as smooth talking…well he's nearly as smooth talking as our old friend Arty, but at least Arty has some conscience."

"I wouldn't be so sure about that," Marilee bluntly stated.

"Don't give up on Arty," Lance protested. "He gets a little off track, but I think it's because he's always trying to prove himself for some reason."

"You're kinder to him than I would be," Marilee remarked. "I don't think Arty's capable of thinking about anyone but himself."

"Arty's bailed me out of a few bad spots in the past," Lance reasoned.

"Like the time he sent you running off to war and stole your girl," Marilee shot back before remembering Mary Sue was in the room.

"I'm sorry," she said looking at Lance and Mary Sue. "That didn't need to be said."

"It's fine," Mary Sue assured. "Lance doesn't keep any secrets from me."

"I don't keep *many* secrets from you dear…I've never claimed to have confessed all my past indiscretions," Lance said while squeezing Mary Sue's hand.

With a mock look of shock, Mary Sue replied, "He's shared enough that I know I don't want to know any more."

"How are Arty and Gwen?" Lance asked.

Marilee and I glanced nervously at each other, neither of us wanting to answer.

"I haven't seen Arty since we bought him out," I finally replied. "We don't exactly travel in the same social circles."

"I'm worried about Gwen," Marilee added. "She's…well she's changed. She's so thin and pale. I worry about her, but she sees anything I say as being judgmental."

"I hate to hear that," Lance said seriously.

"How's Gwen's child?" Mary Sue asked.

"I'm embarrassed to say I don't know much about my nephew," Marilee confessed. "They put him in a home in Oklahoma City, and I haven't seen him."

"Lloyd goes and sees him regularly," I added.

"I didn't know that," Marilee replied.

"I figure there needs to be at least a few things you don't know about, dear," I teased.

"Why is Lloyd so involved?" Lance asked.

"I don't really know," I confessed. "Lloyd lived by Arty and Gwen at the old place for a while. I think he got close to the boy and helped Gwen around the place. Lloyd says the boy's doing better than expected. He's learned to talk, and they're even hopeful they can fix him with some braces and teach him to walk."

"That's great," Lance smiled. "Sounds like Lloyd's taken a real interest."

"I guess so," I said. "I think it gives Lloyd something to do. He's been…well Lloyd's been more reserved since the war."

With a serious tone, Lance said, "The war changed a lot of people."

"So what are you going to do?" I asked, trying to change the topic. "I mean what kind of work are you looking for?"

"I'm not too picky," Lance replied. "I just want to get Mary Sue into town and afford a little house somewhere."

"Have you ever thought of sales?" I asked.

"Not really," Lance answered. "The closest I ever came to selling was talking the sergeant out of sending me to the stockade a few times."

"This sounds like another secret I haven't heard," Mary Sue teased.

"You've reformed me, dear," Lance smiled.

"I think you'd be good at it," I replied, more seriously.

Looking at Marilee to see that she was thinking the same thing, I said, "Why don't you think of coming to work with me? I could use the help, and I think you'd be great with customers. You're a lot like Arty, only more honest…you might have to work on that."

"Are you serious?" Lance asked.

"Sure," I continued. "I can't pay a lot to start, but there's commissions and…well if I can make money, I'll make sure you do all right."

"What do you think?" Lance asked Mary Sue.

"I agree with Gill," she replied. "You can talk me into almost anything."

"You'd really consider letting me work for you?" Lance asked again.

"Lance," I explained, "the secret to a good business relationship is it has to be good for both parties. I don't think I'd be doing you a favor. You're good with people, and I think you'd be doing me the favor coming to work."

Looking at his wife for a reassuring nod, Lance asked, "When do I start?"

CHAPTER 88

A week before Christmas, Lance began working at Brooks & Martin, and it was one of our best seasons ever. Handsome and well spoken, Lance was a natural working with customers. I looked at Lance in his store-bought suit with neatly groomed hair and it was hard to imagine he was the wild boy I had known as a youth.

Lance's aptitude for business should not have been a surprise. He had been conducting business, albeit illegal, since he was a teenager selling moonshine for his father. Lance and Mary Sue rented a small house not far from Marilee and me. By February, they added a beautiful baby girl to their household.

With the addition of Lance, the store finally broke out of the doldrums and business started to improve. Brooks & Martin was not the only business prospering. In the summer of 1926, a huge oil field was discovered a few miles east of Shawnee in Earlsboro. A few months later, an even larger field was discovered south of Salt Creek.

Shawnee, with the railroad infrastructure and business community in place, became an important commerce center for the new oil fields. Even the old Rock Island rail line through Romulus got new life when a switch was opened at a place called Pearson to serve the now-booming oil fields near a town called Saint Louis.

Mr. Martin, who always seemed to be in the right place at the right time, held the mineral rights to 160 acres on the edge of the profitable field. The land my father had once thought of buying also produced a well that would have paid for twenty years of cotton farming. When I asked my father if he was disappointed in missing out on the newfound riches, he just shrugged and claimed the oil boom would not last.

Another opportunity had the town buzzing that year. News of a meatpacking plant locating in the city promised to employ more men than the rail yards. It had been over a year since Arty left the partnership, and there was no sign he would be opening a store to compete with Brooks & Martin. Lance took full advantage of the good economic news, and his sales continued to grow, as did the profits at the store.

On a bright, autumn afternoon, I looked around the store with the acute stress of the previous year now a memory. Lance worked with a customer at the front of the store. The man was tall and nicely dressed. I assumed he was one of the many new businessmen coming to profit from the opportunities in town. As I approached to introduce myself, however, I could tell Lance's tone was not that of a salesman.

"No!" Lance said pointedly. "I'm not signing anything, and I don't appreciate being threatened!"

I had already walked too close to the conversation to turn around, as both men looked at me.

"Is there a problem?" I asked, confused as to why Lance would take such a tone with a customer.

"No," Lance replied. "I was just saying good-bye to Mr. McMurry."

"Hello," the polite man greeted, as he reached out to shake hands. "I'm Taft McMurry…from Tulsa."

"Hi," I said. "Gilbert Brooks."

"The 'Brooks' in Brooks & Martin, I assume," Taft McMurry smiled.

"Yes," I replied. "Can I help you with anything today?"

"No," the polite man replied. "I'm just taking a few minutes to talk business with Mr. Carrington. I'm trying to explain to him the intricacies of land management."

"I'm not a fool," Lance said angrily. "I know what's mine."

"I'm just saying you could save yourself some time and aggravation by taking our generous offer," Taft McMurry explained.

"What kind of aggravation?" Lance hotly asked.

"I'm just saying there's not a lot of law and order in that part of the county," Taft McMurry continued in a calculating tone. "I'd hate to see anything happen to your place…or your family."

For the past year, Lance Carrington had been a changed man. He had been patient, polite, and very much under control at all times. I did not know if his war experience or marriage to Mary Sue created the change, but he had been a transformed man. Taft McMurry, however, stirred something primal inside Lance, and he took on a different demeanor than I had seen in many years.

Squaring up to the dapperly dressed man, Lance said with a flash in his eyes, "You would do well not to threaten my family. I would not hesitate doing you great bodily harm. That land was stolen from my mother, and I bought it back fair and square. I don't know what shenanigans you've pulled elsewhere, but I'm not one of your reservation Indians that's easily intimidated. There's a producing well on the land, and you think you can take it from me. You need to know that I don't care about the oil, but the farm is mine, and I will sign none of it away!"

It took Taft McMurry a second to gather himself to say, "I was just trying to make things easy on you."

Looking at me, Taft McMurry said, "Mr. Brooks, good day."

Without another word, the dashing man left Lance and me standing alone.

"Are you okay?" I asked, as Lance stood staring at the spot where the visitor had been standing.

After a moment, Lance said calmly, "Yes. I'm fine."

"What was that about?" I anxiously quizzed.

"It's about land," Lance sighed. "It's about oil, it's about greed, and about the promises men are willing to make to get it. Some will do anything to get what they want. Leland Holiday filed a quitclaim deed from Haskell on the property saying the land actually belonged to him. He's claiming my purchase is invalid. That land was given to my mother and stolen by the Holidays. I bought back the land when I shouldn't have had to. Now they want it because of the oil…but I'm stubborn and won't give it back."

"What's Mr. McNally say?" I asked.

"He says it's not that unusual to see quitclaim deeds, but that the land could be tied up for a while straightening it out," Lance explained. "I figure Leland wants to drive me off 'cause I bet that well they drilled would produce if the right people own the land, and of course Leland would be the right people."

"What are you going to do?" I asked.

"Nothing," Lance smiled. "I'm going to sell some furniture and hold out as long as it takes."

After a moment, Lance said, "By the way, thanks for the job. I appreciate it."

"Thank you," I replied. "I'm cashing my checks for the first time in two years. What are you and Mary Sue doing for Thanksgiving?"

"We'll go down to her parents for lunch," Lance answered.

"Marilee's got the biggest turkey I've ever seen in my backyard. Why don't you and your family come over Thanksgiving night and eat with us? I know Marilee would love to have you."

"Does she really want to see me…or the baby?" Lance smiled.

Marilee found out a few weeks earlier we would be expecting our first child and did not miss many opportunities to see Lance and Mary Sue's baby daughter, Anna.

"Well," I confessed. "The baby, but I know she'd love to see you enjoy her pecan pie."

"I'll talk to Mary Sue," Lance replied. "But I know I can talk her into Marilee's pecan pie."

CHAPTER 89

"Marilee!" I shouted, as I entered the house. "I invited Lance and Mary Sue over for Thanksgiving."

Stepping out of her kitchen, Marilee looked surprised as she tried to wipe some shortening that had somehow gotten on her chin.

"That'll be interesting," she said.

"It's all right, isn't it?" I asked.

"Sure," Marilee replied. "The more the merrier, but I've got a surprise, too."

"Really?"

"I've invited Arty and Gwen for Thanksgiving."

"That's interesting. Do you think they'll come?"

"Arty said they would," Marilee shrugged.

"You know you can take that to the bank," I sarcastically said.

Hesitating a moment, Marilee added, "They've had a tough time, lately…Arty tried to divorce Gwen."

"What do you mean tried?" I asked.

"Arty was going to divorce her, until Daddy found out," Marilee explained.

"How did your father take that news?" I asked, already knowing the answer.

"Daddy handled it. He told Arty it would be his decision about whether he kept his commitments, but his inheritance would go to Gwen and not to him. Daddy said he would have no trouble treating her as a second daughter."

"Sounds like your dad," I said.

"I think Arty may already have a girl on the side," Marilee said, as if she possessed some secret information.

I had never told Marilee about the times I had caught Arty with other women and did my best to look surprised.

Marilee continued, "After Daddy explained things to him, Arty decided maybe the marriage deserved a second chance. Daddy asked me to make sure to invite them. I hope you don't mind?"

"Not at all," I replied. "I really hope things work out for them this time."

Thanksgiving was a special day for Marilee. The aroma of roasted turkey with dressing, baked yams, a variety of side dishes, and fresh baked pies, including pecan filled the house. Marilee fussed for days making sure every detail was right. She began cooking early in the morning for the evening meal.

Mr. and Mrs. Martin were the first to arrive with Marilee's two younger brothers, who were both teenagers now. Ethan and his wife showed up a while later with their young son. An unspoken tension was in the room as Lance and Mary Sue Carrington came to the house with baby Anna wrapped tight. The Martins, with their tendency to boast, discussed their newfound wealth in the oil fields found under their farm. Eventually, however, their discussions returned to the farming they loved.

Lance and I conducted our own side conversation and occasionally grinned at the boastful Martins. Marilee was busy entertaining, and Mary Sue was happy to help, since she did not know the Martins well. Marilee delayed dinner until it was nearly dark. Her father was becoming impatient at her preparations, but it was clear she was trying to wait for Arty and Gwen to arrive.

Marilee finally gave up and had everyone sit at the two tables she had decorated for the dinner. After the blessing, the younger Martin boys were ready to attack their older sister's cooking when a knock on the door announced the late arrival of Arty and Gwen.

"You're already eating?" Arty pleasantly greeted. "Sorry we're late."

Arty, dressed in a dark suit with a starched shirt, looked as if he were going to a social event instead of coming for a family dinner. Gwen looked more timid as she followed close behind. She wore a pleated, emerald-green dress with a hemline at the knees. An elegant coat with a fur collar hid a neckline low enough to draw a disapproving look from Mrs. Martin.

"The food's already been blessed," Mr. Martin barked. "Have a seat so we can eat."

Arty's smile faded somewhat as he silently obeyed his father. The couple timidly moved to the end of the table close to Marilee and I. Gwen looked as if she had been sick. Her once dimpled cheeks were now gaunt, highlighting her high cheekbones. Her blue eyes seemed almost bloodshot, and her demeanor clearly showed she was uncomfortable with the seating arrangement.

"Things smell wonderful," Arty boldly congratulated his sister.

"Thank you," Marilee politely replied. "It's good to have you here. It's been awhile."

"Yes it has. Hasn't it, Gwen?" Arty cheerfully asked his wife.

"Yes," Gwen said stiffly. "It's very nice, Marilee."

"Thank you," Marilee smiled while looking at me.

Speaking to Lance, Arty asked, "How did you merit an invitation to one of my sister's feasts?"

"We had Thanksgiving with Mary Sue's folks at noon, and Gill invited me at the store," Lance explained.

"You were buying some furniture?" Arty asked as he dished out potatoes.

"No," Lance factually explained. "I've been working for Gill."

Arty dropped the gravy spoon causing a loud crash, which temporarily interrupted the buzz of conversation from the other end of the table. I looked nervously at Marilee, unsure as to how Arty might respond.

Arty's demeanor did not change as he said, "You're working at Brooks & Martin?"

Lance, now realizing it might be a sensitive topic, meekly said, "Yeah."

"That's good," Arty replied. "It was a nice little business."

Looking at Gwen and then speaking as if to the rest of the table, Arty said, "I'm actually involved in a new venture now."

The other conversation came to a hush, as the Martin clan awaited the announcement.

"You may have heard, a meatpacking operation called Packingtown is locating in Shawnee," Arty explained. "It will be the largest in the southwest employing almost a thousand men. Some of my associates clued me in and I've invested my profits from the store into the company's stock."

"A meatpacking company?" Mr. Martin asked.

"It makes perfect sense," Arty continued. "We have all this cattle around here. Why pay to ship 'em off to Chicago when we can process 'em right here."

"You're going to own a meatpacking business?" Mr. Martin asked again.

With a slight sigh, Arty said, "It's complicated, Dad. I'm not the only owner. Packingtown is a corporation owned by many investors. No one person can handle a project this big. I'm one of several stockholders raising the venture capital. Of course, since I got on the ground floor, I got my stock options at a bargain."

"Sounds risky," the elder Martin commented.

"Everything's risky, Dad, but this is a sure thing," Arty continued. "The land's already been purchased north of town, and big money from Chicago and Tulsa is already in it. The corporation's going to invest in land, cattle, stocks, and even oil properties."

After a brief hesitation, Arty said, "I bought my first shares for two dollars and sold half of them for four dollars after only a month to get all my money back plus more. I'm telling you this thing is going up by the day."

"If you sold for four dollars, how do you profit if it goes up?" Mr. Martin asked.

"I didn't sell all my shares," Arty said with a tone of dejection. "Just enough to buy Gwen a new fur and…well, if you look outside, you'll see the newest Cadillac in town."

Mr. Martin looked unconvinced, but when the two youngest Martin boys ran to the front porch to gasp at the shiny new car, Arty could barely contain his broad grin.

After a moment, dinner resumed, and everyone continued with his or her previous conversations.

Arty whispered to Lance and me, "You two ought to look at getting out of that dead-end store and into this Packingtown deal."

"I'm just getting used to settling down," Lance said, while shaking his head.

Before I could tell Arty I did not have the money to invest, Gwen said pointedly to Lance, "So now you decide to settle down?"

The Martins at the other end of the table did not seem to notice Gwen's statement, but Lance, Marilee, and I looked at each other nervously.

"Yes," Lance replied politely. "Gill's been very gracious to give me a chance."

With a sarcastic tone, Gwen said, "What a novel idea…to give someone a second chance."

"Gwen," Arty whispered sternly under his breath.

Gwen bit her lower lip at the subtle scolding and appeared to let the topic drop until she suddenly turned to Mary Sue to say, "I guess we both have something in common."

"Really?" Mary Sue innocently replied.

"Sure," Gwen said with a wicked smile. "The same first husband!"

At this comment, the entire group stopped to listen as Gwen glared at Mary Sue while an uneasy Lance listened silently to the inappropriate remark.

"Gwen!" Arty whispered more urgently. "That's enough."

Gwen looked at her husband with a wild, unstable look as Mary Sue said softly, "I'm very sorry for being here tonight…this must be awkward for you. Lance, I think maybe we should excuse ourselves."

Before Lance could reply, Gwen said sarcastically, "He's good at that…running away."

"Gwendolyn," Arty pleaded. "That's enough."

Desperate to change the topic, I asked, "This meatpacking thing sounds like a windfall. Who put you on to it, Arty?"

Arty stared blankly at me without giving an answer, but Gwen boldly proclaimed, "Leland Holiday, who else?"

Arty looked angrily at his wife while peering down to gauge the reaction from his father. Mr. Martin was engaged in a conversation with his eldest son and did not appear to hear Gwen's revelation.

"How can you do that?" Lance bluntly asked.

"Do what?" Arty nervously replied. "Make money?"

"Be associated with Leland Holiday. Do you have any idea what he's trying to do to people in the south part of the county?" Lance hotly charged.

When Arty did not immediately respond, Lance asked, "Is Taft McMurry the business interest from Tulsa?"

"Just one of many," Arty replied, having regained his composure.

Shaking his head, Lance said, "Why would you have anything to do with Leland Holiday?"

Gwen interrupted and said to Arty, "That's a good question since Leland can't keep his hands off your wife…as if you would care."

"Not now," Arty barked as forcefully as he could without attracting undue attention from his father.

"Gwen," Marilee said softly. "This isn't the right time or place."

"Don't you judge me, Marilee," Gwen replied with her voice now shaking.

Turning to Mary Sue, Gwen then said in a softer tone, "You see, Arty doesn't mind that his business associates put their hands on his wife and propositioned her, but it bothers him to think someone might know, even his old friends from the Cross Timber."

Embarrassed, Mary Sue said pleasantly, "I don't know what your problems might be, but I think Marilee—"

"Don't you patronize me," Gwen interrupted angrily. "You don't know anything about me."

While a stunned Mary Sue looked helplessly, a teary Gwen said, "But wait…I'm sure you've heard all about me."

Seeming to lose complete control, Gwen continued, "So you see, I can't do anything but despise you and your perfect little world."

"Gwen," Marilee said firmly. "Go with me to the kitchen!"

All eyes were now on the spectacle Gwen had made of herself as she looked pitifully at Marilee and said, "I could always count on you to never get ruffled. You were supposed to be my friend, and you put my husband out of the business like we were nothing!"

"Gwen…Now!" Marilee demanded as she rose from the table.

Seeing all eyes were on her, Gwen nervously said in a shaky voice, "No, Marilee…that won't be necessary. Arty…I'm sorry, but I'm not feeling well. Could you take me home?"

Arty, somewhat agitated by his wife's display, seemed anxious to get her away from his family and dutifully rose to retrieve her coat. Gwen rushed outside before Arty returned with her garment, and he quickly followed her to the car.

The shocked silence was broken, when Marilee said, "Gwen wasn't feeling well, but let's enjoy the rest of our dinner. I'm sure she'll be fine."

After a short time, the group resumed their more normal conversation as they continued dinner. The Martins, who still lived miles out of town, had a long drive and left shortly after Marilee served the desserts. Mary Sue helped Marilee with the dishes, while Lance and I sat in the front room to discuss the evening's activity and watch Anna.

"I'm sorry, Gill," Lance offered. "It was nice of you to invite us, but I hate putting you and Marilee in an awkward spot with your family."

"Don't worry," I said. "That's not too different from a typical gathering with Arty and Gwen."

"How long has Gwen been like that?" Lance asked.

Shrugging my shoulders, I said, "At least since they've been in Shawnee. I didn't notice so much when she lived in the country, but they've got different kinds of friends now."

"Like Leland Holiday and Taft McMurry?" Lance quizzed.

"To name a few," I said. "There's been other things, too. I don't think Arty's always been faithful to her."

"You told me about the girl at the store," Lance replied.

"There have been others, I'm afraid. Even before they moved to town," I suggested without going into details.

"Poor Gwen," Lance sighed. "She's always been fragile, and…she's never seemed sure of herself. Now she seems so bitter."

"You're pretty forgiving, considering the way she attacked you tonight," I noted.

"I probably deserve it," Lance said shaking his head. "I'm sure I didn't help things."

"But Arty—" I began to protest.

"Yeah," Lance interrupted. "I'm sure he hasn't helped much either."

"She was drunk tonight," Lance said sadly. "The strong perfume and the cigarettes covered the odor, but she was a little shaky, and I'm bettin' that's not the first time."

"I think you're right," I agreed. "They have an active social life for sure."

"That's not the Gwen I remember," Lance frowned.

"Me either," I said, thinking of the sweet girl who used to bring lunches to the Peaudane General Store.

"I've seen it before," Lance said. "That girl's in a lot of pain. I knew guys in the war that would drink and get that same crazy rant when they got the wrong letter from back home. I'm worried about her."

"So are we," I confessed. "Marilee and I have tried to help without much success."

"I know," Lance said. "It's something she'll have to work out on her own, I guess."

"How about you?" I asked. "How are things working out with that problem at your home place? I haven't seen that McMurry fellow around lately."

"No," Lance said. "I was surprised to hear he's involved in the Packingtown project. I'd hoped he'd left town."

"But he hasn't bothered you again?" I asked.

"No," Lance said with an uneasy grin. "That's what's worrying me."

CHAPTER 90

News of the Packingtown project spread through Shawnee and the surrounding area like wildfire as people scrambled to invest before missing out. The original plan to build a meatpacking plant soon escalated to include a residential district to house the new employees. A development company was formed to take the excess profits to invest in oil production in the county. Investors were making huge returns in a short time, and it seemed everyone enjoyed the oil and property boom.

Although we felt as if we were missing out on the windfall, Lance and I had no time for speculating because all my money was invested in the store and Lance was still battling to save his home place. The bank was now putting pressure on him and threatening to call his note with all the wild speculation happening in the real estate market. He was making good commissions, however, and the furniture store received some residual benefits from the profits being made, as a few people spent their newfound wealth in the local stores.

We enjoyed another profitable Christmas, and prospects looked bright as we entered 1927. The oil fields in Earlsboro and Saint Louis seemed able to pump an unlimited supply of the black gold from the ground. The Martins made enough money that they considered moving west of Shawnee to better farm land closer to town. More people were investing in the Packingtown project, and all anticipated seeing the promised building rise from the prairie in the summer.

"Looks like you made another sale," I complemented Lance, as a customer walked out after a nice order.

"Yeah," Lance smiled. "Her husband is in some kind of business supplying equipment to the oil fields."

"Thank goodness for the oil field workers," I smiled.

"You got that right," Lance nodded.

It was getting late as we began closing up for the day. It was spring, and the days were getting longer, so I looked forward to being home before dark. Marilee had given birth to a baby boy four months previous, so I eagerly looked forward to hearing about the day's events and holding my son. Before we could lock the front door, however, the doorbell dinged indicating we had at least one more customer for the day.

"I'll get this, if you want to head home," Lance said.

"Thanks," I replied, as I locked the safe and headed to get my hat.

"Don't tell me you're leaving early," the chipper voice of Arty Martin shouted from the front.

Putting down my hat, I headed to the front of the store to greet my former partner.

"I never saw you in the store this late in the day," I teased.

It was the first time Arty had been back in the store since the break-up of our partnership. He looked to be doing well, dressed in expensive clothes and wearing a new gold ring.

"Brain power," Arty smiled. "I do my working with my brains so I'm working all the time."

"What's going on?" Lance asked.

"Not much," Arty said. "Just felt the urge to see my old friends."

"How's Gwen?" Lance asked.

With only a hint of a frown, Arty said, "Gwen's fine...she had some health issues, but the doctor has her on some medicine that makes her calm as a kitten."

"Anything serious?" Lance inquired with a tone of concern.

"Naw," Arty assured. "Just nerves."

"Looks like you're doing well," I commented.

"Things couldn't be better," Arty smiled. "The Packingtown stock was up to $22 this morning, and I just checked and it had gone up another $2 by the close. I'm a thousand dollars richer for doing nothing more than breathing God's air today."

"That's great," I smiled, feeling a little jealous of not taking Arty's advice to buy the stock earlier.

"It's not too late for you two," Arty smiled. "That's really why I came by. I hate to see my two best friends slaving away in this place when nearly every person in town is making a bundle besides you. I just bought more shares this morning."

"You never know," I replied. "Business is pretty brisk."

Arty laughed good-naturedly and said, "You boys are making money by addition, but you'll never get ahead unless you learn to leverage and multiply your profits. You've missed out on a ton of growth, but when the ground breaks on this project, the stock's going through the roof. You really need to think about it. We're thinking a stock price of $50 or maybe even $80 per share by the end of the year."

"I still got all my money in this place," I protested.

"You need to scrape up a little," Arty replied. "That boy of yours may want college some day. Get a second mortgage on that old house of yours."

Looking at Lance, Arty said, "How about you? Aren't you tired of taking orders from this guy?"

"Naw," Lance smiled. "I kind of like having someone telling me what to do. Besides, I don't have any money to invest. I'm barely keeping the bank off me as it is."

In a more serious tone, Arty said, "That's kind of what I wanted to talk to you about. I know the group trying to buy your land, and…well, they're determined. They'll give you top price now. You invest it in

Packingtown, and you could triple your money by the end of the year and—"

"Who's going to get me a good price?" Lance asked pointedly.

"An investment company with Packingtown is investing in oil properties, and they're buyin' anything they can get their hands on—"

"The only person been wanting that land is Leland Holiday and that grifter working for him from Tulsa. Are you telling me they're the ones behind this whole Packingtown business?" Lance charged.

"No," Arty defended. "They're not the only ones. They're into it big for sure...that's why they can afford to pay you top dollar. You really need to take the deal."

With an angry stare, Lance said sternly, "You're telling me Leland Holiday's group wants me to sell the land that belonged to my mother—a mother that was forced here from Kansas with the promise of land and opportunity—so I can let a bootlegging bandit like Leland Holiday have it? And on top of that you want me to take the money and invest it back with this Packingtown group?"

"They're going to give you stock for the land, and the way this thing is shooting up, you'll be rich," Arty explained.

Lance looked out the window for a moment, and then asked in a low tone, "Did Leland Holiday send you here?"

Arty, talking quickly and nervously, said, "You don't understand, Lance. These men want that land real bad, and they're bound to get it. I'm trying to save you some grief and put a little cash in your pocket. I'm trying to watch out for you."

"Leland will have that property over my dead body," Lance said defiantly.

In a serious tone of voice, Arty said, "You don't understand, Lance. That's what's at stake. These men...they play for keeps. I don't want to see you get hurt."

"Arty," Lance explained. "I love you like a brother...always have, but you and me...we're not friends any more. You can't seriously think you can run with the devil and not get burned…and trust me…Leland Holiday is the devil. You need to take care of yourself, and for God's sake get Gwen away from here and away from Holiday."

In a pleading voice that did not suit Arty, he said to me, "Gill, you got to talk to him. This is a good deal, and no one gets hurt. I know you and me have had our differences, but you got to explain to him how these things work."

"I don't think I know how these things work," I explained. "I come to work every day and try to pay my bills. I agree with Lance. You've not been the same since you started running with that crowd."

"Lance," Arty pleaded. "I'm begging you, and you know I don't beg from anyone. Take the deal."

In a kind tone, Lance said sincerely, "Get out Arty…you know you're in too deep."

Arty stared at Lance for a moment and then shifted his eyes back to me as he regained his composure.

In his smug tone, Arty said, "I'm just trying to help you boys out…that's all."

Without another word, Arty Martin put on his hat and strolled out the front door.

CHAPTER 91

It was a warm, late spring day and the doors to the furniture store were open to let a few puffs of fresh air into the stuffy store. Fans from the ceiling buzzed overhead and I did not notice the tall man strolling into the front door at first.

"Get out!" I heard the angry voice of Lance Carrington demand.

Looking at Wesley Brown who was working in the back of the store, I quickly moved to the front to see the source of the commotion. Lance was squared off with Taft McMurry, the business associate of Leland Holiday, and I was afraid my friend was about to land a painful punch to the unwanted visitor.

"What's going on?" I demanded, as I stepped between the two men.

Wesley Brown moved close to the front of the store to back me up, if needed. Taft McMurry coolly looked at me before staring at Wesley for a moment.

"I was just trying to help out your friend," the brash young man stated.

"You were threatening me and my family!" Lance charged as his temples throbbed from the excitement.

"Listen," I began. "I'm just trying to run a business here—"

"Then you better explain to this guy that he needs to vacate that land," Taft McMurry interrupted. "Before you're short one salesman."

Taft McMurry's threat was not even veiled.

"I think you better go," I said, while pointing at the door.

"This is your last chance," Taft McMurry said mockingly.

Stepping toward him, Lance said, "I've dealt with your kind before."

"Trust me," Taft smiled. "You haven't dealt with me before."

"I think you better go," I reiterated.

Staring at me as if to size me up, Taft McMurry smiled and said to Lance, "I'll be seeing you."

After he left, I asked hotly, "What was that about?"

"Something's going on," Lance said. "They're desperate for that land. It don't make any sense with all the property they've purchased."

"Listen," I began. "Is that piece of property worth all this hassle?"

Looking at me strangely, Lance said, "Don't tell me they've gotten to you Gill. You can't be on their side?"

"I'm on your side," I confirmed. "I just don't want to see you get hurt. This guy scares me."

"He should scare you," Wesley interrupted.

"You know that man?" I asked.

"Yes, sir," Wesley affirmed. "I knew him back in Tulsa, but I don't think he knows me. His sister-in-law helped my family out…she's as good a person as I ever knew…but that man…he's crooked as a broken snake, mean as a bull, and dangerous as a rabid dog."

"I can take care of myself," Lance boasted.

"I know that," I stated flatly. "I know you can take care of yourself, but you got a family now. You got to think of them."

Looking around for a moment, Lance said, "I know. You're right. I got to keep my head…but…I don't think I can give in to a man like that. He'll just keep taking more and more."

"Lance," I pleaded.

"Don't worry," Lance smiled. "I'll be careful."

CHAPTER 92

The summer of 1927 should have been the best of times in our community, but events were taking place shaking many to their financial foundations and some to their ruin. The wild speculation about the Packingtown project had spawned an unprecedented amount of investment and greed. People investing $100 found they could sell their shares for twice that after as little as 90 days, and many quickly reinvested their profits back into the stocks. Neighbors, not wanting to miss the bonanza, rushed to invest while the ever-increasing stock was still affordable.

By summer, a single share was selling for nearly $50, but no buildings had been erected for the grand project. The week before the Fourth of July celebration, some key investors, like Leland Holiday who had convinced so many people to get into the project, sold their stocks. Two days later, news spread like a devouring locust when the chief architect of the project and president of the corporation left town on a train to Chicago.

Optimism held for a few days as eager investors convinced themselves it must be a sign that construction was finally about to begin. The next day, however, optimism turned to panic as suddenly no one was buying the high-priced stock. People began selling off shares at small losses, but as the panic grew, the price fell back to $10 per share, then to $5 until it became clear the corporation had no assets other than the money the swindler had taken back to Chicago.

By the end of the first week of July, it was apparent the Packingtown project had been a clever pyramid scheme fueled by greed and the hopes of profits similar to those lucky few who owned the mineral rights to the oil fields in the south part of the county. Leland Holiday had sold his shares before the collapse. Marshal McDonald investigated, but Leland had managed to avoid a direct link to the man who had invented the Packingtown ruse, although Leland had personally profited from the scam. He had been content to let others in town, like Arty Martin, find out about the fraud the hard way.

In a sad irony, my father had been one of the very last to be swindled, having bought a single share for $50 a week before the fraud became known.

Although I lost no money in the fraud, the fallout hurt the furniture business for several weeks, as it seemed the only customers coming into the store wanted to gossip about how much everyone had lost. Business had been slow, but we were paying the bills, and I counted myself lucky to have not lost my cash during the Packingtown fraud.

In early August, I drove home for lunch to see Marilee standing on the porch with a familiar person.

"Hey, Gwen," I greeted tentatively. "I didn't expect to see you here."

Apprehensively, Gwen said, "No…no, I don't expect you did. I just needed to see Marilee…good-bye."

Gwen stumbled off the front porch and walked quickly to her car as if she feared being questioned.

As she drove off, I looked at Marilee who was holding our son Billy and asked, "What was that about?"

"Arty's lost everything," Marilee confessed. "He put every cent they had into that Packingtown mess and lost it all."

"Everything?" I quizzed.

"They haven't taken his car yet, but Gwen tells me he even mortgaged their home. They've closed down the upstairs and are trying to rent it out. She's afraid the bank's going to foreclose any day. She asked me for some money. I gave her $40 from my kitchen money. Hope that's okay."

"Sure," I said. "It must have been hard for her to come to you."

"I guess all her new friends have either lost everything or they're afraid Gwen's going to ask for money," Marilee sighed.

"Will your dad help?" I asked.

"Probably," Marilee replied. "But Arty would have to move back to the farm and live with Dad watching him. I'm afraid Arty's too proud for that."

"Too afraid of your dad," I added.

"You're probably right," Marilee admitted.

"It's a bad situation for a lot of folks," I reasoned. "You expect investors to lose money sometimes, but I can't believe how many people lost it all and even borrowed to give money to that crook."

"I felt sorry for Gwen," Marilee said. "I'll have to admit, I didn't think that was possible after all the airs she's put on since coming to town, but...but she really seemed desperate today. I know it must have killed her to come to me for money."

"You're her friend," I reminded.

"That seems a long time ago," Marilee sighed, "and I wonder if I've really been a friend the past few years. It seems all I've been is jealous and a bit resentful of her and her lifestyle."

Smiling at my wife, I said, "You're only human. What have you cooked for lunch?"

Marilee and I ate a sober lunch, as I could tell my wife was concerned for her brother and friend, Gwen. I played with the baby for a few minutes and headed back to work. It was another slow business day, as the summer doldrums seemed to grip the whole town because few cars were on the street and fewer shoppers were in the stores.

CHAPTER 93

August 19th fell on a Friday as Lance and I continued to work to make ends meet at the store. Some of the shock of the Packingtown scandal had subsided, and business was slow but recovering. By late afternoon, I invited Lance and Mary Sue to come to the house for supper. As evening came, Lance and I sat on the front porch giving our opinions about the local news in the community.

"You know what today is?" Lance smiled.

Thinking for a moment, I replied, "August 19th, our day to be on the rock."

"Sitting in the shade with a fishing line would be a good way to spend the afternoon," Lance said.

"As dry as it's been, the fish are probably on the bank," I quipped.

"You're probably right," Lance laughed. "Have you heard from Arty lately?"

"No," I answered.

I had not told Lance about Gwen asking Marilee for money a few weeks earlier. Gwen had actually come by a couple of other times saying she needed small loans, but Marilee and I supposed she was trying to make the mortgage payment and was afraid to ask for such a large sum at one time.

"Hey guys," my brother Lloyd greeted from the street.

"What are you doing here?" Lance asked.

"You're not the only one Gill invites over," Lloyd smiled. "I hear you two will be churning some ice cream this evening."

Lance looked at me and I said, "Marilee's getting things ready now. You didn't think you were going to get a free meal? I need someone to help crank the cream."

"What are you two up to?" Lloyd asked as he took a seat.

"We're just talking about old times in the Cross Timber and our rock at Salt Creek," I reminisced.

"Good times," Lloyd smiled.

"I was asking about Arty," Lance added.

"I hear he lost it all," Lloyd said. "I hear the bank's about to take his house."

"Would you look at that," an excited Lance commented. "Speak of the devil."

Arty Martin walked quickly up the sidewalk toward the house. He was still dressed in an expensive suit, although it looked in need of a good cleaning. His shoes were scuffed, and he had a slightly haggard look as he walked.

"You remembered!" a jubilant Lance greeted.

"Huh?" a confused Arty replied.

"August 19th," Lance reminded. "You came to see us."

"Oh yeah," Arty smiled. "I figured if I can't go back to the Cross Timber on such a miserable day, I can at least watch you guys fanning yourself."

"How you been?" I asked, concerned for Arty's financial well-being.

Looking closely at my old friend, however, I began to worry about his overall health. He looked like he had not shaven, and his cheeks looked lean and hungry. Most of all, the familiar swagger I had come to expect from Arty was gone. Although he was doing his best to put on a brave front, he looked like a beaten man.

"Great," Arty lied. "I had a slight setback with the Packingtown thing, but I've got a couple of things brewing."

"That's good to hear," I replied, sure Arty was not being truthful.

After a moment of silence, Lance asked, "How's Gwen?"

This question made it difficult for Arty to maintain his positive countenance, but he said, "She's fine…she's been getting a little bored around the house, and she's thinking about taking a job."

"Doing what?" Lance asked.

"You know," Arty stammered. "She's a talented girl. She'll probably get into a dress store or something like that. She's got a good eye and…heck, if it keeps her off the street buying clothes, I'll be ahead."

"That'd be good for her, I expect," Lance said.

"How's things at the store?" Arty asked.

"Not bad," I replied. "Things have been a little soft, but the days are getting shorter, and people will start thinking about the inside of their homes in a month or so."

"That's good," Arty said.

After another lull in the conversation, Arty said, "I really came here to talk some business."

"What's up?" I asked.

"I really need to talk with Lance," Arty clarified.

"What kind of business?" Lance asked suspiciously.

Shaking his head, Arty confessed, "I'm in a tough spot. I hate to admit it, but I've got myself a little over-extended. The bank's trying to foreclose on my mortgage, and well, that house is about all I got left besides my car, and…if I could find a buyer, I'd sell the car."

"I don't have a lot of cash," Lance replied. "But I'll help what I can."

"Thanks," Arty groaned. "But what I really need is for you to think about selling that farm of yours. Leland Holiday's got the cash, and he'll pay you a fair price."

"I'm not selling to that man, or any man, for that matter," Lance defiantly stated.

In a defeated tone, Arty said, "Lance…be reasonable. You don't know what these guys are like. I don't want you to get hurt, and Leland says he'll pay me a commission to get my feet back on the ground if you'll just sell."

Lance did not answer as Lloyd glanced at me.

"I'm begging you," Arty said. "I'll get on my knees if I have to, but I need this."

Arty was near tears as he looked pitifully at his old friend Lance.

"I know I haven't always been that great of a friend," Arty confessed, "but I need this. If we can just make this one deal, I'm selling out and getting back to the farm…back where I belong…I…I won't let you down again…just do this one thing."

"Arty," Lance said. "What's going on? Why can't you and Gwen leave tonight? Go back home, your dad's doing well…he'll help…I know he will."

"You don't understand," Arty pleaded. "I've lost everything. The house, the money…Gwen."

"What about Gwen?" Lloyd interrupted before Lance or I could ask.

Arty hesitated to answer as he looked pitifully at us.

"What about Gwen?" Lloyd demanded.

"Tell us," Lance interjected.

"She's with Leland Holiday, now," Arty whimpered as he looked at his feet.

"What?" Lance shouted.

"We lost everything," Arty tried to defend. "Gwen's taken opium since the boy went away. The doctor said it was for the nerves, but when the doctor wouldn't get her more, Leland found a way, and she's addicted. She's been borrowing money from whoever to pay, but we've got nothing now. Leland said if I'd get you to sign, he'd leave her alone. You got to sell, Lance. They're going to kill you if you don't and…Gwen."

"Where is Gwen?" Lloyd asked angrily.

Arty looked at us a second before saying, "She's got a job…she's working at the Potanole."

CHAPTER 94

"Do you have a gun?" Lance asked me seriously.

Before I could tell him no, Lloyd said, "I do."

"What are you doing?" Arty asked worriedly.

Looking at me and then at Lloyd, Lance said, "We're going to get Gwen."

"Don't do this," Arty pleaded. "Just sign the papers, and I'll bring her back and things will be fine."

Stepping up to Arty, Lance said, "Can't you ever think of anyone but yourself?"

"I am," Arty defended. "There will be trouble if you go down there. Sell the property, and it'll be okay."

Looking at Lloyd, Lance said, "You ready to go?"

Lloyd nodded as the two headed to Lance's car. I yelled at Marilee to tell her we would be gone for a while and followed them.

"You don't have to go," Lance said to me. "We can handle things."

"She's my friend, too," I offered, as I climbed into the back seat of the car.

"Are you coming?" Lance asked Arty as we waited in the car.

"I can't," Arty whimpered. "He'd kill me sure…and you guys need to get out of that car."

Without saying another word, Lance sped away leaving Arty behind. After stopping at Lloyd's house to get a shotgun and a pistol, Lance drove into the darkening evening toward the Potanole.

Thoughts of the place haunted me as we drove silently down the dusty roads toward the border of Pottawatomie and Seminole County. I had been at the place only one time, but its reputation was infamous for all types of vice. The thought of Gwen at such a place made my heart sick. We drove in silence for most of the hour-long trip until Lance cut the headlights and coasted to a stop at the edge of the thick woods about two hundred yards from the parking area. Kerosene lamps illuminated the old grist mill, giving it a foreboding appearance. Lance turned to give Lloyd and me instructions.

"Are you ready?" Lance asked, looking more at Lloyd than at me.

Lloyd nodded.

"There's a door around back," Lance explained. "I'm going that way with the shotgun. Give me about five minutes to work my way around back; then you two come in the front. Try to look like customers, and don't show your pistol unless you have to. There'll be armed men inside. If we're lucky, she'll be downstairs serving drinks. If she is, guide her out as quietly as possible, and I'll cover you."

"What if she's not downstairs?" I asked.

Lance and Lloyd looked at each other before Lance said, "Let's hope she's downstairs."

Lance disappeared into the thick woods as Lloyd and I waited in the car before driving to the front.

"Look at this place," I said in disbelief at all the cars. On the one trip I had made with Lance and Arty, there had been far fewer customers or cars.

"This place has boomed since the oil rush," Lloyd explained. "These boys will spend a month's wages on a Friday night."

The Potanole was a dark and forbidding place, and I looked anxiously at the front door we would soon be entering.

"Are you okay?" Lloyd asked.

"Sure," I said uneasily.

"Stay close to me," he instructed.

After five minutes, we drove the car to the parking area in front of the Potanole. Drunken men were already stumbling outside and fighting although the night was still young. Lloyd nodded to the doorman as if he knew exactly how to act in a place like this. I followed close, looking through the dark smoky interior for any sign of Gwen.

"Where is she?" Lloyd demanded forcefully.

I turned to see he was confronting Leland Holiday. Leland stared coldly at Lloyd as he glanced at me.

Talking to me, Leland said in a joking tone, "Need a little break from the wife?"

"Where's Gwen?" Lloyd demanded as the group of men laughed at us.

Looking over Lloyd carefully, Leland took a puff on his cigar and said, "You don't look like you could afford her."

Lloyd looked upstairs for a second before lunging at Leland Holiday. Grabbing Leland by the collar with one hand, Lloyd pointed his pistol with the other.

"What room?" Lloyd glared as Leland Holiday was caught completely off guard at the aggression.

A strange hush fell over the downstairs area as men turned to look at the impending fight. The men sitting with Leland rose to his aid, until a shotgun blast ripped through the room. A second later, Lance Carrington pointed the weapon at Leland's head.

"You fellas need to take a seat, and answer the man's question," Lance said as he moved in front of Leland.

"Carrington?" Leland smirked. "You're some kind of fool. I've been looking to do you in, and you just come to me. There's no way you get out of here alive."

"Where's the girl?" Lance asked again.

Seeing that Lance was not about to flinch, Leland Holiday finally said, "The second door on the right…I think."

Before Lance could move, Lloyd handed me his pistol and headed up the stairs, pushing several men aside who were blocking his way.

Staring at me, Leland Holiday said, "You're way over your head on this thing. Why don't you hand me the gun and leave."

"Gill," Lance calmly instructed. "Hand me the pistol, and see if you can help Lloyd. I don't think Mr. Holiday will worry as much about me being in over my head."

Leland Holiday swallowed nervously as I stepped toward the stairs. Before I reached the foot of the stairs, however, Lloyd had a half-clothed Gwen cradled in his arms.

"Get to the door and start the car," Lloyd demanded forcefully as he carried Gwen with ease.

By the time Lloyd put Gwen in the back seat, Lance was backing out the door while holding Leland Holiday by the collar.

"This isn't over," Leland threatened from his precarious position.

"Maybe," Lance said sternly. "But it's over for tonight."

Lance pushed Leland Holiday roughly into the crowd before firing another shotgun blast into a kerosene lamp, which flashed into a fire causing bedlam in the crowd. Lance sprinted to the car and slammed the door shut as I sped into the dark night. Expecting gunshots at any moment, I was relieved when the lights of the Potanole were in the distance and we drove into the canopy of trees leading to the main road. Looking in the rear view mirror, it appeared no one followed.

"How is she?" Lance asked as he looked at Gwen passed out in Lloyd's arms.

"She's out of it," Lloyd explained with a strange pain to his voice. "She's drunk or something."

"Was she—" Lance began to question.

"Don't ask," Lloyd said solemnly. "It won't do anyone no good."

I drove like a madman back toward Shawnee, while Lloyd gently tried to make Gwen comfortable in the back seat. Once in town, we stopped at the hospital not thinking how three men with a half-dressed woman might look. By that time, Gwen was conscious but incoherent. The doctor believed she was drunk and said she needed to sleep. Driving back to my house, Lloyd carried her into the front room where Marilee and Mary Sue had been waiting anxiously.

"What's wrong with Gwen?" Marilee asked, as she looked at the pitiful woman in Lloyd's arms.

"I'll explain later," I instructed. "Let's put her into the guest room."

Marilee did not ask questions as she quickly prepared the bed before running the men out of the room to make Gwen comfortable.

"What's going on?" Mary Sue asked, as Marilee helped Gwen get ready for bed.

Lance and I both hesitated answering, but Lloyd said bluntly, "Arty Martin has put his wife to work at the Potanole to try to save his own neck."

"The Potanole!" Mary Sue gasped.

"She's drunk," Lance tried to explain, as if that would be the more respectable explanation.

"She looks terrible," Marilee said as she joined us, "but she's sleeping now. What happened?"

"I'll explain everything later," I assured. "Gwen's got to get some help for now."

"What was she doing at the Potanole?" Mary Sue innocently asked.

Marilee, who always seemed to be able to assess situations quickly said, "She was serving as a hostess most likely. Looks like maybe she had too much to drink."

Looking at Marilee, I could tell she knew it was nothing as innocent.

"She needs to rest," Marilee continued. "She can stay here a few days and recover."

"We better be going then," Mary Sue agreed as she and Lance headed to the door.

"If it's okay, Marilee, I'd like to stay for a while," Lloyd asked.

I could tell by looking at Lance that he felt this was a good idea.

"That'll be fine, Lloyd," Marilee assured. "I'll make you a bed here in the front room."

CHAPTER 95

Gwen had been thin and sickly for several years, but the hardships of the past months had taken a toll. Lloyd took off work and stayed at the house just in case any of Leland Holiday's group came looking for Gwen. A concerned Lance came by nearly every day to check on Marilee's new patient, but it was several days before Marilee would allow any visitors into the room.

Marilee cried when she learned Gwen was addicted to opium and borrowed the money to support her habit. A doctor prescribed the medication when her child was sent away, but Gwen had been getting it through Leland Holiday for the past several years. Occasional groaning, screams, and thrashing about were heard for the next few days as Marilee and then Lloyd helped Gwen through the painful process of getting off the drug. Arty was noticeably absent. No one seemed to know where he was, although I believed he was either hiding from Leland Holiday or too embarrassed to see what he had helped do to his wife.

After a week of near constant attention, Marilee said to me, "She's doing better today. Why don't you go in and say hello?"

Anxious to see the patient who had been hidden away, I tentatively stepped into the room to see Gwen looking like a frail skeleton lying in the bed. The room smelled like sickness, and Lloyd was sitting in a chair nearby. If Gwen was having a good day, I cringed to think of what the bad days of the past week had been like. Her pale, blue eyes were sunken and sad, while her cheeks looked bony and weak. Gwen's once-thick hair was matted with sweat beading from her forehead.

"Look who's here," Lloyd encouraged as Gwen struggled to look up.

I sensed an embarrassment and humiliation in the girl I had once so admired as she timidly tried to make eye contact.

"Hey, Gill," she finally said. "Thanks for letting me stay for a while."

"As long as you need," I assured.

"Marilee—" Gwen began emotionally. "Marilee's been so wonderful to look after me…will you please tell her?"

"Sure," I smiled. "She's been worried about you and wants you well."

"I don't know if I'll ever be right," Gwen frowned.

"Sure you will," Lloyd assured. "I've got some errands to do in Oklahoma City today, but I'll be back this evening."

As Lloyd walked away, Gwen watched him carefully and said, "It's like being back at the farm. Lloyd was always looking out for me and the baby…when Arty was out so much."

"Lance came by this morning," I said awkwardly.

"Lance was here?" she said with a surprised look. "He came to see me?"

"He's been by every day, but Marilee's been keeping you to herself," I explained.

"How long have I been here?" Gwen asked.

"A little more than a week," I informed.

"It's been a nightmare, Gill. Like a dream that won't go away," she frowned.

"Things will get better," I tried to assure. "Why don't you rest now?"

"Okay," she said softly as she drifted to sleep.

Walking out the door, Marilee greeted me to ask, "What do you think?"

"She doesn't look well," I said.

"She looks more alert," Marilee affirmed. "But I think she needs to stay here until she's better."

"It's okay with me," I said.

"I don't know what she's going to do," Marilee sighed. "Have you heard from my brother?"

"Not a word," I replied. "Not even a rumor. How about your folks? Have they heard from him?"

"I haven't asked," Marilee confessed. "I figured I'd deal with one problem at a time. She needs to get well for now. Lloyd's been a big help. I don't think I could have managed without him."

As the days went by, Gwen struggled less with the chills and discomfort from her dependence on the drug. It seems the behavior we had associated with the drinking had been her physical dependence on opium. After a few days, she was able to sit up and come to the front room to look out the window at the warm autumn days.

It was one of these pleasant Sundays when Gwen left the house for the first time in weeks to accompany Marilee and me to church. Gwen was clearly exhausted from the short trip, but a hint of her old, sweet smile returned as she sat with me in the front room holding my son Billy while Marilee prepared lunch.

"How are you doing?" I asked, as she quietly held our baby.

"Better," Gwen smiled. "I'm tired, but it was good to get out of bed."

"Marilee said she had a roast for lunch," I said, trying to make conversation.

"It smells wonderful," Gwen smiled. "Why do you think Marilee's been so good to me?"

"She's your friend," I smiled.

"I haven't been friendly with her for years," Gwen said sadly. "In fact, I haven't really treated her well at all."

"Marilee can be blunt at times, but you should know that she's always been a caring person," I reminded.

"Yes," Gwen agreed. "She's proven that to me."

"Who's that?" Gwen asked, as a car pulled up in front of the house.

Looking out the window, I said, "It's Lance and Lloyd. There's someone else with them too."

Gwen looked out the window as they loitered around the car for a moment. A young boy emerged from the back seat with help from Lloyd. Turning to Gwen, I could see her eyes begin to swell into tears as her thin hand covered her mouth. I looked out the window to see her son Jackie with Lloyd.

I was surprised to see the ten-year-old boy walking awkwardly with the assistance of leg braces and crutches.

"It can't be," Gwen cried as she walked to the front porch.

"Look who we've brought," Lloyd said proudly, as the boy continued to walk next to Lloyd.

The boy looked at Lloyd for a moment and then asked, "Mother?"

"Yes," Gwen cried, as she moved as quickly as she could to hug the boy's neck while tears glistened from her face.

The young boy was somewhat embarrassed at the display, but he gently put his arm around his mother's neck.

"Jackie's been staying with me the past week," Lloyd explained. "We wanted to wait 'til you felt better before we came to visit."

"It's really you?" Gwen cried as she continued to hold the boy around the neck. "And look how tall you are and walking—"

The poor boy looked gawky with the weeping woman draped around his neck.

"Why don't we get inside," Lloyd finally said.

Jackie walked awkwardly up the steps to our house while Lance assisted Gwen to the front room. Lloyd had been visiting the boy since he was put in the home. Gwen was speechless as she continued to hold on to her son. As the group went into the house, I noticed Lloyd still standing by the car.

"That was a surprise," I said, as I walked out toward my brother.

"I thought Gwen would like to see how well he's doing," Lloyd smiled.

"How did you get him out?" I questioned.

"I've been looking after him the past year," Lloyd confessed. "Arty quit paying for his care, so I took up the slack."

"Why would you do that?" I asked.

Lloyd smiled and said, "I got close to him when I come back from the war. Arty left 'em alone so much that I kind of looked after Gwen and the baby."

"It was you, wasn't it?" I quizzed with a puzzled look.

"What?" Lloyd replied.

"That night I saw someone in the woods. It was you!" I charged.

"Probably," Lloyd shrugged. "She was left alone so much, I worried about her. I didn't have nothing better to do, so I watched out for the place."

"Do you love her, Lloyd?" I asked pointedly.

Lloyd looked irritated at the question and said, "For a long time, Gill. Even when you used to think she was your girl, but then she married Arty, and that was that. The best I could do was help look after her boy."

"Does Gwen know?" I inquired. "Does she know how you feel?"

"No," Lloyd replied. "She wouldn't have no interest in a guy like me. I just feel sorry for her."

Looking at Lloyd for a moment, I said, "It was a good thing you did...bringing the boy to her and taking care of him. He may be all she has left."

"Still no sign of Arty?" Lloyd asked.

"Haven't heard a word," I confessed.

Shaking his head, Lloyd said, "I don't know how a man could mess up any worse than Arty…he—"

"Gill!" a voice shouted from down the street.

Arty Martin staggered up the street toward Lloyd and me, waving his hands frantically. I looked at Lloyd for a second before we both ran toward him.

"Gill!" Arty shouted again as we approached.

Arty Martin looked like he had not shaved or bathed in days, and it appeared as if he had been sleeping in his clothes. We could only guess what scheme Arty had come to share with us.

CHAPTER 96

"What are you doing here?" Lloyd charged as Arty Martin staggered up the street. "Drunk and looking like that!"

"I'm not here for no trouble," Arty replied.

"What's happened to you?" I asked. "Where have you been?"

Looking pitifully, Arty said, "I've been living down by the rail bridge. I heard you got Gwen."

"No thanks to you!" Lloyd harshly accused.

Arty ignored Lloyd's criticism and asked urgently, "Where's Lance?"

"He's in the house," I said.

"Which house?" Arty demanded.

"My house," I replied impatiently. "What's going on?"

With a sigh of relief, Arty said, "I come to warn Lance. I heard some fellas talking at the bridge that Leland Holiday was going to bomb his house."

Lloyd looked at me, as I said frantically, "Mary Sue and Anna are at the house!"

Lloyd and I sprinted to inform Lance. Before we could make it inside, an explosion rocked the neighborhood. Black smoke bellowed a few blocks away in the direction of Lance's home. Several houses had been dynamited during the contentious railroad strikes, but this blast had everyone's attention on this peaceful Sunday afternoon. People stood outside peering at the smoke coming from the blast, including Lance, who stood on my front porch surveying the smoke.

Staring at the menacing black cloud as he looked in the direction of the bombing, his concern quickly turned to panic as Lance saw Lloyd and me followed by the ragged Arty. Without a word, Lance sprinted toward his car as Lloyd and I scrambled to climb in the back. As Lance sped toward the blast, Arty grabbed the front door handle and piled into the front seat.

"What are you doing here?" a tense Lance asked as he drove toward the commotion. Arty did not reply, as Lance carefully surveyed the smoke to see its location. We all hoped for the best, but it soon became clear the flaming house belonged to Lance Carrington. On a typical Sunday, the Carringtons would have been at church, but today Anna had been running a slight fever, and Mary Sue had kept her home.

Lance did not let the car come to a complete stop before he jumped out of the vehicle and headed toward the flames. The front third of the small, white frame house was missing as shattered lumber and debris was all that was left. The back of the home was more or less intact as small fires danced around the wreckage of the front. Without hesitation, Lance bolted into the chaos with Lloyd close behind.

I looked at Arty Martin, who shook uncontrollably and muttered to himself at the sight. Many people were around the smoldering debris as sirens could be heard in the distance, indicating firefighters were rushing to the scene.

In a moment, Lance emerged from what was left of the house carrying a bloodied and unconscious Mary Sue, while Lloyd carried a now-screaming Anna. The child's shrieks were unnerving and comforting at the same time, because the frightened cries meant the child was alive. Mary Sue on the other hand was limp and lifeless.

Lance was frantic as Lloyd put the screaming Anna in my arms. The small child cried uncontrollably but appeared to have only minor scrapes. Mary Sue's face, however, was covered in blood. It looked as if one arm was badly burned. Lance carried his wife to the car. A calmer

Lloyd drove toward the hospital. Seeing the crowd of people gathering, a nervous Arty walked away, leaving me holding Anna. In a few moments, the firefighters were on the scene, and an ambulance came to take Anna to the hospital.

CHAPTER 97

At the hospital, a nurse took Anna and quickly calmed the child down. Except for a few bruises and cuts, she was fine. The well-being of Mary Sue was unknown when Marilee entered the hospital.

"What's happening?" Marilee frantically asked.

"There was an explosion at the Carrington's house," I solemnly replied.

"Oh no!" Marilee shrieked. "Mary Sue and Anna?"

"Anna's fine," I assured. "I haven't heard about Mary Sue. Lance carried her out of the house, but I don't know."

"There's Lloyd," Marilee pointed, as my brother walked down the hall.

Turning to him, I asked, "How is she?"

"I don't know," Lloyd replied. "She was breathing in the car, but she wasn't conscious. I just don't know."

For the next few hours, Lloyd and I loitered in the small lobby of the hospital waiting for news. Marilee took Anna to the house, where Gwen had been watching Billy. When Lance came out, blood from his wife's wounds still stained his shirt.

"How is she?" I asked, as Lance walked toward us.

"She's going to live," Lance replied.

"Thank goodness," I sighed.

"They don't know if her arm can be saved, and she has some cuts on her face, but other than that, the doctor says she should be fine.

We're lucky I guess," Lance said tearfully. "She's…well she's pretty shook up."

Looking past us, Lance said sharply, "What's he doing here?"

Lloyd and I turned around to see Arty Martin peering inside the front door. Lance marched past us and rushed to the door before Arty could retreat.

"What have you done?" Lance shouted savagely as he grabbed Arty by the collar. "Isn't it bad enough you ruined your wife without trying to kill mine?"

"I didn't do anything," Arty defended. "I was coming to tell you. Honest I was…ask Gill. It was Leland. I was coming to warn you."

"You did a bang-up job of that!" Lance screamed. "My wife is torn up, and the two people I care about more than my own life were nearly killed today because of your friend Leland Holiday! I ought to—"

Lance raised back to punch the defenseless Arty before stopping himself.

"Leland Holiday's not my friend," Arty pleaded. "I came to warn you. I've been living by the tracks, and I heard some guys talking and I came as soon as I could."

Pulling and shaking on Arty's collar to get his full attention, Lance said, "You tell Leland Holiday he's a coward and a cheat. You tell him I'm coming after him and I'm going to end this thing right now."

"I don't have anything to do with him anymore," Arty cried. "He's got men, and he *wants* you to come after him. He'll kill you and say it was self-defense."

"Where's he at?" Lance asked pointedly.

"I don't know," Arty muttered. "But you need to get out of here."

Shaking him again, Lance said, "Where did you get your last drink? You smell like a distillery. Where did you get your booze?"

"He may be down south," Arty muttered. "I don't know."

As Lance let go, Arty fell to his knees. Lance marched off into the night with the wild look in his eye that I had not seen since his youth.

"What are you doing?" I asked.

"I've got business," Lance shot back.

"Not like this," I pleaded.

"The man blew up my house and tried to kill my wife and child. He's got to be stopped," Lance said pointedly.

"Not like this," I repeated. "Let the law handle it. Lance you've got a wife and child depending on you. Come stay with me tonight, and we'll figure things out in the morning."

Lance relaxed a moment and said, "I'll be fine, Gill. Will Marilee watch Anna for a few days?"

"Sure," I said. "But you can stay with her at our house."

"Thanks," Lance said. "I'll be by later."

Before I could protest more, Lance walked to his car and sped into the night.

"I hope you're happy now," Lloyd shouted to the whimpering Arty.

"Gill," Arty said. "You got to go get him. Goin' after Leland's just what they want. They didn't know anyone was in the house. They *want* Lance to come after them so they can kill him."

"How would you know that?" I asked.

"I don't," Arty said as his eyes shifted from side to side. "But that's how those men think. There's oil on the property. Leland wants it, and he won't mind killing Lance to get it. Won't you trust me on this?"

"No, Arty," I said with a sigh. "I can't trust you…I've got to go find Lance."

"I can fix it—" he began before his voice trailed into a pathetic whimper.

Handing Arty five dollars, I said, "Go to the Norwood Hotel and sleep it off."

Arty took the five dollars and said, "You got to believe me, I came to warn Lance. I wouldn't do anything to hurt him. I can still make this right."

"How 'bout Gwen?" Lloyd angrily asked. "How could you do that to your own wife?"

"Things got messed up," Arty said. "But I didn't mean to hurt anyone."

"You never mean to hurt anyone," Lloyd replied. "But you only manage to take care of yourself…and look what that's done for you."

"Go to the hotel," I instructed, as I stepped between Lloyd and Arty. "Sleep it off, and I'll come see you tomorrow."

"I can fix this thing," Arty stated defiantly.

"You can't fix yourself," Lloyd replied.

"Go," I said one more time to Arty.

As Arty staggered into the darkness, I told Lloyd, "We got to find Lance before he does something stupid."

"Let's go," Lloyd agreed.

I took a moment to step into Mary Sue's room to see how she was doing. She was sleeping. The left side of her face was bandaged heavily, and her left arm was in a sling. She seemed to be resting well, so I backed out of the room.

"Is that you, Gill?" she whispered.

"Yes," I whispered back. "How are you feeling?"

"I'm fine," Mary Sue replied. "Where's Lance?"

"He went out for a moment, but I'm going to find him," I tried to assure.

"Do you think Lance will mind?" she asked.

"Mind what?" I replied.

"Look at me," she said sadly. "I must look a mess."

"You'll be fine," I assured. "Lance cares for you more than anything. You're going to be fine."

"Thanks, Gill," she whispered back. "Find Lance for me."

"I will," I promised.

CHAPTER 98

Lloyd and I did not have a car at the hospital, so we walked the ten blocks back to my house. It was already eight o'clock. Marilee and Gwen were sitting in the front room with Gwen's son, Jackie. The two women peacefully rocked the children who were asleep.

"How's Mary Sue?" Marilee whispered.

"She's going to live," I replied. "She's going to be scarred up I'm afraid, and Lance said they're not sure they can save her arm, but considering all, she's doing well."

"Did Lance stay with her?" Gwen asked.

Lloyd and I looked at each other, before Lloyd said, "Lance found out Leland was behind the explosion, and he's out looking for him."

"Oh no," Gwen gasped. "You've got to stop him!"

"We know," I sighed. "Where's the car, Marilee?"

"I parked out front," Marilee replied.

"It's not there," I assured, looking out the window.

"It's got to be," Marilee responded. "I haven't moved since I came in."

Gwen nodded in agreement.

"We'll take my car," Lloyd said, as we headed out the front door.

For the next hour, we patrolled the streets and alleyways of the town looking for any sign of Lance. When we failed to find him in town, Lloyd and I both knew we had to make a trip to the Potanole. We drove quietly into the night, afraid of what we might find.

Even on a Sunday night, cars were parked out front, although there did not seem to be as many people as the night we rescued Gwen from the place.

As Lloyd walked in, it was clear many recognized him as the man who carried Gwen out the front door a few weeks earlier. A charred spot scarred the wall where Lance Carrington had shot the kerosene lamp the night we got Gwen.

A large man walked up to Lloyd and said, "We don't want no trouble tonight."

"Neither do I," Lloyd answered. "But I need to find Leland Holiday."

Looking around the room for a minute, the man smiled and said, "He left here about an hour ago…with your friend."

"Where can I find them?" an anxious Lloyd asked.

The man shrugged and said, "I don't know."

Another man said, "I heard Leland say something about goin' to the Salt Creek Bridge to do some business."

Without saying thank you, Lloyd and I left immediately to stop Leland Holiday from killing Lance. Fearing we were too late, Lloyd drove wildly over the dirt roads and through the thick forest where the railroad crossed the Salt Creek. The Salt Creek Bridge had been a place for illicit business dealings for many years. The bridge was also the spot where Lance Carrington had killed Leland Holiday's cousin.

As we approached, a small crowd of men stood on top of the bridge looking down as flames danced up from the bank of the river. It was apparent a car had crashed off the bridge and was burning below. Lloyd and I jumped out, fearful of what we might find.

After looking at the wreckage for a moment, Lloyd said, "Isn't that your car?"

I studied the car for a second, before asking one of the men to shine a light on the license plate.

"It is," I said in confusion.

A couple of men had scaled down the bridge to attempt a rescue as Lloyd and I scampered down the dark embankment to help. The car was a crushed mess, but I heard someone say, "One's still alive."

Lying next to the driver's side was the mangled body of Arty Martin.

"Arty!" I screamed, as my old friend looked at me.

Arty struggled to breathe, but he flashed a glimpse of the cocky smile from earlier days.

I bent down to hear him say in a pained voice, "Tell Lance I took care of it."

"Leland Holiday's dead," Lloyd said as he stepped from the other side of the car.

Arty smiled strangely, as his eyes closed for the final time.

CHAPTER 99

Lloyd and I were at the scene until the early hours of the morning. The sheriff's deputy said they would pull the car out of the creek later in the day, but he did not think there would be much of it to salvage. It appeared Arty Martin had stolen my car to take Leland to the bridge. Some of the men said he was there to ambush Lance Carrington, and most of the men at the bridge had some association with Leland Holiday. Arty drove off the bridge at a high rate of speed, killing Leland immediately.

The men on the bridge assumed Arty had been drunk, but I will always believe he had more selfless motives. One thing I salvaged from the car was an old leather string with a three-inch boar's tusk tied to it. Arty and Lance were the only ones to share this prize, and Arty must have taken this trinket with him that night.

As we drove past the hospital, Lance Carrington's car was parked outside. We slipped into Mary Sue's room to find Lance by her side.

"He's sleeping," the pained voice of Mary Sue whispered in the dark.

"Sorry to bother you," I apologized.

"I can't sleep," Mary Sue replied.

"How long has Lance been here?" I questioned.

"Gill?" Lance asked in sleepy confusion.

"He came shortly after you left," Mary Sue answered. "Thanks for finding him."

"Try to sleep, Mary Sue," Lance said while reaching out to touch her hand. "Are you in pain?"

"A little," Mary Sue confessed.

"I'll get the nurse," Lance said, as he rose to exit the room.

"Lance has been here all night?" I asked.

"Yes, he fell asleep a little while ago," Mary Sue whispered.

"What are you men doing in here!" the nurse barked in a loud whisper. "Get out, this woman needs her rest."

Lance followed Lloyd and I out of the room and asked, "What are you doing here?"

"We've been looking for you," I replied.

"We thought you were going after Leland Holiday tonight," Lloyd added.

"I went to check on what was left of my house and to change shirts," Lance informed. "I got a cup of coffee, and I'm settled down now. What time is it?"

"Nearly three," I replied.

"You've been looking this long?" Lance questioned. "I've been right here."

"We've got some bad news," I sighed. "We went down to the Potanole."

"What?" Lance gasped.

"We thought you would be looking for Leland," I said. "Arty…well, Arty stole my car and…he drove off the Salt Creek Bridge with Leland inside."

The news caused Lance to turn pale with a blank, shocked look in his eyes.

"Is Arty—" he began to ask.

"Arty's dead," I interrupted. "Leland Holiday, too."

Lance stumbled back and found a place to sit before saying, "Arty's dead?"

"I saw him before he passed," I explained. "He…he asked for…he was worried about you."

"Arty was always worrying about the wrong things," Lance said, as tears flowed down his cheeks. "I can't believe he's gone."

"I think Arty wanted to make things right," I said. "He was afraid Leland was going to ambush you."

"Arty's dead," Lance repeated again, almost to himself.

"Are you okay?" I asked.

Lance looked up and said, "I…I can't believe it…Arty's gone. I said some things—"

"Arty understood," I explained. "I think he thought he had to make some things right. You know Arty."

Lance did not answer but wept into his hands at the death of his old friend.

CHAPTER 100

The hot August sun scorched the top of my head through my thinning hair, as I stood on the flat rock overlooking Salt Creek. A persistent drought left little more than a trickle in the dried creek bed. It was Sunday and the day before August 19, 1935. It was always Arty's idea to meet back at this place every ten years. Although he had died several years earlier, Lance and I made the drive into the Cross Timber to remember the times, remember the place, and more importantly remember our friend.

"I don't think there's any fish in the creek!" Lloyd yelled as he walked out of the thick Cross Timber forest and toward our spot.

"How you doing, Lloyd?" Lance shouted back.

Lloyd carried his five-year-old son on his shoulders while strolling lazily toward us.

"It's too hot to be down here," Lloyd complained. "Are you boys heading back to the house later? We're churning ice cream."

"You know I'll be there," I replied.

Looking at my protruding mid-section, Lloyd quipped, "I didn't think you would turn down ice cream."

"How's this little man?" I asked the young boy perched on top of Lloyd's shoulders.

"Can you say, hello?" Lloyd prodded the shy boy.

"Hello, Uncle Gill," the voice squeaked.

"Are you keeping your daddy in line?" I asked the boy playfully.

The young boy bashfully hid his face behind Lloyd's head.

"How's farming?" Lance asked.

"It's a bust," Lloyd frowned. "I've never seen it this dry. Look at the creek."

"Looks bleak," Lance sighed.

"We're making it okay," Lloyd shrugged. "I'm finding plenty of work as a pumper…trying to keep your wells running."

"I appreciate that," Lance smiled. "How's Gwen?"

"She's fine," Lloyd assured.

Lloyd and Gwen married after Arty passed away. Lloyd moved them back to the country and tried to farm part of the old Brooks place. Lance still owned his mother's old farm, although the house had been torn down years earlier. The property produced three wells, and Lloyd worked maintaining several oil wells in the area for the Deep Rock Oil Company.

"Gwen looks good." Lance said.

"Always did to me," Lloyd smiled.

A loud rustling came from the woods as a group of women and children emerged from the old trail out of the Cross Timber. My oldest son Billy, daughter Laura, and youngest son Bobby followed Marilee. Mary Sue had Anna and her younger daughter Christy trailing behind, while Gwen followed with her son, Jackie, who was now seventeen years old and walking without his braces.

Mary Sue had scars on her arm from the burns. The left side of her face was also scarred from the explosion, but her personality was as fresh as the first day I had met her. The marks on her face now appeared to be part of her ever-present smile. The nation had been in the midst of a great economic depression, but our families had been able to weather the storm. Lance and I lived in Shawnee with our families, while Lloyd and Gwen seemed to enjoy being back in the Cross Timber.

Although Leland Holiday died at the Salt Creek Bridge years earlier, the county and the Cross Timber could not seem to get away from conflicts and controversy. In a county forged by wild saloon towns and the challenges of four Indian nations sharing the once-rugged Cross Timber, the two towns of Shawnee and Tecumseh feuded for nearly thirty years about the county seat. Shawnee finally won the battle although the citizens of Tecumseh protested vigorously. Governor E.W. Marland dedicated the new courthouse in Shawnee the month earlier, and it was now certain Shawnee would be the center of county government in the future.

Our group stood under the blazing sun until the children complained and the women urged us back to Lloyd's house for ice cream. The simple marker with Lance Carrington's name carved as a memorial now had Arty Martin's named etched underneath. I expected some day for my name to be reunited with theirs at this spot.

Gwen once said, Arty had the personality, Lance the passion, and I had been the constant. I missed my friend Arty Martin. We had our differences, but he had helped mold Lance Carrington and me into the men we eventually became. Arty's selfishness caused him ruin, but in the end, he was looking out for a friend with one selfless act of desperation. I guess it was all Arty thought he had left to give.

Trust is the great compliment to love. Marilee always believed in me. She had been my blessing and partner in life. Gwen had exorcised the demons of her past and found someone she could trust in Lloyd. To see her back at the farm with a radiant glow to her cheeks seemed somehow to bring me closer home to the Cross Timber of my youth.

"Are you ready to go?" I asked Lance, as we stood alone, the rest of our families leaving earlier for the shade of Lloyd's back porch.

"In a minute," Lance answered, as he looked around one more time.

"Do you miss it?" I asked.

"Miss what?" he replied.

"Our days in the Cross Timber…the days of our youth," I explained.

"Youth's for the young," Lance smiled. "I miss it, but I wouldn't change much. I wish I'd helped Arty have more courage. A true friend is a friend at all times. Some pretend to be friends, but there are some friends who are closer than brothers. You, Arty, and even Lloyd have been like that to me. I'd done anything for Arty, and I guess Arty did all he thought he could do for me in the end."

"You think we'll make it back in ten years?" I asked.

"Sure," Lance replied. "We promised Arty. Remember?"

"Can't forget it," I replied.

"We've done pretty good beyond the Cross Timber, haven't we?" Lance reflected. "Not bad for a couple of boys who went to town in overalls."

"I miss it too," I confessed.

"Yeah. It seems a part of me's still in the Cross Timber," Lance added.

"We'll always have the memories," I suggested.

"Memories are the best part…and the worst sometimes," Lance said, as the sun reflected off his tanned skin and infectious smile. "We make memories today, so we'll have them always."

"Let's go make some memories at Lloyd's ice cream freezer," I suggested.

"I hope Marilee made the cream instead of Gwen," Lance smiled.

"Me too," I replied.

THE END

FACT FROM FICTION

Brothers of the Cross Timber is a story of fiction based on some real-life events happening in and around Pottawatomie County, in Oklahoma.

FICTION

All major characters are fictional as well as many of the places in the story, including the flat rock on Salt Creek, the Potanole speakeasy, Unity School, the Peaudane General Store, and the Brooks & Martin Store. Most of the characters in the story are fictional including the Brooks family, the Martin family, the Peaudane family, Lance Carrington, Mary Sue McNally, Mr. McNally, Laura Jones, Leland Holiday, Haskell Holiday, and Ginn.

FACT

Remnants of the Cross Timber run across most of Oklahoma from Texas to Kansas separating the western prairie from the eastern hills. The Cross Timber forest is mainly post oak and blackjack trees that are able to survive grass fires and thrive in the clay soil. The forest is very short, but thick making it difficult to travel through. Washington Irving in his travels through the region in 1835 described it as "struggling through forests of cast iron." The Cross Timber is also referred to as the "Emerald Wall" because the forest often starts abruptly from open pasture or prairie. Although the term "Cross Timber" is used throughout the story, most people from that area and era would have probably referred to the region as "South Pott County" or "the country."

Pottawatomie County was one of the last areas in Oklahoma to be settled and it represented the final reservations for the Citizen Potawatomi, Absentee Shawnee, Sac & Fox, and Kickapoo tribes. Pottawatomie County was on the border of the Indian Territory and the towns of Violet Springs and Corner were notorious bootlegging towns. Frank Starr and Hookie Miller were gunfighters who served as bartenders in the saloons of Corner. Hookie Miller got his name from a hay-hook that replaced his left hand. He was killed in a gunfight in a place called Three Sands in 1924.

The Great Railroad Strike of 1922 was one of the largest national strikes in history. The strike was particularly contentious in Shawnee where at least three houses were dynamited and many strikebreakers were robbed. United States Marshal, Alva S. McDonald arrested a gang of 15 men for bombings in Texas and Oklahoma related to the strike. Several elected officials were also implicated in the bombings and the group was called a "terror squad" in the March 5, 1923 edition of the *Daily Oklahoman.*

The "Baptist University" mentioned in the story became Oklahoma Baptist University. The "Catholic University" would become St. Gregory's University. Neither school was universally known by its contemporary name in 1915. Both universities are located close to each other in Shawnee, Oklahoma, and each school completed the first major buildings on their campuses about 1915.

The battle for the county seat between the towns of Tecumseh and Shawnee lasted nearly thirty years and involved several spirited elections and the intervention of the state's Supreme Court. The larger city of Shawnee finally won the battle and the courthouse was dedicated on July 3, 1935 by the tenth governor of Oklahoma, E.W. Marland.

If you enjoyed
Brothers of the Cross Timber,
look for these other Bob Perry novels:

The Broken Statue

Mimosa Lane

Guilt's Echo

Lydie's Ghost

The Nephilim Code

www.bobp.biz

Made in the USA
Charleston, SC
23 January 2013